THE VALLEY

THE VALLEY

A LEE HARDEN NOVEL

D.J. MOLLES

Copyright © 2023 by D.J. Molles Books LLC

All rights reserved.

No part of this publication may be reproduced, distributed, or transmitted in any form or by any means, including photocopying, recording, or other electronic or mechanical methods, without the prior written permission of the publisher, except as permitted by U.S. copyright law.

For permission requests, contact djmollesbooks@gmail.com.

The story, all names, characters, and incidents portrayed in this production are fictitious. No identification with actual persons (living or deceased), places, buildings, and products is intended or should be inferred.

Book Cover by James T. Egan, Bookfly Designs

ISBN Print Paperback: 979-8386061234

ASIN: B0C1FDJNJX

First edition 2023

*For Jim Hetrick,
whose voice I still hear,
telling me to run faster,
fight harder, and shoot straighter.*

Chapter 1

If there was one thing Bran Potter wished for that day, it was to discover some miraculous means by which he wouldn't have to murder an entire settlement of people. But, as was so often the case, things were not looking good for Bran's wishes. Like his ma always said: "If wishes were fishes, Bran, we'd all cast nets."

If there was a bright spot to any of this, it was that he got to drive the little electric side-by-side ATV, which was always a blast. The sun was hot, and the wind was dry, so while he should have been sweating like a pig, he actually felt quite nice. And, of course, there was Kat to keep him company. Not that she was much of a talker, but they got on well enough.

He cast a sidelong look at her as he piloted the little vehicle through a field of corn that had lost its battle with the drought. She was young, but built like an athlete. Everything from the nose up was quite pretty—large, copper-colored eyes, and a mane of thick, reddish-brown hair. Everything from the nose down was covered by the blue bandana she perpetually wore.

Bran sighed, looking back out at the drought-stricken landscape as they emerged from the sad remains of the corn field into a big field of Bermuda grass that was only *just* staying green. When even the Bermuda grass is thirsty, then you know it's a drought.

"Whaddaya think the odds are the old hag has the goods?" Bran asked. He didn't even have to raise his voice much to be heard over the wind and the tires. Kat's hearing was like...well...a cat's.

She didn't even twitch. Just sat there, staring straight ahead. Two words, in her usual throaty husk: "Dark Mode."

Bran cringed. "Well, fuck, Kat. It ain't always gotta go that way, you know."

She grunted in response. Bran had become quite the expert on Kat's various grunts, and successfully intuited what was meant: *Fat fucking chance.*

"It ever occur to you that I *don't like* Dark Mode?"

She finally turned, those copper-colored eyes boring into him. Yes, they were a lovely shape and color. But damn, they had a ferocity to them that gave people the willies, and Bran was no exception. She arched a single eyebrow.

Bran huffed and shifted in his seat. The wind might be scouring the sweat from everywhere it touched, but it didn't touch his back, and his sodden shirt stuck to his skin as he peeled it off the vinyl seatback.

"Yeah, well, I don't. Okay? It's not my idea of a good time." He squeezed the steering wheel in his grip. "When I came to work for your dad after I got out, I thought it'd be all horseback riding through the hills and shit."

And it had been. For a time. Until the world went to utter shit six years ago.

Bran shook his head. "Seems no matter how hard you run from your past, you always wind up right back where you started."

Kat grunted. *I wouldn't know.*

They drove on for a moment in silence. Bran checked the battery life on their little vehicle, as was his endless compulsion—nothing quite takes the wind out of your sails like a dead battery and having to hoof it ten miles back to the ranch. But it was still two-thirds full. Plenty to get to Camperland and back.

"I'm just saying," Bran broke the silence, because, while Kat might not be a great conversationalist, Bran got chatty when he was uncomfortable. "Maybe this time you don't get her little rat dog all fired up, huh?"

Kat didn't respond. Which had its own interpretation.

She was going to stomp the little rat dog the first chance she got.

Poor mutt. Its only sin was being owned by the wrong lady. That, and being annoying as fuck to be around.

Up ahead, the rolling hills of the Valley fell away, and there it was: Camperland.

Eighty-four men, women, and children, all crammed into a collection of forty-some-odd recreational vehicles, including camper vans, pop-up campers, tow-behind campers, and one retrofitted school bus that some Godless hippy had intended to drive to Alaska before the world went into meltdown.

Camperland had been in the Valley for four of the six years since the plague swept society into the dustbin. It had started out as a handful of squatters—a Winnebago and an Airstream. But others had slowly coalesced around them over the years, and now the whole area looked like a blight. One big circle of dusty earth, trampled to death by a million footfalls.

And there, right in the middle of it all and watching them approach, was the old hag herself, bedecked in her usual sweat-stained, floral muumuu. The thing was big enough to fashion a five-person tent. But she didn't fill it out as much as she used to—years of hand-to-mouth subsistence had leaned her out a great deal.

Bran pulled the ATV up short of the dusty circle in which Camperland huddled in all its drab, derelict glory. The Jenkins family's brood of half-witted, ill-fed children huddled in the shade of their tow-behind, peering out suspiciously, like feral cats. Bran grimaced and looked away from them.

Terrible children, but...

Still children.

He thrust open the little door on the side of the ATV and grabbed his chopped-down shotgun from between the seats. He didn't bother to menace the denizens of Camperland with it.

There was no need. His presence was threat enough. He held it casually in his right hand as he approached, Kat falling in step beside him.

The old hag—her name was Missus Beetle, just like Beetle Bailey—raised one tremulous finger at them. "You said two weeks! It's only been ten days!"

Her other arm held the little rat dog that she called "Pooks" or "Pooksie-boo." Wirey white hair, too thin to hide the sunburned skin beneath, and cloudy eyes that Bran wasn't even sure could see much further than the end of its little black nose. But the nose worked well enough, and old Pooksie-boo caught the scent of Kat on the air and started growling and trembling.

"Yeah, well," Bran scuffed his heels to a halt a few yards away from Missus Beetle. "That's where you're off by about four days. I told you two weeks, two weeks ago. Then I *reminded* you ten days ago." He shook his head. "The two weeks doesn't just restart every time I show up. And, in fact, it's run out."

"How're we supposed to grow fucking corn when you keep driving through it?" Missus Beetle shrilled.

Pooks began to yap.

Kat stiffened. Bran glanced at her and saw the way she'd fixated on the dog. Jesus, what was with her and that dog?

Bran had learned long ago not to even bother telling Missus Beetle to shut the thing up. It wouldn't, or she couldn't, didn't much matter which.

"Missus Beetle," Bran said, rubbing his brow tiredly. "That corn is dead as fuck. Been dead for the last month."

"Can't grow corn without water!" Her voice, if possible, had pitched even higher. Any higher, and only Pooks would be able to hear it.

"Yeah, well. Drought's been shit. What do you want me to say?"

"Look!" Her crepey-skinned hand trembled in a new direction, off to Bran's left. He didn't bother looking. "This ain't about rain! Look at the river!"

"I'm not gonna look at the river." It wasn't a river anymore. Just a bone-dry ditch.

"It's fucking dry!"

"I know it's dry."

"Does Colin know it's dry? Maybe you should have Colin come down here and look for hisself and tell me how the fuck he thinks I'm supposed to water crops when he don't open the goddamned floodgate!"

"Mr. Horner don't open the goddamned floodgate until he gets paid."

Missus Beetle's wrinkly old mouth worked into a panic, her fatless jowls swaying like a chicken's wattles, froth building up in the corners of her lips. "How...?" She seemed at a loss for words. And, admittedly, Bran knew it was a bit of a paradox. "How'm I supposed to pay him? He wants corn as payment, but I can't grow corn without water. He won't open the floodgates without the corn. But I can't grow it until he opens 'em."

"Yeah, it's quite the pickle," Bran sighed.

It all seemed completely illogical. But it wasn't. It was actually very simple: Colin Horner didn't want them there anymore. Colin Horner was tired of the useless drain on his pastureland. The only thing that could possibly make Camperland's continued presence worth it, was if they could grow enough grain to offset the loss of pasture. Which they couldn't, never could, and never would. Colin knew that. Bran knew that. Presumably, Kat had some idea of it.

Only Missus Beetle seemed unable to connect the dots.

"Missus Beetle," Bran said, gazing up at the sky and spotting a lonely little cloud that would never have a chance to grow big enough to precipitate. He smiled wistfully at it. Then dropped his gaze to the old hag. "I need five hundred pounds of corn."

Missus Beetle provided him only with a frothy gob of spittle which landed too far shy of Bran to even be insulting. "You tell Colin that he can open up his fucking dam if he wants that corn. Shoulda known how all this was gonna go when he built the stupid thing in the first place. Who does that? Who cuts off water to settlements full of good people?"

"The guy that owns the river it comes from, I guess," Bran answered.

"Nobody owns shit anymore!" Missus Beetle spread her arm grandly. "This is the *earth*! You don't get to own the *earth*! It's for everybody!"

"I'm not having this conversation again."

"Colin Horner don't own shit! He don't own the water, or the mountain it come out of!"

"Jesus Christ."

"We're all free people here! Children of the earth and—"

And just like that, Bran went into Dark Mode. He'd wanted to avoid it, if at all possible. But these fucking people...they just kept pushing.

He fired his shotgun at Missus Beetle's feet. He had no idea whether the buckshot skipped up and got her, or if it was just bits of rock and dirt, but down she went with a howl, poor old Pooksie-boo flying out of her arms and tumbling through the dirt.

A great cry of indignation went up from the Camperlanders all around them, but Bran didn't bother to spare them a glance. They didn't have the balls to do anything. If they did, they'd've done it a long time ago.

While Missus Beetle wallowed on the ground, and Pooks got unsteadily to his twiggy little legs and ran off, yapping like his tail was on fire, Bran pumped a fresh round into the shotgun. The smell of the spent shotgun shell hit him, acrid and sweet. God, he'd always loved that smell.

Missus Beetle seemed unable to rise from the ground. She looked as helpless as a turtle on its back. She wasn't even injured all that bad—just a few bloody pock marks in her blue-veined legs. The cry of outrage from the others died rather quickly, as outrage has the tendency to do amongst cowards. Now they just watched.

Bran squatted down next to Missus Beetle, any semblance of diplomacy blown out like a candle in the wind. His face peered down at the old woman, expressionless.

"You don't have five hundred pounds of corn, do you?"

"You shot me!" Missus Beetle keened.

"Only a little."

"I'm dying!"

"Well, that depends."

"My heart! I can't breathe!"

"You don't breathe with your heart, Missus Beetle."

"I can't breathe!"

"You're talking well enough."

She went into paroxysms of gasping.

Bran shook his head, reached down, and slapped her on the face. Didn't like the texture of her skin across his palm. Didn't like the old, sour smell of her. "Hey. Hey. Missus Beetle. You need to listen."

She gasped some more. Eyes rolling.

"I'm going to kill everyone here if you don't listen."

"Oh Lord! Oh, Jesus!"

"Shouldn't you call out to Mother Earth or some shit?" Bran mused. "Anyway. Missus Beetle, you have to go. You have to get your people and get gone, campers and all. I want this place to look like you were never here." He considered this, and then shrugged. "Well. You know. Except for the big patch of Mr. Horner's pasture that you've trampled to dust."

"We're not going anywhere!" Missus Beetle wheezed, her wild eyes honing in on him again. "We've just as much right to be here as your fucking boss!"

"No. No, you don't."

"The land don't belong to—"

"Stop. Stop that." He put his hand on her chest and leaned his weight on it, which set her to gasping again. Her arms batted at him, but they were weak and ineffective. "You're going to leave, or you're going to die. You and everyone here. No one will be spared. You know how this works."

Missus Beetle worked hard to gather enough air past the weight he was putting on her chest. Her head rose up off the ground, greasy gray hair standing out in an unkempt corona around her pinched face. She thrust her wrinkly chins at him, the picture of geriatric defiance.

"Fuck you, and fuck Colin Horner."

Ten minutes ago, this would have made Bran sad. Now he just smiled. Then shrugged.

"Whatever."

Kat watched him work, and it was beautiful. He told her he hated going Dark Mode, but every time he did, he seemed so wild and free. Just like Kat wanted to be.

She wasn't really paying attention to everything that was said. She understood enough to get by, but language wasn't her strong suit, and when people got into a rapid back and forth, she struggled to keep up with their flapping tongues.

So, while Bran stood over the old sack of flesh and they yammered at each other, Kat paced back and forth, her empty hands clenching and unclenching, her savage gaze whisking back and forth between the faces of the people watching.

She could smell them, those people. Even through her bandanna. She could smell their sweat. Their unwashed bodies. She could smell the remnants of what they'd eaten, and the coating of woodsmoke over everything. She could even smell their fear.

It made her mouth water.

Bran said something that had the sound of finality to it. Missus Beetle said something back that sounded like a pathetic attempt to look strong, even as she was flat on her back. And then Bran shrugged and stood up and said "Whatever."

Then he turned to Kat and nodded.

Joy welled up in her. Relief. Release. The feeling of running downhill on sure feet.

She tilted her head back and howled at the sky, long and loud, and the fear-stinking people all around them began to scream. Some tried to run, but they wouldn't get far. Some tried to hide in their campers, but they would be found.

When all the breath had been expelled from her lungs, she lowered her head again, no longer Kat, Colin Horner's daughter. She was just herself. She was free.

Now...

Where was that dog?

Chapter 2

Beatrice Drye stood in the lookout, peering west, towards Camperland, and searching vainly for even just a wisp of smoke. "It's almost ten o'clock," she said, spitting a strand of brown hair out of her mouth that the breeze had just tossed into her lips. "They should've started their cookfires a long time ago."

Beside her, Ted Foley squirmed with obvious apprehension. He stood very close to her, and when she turned to glance at him, she had to crane her neck to look up. He was tall. But she was also a bit short. She could see straight up his nose.

He was handsome, though kind of bookish, which was made worse by the tortoise-shell glasses he wore. His features were all screwed up with worry. Mouth tight. Eyebrows drawn in.

"You sure it's not just too thin to see?" he asked, though it had the sound of grasping at straws. Because it was.

Beatrice shook her head. "I've been up here since dawn. I would've seen something."

"Shit." Ted leaned forward, placing his hands gingerly on the sharp-edged steel wall that enclosed the lookout—which was a lofty name for a metal box on stilts. But everything in the Redoubt was made out of metal boxes. The entire settlement was shipping containers—what Ted called "Conex boxes."

"You think they finally did it?" she wondered, feeling sick.

Ted grimaced. "Well, they've been threatening to."

"He won't stop with Camperland."

Ted turned his eyes on her. Sharply blue in his tanned face. She felt a little flitter of something in her stomach, and immediately felt a wash of guilt that made her look away from him again. It had been three years since James, and yet it still felt too soon.

"You think Colin's gonna try the same shit with us?" Ted asked, quietly.

Beatrice—really, it was Bea; only James had ever called her by her full name—nodded. "Come on, Ted. Five hundred pounds of corn in two weeks? In the middle of a drought? And he won't open the dam?" Now she shook her head, embittered by the cruelty of it. "That wasn't a deal. Colin knew they'd never be able to deliver. He just wanted them gone."

"Well, he hasn't given *us* a timeline."

"He will," Bea huffed, then flung a hand out at the expanse of rolling hills all around them. "He wants the whole damn Valley to himself."

A warm hand settled on her shoulder. "Beatrice."

She almost winced when he said it. He shouldn't be using her name like James had.

She met his gaze, searching his face. He was trying to look confident, but she could see the fear in him.

"I won't let him hurt you," Ted said.

Bea drew back from him, frowning. "Hurt *me*? What about the rest of the Redoubt?"

Ted blinked a few times and straightened, seeming off kilter. "Well, yes. That's what I meant. I won't let him hurt *anyone* here."

"You can't make that promise, Ted." She saw that she'd struck a sore spot and turned to look out towards Camperland again, before he could try to argue with her. She'd been stupid to even entertain the thought of Ted as anything more than her friend, and the leader of their settlement. James hadn't been in the ground for a week before Ted had started eyeing her, and now he was laying his hands on her and telling her he'd protect her. As though she needed him to. As though he *could*.

Ted was nice enough. But he wasn't as tough as he thought. James had been tougher. And stronger. And James hadn't even been able to protect himself, let alone her.

The puckered scar on her left cheek was a constant reminder. But it wasn't James's fault. He'd tried. He'd lied for her. And it had saved her life, even as it doomed him. The thought wracked her with that old familiar guilt. And bitterness towards herself.

Her eyes scanned the horizon and fell upon a small, tan smudge in the distance. For the span of a few hopeful heartbeats, she thought it might be smoke from Camperland. But it was too far to the south.

And it wasn't smoke, she realized. It was dust.

She jabbed a finger out at the horizon. "What's that?"

Even as she said it, leaning forward and squinting, something emerged from the dust cloud, just barely visible. Sunlight glinted off of a windshield.

"It's a vehicle," she answered her own question, feeling her heartrate ramp up. "White pickup truck."

"Ah, hell." Ted knuckled his glasses further up onto his nose, squinting into the distance. "Your eyes are better than mine."

Which wasn't saying much. Ted's eyesight had worsened the last few years, and his prescription glasses no longer gave him 20/20 vision. But it wasn't like he could just go to the optometrist and get new ones.

"Is it coming here?" he asked, worry evident in his voice.

Bea didn't answer for a moment. With Camperland presumably wiped out, she was on edge, but still hoping that their inevitable conflict with Colin Horner could be postponed for just a little while longer.

She watched the distant vehicle make its way around a lonely hill, then roll to a stop for a moment, positioned in a way that made her hold her breath. The way it was facing, it could just as easily spin eastward, towards Horner's Peak. Or it could spin north, and come for them.

It started moving again.

And began to turn towards them.

"Shit," Bea snapped, then reached down and snatched up the bolt-action rifle leaning against the wall of the lookout. "It's coming towards us."

Ted didn't waste a single moment. He immediately spun and hammered his fist against the inside of the metal walls, causing them to reverberate like a drum. A warning noise for everyone in the Redoubt: Danger incoming.

Ted was halfway out of the lookout by the time Bea got the rifle shouldered. "Keep them in your sights," he said as he clambered down the ladder to the ground. "You know the drill. I'll get everyone else into position."

Bea didn't like the look of them one bit. She didn't have much to base this on, except for the fact that there seemed to be five men in that pickup truck, and anytime a vehicle had an ass in every seat, it made her think that they wanted manpower. And when you have manpower, what do you do with it?

In her experience, violence.

Had Colin Horner sent them? That was where her mind went first. And she wasn't about to dismiss it as a possibility. Horner's Peak typically sent their goons out in one of two ways: Either on horseback, or, if it was their worst two—Kat and Bran—they came in a side-by-side ATV.

But Bea also knew that Horner's Peak had *some* supply of fuel, though she didn't know how they got it. Had they gassed up one of their vehicles and sent it as a show of power?

Down below the lookout, the Redoubters were either hiding in their Conex boxes, or they were armed with the few weapons they had ammunition for, and huddled in ready positions all around what they affectionately called "Main Street," which was essentially the narrow lane that bisected the grid of steel boxes.

If Colin meant to throw his weight around, he was going to get a helluva shock in response.

That was, if Ted had the balls to open fire on them.

As the vehicle slowed and approached their Main Street, Bea smooshed her cheek against the buttstock of her rifle. It was James's rifle, actually. A .308 that he'd purchased on some wild idea that he was going to hunt mule deer, but never got around to it. She had exactly five rounds for it—one in the chamber, three in the little detachable magazine, and one extra in her pocket.

She tracked the vehicle as it approached, the reticle of the scope hovering right over the driver, but the reflection on the windshield prevented her from getting a clear view. She could only make out the ghostly outline of head and shoulders.

Sweat trickled down the small of her back. Damn, but the lookout was getting hot as the sun reached its zenith. Her moist palms clutched the polymer stock of her weapon, the muscles in her arms beginning to tremble with the strain of adrenaline.

They should just shoot them now and get it over with. Why wait for them to get out and issue whatever threat they'd been sent to deliver? Sure, it would start a war between the Redoubt and Horner's Peak. But that war was an inevitability, so they might as well strike first.

Her gaze flicked down to the ground and spotted Ted with his rather ludicrously big, chrome-plated revolver in hand, lurking around the corner of a box, just his head protruding and watching the pickup approach.

As much as Bea wanted to pull her trigger, she would wait until Ted gave the order. She just hoped that he wouldn't wait until it was too late.

The pickup slowed to a crawl as it entered their Main Street. She could see the occupants inside moving about, looking out the windows, spotting some of the armed people in their ambush positions.

The pickup trundled along the length of Main Street at a rolling idle until it was right about at the midpoint, and then rocked to a stop, less than twenty-five yards from Bea.

For a long moment, the only noise was the thrum of the pickup's engine. The occupants of the vehicle seemed to be in conversation with each other. She still couldn't make out much through the windshield, and now, with it so close, and below her, the roof of the vehicle blocked the three people she'd seen in the back. Of the front-seat occupants, she could only make out the chest and below.

Shit. Were they wearing armor?

Her knees began to quake. If the target hadn't been only twenty-five yards from her, she would have been concerned that she could hit anything at all. But at this distance, there was no way to miss.

She stayed focused on the driver. Slipped her finger inside the trigger guard and rested the tip of it against the trigger. She held the crosshairs just above the collar of the man's armor. One wrong move—or a signal from Ted—and she'd blow that man's clavicle straight through his spine.

The driver's door eased open.

Bea clenched her breath. Every pulse sent the crosshairs jumping. Sweat beaded on her forehead and tickled as it ran down to her eyebrows.

The driver stepped out. She half expected it to be Bran, or one of Colin's other top goons, but she did not recognize this man. He was tall and rangy, with a short crop of sandy-brown hair, and a few days of stubble on his face. He wore a battered and faded pair of jeans, and a black t-shirt under his armor. He had rifle magazines stowed in that armor, but no rifle. Only a pistol on his hip.

He eased his door closed behind him, then turned a slow circle, taking in the Redoubt. Bea noted that he had a pronounced limp—his left leg seemed stiff and unwieldy. As he turned all the way around, she raised her reticle and settled the crosshairs right on his face.

She got the impression that he'd been a somewhat handsome man in the past, but his face was marred with old scars, and his expression didn't help: Mouth stern and drawn down at the corners, beetled brows casting his eyes into stark shadows. Then she realized with a start, that what she'd taken for a severe squint, was in fact a missing left eye.

After completing one full circle to take in the Redoubt, he took one step away from the truck and raised his right hand in a little wave, to no one in particular.

"Hello!" the man called out, with a voice to match his scars—low, and harsh, and husky. "First thing's first: We're not here to cause any problems, so, if you don't mind, please take your fingers off your triggers. As you can see, I do not have a weapon in my hands, and I'm really not in the mood to get shot today."

Bea did not remove her finger from the trigger. But she did blink, and then, with a bit of confusion mixed with hope, raised her eye from the rifle's optic. Was this some sort of trick? A ruse to get them to lower their guard?

But for the life of her, she couldn't remember seeing this man around the Valley. He was a complete stranger to her. And while she didn't trust strangers, the fact that he might not be sent from Colin Horner gave her a tiny ray of hope.

The scarred man lowered his hand. Raised his right eyebrow and peered around with his good eye. "I'd like to speak to whoever's in charge of your settlement."

A long pause as he waited for some sort of response and got nothing.

"Do y'all have a leader? A mayor?"

More silence.

"A chieftain?"

Movement from the corner of Bea's eye: Ted stepped out, and her heart jumped and then dropped, not sure whether he should be exposing himself to these strangers or not.

"That's me," Ted announced, not approaching the man, but standing in plain view with his big revolver still in his hands.

From Bea's vantage point, she couldn't be positive, but it seemed like the scarred man's good eye was focused on that revolver. He was very still for the span of a few heartbeats. Then he gave a slow nod.

"You wanna put that thing away?" the scarred man asked. "Or are you still thinking about shooting me?"

The revolver twitched in Ted's hand, but he didn't put it away. "I'll keep it right here, if it's all the same to you."

The scarred man's face split into a grin without a lot of humor in it. "Yeah, well, it's not all the same to me. It is, in fact, very different. You can hold onto that thing if it makes you feel better. And then me and my people will move on to some other place where the folks are little more friendly." Then he shrugged, casually. "Or you can put it away and we can talk like civilized people."

Ted took a half step forward. "Why would we want to talk to you?"

The scarred man made a face and turned his head, inclining his ear. "I'm sorry. Bit deaf in the left ear. I can't hear you when you mumble from twenty yards away."

Ted took another step forward and raised his voice, his tone piqued. "I said, why would we want to talk to you?"

"Ah." The scarred man nodded. "Good question." He put his hands on his hips. Twisted to the left. Twisted to the right. He was looking at their hastily-prepared ambush. "Sure seems like y'all are loaded up for a party. Expecting trouble?"

Ted shifted his weight. "That's none of your business."

The scarred man shrugged. "Well, if you think you got it handled with a few shotguns and deer rifles, then I guess you don't need our help."

He turned and stepped back towards the pickup truck.

Ted lurched forward. "Wait."

The scarred man stopped. Turned. One eye peering at Ted. Waiting.

Ted seemed to struggle with his words for a moment. "Are you saying...?"

"I'm saying," the scarred man's voice suddenly turned hard. "That you need to holster up. I gave you the benefit of the doubt by driving right into your shitty-ass ambush and stepping out without my rifle in hand. And I don't take kindly to people that brandish weapons at me when I've already told them I mean no harm."

Ted scoffed and shuffled uncomfortably. "Well, you can't just roll into the middle of someone's settlement and expect them to give you a warm welcome!"

"It's weird. You seem like you want to talk. And yet, you're still holding that revolver."

Ted tapped the side of his thigh with the long barrel of his revolver. "You never told me why I should want to talk to you."

The scarred man regarded Ted in silence for a moment, as though he was considering whether to drive off, or keep talking. Bea wasn't sure what she wanted him to do. The defensive, animal portion of her brain just wanted the strangers to leave. But the more logical part of her had become curious. Had he just implied that he could help them? And was it so obvious that they needed it?

That thought gave her pause. If a group of strangers could show up and know within a minute of laying eyes on them that they were woefully unprepared to mount a defense...well, that was a bad sign.

Finally, the scarred man spoke again: "I'm gonna shoot straight with you. It's obvious to me that your settlement is in some sort of trouble. And it is even more obvious that you don't know how to handle it."

Ted bristled. "You don't know shit. We can handle ourselves just fine."

The scarred man let out a lengthy sigh and turned to gesture lazily at either side of the Main Street. "You got shooters positioned directly across from each other. Everyone's backdrop is a friendly. You start shooting, you're going to kill more of your own people than whoever you intended to ambush. And how much ammunition do you have for those shotties and bolt-guns? Enough for one volley of fire?" The scarred man clucked his tongue. "You seem to be in bad straits, with minimal weapons and nonexistent training." He leaned toward Ted. "If I were you, I would think about holstering up and talking to me."

Ted stood very still, baking in the midmorning sun, the shirt along his spine dark with sweat. "Who are you?"

Rather than answer, the scarred man just dropped his good eye to the revolver in Ted's hand and raised his brows expectantly.

"Alright," Ted suddenly snapped. Bea stared in horror as Ted stuck the revolver into the back of his waistband, because he didn't have an actual holster for the monstrosity. It was so big it made his pants look like they might fall off his ass.

She almost yelled out to him not to give into these strangers. But then found that she was mighty curious to see what they had to offer. She still had a whole lot of reservations, but their situation was desperate. Maybe Ted was right.

"There." Ted raised his hands to show their emptiness. "Now. Who are you?"

The scarred man visibly relaxed and a new expression came to his face, like a fresh breeze scouring away storm clouds and letting the sunlight through. He smiled, and it was filled with such genuine good-humor that Bea noticed her grip on the rifle softening, and the muzzle rising away from the man's face.

"Name's Jackson," the scarred man announced, stepping towards Ted with a slow, methodical limp. "But my friends call me Jax." He extended his hand to Ted. "And you are?"

Ted looked at the hand for a long moment, then took it and gave it a single, brisk pump. "Ted Foley. And this is the Redoubt."

"Good to meet you, Ted," Jax said, then nodded towards the truck. "Would it be too much to ask that my companions be allowed to exit the vehicle and stretch their legs? We've been on the road for quite a while."

Ted craned his neck to see inside the vehicle. Then he twisted and glanced up at Bea again. The man named Jax followed his gaze and spotted her in the lookout. Ted gave her a small nod, and she sunk into her sights again, angling the rifle towards the vehicle. If Jax minded having his people under the gun, he didn't make a fuss over it.

"Go ahead," Ted said, with a small wave.

Jax turned and motioned to the rest of the people in the vehicle. Immediately, the doors opened, and four more individuals slid out.

Bea realized that she'd been mistaken thinking that it was five men in the vehicle—one was a woman. She was rail-thin and sharp-featured: Sharp nose, sharp chin, and sharp cheekbones. Discerning eyes that took in everything with a single pass. She had a head of thick brown hair that looked like it might be a mess of curls if it weren't braided so tightly to her scalp. She, as well as all the others, wore armor, and seemed generally well-equipped. Unlike Jax, they all exited with rifles strapped to their chests, as well as pistols on their hips.

The man from the front passenger seat seemed to be of an age with Jax, but that was the only similarity. Where Jax was tall and lean, this man was stockier and powerfully built. Thick black hair stood out almost like a short afro, and his face was ensconced in a bushy, black beard, shot through with silver around the jawline. Where Jax seemed to vacillate between sternness and good humor, this man looked flat-out mean.

From the backseat, immediately following the sharp-featured woman, two younger men got out. One was light-skinned, with a ruddy, sunburnt complexion, and a general way about him—the set of his face, the swagger of his walk—that pegged him as a willful clown.

The other young man was far more serious. He had shaggy black hair, and brown skin, and seemed to be of middle-eastern ethnicity. Bea found herself staring at this young man, fascinated by what she saw as a strange contradiction: He couldn't have been more than eighteen years old, and everything about his face was youthful. And yet, there was something in the hard set of his eyes and mouth that told her he had the experience of a much older man.

Bea was so momentarily distracted by this dichotomy, that she started when she realized the young man was looking right at her. Her heart did an uncomfortable little jig, feeling like his eyes were boring into her, and almost as a reaction to this, she pulled back from her scope, not liking how it magnified his face and made them feel oddly close.

He kept his eyes on her, and tilted his head when she pulled back to look at him with her naked eye. He seemed to be evaluating her as hard as she'd evaluated him.

And then he did something very strange: He smiled at her. A big, warm, guileless grin, that made the hardness seem to fall away from him like a skin he'd just shed.

And then he winked at her.

Chapter 3

It was obvious to Sam Ryder that he'd made the woman uncomfortable when he winked. Rather than respond in kind, which would have been a bit too much to hope for, she made a little recoiling motion with her head and scowled at him.

Which only made Sam smile wider. It was only when she shook her head with a note of dismissive irritation and focused back in on the others that Sam felt momentarily out of place. No one had ever accused him of being a charmer, and it wasn't something he typically tried his hand at.

But after everything they'd just been through over the last month, after all that bloodshed and loss, he'd been in a somber frame of mind, and heavy thoughts of regret and loss had chased him all the way north to this little corner of California.

When they'd pulled into this little settlement comprised of a bunch of shipping containers—not so different from the settlement that Sam had grown up in—he hadn't been expecting much.

But when he'd looked up and seen that pretty face staring down at him, it had taken him by surprise. After all the ugliness lurking in the background of his mind, even something so simple as a beautiful woman had been like stepping into the warm, spring sun after a cold, hard winter.

In this life, Sam had realized that you had to appreciate what beauty there was to be found.

"Oh-ho," Jones murmured at Sam's shoulder, giving him a nudge. "I see you're already building inroads with the ladies." He wiggled his eyebrows suggestively. "Nice."

Well. That hadn't taken long.

"Careful, Jonesy," Sam remarked, turning his attention to the others. "She's got a gun."

"Pff. Everybody's got guns."

The apparent leader of this settlement, a lanky guy that looked like he'd be more at home behind some accounting books than leading a fellowship of survivors through the end of the world, was watching Sam and his teammates with a concerned look. He also seemed inordinately impressed by their armor and weapons—a sign that this much firepower was unusual in these parts.

"Who are you people?" the man asked.

And with that, Jax turned and smiled knowingly at his team.

He hadn't exactly been lying when he'd introduced himself as "Jackson, but my friends call me Jax." His name was indeed Jackson, but that was his middle name, and none of his actual friends called him either Jackson or Jax. His name was Lee Harden, and they all called him Lee. But only in private.

Why the subterfuge? Because Lee Harden was not a name you wanted to introduce yourself by. Partly because they'd promised never to buck the official story that he was dead. But also because the name came with a whole slew of baggage that was best left buried.

"This," Lee/Jax said, gesturing to the nearest team member. "Is my second in command, so to speak. His name is Lincoln."

His name wasn't Lincoln at all, not even his middle name. He of the fierce demeanor and bushy black beard was Abram Darabie, but they all called him Abe when in private, and since they called him Abe, they decided that Lincoln was an easy enough pseudonym to remember. As it so happened, the name of Abe Darabie carried almost as much baggage as Lee Harden.

"And this," Lee now pointed to she of the sharp features and keen eyes. "Is kind of my *other* second in command, Marie. We call her 'Ma.' But she's not really anyone's mom."

It was actually just Jones that called her 'Ma,' but Lee liked to introduce her that way because it sounded friendlier. In the very beginning of all this, Jones had insisted that she was the "Team Mom," and began to call her that, which, over time, got truncated to Ma.

"And these young men over here are Sam and Jones." Lee flicked a finger between them. "Sam's the dark-skinned one. Jones is the sunburnt one."

They weren't important enough to have pseudonyms. Though, in truth, Sam Ryder was an adopted name, of sorts.

Six years ago, as the plague burned through the populace like a wildfire, Sam Ryder had been Sameer Balawi, the son of immigrants from Afghanistan. He was only twelve years old when the world changed. And he'd changed with it.

Gone were his parents. Gone were his sisters. Gone were his obsessions with video games and social media. He'd been stripped down, shaken up, and scattered, and when he'd finally pulled the pieces of himself back together, he'd become something very different. He'd become Sam Ryder.

"So..." Lee clapped his hands together and turned back to the leader of the settlement. "You got any place we can talk?"

The leader of the settlement looked around, as though he wasn't sure that such a place existed. "Like...in private?"

Lee bobbed his head. "Private would be best."

The other man's face clouded. "Would you be willing to disarm yourselves?"

"No," Lee said, simply. "But I'll meet you in the middle." He flicked a finger at Marie and Abe, who shared a brief roll of the eyes, but acquiesced to the unspoken command and doffed their rifles, placing them on the hood of the truck.

Lee looked back to the leader. "I'll be accompanied by Ma and Lincoln. Sam and Jones will remain out here with the truck, fully armed. But the three of us only have pistols, just like you. Fair enough?"

The leader either didn't have the guts to demand more from them, or he stupidly thought that it actually was fair. Luckily for him, they really weren't there for nefarious reasons. They always remained civil, until given a reason not to be.

The leader nodded. "Alright, then. We can talk in my...house."

Lee quirked a brow. "Anyone you'd like to accompany you?"

The leader, halfway to turning around and leading them to his "house," stopped and glanced back. "I'll be fine by myself."

Sam thought that was interesting. It wasn't good for the leader of a settlement to be an island unto themselves. Did this man not have a support network? Or did he fancy himself so smart that he didn't need any outside counsel?

Marie turned to Sam and Jones and raised a thumbs-up as she fell in behind Lee and Abe. "You boys good?"

"I want a juice box, Ma," Jones immediately replied.

Marie just ignored him and turned back around.

"Ma!" Jones called at her back, for no other reason than it was his eternal pleasure to disrupt the seriousness of every occasion, trampling gravitas underfoot wherever he found it. "Come on, Ma!"

Marie never turned back around.

Jones slumped and scuffed his heel in the dust. "Well, shit. Just wanted a fuckin' juice box."

Sam sighed at his friend, but smiled, because what else were you going to do with him?

His gaze drifted up to the lookout again, and noticed the woman behind the rifle peering down at him with a curious, evaluating stare. When their eyes met, she flushed and turned away.

"Alright," Lee grunted, easing himself into the folding chair that had been offered. It was the only other chair at the chintzy little card table besides the one in which Ted Foley had seated himself. Abe and Marie were content to stand. "First thing's first." Lee leaned his elbows on the table, careful not to overload the flimsy thing with his weight. "What do you call 'em?"

Ted, who sat stiffly across from Lee, frowned. "Beg pardon?"

Beg pardon? Lee almost laughed. He hadn't heard that formalization in God-knew how many years. This guy was a peach.

Smiling with private amusement, Lee drew a circle in the air. "The people infected by the plague. What do you call them around here? Always easiest if we work off of the same terms."

"Oh. Uh...we just call them 'infected.' Or 'crazies.'"

"First generation or second generation?" Lee's gaze zipped around the room as he spoke, cataloguing what it contained, the state of everything, and what that all said about the man who called it his home. "Do you call them the same thing?"

Ted's face pinched up. "What?"

Lee looked at him sharply, a note of irritation blooming right behind his sternum. Ted had seemed like he'd be more brains than brawn, but so far Lee had seen neither. But maybe he was just off his game. That was understandable.

"Most folks discriminate between the first and second generations," Lee explained. "The original ones and the new ones that mutated?" Ted's expression was still rather vacant. Lee felt the need to clarify. "First generation would be all the people that got sick at the start of the plague and went batshit crazy. Most folks just call those infected. When I refer to the second generation, I'm talking about the big bastards that evolved to become our perennial pain in the ass. So do you have a different name for them, or do you just call them all 'infected'?"

Ted leaned forward a bit. "I thought all the original ones died out."

Lee shook his head. "Mostly. But not entirely. They're still out there." Eyes wandering again while he spoke. The room was dimly lit by a single solar-charged lantern. Most of the floor space seemed to be a storage area for a variety of bric-a-brac—all the things that they didn't have a current use for, but might in the future. Engine parts, scraps of steel, power tools with no power to plug into, a set of bald tires, and a collection of storage bins.

All in all, though, Ted kept it surprisingly tidy. The floors looked like they were swept regularly. There was no trash. No stink of rank body-odor. Or the stink of rodents, for that matter. The snug area at the front of the box contained only the table and two chairs, and what looked like a futon cushion for a bed, a single blanket folded neatly at its foot. Leaning against the wall was a mountain bike that looked like it was still in good repair. Lee hadn't seen any vehicles in the settlement—maybe this was how Ted got around?

Lee continued, tapping a finger to his forehead. "The plague all but destroyed the frontal lobe of the first generation of infected. They don't do much but run around and eat whatever they can get their hands on. Basically, they don't take care of themselves like a normal animal would do. In cold climates, they died out after the first winter. But they're still around in more temperate areas where they don't freeze to death. And where they can scavenge enough food."

Ted shook his head. "I haven't seen any of them in years."

"But you do have the new ones around here? The ones that mutated?"

"Yes. We just call them 'infected'."

Well. That showed a marked lack of imagination. Without exception, every settlement that Lee had been to had their own name for them. Big'uns, teepios, hunters, eaters. Hell, one particularly superstitious group had even called them demons.

"Well, if you don't have a name for them," Lee said, returning his gaze to the room. "Then we do. We call them primals. To keep things simple, we'll be using that term from here on out. The primals hunt in packs led by an Alpha, but as a whole colony, they're matriarchal—the females run the show. We call the females Omegas." Lee ticked off three fingers. "So, primals, Alphas, and Omegas. You got all that?"

Ted blinked a few times, and seemed to be re-evaluating Lee. "You guys have done this before."

"Done what?"

"Travelled to different settlements."

Lee chuffed and gave an amused glance over his shoulder at Marie and Abe. "Yeah, we've done it a time or two."

Ted placed his hands on the table and folded his fingers together. "And what exactly is it that you do at these different settlements?"

Lee gave him a level stare. "We identify problems, and then solve them."

Ted's brow furrowed and he leaned back. "Who do you work for?"

"Would you believe me if I said the Interim Government?"

Ted actually laughed. "No. I would not believe you."

Lee smiled and shrugged. "Well, in that case, we're private contractors."

Ted let out a disconsolate sigh and then stood up. "I'm sorry. There's been a misunderstanding."

Lee remained seated. "Oh?"

"We barely have enough to get by ourselves," Ted said. "We have nothing extra to pay you with. So I don't see the purpose in continuing these talks."

"Ah." Lee had no intention of leaving just yet, and chose to let Ted know by wrangling his bum leg up and crossing it over his good one, then began to massage the knot in his hip. Old bullet wound. Standing hurt more than sitting, but God, sitting sure made it tighten up.

Ted stared down at him, looking a little put out that Lee hadn't allowed himself to be dismissed.

Lee found a little speck of dried something-or-other on the table and began to scrape at it with a fingernail. "What keeps you up at night, Ted Foley? Is it thoughts of the primals, coming in and tearing your people to shreds? Or is it other people you're afraid of?"

That seemed to give Ted pause. His fingers worked nervously where they hung at his sides. His jaw muscles pulsed. His eyes were looking at Lee, but he seemed to be picturing something else.

"I'd say it's fifty-fifty," Ted finally answered, his voice a tad rough.

"Well, it just so happens that I am in possession of some things that have been proven mighty effective against both."

"What's that?"

Lee smiled sanguinely and spread his hands. "Guns and ammunition, of course."

Ted looked exasperated. "I already told you: we have nothing of value to trade."

"Yes, you did already mention that." Lee gestured to the empty seat across from him. "Could you sit down? You're looming and it's making me nervous."

Ted quirked his head. "You don't seem like the type to get nervous."

"Anyone that doesn't get nervous died a long time ago. Please. Sit down."

Ted grunted and seemed like he'd make a deal out of it, but then just crossed back over to his chair and slumped into it, looking defeated. "If this is a sales pitch, you can stop. I know we need more weapons. Better defenses. Hell, better training. But, again, we can't pay you."

"I'm not a travelling salesman, Ted, and this is not a sales pitch."

"How, then? How do we make a deal?"

"Well, for starters, do you have a place we can sleep?"

Ted considered this for a moment. Then chuckled dubiously. "You mean you're going to give us weapons and ammunition in exchange for room and board?"

"Let's just start with a place to sleep, and we'll see where we go from there."

Ted rapped his fingertips on the table. "Okay. Yeah. I'm sure we can find some room for you."

"Great. In exchange for a place to lay our heads for a few nights, we'll...consult."

"Consult," Ted echoed, as though the word were a trap door.

"Yes, consult," Lee said, waving the man's suspicions away like fruit flies from a rotting apple. "And we can start with who you thought we were when you set up that ambush."

Ted fidgeted in his seat. "You're strangers. We didn't know *who* you were. Hence, the ambush."

Lee clucked his tongue. "It's a lot easier to identify problems when the people with the problems are forthcoming about them." He skewered Ted with a look that made it plain he saw past the bullshit. "You thought we were someone else when you saw us coming. Who did you think we were?"

Ted chewed on that for a minute. Fidgeted again. Damn, but he was a squirmy motherfucker.

Eventually, Ted let out a laborious sigh, and with it, all the bullshit evaporated. "There's a man. His name's Colin Horner."

Chapter 4

Sam was supposed to be scanning his surroundings, but, really, there's only so many times you can look at the same cluster of Conex boxes and curious-suspicious faces. Not that he was being a complete slack-ass. Only that there was a magnetic pull to his vision, that kept sucking his eyes back to the woman in the lookout.

It seemed to happen without him even realizing it, until his eyes glanced off of hers like ricochets and they both looked away with mild embarrassment.

But she'd been looking too.

Sam sighed and forced his eyes over his surroundings again. Dusty dirt. Metal boxes. Strangers' faces. Rolling hills of patchy, emaciated green. A hazy, hot sky.

Back to the woman again.

This time she wasn't looking at him. He found himself mildly disappointed by that, and yet pleased to be able to study her. Dark brown hair. Skin that looked like it did not get along with the sun—probably why she wore long sleeves, despite the warm day, and the wide-brimmed hat she had pushed back off her head. In that pale, flushed face, her blue eyes stood out starkly, even from a distance.

And then they swiveled and caught him.

He huffed out another sigh and looked down, scuffing his boot in the dirt. "Aw, hell, Jonesy."

"What?"

Sam righted himself, bringing his gaze back to the woman in the lookout, meeting her eyes and not flinching away this time. "Guess I'm gonna go talk to her."

Jones scoffed. "What is this? A high school dance? I don't give a fuck who you talk to."

"I never had a high school dance," Sam admitted, pulling the sling of his rifle away from the skin of his neck. "Never went to high school."

"Aw," Jones sang. "Such a babe in the woods."

Sam glanced down at himself. Dusty boots with the soles starting to split from hard use. Pants with faded bloodstains on them. Plate carrier with who-knew-what staining every nook and cranny of it. Battered rifle, held in calloused hands, the knuckles still cracked and scabbed over.

Babe in the woods, indeed.

He smirked up at Jones, then started walking towards the lookout. Over his shoulder he said, "How's it go again?"

"What?"

"Talking to girls."

Jones sighed theatrically. "Bro, it's easy. Just swagger on up there and tell her you got two tickets to Poundtown."

"Right." Sam gave him a finger gun. "Got it."

Leaning lazily against the front of the truck, Jones called after him: "If it doesn't work, it's because you didn't do it right."

Sam walked the rest of the way in silence. It was only twenty yards or so to the base of the lookout, but he could feel her attention shift to him, and then become sharp with focus. It was obvious that he was walking towards her, and it was also obvious that she didn't want him to.

Sam didn't know what else to do but raise his hands. And that struck him as funny: The new courtship rituals of humans started with convincing them not to shoot you.

What exactly did he think was going to happen? Hell, he didn't know. But life was short, and if he knew one thing, it was that tomorrow was not guaranteed—not for him, and not for anyone he had an eye for. He'd learned that lesson the hard way, and been forced to take a refresher course multiple times.

Fuck decorum. Fuck courtship rituals.

There simply wasn't time for it.

He stopped at the base of the lookout and peered up, squinting against the bright sky. She frowned down at him like a barbarian at her gates. He realized that, from the truck, he hadn't been able to see the scar that ran down the left side of her face. Seeing it now, it came and went through his consciousness, barely raising a stir outside of a mild curiosity of how she'd gotten it. Everyone had scars these days. Sam had seen some doozies—*had* some doozies—and this one was pretty tame by comparison.

"Hey," he said. No charm or seduction to it. Just a frank greeting between two people that didn't know each other.

"What do you want?" she demanded.

Prickly. But that's to be expected, isn't it? At least she wasn't pointing the rifle at him. So things were already looking pretty good.

"I'm Sam."

"I didn't ask you for your name."

"Well, I gave it to you."

Her eyes narrowed. "Well, I'm not giving you mine."

"Oh, that's fine," Sam said, turning around to look back at Jones. The lookout was just tall enough to cast a decent shadow, which Sam was currently in, and it felt twenty degrees cooler. "I was just grabbing some shade anyway. I'm sure you can appreciate that."

She didn't respond outside of a soft snort.

Sam smiled to himself. Caught Jones looking at him. Jones gave him a hopeful thumbs up, clearly in plain view of the woman eight feet over Sam's shoulder, and then made it worse by suggestively pumping his fist back and forth in what Sam assumed to be a mime of "Poundtown."

It was not missed by the woman, who breathed out a derisive "Christ."

"Yeah, he's a gem, isn't he?" Sam said absently. "Hey, you know, there's probably a good chance that we're going to be here for a while. I'm going to end up learning your name anyway."

"Well, good for you."

Sam leaned back against the metal wall. "You strike me as somewhat hostile. Can I ask why?"

"Just not in the mood, Sam."

"Oh, hey, that's good. You used my name. What are you not in the mood for? Conversation?"

"Men."

"Ah. Well. Does it help if I tell you I'm very young?"

"No. That makes it worse."

Sam snickered. "Alright, I can appreciate that. How old are you anyway?"

"Too old for you, hotshot."

"Alright," Sam said, smiling evenly back up at her. "Well, I won't try to climb your walls if you don't want me to, and it sure doesn't seem like you want me to." He dipped his head towards her and flicked a salute off of his sweaty brow, then turned.

He took two steps before stopping, his gut giving him just the tiniest twist of regret.

Aw, hell.

He turned and looked at her over his shoulder. Her face was every flavor of *go fuck yourself*. But that was okay. This part was for his own peace of mind.

"Don't take this as weird, but I learned a long time ago not to hold back what I wanna say, 'cause I might never get another chance. So, since you're here and I'm here, and neither of us are dead yet...You're beautiful. It was a pleasant surprise."

She blinked a few times, her face caught in some sort of dilemma on whether to continue to be hard and unyielding, or to let herself be flattered. He didn't see which one she went with. He'd already turned back around and strode the rest of the way to Jones.

Who was shaking his head. "You didn't say the line. I told you to say the line."

"No, I said it," Sam lied, knowing that Jones knew it was a lie. Knowing that Jones didn't actually want him to say the line. Knowing that Jones probably had never said that line to a woman before, unless perhaps on a dare. But this was the act they played at, and it was a familiar call and response: Jones, the wild jester who fancied himself wise, though everyone knew he was an idiot; and Sam, the naïve kid who didn't know any better than to listen to the jester.

"Must not have said it right," Jones sighed.

"Maybe it was something with the cadence?"

"Yeah, it's a very specific cadence. You gotta get the beat right. It's the rhythm of it that lulls them into having sex with you." Jones shook his head. "Welp. Keep practicing, young padawan."

"Damn." Sam snapped his fingers. "One of these days, Jonesy. One of these days I'll lose my virginity."

Jones put his hand on Sam's shoulder. "I know you will, son. And when you do? I'll be right there, cheering you on."

"Thanks, Dad. I can't wait until I can be just like you."

"Me neither."

"Hey! Hotshot!"

Sam jerked his head up to the lookout.

The woman had her rifle shouldered with one hand, and with the other was pointing.

"We got incoming!" she snapped.

Sam whirled around, hands snatching up his rifle without thinking about it, and angling closer to the engine block of the truck. Distantly, he worried about his pack in the bed—it contained everything he owned in the world, and he really didn't want it shot up. Secondarily, he worried about his own skull and brain matter, and thought about his helmet in the backseat.

Jones had already started moving towards the engine block of the truck as well, but when he saw what the woman had pointed at, he slowed. It was a tiny little dust cloud, cresting a hill maybe two miles distant. No need to rush.

Sam moved for the cab of the pickup, wondering how worried he should be. "Ma'am?" he called behind him.

"What?" the woman hollered from the lookout.

"You got any idea who that is and whether we should be worried?" Sam yanked open the back door, snatched Jones's lid and shoved it at him, then grabbed his own and plopped it onto his head.

"Worried? Always. And as for who it is? Yeah, I've got a pretty good idea."

Sam buckled the chin strap. Considered his pack in the bed, but if he tried to secure it under the engine block, it'd either get in the way, or get left behind. It surprised him how badly he didn't want the things in that pack to get perforated.

He slammed the door behind him and moved with Jones towards the engine block.

"Someone wanna tell Lee?" Jones murmured under his breath.

Sam just shrugged. "Let's see what we're dealing with first." Then, over his shoulder. "Ma'am, who is it that you—"

He jerked in surprise to see the woman running up to him, her eyes fixed in the distance.

"Listen!" the woman hissed. "I just scoped them. It's these two—"

"Wait-wait-wait," Sam hissed.

"What?" she demanded.

"I can't just keep calling you 'ma'am'."

The woman's eyes widened. And again, that moment of indecision that he could see so plainly written on her face: Tell him to go fuck himself, or just acquiesce for the sake of expediency?

She acquiesced. "It's Bea. Now, are you listening?"

Sam nodded, smiling at this small victory. "Roger that, Bea, I'm listening."

She thrust her finger towards the horizon. "That's Bran and Kat. They're bad news. And they're coming this way. Which is even worse news. They only ever come around if they've got a bone to pick. I'm going to run and warn Ted."

"What do you want me to do when they get here?" Sam asked.

"Just stall them. And…" Bea started backpedaling, looking worried. "And don't piss them off too much, okay? Trust me. You do *not* want to make them mad!"

Sam frowned as she twirled and sprinted away.

Jones stared after her. "What? Is one of them the Hulk?" He glanced at Sam. "But seriously, if we're not supposed to piss them off…"

"Yeah, you probably shouldn't speak," Sam preemptively agreed.

Jones coughed out a laugh that turned into an actual cough, then a throaty hack, then he spit a glob of phlegm off to the side, and then, as though that had all been an eloquent speech, he said, a little hoarsely, "But I digress. Really. It's just the two of them. Why don't we just wax 'em?"

"Oh, you know," Sam said, hiking a weathered boot up onto the front bumper of the truck. "Geopolitics being what it is, we usually refrain from 'waxing 'em' until we have a better idea of what's going on in the area."

"Okay, alright. I'm just sayin', your girl didn't look too happy that they were coming. These obviously aren't friendlies. What'd she call them?"

"I don't recall, but there's a cat in there somewhere."

"I think the other one was Bran."

"Short for Brandon or something?"

Jones shrugged. "That, or Bran Flakes"

"Or Bran Muffins."

"Oat Bran."

"Brannnnn…" Sam drew a blank. "…nanas?"

"Brananas?" Jones looked pained. "I can't even look at you."

"I'm sorry. It got away from me."

"You sure you wanna do the talking here?"

"Oh, yes. I'm sure."

"Why'd you say it like that?"

"Because you're an idiot."

"Oh. My. God." Jones shook his head. "There's so many times I can think of when I've been way smarter than you. But now's not the time, because they're here."

Sure enough, the dust cloud had coalesced into a quiet little side-by-side ATV that trundled into the main drag of the settlement, slowing its roll while the cloud of dust in its wake was swept up by the breeze and pushed away. It was a dust-coated white, with black accents. Two occupants, just like Bea had warned them. An older male that didn't look all that scary, and a younger woman with a blue bandana that covered everything from her nose down.

"Ooh," Jones murmured as the ATV slowed to a stop, about ten yards shy of their truck. "What's she supposed to be? An old-timey bank robber?"

Sam lowered his boot from the bumper and took a miniscule step out from the truck—not enough to fully expose himself, but enough to be visible. He didn't want to give whoever these people were the impression that he was cowering behind the truck. He also didn't want to hide and then accidentally surprise them. Sometimes people started shooting when they got surprised.

Taking a cue from Lee's book, Sam decided to go with what he considered to be the most effective tactic for dealing with unknown parties: Being overly friendly. So he raised a hand and gave them a little wave.

Both pairs of eyes locked onto him, and Sam had the fleeting notion that he was a piece of meat dangling over an alligator pond.

But he still kept his hand upraised, a sunny smile on his face.

There was a reason this technique was so effective. People just generally had at least a *slight* mental block about trying to kill someone who seems happy to see them. And maybe-just-maybe you'd exchange only words and not gunfire.

In Sam's opinion, that was always worth a shot.

The small side doors of the ATV swung out and both the man and the woman stepped out at the same time, the man grabbing a shotgun from between the seats. The woman didn't seem to have a weapon at all.

The fact that they were not very heavily armed only alarmed Sam more. Bea was clearly terrified of these two—as was the rest of the settlement, considering how they all shrunk back and gripped their weapons a little tighter. It'd be foolish to assume their fear was baseless.

The man and the woman approached and stopped a few yards shy of Sam, right about at the tailgate of the truck. The masked woman peered around her with squinted, predatory eyes, while the man stayed locked onto Sam with a look on his face like Sam was a mysterious monolith sculpted entirely out of dog shit.

"Who the fuck are you?" the man demanded.

"I'm Sam. This is Jones. We're just visiting." He considered extending his hand, but decided against it. "Are you Bran?"

The guy tilted his head, the side of his mouth curling up slightly. His grip on the shotgun worked, but it remained pointed at the ground. "Visiting, huh?" He chuckled softly and raised an eyebrow. "Like, you got an auntie in the neighborhood or something?"

"Oh, you know," Sam said, still smiling. "Just passin' through."

"Huh." The guy spat off to the side. "See, when you say that, I get all hinky inside because it really feels like you're hiding something."

"Well, I really wish you wouldn't get hinky, because I was explicitly told not to piss you off."

"That's nice. But I'm just trying to figure out why I'm even talking to you and not Ted."

Sam pointed helpfully in the direction of Ted's Conex box. "Oh, Ted's in a meeting with my boss. I'm sure they'll be out in just a minute. We were just standing out here, guarding our truck. And then you pulled up. And now we're talking."

The guy's eyes narrowed. "I can't figure out if you're being dense or a smartass."

"Neither. I'm trying to be civil." He tried to get his name again: "Are you Bran?"

The man seemed wholly unable to make heads or tails of Sam, but eventually sighed. "Alright, kid. Yeah, I'm Bran. Now, I don't know what kind of comedy routine this is supposed to be, or who put you up to this, but I'm going to issue a word to the wise here..." he lowered his voice and leaned in. "You don't know what the fuck you're dealing with right now, and it is in your best interest to get the fuck out of my way."

Sam looked down at the ground, then to either side of him, as though making the point that he really wasn't in anyone's way. "Well, Mr. Bran, sir, my boss parked the truck right here, and told me to guard it. Sooooo..." He smiled again. And shrugged. "I can't just walk away from the truck. I'm sure you understand. You have a boss too, don't you?"

Bran studied him for a moment, his smile widening. Then he chuckled and shook his head and started moving forward again, angling around Sam. "Alright, kid. You guard your truck. Me and Kat are just gonna go have a word with Ted."

Sam made a regretful noise and stepped into Bran's path. "Oof. Well, I can't really let you interrupt my boss's meeting either."

Any good humor fled from Bran's face. The woman beside him—Kat, presumably—issued a low growl.

"Kid," Bran said, his voice husky and low. "You remember how you weren't supposed to piss me off?"

Sam nodded. "I do."

"Well, you're pissing me off right now."

Sam made a cringe-y face. "Ah, man. I wish you weren't getting pissed off right now. Because I'm really just trying to do my job, you know? I'm sure you're trying to do your job too. Sucks that our jobs are kind of...butting heads right now."

Bran stared at him, unmoving. Sam couldn't even see the pulse of his carotids in his neck. Either this guy had the lowest blood pressure on the planet, or he was dead calm. Which was impressive, because, despite his cool demeanor, Sam was starting to freak out just a little bit, wondering where the hell Bea was and why it was taking her so long to get Ted. How far was he supposed to take this stalling tactic?

Sam had seen a lot of mean, screwed up people in his life. But there was something about this guy that set off instinctive warning bells in his head. It was like the guy knew he was untouchable. Like he was confident that if things went bad, he'd be on the winning side.

Standing so close to him now, Sam could see that Bran's confidence was not bravado. He knew something Sam didn't. There was a danger here that Sam wasn't seeing.

Tread carefully, Sam warned himself, wondering if he'd made a mistake by acting too casual.

But then Bran's eyes shot off to something over Sam's shoulder, and a worried voice hollered out, "Bran! Kat! I'm coming!"

It was Ted, sounding like he was in a hurry to get there.

"Let's all just take a few deep breaths! Sorry for making you wait!"

Slowly, humanity crept back into Bran's face, and when it was fully there again, it left Sam feeling queasy and strange. As Bran relaxed and took a step back, Sam allowed himself a quick glance over his shoulder. Ted was front and center, hustling along with Bea at his side, Lee and Marie trailing...

A frown crossed over Sam's eyes as they darted around. Where the hell was Abe?

It took him about two seconds before he made eye contact with Lee and got a stern, *hush-hush* look from that one eye.

But of course. Abe had squirreled around somewhere and probably had his rifle trained on Bran's nose.

Ted and Bea stopped, more or less abreast of Sam, looking terrified and out of breath. Lee and Marie hung back a few paces, close to the engine block with Jones.

"Ted," Bran crooned, drawing out the name like they were longtime pals. And then he got serious again. "Mind telling me what the fuck's going on here?"

Ted held out a staying hand, as though Bran was a bull that might charge him. Sam noted that the fingers trembled. Good God. How had this guy become the leader of the settlement?

"Look. Bran. We're very close, okay? If you can just give us a little more time—or better yet, if you can convince Colin to open the dam, then—"

"Christ," Bran spat. "No, he's not gonna open the fuckin' dam, and don't ask again. But that's not what I'm asking you about right now." Bran had his gaze clamped onto Ted's like a bulldog on a jugular and stabbed a finger so close to Sam that it nearly touched his nose. "I wanna know who the fuck these guys are."

Sam only did what he did next because he knew Abe would splash the man's brains if it came down to it. He gently pushed the finger out of his face and said, "Oh, I already introduced myself. I'm Sam. That's okay. I'm bad with names too."

Bran turned a face on Sam that looked for all the world like lightning would come shooting out of his pupils. Sam couldn't tell if it was his nonchalance, his words, or the fact that he'd pushed Bran's finger away.

But Bran didn't burst. Got right up to the edge, it looked like—if the redness along his scalp and the protruding vein in his temple were any indicator—but then spoke quietly. "Who's this kid's boss?"

Lee let out a sigh and shuffled around Ted and Bea. "Yeah, that's me," he said, like a parent that's been called out for their unruly child. He made no effort to hide his limp. He didn't stand tall and imposing as he could when he wanted to, but rather approached with a bit of a slouch, eyes on the ground in front of him.

Lee stopped when he was shoulder to shoulder with Sam, then drew himself up with a grunt and looked tiredly at Bran. "Has he done something wrong?"

Bran's eyes narrowed, and Sam could see all kinds of calculations zipping around in that guy's brain, trying to make sense of Lee. Sam almost felt bad for him. To the freshly-introduced, Lee could seem like a jumble of contradictions. He was battered and scarred up and missing bits of himself, and yet he projected the attitude of a man completely confident in his body. His musculature wasn't pronounced, but you could see the hard edges of it, and it didn't take a genius to know that Lee could exert mean amounts of force on a fleshy target if he chose to. He acted all good-humored and friendly, but you only needed to make eye contact with him for a few seconds to know that he could turn that off like a switch.

But Bran was savvy. He took Lee's measure, and instantly knew what he was dealing with.

He sniffed and tilted his head back, peering at Lee. "I have no clue who you are. But..." Bran lifted two fingers and waggled them at Lee in an *I-see-you* gesture. "I know *what* you are."

Lee smiled back, but with much less genuine feeling. "I'm a traveling merchant. Name's Jackson, but you can call me Jax."

The girl—and she *was* a girl, Sam realized; she couldn't possibly be more than fifteen or sixteen, judging by her eyes—let out a protracted hiss, and then spoke in a rough, husky voice: "Dark mode."

Sam had no idea what the hell that meant, but Bran obviously did, because his hand shot up, palm to Kat, silencing her. "Not now, Kat."

Lee pulled his head back. "Sure wish I knew what y'all were talking about."

"Oh, it don't matter anyhow," Bran said, taking a step back from Lee. Sam watched his eyes stray from Lee's and go ranging all over. And he realized what Bran was looking for. "So, where's your other guy, Jax?"

Lee sighed, but didn't otherwise respond.

Bran waved a dismissive hand at the truck, eyes still searching. "Three helmets in there," he said, then nodded at Sam and Jones. "Two helmets on your boys here. So where's your fifth guy?"

"Well, I'll be honest," Lee said. "I don't really know *where* he is, exactly. But I do know that there's only eight ounces of finger pressure between a bullet and your brain, so you do with that what you will."

"Huh," was all Bran replied.

Sam guessed Bran never did spot Abe, because he gave up after a moment and his gaze skipped across all of them and landed back on Ted. The expression on his face was one of rueful disbelief. And maybe a bit of warning.

"This really how you want to play this one, Ted?"

Ted took a halting step forward. "Hey, whoa. It's not like that, okay? We'll have Colin's payment. We just need a little more time."

"And this was your plan to get more time?" Bran asked, almost sounding disappointed in Ted. "Hire some outside guns?"

"No," Ted said quickly. "That's not it at all."

"Camperland's done."

The words came out of Bran so flat and understated that, for a moment, everyone was silent. Even the residents that presumably had the inside track on things seemed a bit confused by that.

Ted frowned like he was trying to piece it together. And when he did, his face blanched. "Done? Like...*done* done?"

Bran surprised Sam by wincing and glancing away. "Well, they didn't leave me a whole lotta options, Ted." Eyes sad, almost plaintive. "Is that what you're doing to me right now?"

Ted swallowed and shook his head. "I'm not doing anything to you, Bran."

Bran chewed on that for a moment. Nothing but the sound of the wind. Then Bran nodded. "Alright then."

"Alright?"

But Bran just tapped Kat on the shoulder and they both turned back to their ATV.

Ted skittered forward a few steps. "Alright, like, everything's cool now?"

"No, Ted," Bran called over his shoulder. "Everything is not cool."

"Shit," Ted hissed. "You're not gonna call them, are you?"

Bran swung into the driver's seat. Slumped back and regarded Ted over the steering wheel. "Three days, Ted. I'll be back in three days. You know what I want. Please have it ready." His face clouding over, Bran yanked the ATV into gear. "I don't wanna do to you what I did to them."

And with that, Bran gunned out a rapid turn, stirring up dust, and disappeared into it.

Chapter 5

Lee watched the ATV until it crested a rise and disappeared over the other side.

At this point in Lee's life, he'd been a lot of places, and dealt with a lot of bad men. Sometimes he'd been the bad man, depending on your perspective. He'd been shot up a bit. Blown up. Stabbed. Burned. Mauled. Pretty much all the ways you could wreck your body going toe to toe with things that wanted to kill you.

You'd think by now he'd be the coolest cucumber in the pickle patch. But God, were his guts torqued up. Pulse hitting hard enough to feel it in his throat. Mouth dry. Shoulders tense.

It wasn't just fear, though. Lee wasn't immune to fear—nobody was. But fear of death didn't hold the edge that it used to for him. That old blade had been notched and dulled from years of hard use. It'd become a blunt instrument, and easy for him to ignore.

And yet his body still dumped adrenaline into his system for other reasons. More than any other factor, it was the tension of restrained desire. It was a twitchy horse, locked into the starting blocks, and just wanting to run. It was knowing he shouldn't be the one to strike first, and trembling as he prayed for the other to do it, do it, *do it!*

It was his body gearing up for yet another fight to the death.

Which was great—when there was an actual fight.

But when there wasn't, that dump of potent brain chemicals would just sit and simmer, with no outlet. They had to be worked out slowly with deep breaths, and shaking hands, and twitching calf muscles.

He fucking hated it. Wished that he could just be stoic and calm. Sure, he presented that on the outside. But he just wished he could feel it on the inside.

Now he was going to have a headache.

"Well," Lee gruffed, then spat off to the side. "They seem nice."

Ted twisted to look at him, his face blank.

Lee just shrugged. "I mean, he wasn't a dick about it. Although, I dunno about the young woman."

Something strange crossed over Ted's face. "Don't let her age fool you. She's dangerous."

"That's why I said I don't know about her."

"Bran's dangerous too."

"Maybe. But he doesn't *want* to hurt you. The girl does."

"They both work for Colin Horner," Ted said, as though changing the subject.

"And Colin Horner wants five hundred pounds of feed corn," Lee recalled from their meeting. "Of which you are far short, correct?"

Beside Ted, the woman with the scar on her face who had been in the lookout bristled and cinched closer to him. "You told them?"

"Yes, I told them," Ted snapped. Then, to Lee: "Five hundred pounds short."

"Oh dear," Jones quipped from off to the side.

"Ah." Lee tilted his head back, working the aching fingers of his left hand. Three years ago, he'd made a brave but ultimately stupid decision, and gone running after a primal that was trying to carry a wounded woman away. That was the "brave" part. But he'd only had his pistol. And that was the stupid part. The primal had latched onto his wrist. It had received a 9mm to the brainstem, and Lee had received severed tendons and a hand that didn't quite work right anymore.

All for nothing, as it turned out. The woman had died anyway.

That was a long time ago. Back on the East Coast. Back when he'd been Major Lee Harden, and his name had meant something.

He dragged his good eye over to Ted. "Just gonna hazard a guess here, but I'm assuming you're not going to magically come up with five hundred pounds of corn in three days, are you?"

"Is magical corn one of the things you sell?" Ted let out a desperate titter, then choked it off and cleared his throat. "No."

The sound of a heavy *thunk* drew Lee's attention to the truck. Abe, sweating profusely and looking like he'd just completed a hard run, had slapped his Mk-12 Designated Marksman Rifle on the hood of the truck and was now glaring at Ted.

"So did you actually have a plan to deal with this problem of yours?" Abe's tone gave no quarter. Abe was not the best at being gentle with his words. But then again, nobody had ever accused Lee himself of being terribly diplomatic.

"We were figuring it out," the woman beside Ted answered sharply.

"I'm sorry," Abe snapped back, stepping forward with his hands on his hips. "Who are you again? Besides the woman that pointed a rifle at me when I first got here?"

"Name's Bea," she stated, as though her name were a throwing knife.

"Well, good for you, Bea and Ted," Abe growled. "I'm so glad you were *figuring it out*, but now your time's up."

Bea's eyes widened and her teeth flashed. "*You* came *here*—" she spun to Ted. "—we don't have to listen to this bullshit."

Ted stood there, looking at them thoughtfully.

"Ted!" Bea pressed.

He held up a hand. "Now, hold on a minute, Bea."

"These guys are nothing but trouble!" she spat.

"Aw," Jones said, hurt.

"They've been here for ten minutes and they already got Bran and Kat all pissed!" She whirled on Sam. "Like I told them *not* to!"

Marie sniffed loudly and leaned against the hood of the truck. "And how do you think that would have gone *without* us here?"

Bea blinked rapidly like Marie's words were a bit of sand in her eyes. "That's a stupid rhetorical question, lady. All I know is that we were fine, and then you showed up, and now we've got three days before all unholy hell gets unleashed on us."

"Right," Lee said loudly, clapping his hands, and forcing everyone's eyes to him. "You've got three days, and we're here. Those are the facts. So, what happens in three days? That's really up to you." He smiled and leaned in, lowering his voice. "But if I were you, I'd think about maybe asking us how we might be able to help."

Bea drew her head back. "What? Is this your schtick? Show up to random places and cause problems, then sell the solution?"

"Seems like you had this problem before we got here."

"Ted!" Bea said again.

But Ted just looked right at Lee, without a breath of guile in his face, and said, "How can you help?"

"What a great question," Lee said. "Marie?"

Still lazing on the side of the truck, Marie said it like a bored fast-food clerk reading a menu: "Weapons, ammunition, training, consulting."

Silence.

A wave of realization. Not just over Bea and Ted, but over all of the onlookers slowly inching closer to hear the exchange. The realization that, regardless of whose fault the problem was, these strangers were a solution. Possibly the only solution they were ever going to get.

"What do you want for all that?" Bea asked, her voice much quieter now.

It was Ted that answered: "For now, they want a place to stay." He gave her a cautious sidelong glance, but Bea remained focused on them.

A shadow of disbelief crossed over her eyes. "So, you're gonna give us weapons, ammunition, training, and consulting, and all you want in return is a crash pad?"

Lee gave a facial shrug. "That a problem for you?"

Bea whirled on Ted. "Well, who the hell are they gonna..." she trailed off, answering her own question, and apparently not liking it.

Ted gave her a pleading look. "I'm sorry, Bea. I was going to talk to you about it first, but then all this happened."

"Really?" Bea's eyes sparked. "You're gonna put a buncha strangers in with me? What the hell, Ted?"

"You're the only one in the Redoubt with room, ever since..." he cut himself off and swallowed, waving his hand in front of his face. "I'd put them up at my place, but I can barely move around in there as it is with all the crap we have in storage."

Bea looked like she might start shaking with rage.

Sam leaned in. "I promise we're housebroken. And we won't chew your shoes." He made an X across the front of his plate carrier. "Cross my heart."

Lee inspected his teammate's face and frowned. Was he imagining things, or was Sam a little sweet on this lady?

Sam's sense of humor did nothing to douse Bea's anger. She started to open her mouth, but really, Lee wasn't in the mood for more arguing—that post-adrenaline headache was already coming on.

"Actually," he said, jumping in before Bea could get started on whatever tirade she had brewing. "Nothing's for sure and certain just yet." Lee jerked his head towards his team. "We still need to talk amongst ourselves and decide if we really do wanna stick around here and help."

Ted's eyes went a little wider and his mouth popped open. He struggled to make sounds with it for a few seconds, and then finally managed, "You still have to decide? I thought it was already decided. Why the hell have you been arguing this whole time if you haven't even decided?"

Lee squinted at Ted. "Well, frankly, Ted, we haven't decided *because* we've been arguing this whole time."

Ted's face screwed up. "What does that even mean?"

Lee sidled up closer to him. "Let me put it to you like this, Ted. How bad a community wants our help is a big indicator of how successful we're going to be. And so far? I can't say with much certainty that anyone besides you actually wants us to be here."

Ted considered this for a long moment. Once or twice, his eyes jagged in Bea's direction with a definite note of resentment.

Lee didn't want to build any bad blood between the people of this settlement, so he put on another smile and gave Ted a pat on the shoulder. "Just give us a few minutes, Ted. We'll work everything out."

Chapter 6

Lee slammed the door to the truck. Everyone else was already in their seats, doing a great job of avoiding eye contact with the people outside of the vehicle. And there were quite a few at this point.

Bea and Ted had retreated. But the rest of the denizens of the Redoubt had now relaxed a good bit and come sauntering out into the open, where they now lounged in the shade and stared at the newcomers like they'd never considered that staring at others might make them uncomfortable.

Lee felt like a fish in a bowl.

A betta fish, to be exact.

"Alright," Abe grumped from the front passenger seat. "I'll go ahead and get this ball rolling. I say we ghost this shitheap and head on to the next town."

"Bold statement," Lee noted. "You seem very sure of your decision."

Abe shook his head, eyeing the people outside. "Man, fuck these asshats. I don't know what's going on between them and this Colin Horner guy, but maybe he's got a good reason to be pissed at them. I feel strongly that we just saved their asses, and that little bitch with the rifle can't say a damn nice thing to us."

"She's just worried," Sam said from the backseat.

Lee raised his eye to the rearview mirror and looked at the younger guy. Sam didn't look terribly offended by what Abe had said, but if you were the type to get offended, then you probably wouldn't last long on a team with Abe Darabie. Sam was looking out the side window at nothing in particular, but he had a set to his face that looked to Lee like concern. Like he was concerned for this place.

Or maybe just Bea.

"Well, she should be worried about Colin Horner, not us," Abe huffed.

Lee's gaze lingered on Sam for a moment more before he shifted to Marie. "What's the matriarch say?"

Marie took a deep breath, her expression neutral. "I'm tempted to side with Abe on this one. Like you said, Lee, cooperation from the settlement is the most important element of success. And I'm not getting overly cooperative vibes."

Jones stretched his back and sighed. "Don't y'all think you're getting a little assed up over nothing? You're painting it like this entire settlement came out to haggle with us. But the only person that's had anything bad to say to us is Sam's new girlfriend."

Sam made a small noise of exasperation.

Abe jerked around in his seat, eyeing Sam. "What's he talking about? You got a thing for the Scarface girl?"

"Jesus," Marie hissed, shaking her head. "You are an offensive twat."

Abe looked briefly put-upon. Which was something only Marie had the power to do to him. "I was just trying to figure out if he was legit into her, so I could filter any further derogatory comments about her. I was trying to be *sensitive*."

"Oh, yeah. Sensitive. That's you."

"She's not my girlfriend," Sam said, as though it was something he'd already addressed several thousand times. "And I'm shocked at you for taking anything Jones says seriously. But, to Jones's *actual* point...I mean, yeah, we've really only talked to Ted and Bea at this point. We can't just go making broad statements about the entire community."

Abe sat back in his chair with a disconsolate grunt. "Don't like 'em."

Marie gave him a pat on the shoulder. "Hon, when do you ever like them?"

Jones, all relaxed into his seat with his head lolling on the headrest, rolled it over to look at Lee in the mirror. "What about you, Boss?"

Lee saw Jones looking at him, and then he caught the barest little glance from Sam, and saw the hope in it before Sam quickly looked away. He considered that for a moment before answering. Ran his rough hands over the steering wheel. Feeling how smooth the vinyl had been worn in the three years of driving it.

Abe and Marie would only ever be convinced with hard facts and logic. They were supreme pragmatists. And that wasn't a bad thing to be. In fact, it was great. Great for the team, and great for Lee.

Was Lee a pragmatist? Well...no.

Everyone likes to think of themselves as a pragmatist. Because what's the alternative? To be some plastic-bag-caught-in-a-breeze-type jackass that just goes with how he "feels" about every situation? No one wanted to be that guy. Certainly not Lee.

And yet, Lee had been forced to realize a whole lot of things about himself. That happens when you confront your own mortality on a regular basis. He was absolutely capable of rational judgment, and the majority of the time, that was how he operated.

But if Lee were being honest with himself—and he always tried to be—then when he looked back at the pattern of his life, at all the decisions that had led him down the path to where he currently was, he couldn't help but notice that a lot of those decisions had been emotional ones.

Not weepy emotional, or flying into a rage emotional. Because Lee was always controlled. But you could control emotions and still make decisions by them.

Running after that woman who was being carried away by the primals? That'd been an emotional decision. He'd been furious at the creature, and scared for the woman. A pragmatist would have said, "I only have a pistol, and there's too many threats." But Lee ran out there anyway.

And years before that, when Lee had been a member of the tiny, secretive Project Hometown, and was sequestered in his underground bunker while the plague ran rampant on the surface, Lee made the decision to break protocol and leave his bunker early. That particular decision had some logic to it—he wanted to recon his area of operations. But it was still a decision based on worries of what awaited him topside. Ultimately, it was an emotional decision, and it altered the course of his life. He was blackballed by the remnants of the US government, and labeled a "nonviable asset" and a domestic terrorist. Which was no small part of why he didn't go by Lee anymore.

But not every emotional decision was a bad one. Soon after leaving his bunker, he stumbled across a young man and his father, being hounded by a group of men. Watching them kill that kid's father, Lee made another emotional decision. The pragmatic decision would have been, "Oh well, there's too many of them, and only one of me." But instead, Lee went with "Fuck that," killed them all, and saved the boy's life.

That boy now sat in the seat behind him, no longer a boy, and no longer the Sameer Balawi that he'd been. Somewhere along the line, he'd grown up, and now he was Sam Ryder.

It's funny how emotions and logic eddy and swirl around each other to create the paths our lives flow through. Seeing the hope to stay in Sam's eyes, Lee knew what his decision would be, and he knew it was an emotional one. But he also knew he'd have to defend it with logic.

"We need a win," Lee finally sighed, staring straight ahead. "Northern California, Oregon, Washington—they were all great. Everything after San Diego? Complete trash." He let his hands flop down onto his thighs. "We need a win. And I'm not just talking about morale."

He twisted to put his one good eye on his team. First Abe. Then Sam, Marie, and Jones in the back. "The border? Rampart? I know we did everything we could, but we still got our shit pushed in. And it doesn't reflect well. If it keeps happening, we might get cut off. We might lose The Deal."

Oh, The Deal, The Deal. Lee's perennial blessing and eternal curse. One that he'd conjured up himself, starting from the moment he'd broken protocol and left his bunker ahead of schedule. He had one job as a Project Hometown operative. Their motto was *Subvenire Refectus*—Rescue and Rebuild. The state that he was assigned was North Carolina, and it was his job to save who he could, and try to re-establish a constitutional democracy in the event of complete social collapse.

But then things got out of control. Almost as though he were caught up in a strange tide against his will, he found himself leading a rebellion against the former Secretary of State—a man named Erwin Briggs, who'd appointed himself as the President of the United States, and then tried to run it like a fiefdom.

When Canada and the United Kingdom got involved, Lee hoped and prayed and tried his damndest to get them on his side of the conflict. But he made the mistake of giving one of his men a little too much leash, and a few civilian massacres later, Lee was branded a war criminal, and lost any chance for foreign aid.

The Canadians and Brits didn't back Erwin Briggs, though. By that time, Lee had already tracked him down, and Abe had put a bullet between his eyes. Instead, they backed another Project Hometown operative named Griffin. A former friend of Lee's, who had become the commander of Briggs's army, and then spent years trying to track Lee down and kill him.

But then a funny thing had happened. When Griffin finally had Lee dead to rights, he didn't do the deed like Lee thought he would. Instead, he offered Lee and his team the chance to redeem themselves.

Officially, they were considered dead. Incinerated in the blast of a small-yield nuclear warhead, courtesy of the Brits. Unofficially, they worked for Griffin, though they never spoke to him directly—only ever through a secret liaison stationed in Colorado.

By that time, three years after the complete collapse of American society and government, warlords and two-bit dictators had popped up like mushrooms in a damp back yard, particularly along the coastal states. Griffin knew that he'd have to eventually oust those people, once he shored up some semblance of democracy in the slightly-calmer Interior States. But the longer he left them, the stronger and more entrenched they'd become.

Griffin found his solution in the man he'd hunted for so long. A man who'd been damn near impossible to catch, and left a trail of bodies and destruction behind him every time Griffin got close. But that was just what Griffin needed—someone who knew how to do a lot with a little, stay under the radar, and operate without oversight.

And just like that, yesterday's bitter enemies became today's unlikely allies.

And that was The Deal: Lee would go out and find the problem children of America, and correct them, by any means necessary. Pave the way for whenever the hell Griffin finally decided to expand civilization back to the edges of this wrecked country. And any time Lee needed anything—weapons, ammo, ordnance, medical supplies, food, fuel, etcetera—all he had to do was pick up the battered old satellite phone, and call his liaison in Colorado.

The prospect of losing The Deal and getting cut off was a heavy thing for them all to consider.

Lee pressed on. "I'm here for a reason—because this is what I'm good at. I'm not going to find some place to hide in a hole. As bad as this sometimes is, this is our life. And if you didn't love it, you'd've been gone a long time ago."

No one said anything for a moment. Lee could tell that his words had struck a thoughtful chord in them. No one challenged him on the fact that they loved it, as odd as that sounded. Lee and his team, they were born fighters. Without a fight to fight, what were they going to do with themselves?

The world was a fucked-up place, and in that truck there were five people who were driven by their desire to pull the shattered pieces of it back together.

It was a wonderful fantasy to believe that you could be happy living a peaceful life. Lee had wanted to believe that about himself for a long time. But right around the time when Griffin hadn't executed him outright, and had offered him The Deal, Lee had realized that a quiet existence was, for him, just as much a prison as if it were made of concrete and iron bars.

Besides all that, they were *good* at this—recent failures notwithstanding. And people like to do what they're good at.

Abe made a weird face, glowering out the windshield at Ted and Bea, with his lips pursed so they stuck out from the confines of his beard. "You're talking like this is going to be an easy win."

Lee shrugged. "I guess I am."

Abe flicked a look at him. "What makes you think it will be easy?"

"Well, easy's a relative term," Lee answered, shifting his bum leg around to a more comfortable spot. "Compared to Rampart on the Border, though? This looks easy."

Marie sniffed. "Looks can be deceiving."

"They can," Lee admitted. "At Rampart, we faced down a whole lot of cartel and ex-military. And, yeah, we had to cut and run. But we gave them something to think about. This?" Lee waved a hand at their environment. "I'm seeing some asshole ranch owner, whose toughs are a teenage girl that don't talk, and a middle-aged man with a shotgun."

Abe's gaze listed to him, laconic. "*We're* middle-aged."

Lee reached across and patted the rifle strapped to Abe's chest. "But with rifles. And armor. And explosives."

Abe made a dissatisfied noise, but then said, "Alright, fine. Fuck it. We'll save these bastards, even if they don't want to be saved."

Lee smiled. "Oh, I'm sure they want to be saved. They'll just be weird about it."

Jones clapped his hands and rubbed them together. "It's only weird if you make it weird, Boss."

Lee looked to the back, cognizant of the fact that he hadn't heard fully from Marie. "Are we all on board, then? We gonna do this?"

Marie squinted past Lee to the outside world. "Meh. I was tired of driving anyway. One oppressed shithole is as good as the next, huh?"

"Well then." Lee turned forward again and looked at Bea, their new host. She was standing a good distance away, with her arms crossed over her chest, mouth shuttered up tight, staring right back at him. "This should be fun."

Chapter 7

Here's something funny: Growing up, Bran had thought he wanted to be a cop. His dad had been a cop, and when he had his guys come over and they got to smoking and drinking, they'd tell all their hilarious stories about the job, and Bran thought that it sounded real nice to do all that crazy shit, and have friends as close as the ones his dad had.

But then his dad had a massive heart attack and died when Bran was in his freshman year of high school. And Bran learned all about the other side of things—how that job ate away at the good parts of you, and left a whole mess of resentment and bitterness that eventually stopped your heart. And then being a cop didn't sound so great anymore.

Throughout high school, Bran discovered that his second-hand knowledge of policework made him a popular guy amongst other kids that maybe wanted to avoid being the subject of policework. One thing leads to another, and before you know it, you're twenty-two years old, standing over some asshole you just shot in the leg during the course of knocking over an ATM. Everything was all in a panic, and the next hour went by like a nightmare, and wound up with Bran in a high-speed chase. It ended in their getaway car being upside down on the interstate, and him being face-planted onto the blacktop by a very pissed-off State Trooper that, oddly enough, reminded him of his dad.

The armed guard that had stupidly tried to be a hero survived his leg wound, and Bran ended up with a prison sentence of 150 months, which he served every damn day of, despite his impeccable behavior—except for that one time, but that wasn't his fault. You can't stop every idiot from picking a fight with you, and sometimes you have to fracture a man's skull to convince him to leave you alone.

Being a thirty-five-year-old felon, there weren't many prospects for Bran after he got out. Work release had him shoveling cow shit at a stockyard and cattle auction for minimum wage. And that's where he met Colin Horner, who, owning a ranch in a fine area of California, found himself beset on all sides by land developers, and needing someone who didn't mind doing some shady shit.

Bran was tired of shoveling cow shit, and he needed the money. Whaddaya gonna do?

That was only two years before the plague came stateside and everything went to shit with such surprising speed. He remembered watching it spread on the news, how it started at the major airports and cities, and bled out from there. Entire population centers turned into seething masses of insanity, people rendered down to vicious animals that seemed to want to do nothing but feed.

And then there wasn't any news anymore.

On the one hand, the plague certainly solved the problem of the land developers. On the other hand, that kind of put Bran out of a job. But, as it would turn out, Bran was still very useful to Colin when it came to dealing with the streams of refugees that thought a quiet place in the California countryside was just the spot to escape to. Colin, for his part, had no intention of letting such a trivial thing as a society-ending plague ruin his family's three-generation hold on the land.

"Just weather the storm," Colin was fond of saying. That, and, "People are always gonna need meat."

See, Colin didn't see himself as a man bitterly clinging to his birthright. He saw himself as the scrappy progeny of his ancestors, who, upon encountering trying times, made lemonade out of lemons.

In Bran's opinion, Colin was the type of person that would have come out the other end of the Great Depression richer than he'd been going into it. He was a pragmatist to the core, and a genuine opportunist.

Not that any of that had necessarily worked out for Colin. The storm hadn't ended, and, outside of a few trips to larger nearby settlements—all of which garnered lackluster profits—no one was buying beef. Which wasn't particularly shocking to Bran, but he wasn't the one running the show, so he kept his mouth shut about it.

Now, as Bran drove the little ATV over the crest of a hill, and saw the ranch appear in the mirage-rippled distance, he wondered how long Colin was going to keep trying to weather a storm that had raged for six years straight, and showed no signs of letting up.

Oh, sure, the hordes of crazy people pouring out of the city centers were no longer a problem. They'd all died out within the first year or so, due to starvation and exposure. They were just people, after all—people that'd had a bacteria burrow its way through their frontal lobe, leaving them incapable of much outside of the instinctive need to feed and fuck.

And, much to Bran and Colin's chagrin, fuck they did. And the new generations weren't like the stupid urbanites that'd just gone crazy and roamed around chasing anything that moved and eating anything that was edible. These new creatures were born into this world, running after their first day, and ready to fuck shit up by the time they were a year old. Oh, and also, spawn more feral animal-babies.

He glanced at Kat, sitting in the seat next to him, with that neutral expression in her pretty eyes. "When you think your dad's gonna realize that there's nobody around to buy his beef?"

She blinked, languidly—the only sign that she'd even heard him.

Bran looked forward again at the dusty trail to his home. "Least, there won't be within our lifetimes. Well, maybe *yours*. But not us old bastards. And your dad's older than me."

Kat finally swiveled her head and fixed him with those eyes. So beautiful. And yet, creepy as hell, because of what was in them.

"Interior," she said, the word coming out a little unwieldy.

"Pssh," Bran waved a hand at her. "Can't drive all these cattle to the Interior States."

She frowned, like he was arguing with her. He guessed he was. She thrust a hand out in the general direction of east, where the promise of civilization and cities run by an actual, functioning government—albeit an interim one—was only a thousand miles and one helluva mountain range away.

"Safe," she said.

"No, yeah, sure, the *cities* might be safe. Least, that's what they say. But how we gonna drive all those cattle there? If they didn't freeze to death in the Rockies, they'd get picked off by packs of infected. Or just regular folks who're hungry." He shook his head again. "Ain't no way."

Kat frowned, considering it, then just shrugged and looked forward again, like it didn't concern her. And why should it? She worked for her dad, just as much as Bran did, but where Bran had a mostly-friendly relationship towards his boss—and a sense of loyalty to the guy that'd gotten him out of that work-release hell—there was really no love lost between Colin and Kat.

Colin wasn't really father material to begin with. Too harsh. Too focused on the ranch. Too set in his ways to budge for the likes of a daughter.

Not to let Colin off the hook for generally being a dick to her, but Kat didn't make it easy on him. She could be difficult to handle. She had…issues.

You might say she got them from her mother.

"Well, suppose we can't complain, huh?" Bran said, as he drove the ATV through the front gates—checking the battery and satisfied to note that he'd made the day's rounds with 10% battery left to spare. "We got a nice place to live, we're relatively safe, and we got all the beef we could ever eat."

"Mm," Kat grunted, looking at a corral of young bulls, herded in for castration. "Cow."

"'Course, we all probably have ridiculously high cholesterol," Bran said, steering his way for the Big House. "But who gives a shit about *that* anymore?"

Kat shook her head. "Not me."

"Wow, two words in a row?" Bran shoved the shifter into park and yanked on the emergency brake, smiling at her. "Don't turn into a chatterbox now. I won't have as much fun if I don't get to talk all the time."

He hoisted himself out with tired old grumble and slammed the door behind him. Grabbed the charger that was hooked up to the bank of solar panels along the south-facing roof of the house and plugged the ATV in.

Colin Horner had bought the electric ATV and the solar panels the year before the plague hit. He'd grown tired of paying out the ass for fuel and having to drive to get it. He'd called it "dependence on an unreliable system." Which turned out to be a shockingly accurate assessment.

Too bad society had gone belly up before he'd been able to buy a whole fleet of them.

Bran angled himself for the front door of the Big House. Then stopped. Looked back over his shoulder.

Kat was still sitting there. Glaring at the house.

Bran sighed. "Don't be like this again, Kat."

"Shithead."

He knew it wasn't directed at him. "Come on, Kat. You gonna make me talk to the shithead on my own?"

A low growl came from under her bandanna. And then, locking every bit the petulant teenager, she shoved her way out of the ATV and slammed the door aggressively behind her. Loud enough to garner a look from two nearby ranch hands hanging on a fence. When they saw who it was, they wisely looked away.

"You know," Bran said, as Kat came abreast of him and they started up the front steps. "You probably shouldn't call your old man a shithead. It's very disrespectful."

She gave him a side-eye that spoke volumes about who disrespected who. But Bran didn't have that kind of relationship with Colin. He couldn't just call him out when he was an asshole to Kat. All Bran could do was talk to Kat, and try to keep her from making it worse.

"He's got a lot on his mind, alright?" Bran said, kicking the dust off his boots on the last tread. "Makes him less patient. Makes him a bit snippy. It's not okay that he takes it out on you, but you should at least try to understand the tough spot he's in."

Kat caught his arm as he reached for the doorknob, stopping him.

He looked at her and was surprised to see a rare depth of emotion in her eyes. She jammed a finger into her chest, and then pointed at the house, and all around them, as though gesturing to existence itself. "I," she said. "Didn't ask. For this."

Bran was so surprised that she'd struggled through an actual full sentence, that it took him a moment to catch what she'd actually said. And the feelings behind it.

Something in his chest ached for the girl. His shoulders slumped.

If Kat had been cooler with physical contact, he might've laid a hand on her shoulder, but he held back. "I know you didn't, Hon. But we're here anyway. So let's try to make the best of it."

Unconvinced, her eyes narrowed and she turned to the door.

Well, Bran guessed that was that, and went in.

As Big Houses on large ranches went, Bran had only seen a few, and knew that this one was "humble." But compared to a regular person's house, it was large and nicely decorated, with all the wood and leather a cowboy could hope for. And plenty of stone. Stone everywhere. Can't put wood or leather there? Have some stone.

The foyer opened up into a great room, the tall ceiling held up by massive pine timbers stained a warm chestnut. Two of Colin's men sat in plush leather chairs with a table between them, a chess game in full swing.

The guy whose pieces had all been slain was Darryl, and he was nice, though a bit dull. The guy who had slain all those pieces was Joaquin, and he was whip smart, but broody and generally mean.

Joaquin was facing Bran as he walked into the great room and peered at him over steepled fingers. Gave no greeting. Just stared.

Darryl, on the other hand, turned and grinned. "Oh, hey, Bran." Slightly less jovially: "Hey, Kat." Jovial again, to Bran: "Y'all looking for Mr. Horner?"

Bran just kept on walking through the great room. "He in his office?" he asked without really needing to. Colin was in his office more often than not. More and more, lately.

"Yeah," Darryl called back. "But—"

Joaquin's low, cold voice: "He asked not to be disturbed."

Bran pulled up short of the door to the office and turned to look at Joaquin. Both he and Kat, glaring at the man at once. But Joaquin seemed more disconcerted with Kat's attention than Bran's.

"He told me to see him as soon as I got back," Bran said, evenly. Then clicked a finger-gun at him. "But thanks for doing such a fine job in guarding our fearless leader from...you know...chess champions or whatever."

Colin hadn't always had two of his ranch hands in the house with him at all times for protection. That was a more recent development. Darryl seemed as flummoxed by it as the rest of the ranch. Joaquin seemed to be deadly serious about it. As though there was some sort of war going on, and any one of them, Bran and Kat included, might have turned coat and become spies for the other side.

Colin's getting paranoid, Bran thought. Again. For the thousandth time.

Then he rapped a knuckle on the door and announced himself. "Boss. It's Bran. And Kat."

From behind the big wooden door, the sound of a chair creaking. Movement. Shuffling. A drawer closing. Then, "Come on."

Bran pushed his way in, making space for Kat to get by, then closed the door behind him, not failing to give Joaquin a passive-aggressive little smirk.

The office was spacious, but not cavernous. A couple of leather chairs, situated around a desk that was not drastically large, but nice enough to make the statement that you were talking to The Man.

The Man himself was standing behind the desk, his broad shoulders framed by a painting of a pair of cowpokes wrangling a steer, and above the painting, a set of horns that Bran had always thought were a bit out of place, seeing as how they didn't even raise longhorns here.

Colin was a large individual, but Bran somehow couldn't see him as anything but withered. He'd known the man before the world went into the shitter, and he'd been filled out to proportions that most would consider bear-like. Now, though, his worn-out shirts hung loose on his deflated chest, tucked into faded and oft-mended jeans. The waists of those jeans were folded over in places to accommodate the use of the extra notches Colin had put into his belt.

Most people still found him intimidating, on account of his height and broadness, and...well, everything about him, really. His hair was gray and bristly, as though it were made out of wire brushes. His brows were thick and stern, and often sat hooded—as they did now—over cold gray eyes that always looked like they were squinting into the sun. Or squinting at something he found mildly distasteful. His arms, visible due to his rolled-up sleeves, were thinner than they once were, but still corded with lean muscle, and his hands had the gnarled hardness of tools that saw a lot of use.

Bran stuck his thumbs in his belt and sauntered over to the other side of the desk. Kat followed, looking around the office as though she'd never seen it before, though Bran knew that was just what she did to avoid looking at her father. Colin didn't like it when she looked at him.

"What's the word?" Colin said, his voice sounding as it always did—dry and harsh, like something being dragged through gravel.

Before answering, Bran glanced hopefully at a decanter on the corner of Colin's desk, to assess if there was enough whiskey in there that he could bum a small pour. But only a thin base of amber sat at the bottom. A couple of the ranch hands brewed it and distilled it, but with the drought hitting them hard in their grain reserves, whiskey production had been impacted. Colin let the ranch hands have what they did manage to make, to keep morale up.

Bran let out a mostly-inaudible sigh. "Camperland couldn't pay."

"And?" Colin prompted.

"And they're gone."

"What about the Redoubt?"

"Not gone. Yet. But they probably won't pay. Asked for more time. But I got the distinct sense that extra time wouldn't make a difference. They're just stalling."

"Uh," Colin grunted, frowning out the large window to the left of his desk. "Well, that's just fine by me. Corn or no corn, I'll get what I want."

"Yeah, so..." Bran leaned his hip against the arm of one of the leather chairs. "There's a thing about that. With the Redoubt, I mean."

Colin looked up sharply, a question in his eyes.

Bran elaborated. "Some strangers rolled into the Redoubt just before we got there. They were in some sort of talks with Ted. There were five of them—two older guys, two younger guys, and a woman." He looked significantly at his boss. "All with armor, rifles, and what looked like plenty of ammo."

Colin leaned back from his desk and crossed his arms over his chest. "They planning to make a stink about things?"

"That wasn't clear," Bran said. "I talked to the lead guy—battered fucker with only one eye. He says they're just traveling merchants, passing through, looking to make some deals. He didn't elaborate on what he was selling."

Colin sniffed and gazed out the window again. "You sure there were only five of them?"

"I only saw five," Bran admitted. "And they only had one vehicle—crew cab truck. Guess there coulda been more hiding, but that'd be an awful cramped pickup if there were more of them." Bran snapped his fingers. "Oh, and one of them I didn't even see."

"Thought you said you saw five."

"I misspoke. I saw four, and it was implied that there was a fifth, aiming a rifle at me from somewhere."

"Motherfuckers."

"My thoughts exactly."

Colin shook his head and turned back to Bran. "Doesn't matter anyhow. There's only five of them."

"Five, heavily armed."

Colin made a face and waved it away. "I don't care if they're goddamned Navy SEALs, Bran. There's only five of them. Only so much five people can do, no matter who they are, and something makes me doubt they're anything special."

Bran shrugged, knowing better than to argue with his boss. He wanted to tell him that there was something hard about that guy with the one eye, something dangerous about him that Bran didn't care for. But he kept it to himself. Because, really, Colin was mostly right. It didn't matter who they were. Five of them couldn't hold out. Not against what Colin could throw at them.

Bran realized, after a moment, that Colin was inspecting him hard. Those cold eyes just soaking him in. He felt like he couldn't move when Colin was staring at him like that. As though Colin were a snake and Bran had to stay still to keep from being bitten.

"What's the problem, Bran?"

"I don't have a problem."

Colin huffed, mirthlessly. "You come in all sighing and down around the mouth, talking about Camperland being gone like they were your friends or some shit. You been ruminating a bit too much again lately?"

Bran smiled, despite not feeling like it. "What can I say, boss? I'm a thoughtful guy."

"Well, spill it, then. Don't hold me in suspense."

"I'm just gonna piss you off."

"Then piss me off. But don't just stand there keeping it buttoned up like a bitch." A pointed glance at Kat. Then back to Bran. "Speak."

"Woof," Bran said, before he could really stop himself.

The outside of Colin's brows arched up, while the centers cinched down a bit more. An expression that Colin reserved only for moments when he needed the other party to know he wasn't fucking around. Bran took his point, and dipped his head, half in apology, and half in acquiescence.

Bran chose to look at the floor. "What're we doin' here, boss?"

"There's a lot of ways to interpret that question."

"I'm saying, what are we doing with these people? Why are we doing this whole thing? With the dam, and the water tax, and the..." he waved a hand. "*Slaughter*. I mean, I get it, it's your land, it's your family's land, yada yada. But it seems like a whole lot of mess for not much gain. You get your pastureland back, sure, but for what? Ain't nobody buyin' beef, boss." Bran thumped his heel against the ground and reluctantly hazarded a glance at his boss's face to see how much shit he'd just buried himself in. "Guess I just wanna know why I gotta do this shit."

"Violent felon with a conscience," Colin growled. "It's a real charming act."

Bran bristled inwardly, but kept his expression neutral. "Man shouldn't be shamed for having a conscience. And yeah, maybe I do feel a little bad. There was kids in Camperland. And there's kids in the Redoubt, too."

"There's kids every damn place there's people. What's your point?"

"My point is, have I ever said no to you?"

Colin seemed taken aback. He raised his chin, evaluating Bran again. Then he slowly shook his head. "Don't suppose you ever have."

Bran nodded. "I haven't. And I'm not planning to. But I do want to know *why*. And if you won't tell me just to assuage my conscience, then maybe just tell me why because I'm loyal, I've stuck by you all these years, and I never say no."

Colin let out the wheezy, windy chuckle. The one that came with no accompanying smile, and only the very slightest twinkle of amusement in his eyes. "Alright, fine," he said. "Guess I owe you that much."

Colin hitched his thumbs behind his belt and gave them an upward tug. "You think the world gone and ended. But it didn't. It just restarted." He raised a hand and twirled a finger in a circle. "All this shit? It's just the Wild West again. Who owns the land? Nobody owns shit anymore, except whoever can keep it by force. Now, there's civilization coming, Bran. It's coming again, sure as shit. The Interim Government ain't gonna stay on the other side of the Rockies forever. And once they get here, there'll be rules that come with them. But for now, there are no rules. Which means I have between now, and whenever the new government finally crosses the Great Divide and brings their laws to us, to become the biggest land and cattle owner in the country."

Christ. He really *would* have come out of the Great Depression a millionaire. The type of guy that didn't look at the fall of society as the end of the world, but instead, as an opportunity. Bran found that he admired it. And was also somewhat terrified by the implications.

Colin finally let a smile range across his face, making his lips look taut, like the expression put too much tension on them. "I don't give a shit about selling beef to people right now. I'm growing the herd, Bran. And I'll just keep on growing it until people *are* ready to buy beef again. And when that happens, won't we be sitting pretty?"

Bran pursed his lips and considered the logic of it. Oh, yes, plenty of logic. It all made sense. It was just a tad heavy on the Machiavelli and a hair light on scruples.

Colin didn't wait to see if Bran approved of his plan, likely because he really didn't care. He swiveled his gaze to Kat, and it became harsh and mirthless again. "Which reminds me of something else." He rapped a finger on the desktop—a single, hard thump, surprisingly loud, like his fingers were made of stone. "Two head of cattle. Dead. Torn up. Down by the gorge."

Bran felt his stomach twist up in sympathetic anxiety for Kat. "Coulda been wolves. Or coyotes."

Colin hit Bran with his eyes and made it feel like a physical blow. "It weren't wolves or coyotes. It was infected. I know the fucking difference." Back to Kat, his face getting even harsher, the veins beginning to stand out on his forehead, and an unhealthy flush coming to his scalp. "Now, you got two fucking jobs around here, Kat. Two." Raising a mean rod of a finger with each point: "You go with Bran on his rounds. And you keep my cattle from being preyed on. Any particular reason why you couldn't do your damn job last night?"

It wasn't very obvious with the bandanna over her face, but Bran knew Kat well enough to see that her jaws were clenching hard. Clenching and unclenching. Like she was gnawing on her own hatred.

Finally, she spoke: "No."

And Bran knew that wasn't quite true. There was a *very* good reason she couldn't have protected those two head of cattle last night. Because the gorge was damn near five miles away from where she'd been watching over the *rest* of the herd. If those two got taken down by the gorge, it was because they'd wandered off from the others, not because Kat hadn't done her job.

But Kat knew as well as Bran not to argue with Colin. Colin would tolerate a little bit from Bran. But he didn't tolerate shit from Kat. Hell, she still wasn't even looking at him, because they all knew he'd lose his shit if she did.

"No," Colin echoed, then punched the table. Didn't even punch it hard. Almost like he just let his fist fall on it. But it still sounded like he'd dropped an anvil on the desk. "Well, if you haven't done your fucking job, then why should I pay you?"

She looked up sharply, and Bran's stomach dropped even further. She was looking square at her dad now, all fire and defiance in her eyes, which was just the sort of thing that set Colin off. She knew it, and did it anyway.

Colin didn't immediately react to it, though all the muscles in his arms suddenly stood out sharply. Tense through his entire body, like a dog getting ready to fight. "Why you lookin' at me, girl? You got a problem with my rules? You thinking of doing something about it?"

Now Kat's body matched her father's: Tense and ready for battle. Fists not clenching, like a man thinking of throwing punches. But opening like claws, ready to tear at something.

Bran let out a dusty cough. "What about the Redoubt?"

Colin snapped to him and looked damn ready to hurl something from his desk at Bran's face.

Bran raised a defensive hand. "Reason I ask, Boss, is that if you want something handled tonight...well, she can't handle it and watch the herd at the same time."

Colin's eyes narrowed. "Two minutes ago, you were crying a river for the Redoubt and all its children."

Bran felt like he'd betrayed himself somehow. But what was he going to do? He didn't want to keep on with this Dark Mode bullshit. But he also didn't want to watch Colin beat his daughter. Again.

"Well," Bran huffed. "Sounded like you made up your mind about it is all. Haven't you?"

Colin straightened. Loosened up. Shrugged the tension out of his shoulders and neck. Gave Kat one more castigating glare, and then took a deep breath. "Yeah, my mind's made up." He thrust a hand at Kat without looking at her. "Take...her. And get it done."

Bran couldn't tell if he was relieved or disappointed. Bit of both, he supposed.

Colin looked at his daughter again, who had retracted her gaze to the floor once more. "Don't think you're sleeping in my house for the next week. You learn to do your fucking job and appreciate the life I provide for you, then you can come back under my roof. And I think that'll take at least a week. Whether or not you need more time to come to your senses is up to you. You understand?"

Still looking murderous, but at least directing it at the floor, Kat nodded. "Yes."

"Yes, *what*?"

Fingers tensing into claws again.

"Yes, *sir*."

Chapter 8

"You know," Lee said, standing in the doorway of Bea's Conex box and looking at all the others, now shuttered up tight, and nary a person to be seen outside in the ochre sunset. "I got enough food for everybody. But it doesn't seem like they're all that interested."

"They're not," Bea stated brusquely from beside him. He turned and noticed her standing close enough to him that he got the picture: she wanted him to move so she could close the door.

He shuffled to the side and she quickly swung the door closed. She lowered a large iron bar into place, creating a crossbeam that settled securely into a cradle welded to the hinge side of the door. Nothing short of a bulldozer—or an angle grinder and a lot of time—was getting through that door.

Bea brushed past Lee without looking him in the face. Perhaps because she found the empty eye socket disconcerting. But Lee thought it more likely that she was just pissed at having her home invaded.

She bustled about, trying desperately to find things to do, such as kicking some pebbles into a corner and aggressively swiping a thin layer of dust from a rickety wooden table that wobbled threateningly as she did it.

Lee tracked her movements around the interior of her home, taking it in as he did. Yup. It was a Conex box. Identical in dimension to Ted's, and a rather commonplace way to make a secure structure on the cheap. Lee had been in his fair share of them over the years.

Bea's home was lit by two solar lanterns that looked like they'd been a part of someone's pre-collapse landscaping. There was little else to make note of: The wooden table in the center, an additional folding table that looked like it served as kitchen counter and general catch-all. Two folding chairs. A queen-sized mattress in the back.

Frowning, Lee looked the room over again for more detail. On the ledge of a shelf posted to the wall, he spotted what looked like a man's jacket. On the floor near the bed, pushed up against the wall, but otherwise looking almost like they had been carefully preserved, a pair of boots far too large for Bea.

"Whoop," Jones said, from where he was crouching over his gear in a nearby corner. "That was it."

Lee glanced at him. "What?"

"That was my daily limit of uncomfortable silence. Now I've gotta talk." He glanced up to the big vacuum-sealed bag in Lee's hand. A look of ecstasy came over his face. "Oh, God. Please tell me…"

Lee hefted the package and put on his most charming smile—which was not all that charming, he had to admit, but there just weren't a lot of angles he could turn his head where a nasty scar didn't ruin his once-upon-a-time decent looks. "Bea, our gracious hostess?"

Bea was not in the mood for levity and only looked at him with irritation.

Making peace with his new roommate was going to be harder than he thought.

Still, he pressed on. "When's the last time you had chicken-mac-and-cheese?"

A look of genuine shock came over her face and Lee felt his hopes rise…and then were dashed when she wiped the expression away like an annoying drip of sweat and replaced it with stony disregard.

"I'm lactose intolerant," she said.

"Oh, well, that's good, because it's not actually cheese." Lee took the package over towards where Marie was hooking up their little portable stove. "Don't ask me what it is, because I can't tell you anything about it. Except that it's wildly delicious. I am, however, fairly certain that the chicken is actual chicken."

The vacuum sealed bag was clear, and Lee could see the pieces of pasta, and the freeze-dried chunks of chicken, all coated in a yellowish powder that would make any health nut of yesteryear recoil like a vampire from a crucifix. Nowadays, other health concerns took priority. Like starvation. Or being murdered.

There was enough in the package to create quite a feast. It was one of Lee's go-to moves for introducing himself to a new settlement. After all, when you've been living on beans and rainwater, who doesn't love the guy that shows up with a big pot of every childhood's most beloved food?

That would not be the case today, apparently. The Redoubt was still fairly hesitant with Lee and his team. None of them had interacted with any of Lee's team except for Bea and Ted.

Bea sauntered over, still trying to look disinterested. Lee handed the package to Marie. The first time Lee had met Marie, she'd been cooking for people. That had been over six years ago. She'd never stopped. If she had the means, the time, and the ingredients, she was making food for people.

Lee had offered to take over—not that he was a great cook, but, hell, it doesn't take much to add water to a freeze-dried meal and heat it up. Marie always declined, and Lee had eventually realized that this was her way of making peace with the world. In a reality so filled with conflict and violence, opportunities to do a kindness for others were few and far between. This was Marie's way of feeling like her contribution to the Universe wasn't *just* shooting people.

Bea stood to the side of Marie as she finished hooking up her portable stove. Bea crossed her arms over her chest and gave Lee the look of a person who thinks things are just a little too good to be true.

"So," she said. "You have guns, you have ammo, and you even have freeze-dried foods."

Lee nodded. "I try to keep us well-supplied."

"Oh?" All sorts of suspicion radiating from her. "Doesn't freeze-drying foods require pretty heavy-duty equipment?"

"Does it?" He knew that it did.

"It does."

"Huh. Interesting."

"And all that ammunition you claim to have. Doesn't that require a lot of equipment to make?"

"Oh, yes. All kinds of equipment."

Bea blinked rapidly at him, like she thought he was being dense.

Finally, she had out with it. "Where's all this stuff come from, Jax?"

"Let's call them friends in high places," Lee answered.

"What's that even supposed to mean? What kind of high places are you talking about?"

"Sweetheart," Marie put in, not looking up as she deftly knifed open the package and began pouring a portion into her cookpot. "Usually when someone says 'friends in high places,' it's a polite way of saying 'ask me no questions and I'll tell you no lies.'" Marie looked up and gave Bea a smile that was most of the way to being nice. "Now hand me that jug of water right there by your feet, would you?"

Bea looked like she might just up and refuse, and Lee was about to grab the water for Marie, but Bea hooked the jug with her foot and slid it over to Marie's waiting hand. A somewhat surly way to comply with the request, one could argue.

"So that's it?" Bea said, eyeing both of them now. "If I ask questions, I'll just get lies and half answers?"

Marie just shrugged. "I guess that depends on the questions. When they have to do with who is backing us, yeah, you'll get lies. Not because we're dishonest people, but because we gave someone our word that we wouldn't tell the truth. But you're welcome to ask other questions. Such as, 'Marie, what's it like to be crammed into a truck with these four cocks day in and day out?'"

Lee snickered. Boy, did Marie have a way with people.

Bea tried to stay hard, but her expression softened. Not by much, but Lee was watching for it, and saw it. Marie had touched on a little point of connection between them.

"And what would be your answer to that?" Bea asked.

"Meh." Marie shrugged and stirred the water in with the freeze-dried mix. "They stink. They're loud. They're crass. And Jones never stops talking. But I love 'em anyway."

Lee squinted at the ceiling. "I feel like all of that was just about Jones."

Marie leaned back and consider this. "No. You definitely stink."

"Well, I mean, besides that one."

"You're no rose yourself after three days on the road," Abe quipped from where he had seated himself and his gear against one of the walls, legs sprawled out in front of him.

Marie gave him a look over her shoulder. "I can always roll my bed out somewhere else, if you'd prefer, Hon."

Abe raked his fingers through his beard, watching her with a faint twinkle in his eyes. "I didn't say I minded."

As Marie smirked at Abe and returned to her meal prep, Lee cast a look over to Sam, who'd stayed uncharacteristically quiet this whole time. He was seated directly across from Abe, his pack and his doffed armor creating a sort of throne in which he was ensconced.

Lee found himself a smidge disappointed that Sam wasn't really putting any effort into getting to know Bea. Not that she was really flinging the doors open for any of them, but still. Had he read the situation wrong? That'd be a shame, Lee realized. He wanted the kid to have something beautiful. But maybe it just wasn't in the cards.

Jones sauntered over to Lee and stood, looking expectant.

Lee frowned at him, not knowing what he wanted.

Jones frowned back. "Isn't this where we're staying?"

"Seems that way," Lee said with a glance in Bea's direction.

Jones peddled his hand slowly through the air. "Then aren't we missing something?"

Lee snapped his finger. "Oh, right." He couldn't believe he'd forgot. He dove into the pants pocket of his jeans. Fingers touched the little lump of plastic. He drew it out.

Bea had grown curious and was leaning over the table.

"There he is," Jones said, satisfied.

Grasped in Lee's fingers was a plastic figurine of a German Shepherd dog, standing with head up and ears pricked. Alert. Like it was looking for threats. Lee smiled at the figurine, but there was some melancholy in it. He ran a thumb over the faded paint, then brought it to his lips and kissed it like a good luck charm. Which it was.

He handed it to Jones, who repeated the ritual, adding a "Good boy," at the end, as though it were a real dog. Then he tossed it to Abe. It was customary that everyone kissed the figurine for good luck.

Bea looked highly confused. "What is that? A toy dog?"

Jones gave her a hooded look and turned away.

Lee, trying to be more diplomatic, gave her a wan smile. "That's Deuce. Deuce was our dog. Team dog. Great animal."

"He was a very good boy," Abe said, kissing the figurine then tossing it to Sam.

Lee nodded. "He could smell primals coming from a mile away. Invaluable."

Bea nodded, realization coming to her face with a modicum of sadness. "I'm sorry."

Lee shook his head. "Oh, he's not dead." He heaved a sigh, missing his canine companion. "He just got old. Started getting hip dysplasia—it's common in the breed. He couldn't keep up with our operations anymore. We left him with a very nice family in a settlement we helped, about a year back."

Marie received the Deuce figurine, dutifully kissed it, then handed it back to Lee.

Lee inspected it lovingly for a moment, then set it on the table in front of him. "Family had a daughter. This was one of her favorite toys—which is why she took to Deuce so much when we showed up. Deuce was never keen on strangers, but man, he loved that little girl." Damn, but Lee was gonna get misty if he kept going. He cleared his throat. "Anyway. When we left Deuce with them, she gave us her toy. Now it's our lucky charm."

Bea took a moment to eye them all, ending on Lee. "So, how long have y'all been doing..." she waved a hand about as though conjuring something. "...whatever it is you do?"

Lee gave a small shrug at that. "Kind of depends. We've been together for sixish years. Been working as a team for a good part of that. But as far as just the five of us, doing what we do? Three years."

"And as far as *what* it is you do," she said, cocking an eyebrow at Lee. "Are you gonna stick with the whole 'identify problems and solve them' line?"

"I am. Because it's the truth."

"Well, you do seem to have the equipment for it. Which you get from your friends in high places, right?"

"Precisely."

"High places in the US government?"

Lee scoffed. "The US government has only just managed to consolidate itself and build a sturdy base. I don't reckon they have any high places just yet."

"So, you *don't* work for the US government?"

Lee made a noncommittal noise, neither confirming nor denying.

"I feel like you're being intentionally obtuse."

Lee shrugged. "The cost of keeping secrets is that, to the uninformed, you might often come across as obtuse. But I'll throw you a bone, Bea, because you're kind enough to welcome us into your home. I work for an anonymous benefactor that has a vested interest in stabilizing those areas of the country that are too out of the way to receive aid from the Interim Government."

"Sounds like charity."

Lee smiled. "It's not."

A smugly savvy expression shaded Bea's face. "So, there *is* a cost."

Lee's smile faded. "There's always a cost to what we do, ma'am. Sometimes our benefactor pays that cost. Sometimes the settlement we're helping. Sometimes we pay it. But it's never free." He took a deep breath. "But if you're worried about us suddenly demanding your settlement's valuables, don't be. Like I already said, all we want from you is a place to sleep, and your cooperation." He squinted at her. "As begrudging as it may be."

Chapter 9

Thirty minutes later, Bea sat at her own table, surrounded by strangers, as the woman named Marie spooned out generous portions of steaming chicken mac and cheese. Her new house guests brought their own mess kits—high-sided metal plates that were deep enough to function as shallow bowls.

As for Bea, she'd taken one of the two plastic plates that she owned. The other had belonged to James. She left his where it was—where it always stayed. It was never her intention to memorialize something so silly as the plate he ate from. But she'd spent so many years cleaning her own plate immediately after using it, that she never had to use his. She only kept his around just in case hers broke one day.

And she'd only kept his boots because someone might need them. Though, Will from two boxes down wore the same size, and had been complaining about the soles of his own boots wearing out, and she hadn't offered them up yet.

She'd only kept his jacket because…well, because she liked to put it on when the nights got chilly. Even though the smell of him had long since faded. Even though it never made her feel better about things. Seemed she put it on when she was already feeling down, and it only drove her into a deeper melancholy. And yet she kept doing it. As though to punish herself. As though the grief she felt wasn't enough.

"Something wrong, Hon?" Marie asked from over her shoulder.

Bea realized she'd been staring down into the steaming mound of yellowy-orange. She blinked and pulled her head up. Forced a smile. "Yes, fine. I was just…it's been a long time since someone else cooked for me." She felt the smile strain at her mouth, her teeth clamping down. Just that one, small compliment—if you could call it that—felt like she'd betrayed her decision to protest their presence by giving them the cold shoulder.

For a moment, she considered doubling down on that and claiming that she wasn't hungry this evening. But what would she prove by doing that? That she was an idiot, with too much pride to accept the first good meal she'd had in…oh, probably since the world went to shit.

"It smells good," she mumbled, looking down at her plate again. "And you gave me so much."

"We've got plenty," Marie said, putting the cookpot back on her stove and stepping over to seat herself at her own place. "If no one has the balls to join us this evening, then there's no reason we shouldn't fill up ourselves."

The table was a tight fit for all six of them. Shoulders scrunched, and elbows touching. Only two chairs, and Bea noticed that they were occupied by herself and Marie. Jones had appropriated an empty plastic crate, and Sam, Jax, and Lincoln—the guy with the big beard—were all sitting on their packs. It almost made her laugh. She hadn't seen a nod to chivalry in God-knew how long. Probably about as long as it'd been since she'd had a good meal.

Funny, she was almost insulted by it. But that may have been her residual prickliness at the invasion of her personal space. It seemed she was determined to interpret everything they did in the worst possible light.

Maybe she was being unfair.

In the midst of all this, she realized that they weren't eating. They were all sitting there with their spork utensils in hand, watching her patiently.

Bea frowned, picking up her own fork. "I'm sorry, am I supposed to bless the meal or something?"

Jax shrugged languidly. "Is that what you normally do?"

"No," she said. "I usually just eat."

Jax nodded, and without further comment, everyone else dug in.

Still frowning, Bea hefted a forkful, her mouth betraying her by watering profusely. She swallowed it back and said, "But if you're the praying sort, don't let me stop you."

Jax shook his head as he shoveled food in. Waved her off as he chewed, and then spoke around the mouthful. "We've stayed with some more…religious settlements. We try to be respectful of folks' customs."

"Plus," Jones put in. "If you make a good show of praying over your food, they're much less likely to try to convert you."

Sam gave him a wry look. "You didn't mind it when Misty tried to convert you."

Jones gazed at the ceiling. "Oh, sweet Misty. If only she'd had looser morals."

"And lower standards," Marie said.

Jones looked at Bea. "You see what I have to deal with? The constant insults. Always being beaten down. It hurts."

Bea raised an eyebrow. "You seem to ask for it a lot."

Lincoln barked out a laugh, using the back of his wrist to scrub not-really-cheese sauce from his chin. "She's only known you a few hours, and she's already got you pegged."

"I am what I am," Jones announced, flourishing his spork. "These other four, they like to be all mysterious. But not me. I'm an open book. You'll always get a straight answer out of me. I'm honest to a fault."

Bea considered asking him about who they worked for, but even as a joke, it was a little too soon after being stonewalled. She wasn't trying to make her evening any more awkward than it already was.

"Bea—" Jax started, then stopped. "Can I call you Bea?"

"You already have been."

A rather stale smile stretched Jax's lips. "Can I *continue* to call you Bea, then?"

"Well, that is my name, and I don't have another."

"No last name?"

"Drye," she said, warily.

His eye strayed over her shoulder. Was he looking at the jacket? "Missus Drye?"

Everything cinched up tight in her chest. Her fork stopped, halfway to her mouth. She eyed Jax. He stared back, waiting. "Bea is fine," she said, rigidly.

"Well, Bea," Jax said, returning to his food. "I don't want to impose any more than we already have, but it's usually good to get to know the folks you're staying with. What's your story? Or, at least, the parts of it you're willing to share."

"What makes you think I've got secrets to keep?"

Jax hefted a sporkful. "It doesn't have to be a secret to be something you just don't feel like talking about. At this point in pretty much everyone's life, we all have a few parts of our story that we'd rather skip over." He ate and chewed in silence for a moment. "Point being, I don't want to pry. I only want to know who you are."

Bea considered this for a moment. It was a reasonable request, objectively. Subjectively, she didn't like handing out information about herself to people she knew so little about, and who were so close-mouthed about their own details.

"Alright," she finally decided. "How about this? You ask me something, then I get to ask you something. I'll keep my answers as honest as I feel you're keeping yours."

Jax smiled again, but this time with some genuine humor. And maybe a little mischief. "Sounds fair. But I still won't tell you who we work for."

"We'll leave that out for now." She took a big bite and nodded at him. "Shoot."

Casually enough, he said, "How old are you?"

"Twenty-five."

"Damn. So you were only nineteen when everything happened."

"I was," she said, then immediately took her own shot. "Where are you from?"

Jax pushed a hand to his chest. "Me, specifically? Or us, generally?"

Bea glanced at the others. "Let's start with you, specifically."

"North Carolina."

"Long way from home."

Jax shrugged. "These days, my home is wherever I lay my head."

"Oh, a vagabond, then?"

"Vagabond," Jax mused, tasting the word. "I like it. It's got...romance. What about you?"

"Where am I from?"

He nodded.

"Here," she answered. "California." She could have been more specific and said Encinitas, but he'd only given a state, so she repaid him in turn. "What was the last settlement you were at before us?"

That got a reaction she hadn't been expecting. Sporks stilled. Chewing slowed. Eyes glanced around, and connected, and spoke entire conversations in brief moments of contact. This was not a topic they were comfortable with, for some reason. Which, of course, only made Bea more intrigued.

"The border," Jax eventually said, slightly stiffer than before, but trying to sound nonchalant. "Place called Rampart. Have you been here in the Redoubt the whole time?"

"Pretty much. A few weeks in a FEMA camp before it got overrun. We barely made it out. Wandered around the hills for a while before we found this place." She realized her mistake only after she'd finished speaking. It seemed that Jax had realized it too.

Feeling vulnerable now, Bea leveled a cold look at him and poked at the discomfort that she'd seen in the group. "What happened to Rampart?"

That same reaction, but moreso. Lincoln stabbed his spork into his plate with unnecessary force and leaned back in his seat, giving her a hard look. She held it, defiantly, until she realized that it wasn't anger she was seeing in his eyes. It was pain.

Abruptly feeling unsure of herself, she looked away from Lincoln. Found Jones staring at his food like a kid that's been scolded by their parents at the dinner table. Sam was watching her carefully, but when she caught his look he glanced away.

Marie, for her part, had continued to eat, but it looked forced. Robotic. Like she couldn't taste the food anymore.

Bea's eyes wound up back on Jax, who was slowly stirring his spork around in his food. Chin lifted slightly as he looked contemplatively at the ceiling. The light from the lantern caught his face sharply at that angle, causing the mess of scars along his left jawline to stand out.

The silence drew on to the point that Bea almost—*almost*—told him to forget it. But then she thought, *fuck this guy*. He'd come swaggering into their settlement talking like he was God's gift to oppressed peoples, but it sure as shit seemed like the last settlement that they'd "helped" hadn't wound up too good. Bea had a right to know if the Redoubt was headed in the same direction.

"Well," Jax said with a small smack of his lips, looking back to his food like it had suddenly lost its appeal. "They didn't make it."

Bea waited for more, but Jax just languidly took up another sporkful of food and ate it without relish.

"Care to elaborate?" Bea said, forcing some steel into her voice, though she now felt a little awkward. And a lot outnumbered. She was sitting at a table with five other people that clearly *didn't* want to elaborate.

Annoyingly, Jax gave no indication that he'd even heard her. He just stared down at his plate with a smile so wan it might've been a cringe.

Bea leaned forward on her elbows. "Shove the question game for now. As a member of this settlement, I think I've got a bit of a duty to ask for more details. And I think I'm entitled to an answer."

"Oh, you're entitled?" Jax echoed, softly, still not looking at her.

"I'm entitled to know your success rate, especially if you want everyone to hop on board and cooperate with whatever it is you have planned."

Jax's one eye did the job of two and skewered her hard. "Our success rate? Well, let's see." He leaned forward on his elbows, matching Bea's posture. Except that he hadn't been very intimidated when she'd done it to him, but with the lantern light turning both his good and his ruined eye into shadowy caves, Bea felt downright frightened of him.

"Over the course of three years," Jax said, his voice grinding out without any hint of the friendliness he'd shown up to then. "We've been with seventeen settlements, up and down the west coast. Of those seventeen, there've been two instances that I would categorize as abject failures."

Bea summoned some intestinal fortitude and didn't back down. "Abject failures on *your* part?"

Lincoln slapped his spork down, causing Bea to jump. He glared at her, shifting about on his pack like he couldn't decide whether to stick to the table and argue it out, or get up and walk away. "And what have *you* been doing, huh?"

Bea swallowed. "This isn't about me."

Lincoln leaned in, expression severe. "No, it is. Because right now you're sitting atop your high horse, judging us pretty hard over some shit you have no clue about."

"Lincoln," Jax warned, quietly.

Bea stuck her chin out. "You're right. I don't have a clue about it. That's why I'm asking. You want us to cooperate with you?

There's going to need to be some transparency. And I'd sure like to know how two other settlements that cooperated with you wound up dead."

Lincoln's hands balled together into a single clenched fist, from which one finger protruded, pointing right at her. "Nah, see, you're dodging *my* question now. My question was, what the fuck have *you* been doing this whole time? Because while we've been out trying to make life better for other people, you've been here, doing…what, exactly?"

"Lincoln," Jax said, slightly sterner.

"No." Lincoln shook his head at Jax. "I wanna know. I want her to tell me what she's been doing that makes her so goddamned righteous." Back to her. "Scraping out a living? Trying to survive? Looking out for number one? And then you have the fucking balls to try to come down on a group of people that have actually been trying to fix shit? You think you've uncovered some deep dark secret? Guess what? It's not a secret. Sometimes we fail. Sometimes the best laid plans get torn the fuck up and shit goes sideways." He sneered at her, shoving himself back from the table. "But I guess I can't really expect some civvy hiding in a metal box to understand that shit."

Jax's hand moved quickly, grasping Lincoln's wrist. The two stared at each other for a moment. There wasn't any aggression in that look. Jax simply looked up at his friend, mild but serious.

"That's enough," Jax said.

Lincoln grunted, pulling his wrist away from Jax. "Didn't want to stay here in the first place," he murmured, then snatched up his plate and spork. "I'm gonna get some air."

Bea almost came out of her seat. "It's not safe out there."

Lincoln cast a withering glance over his shoulder. "Primals would be better company."

No one spoke as Lincoln stalked over to the door, undid the security bar, and disappeared outside.

Jones rose. "I'll lock it back," he said with a voice a tad too eager.

He took his time doing it, too, like he wanted to waste as much time as possible before returning to the table. So the rest of them—Bea, with Sam to her left, Jax directly across from her, and Marie between them—sat in tense silence. A cloud of emotions and recriminations hovered around Bea's head like gnats, occasionally dive-bombing her with thoughts of *Screw this shit, go tell Ted to get rid of these idiots*, or *Dammit, did I just fuck over the entire settlement because I couldn't play nice?*

It was Sam that broke the silence, leaning on a single elbow and scooting a few sodden macaroni pieces around his plate. "There's a cartel down south. They call themselves *Nuevas Fronteras*. It mean's 'new frontiers.' For a while, they were in the fuel business—pirating refineries and pumping stations along the Gulf, and trying to expand further north and lay claim to the country while it was down. Hence their name."

He laid his spork down. Wiped a bit of something on his pants.

"Rampart on the Border had sixty-eight people," Sam continued. "They were being pressed by the cartel to be a new outpost for them, because Rampart was decently defended, had solar power, and was positioned pretty ideally just north of the cartel's territory. They were giving the people the old *plato o plomo* schtick—silver, or lead. Basically, you cooperate, they make you rich. You don't cooperate, you die.

"When we got there, they were right on the cusp of giving in, and..." Sam sighed and looked skyward with a faint, grim smile. "...and it was like a sign from the Universe. Because we just happened upon Rampart. We didn't know about the cartel until after we'd already introduced ourselves and offered to help. And the whole sign from the Universe thing was that...well..." Finally, he lowered his eyes to hers. "We'd dealt with *Nuevas Fronteras* before. Or, at least, Jax and Lincoln had. It all just seemed so obvious. Like this was a path that had been laid out for us. Here were these people, dealing with this threat, but it was a threat that we knew, and a threat that we'd beaten before. I remember feeling so optimistic about it. Serendipitous. Like it was meant to be, and we couldn't fail."

He smiled again, and it was a haggard, desperate thing. "But we did fail. Five of us. And forty-three others that could fight. We brought everything we had to that fight. But it wasn't enough. Cartel found out about Jax and Lincoln being involved. It got personal for them, and they threw everything they had at us. Which included several hundred fighters, and a whole lot of armored vehicles that they'd scooped up after the Mexican government fell."

Sam turned and looked at Jax, who was watching his young teammate with a strange expression of loss, and bad memories, and powerlessness, all rolled into one. "Jax saw the way it was going and tried to get Rampart to fall back with us. It was obvious we were gonna get our shit kicked in. But they just didn't want to hear it. They didn't want to leave their homes. We told them they'd die if they stayed. They told us to stay and die with them. We told them that didn't make any sense." Another big breath, and another big exhale. "And then we left, and they stayed. And they died."

Bea swallowed hard. "If you left, you don't know if they all died."

"No, they did," Sam said, simply. "I watched it happen." He made a pained face and a grunt, like something had just pricked him. "We set up an overwatch, in case anybody from Rampart came to their senses and decided to retreat, so we could cover their escape." A slow shake of his head. "But no one retreated. They all hunkered down and fought it out to the last person." He sniffed, then tilted his head towards Bea, his eyes looking hollowed out of any youth that she might've seen in them before. "I say fought, but it was just a slaughter. And once the people with guns had all been slaughtered, they gathered up what was left—every old man, old woman, and every kid—and they decapitated them. Right there in the middle of Rampart. Right where we could see it happen. Like they knew we were out there, watching."

Sam craned his neck around, his vertebrae audibly popping. "And that," he said, tapping his spork onto his plate. "Is how we lost Rampart."

Jones had wandered back by then, and stood over his place, his arms crossed over his chest, looking at Sam. "We tried to take shots from our overwatch," he said, quietly. "But we'd positioned ourselves to cover a retreat, not cover the settlement, and they were..." he bared his teeth and held up a thumb and forefinger, nearly touching. "*Just* too far out of range."

Bea realized that she'd barely eaten her food with all the talking back and forth. She could feel the emptiness of hunger still holding onto her belly, but her appetite had fled. She fully intended to eat that plate of food at some point this evening, but for now she couldn't bear to stuff her face.

She thought about apologizing, but stopped herself. What would she be apologizing for? For asking about their failures? The humanity in them was hurt by the recollection, and she was not numb to that. But she still held to the fact that she, and everyone in the Redoubt, needed to know these things to make an informed decision.

Sam stretched his back and tendered a mild smirk in Bea's direction. "So, what now, Bea?"

"What do you mean?"

He shrugged. "Now that you know we can't guarantee success, are you even more opposed to us being here?"

"Not sure I have much of a choice in the matter."

"You do," Sam said, simply. He looked to Jax and a silent conversation ensued in raised eyebrows and subtle looks. It concluded with Jax giving Sam a small nod, and he turned back to Bea. "You make the call, Bea. You are now the person in the Redoubt who knows the most about us. If you tell us that we're not welcome, we'll leave in the morning."

Bea snorted, but then realized that Sam was serious. She looked to Marie and Jax, but they gave no indication of superseding Sam's offer. They were waiting for her response.

"Well..." she stammered. "What would I tell Ted?"

Jax made a face like she'd said something nonsensical. "You can tell him whatever you want. Tell him we were a bad bet. Tell him we didn't have what we promised. Hell, you can tell him we're swindlers or marauders or whatever you think will get the job done. It doesn't matter to me." Jax leaned forward again. "Bea, we've done this enough to know that when a settlement has an outspoken opposition to our presence, we've only got two options: Win that person over, or get to steppin'. Not to put too fine a point on it, but if you just can't stand us, and we stay anyway? Well, you'll sour the whole damn thing. So either you're in, or you're out, Bea. And right now, you speak for the Redoubt."

She scoffed, uncomfortably. "I can't speak for the Redoubt."

"Tonight you can," Jax stated flatly. "And you are. Like it or not, the decision is now on you."

"I didn't ask to make the decision."

Jax spread his hands. "Doesn't matter. By being that outspoken opposition, you made it yours. So what'll it be? Should we stay or should we go?"

Bea felt heat rising up her neck and flushing her cheeks. She felt put on the spot, but she also felt that, in a way, she'd done it to herself. Dammit, but if she just could have played nicer, none of this would have wound up at this point. Now she was sitting there, forced to weigh the welfare of her settlement in the balance while she tried to suss out whether this man Jax was capable of doing what he claimed.

Oddly, she realized that his admission of failure had changed her opinion of them. Not necessarily to a positive opinion. But she'd been very concerned at the outset that they were, as Jax had put it, swindlers. A group of con artists that showed up looking good in their battle rattle, and promising to help settlements with their backs against the wall, only to drain them of supplies and move on in the middle of the night.

But their story had too many details in it. Too much obvious emotional baggage to have been made up. That, or she was dealing with world-class liars.

And if they really were there to con the Redoubt, then why would Jax have laid this decision in the lap of the one person that clearly didn't want them there?

She still didn't know if she could trust them. But she at least felt confident that they weren't swindlers.

"Stay," she suddenly said, the decision made at right about the same moment that the word came out of her mouth, leaving her feeling like she'd either done something great, or been suckered into doing something pitifully stupid.

"Alright," was Jax's only reply, given with a small nod.

Bea shifted uncomfortably in her chair. "You can ask me something now."

"Oh, I think that game's over with."

Bea gave him a look that was not to be denied. "No, I pried. I asked a hard question, and you gave me a hard answer. It's your turn."

Jax considered her for a long moment. He seemed to be re-evaluating her, and she felt his scrutiny like a spotlight glaring in her face. "Okay. I'll ask you one more question. A hard question for a hard question."

Bea swallowed, but nodded, knowing what was coming.

"When you talked about escaping the FEMA camp, you said 'we.' And, not to make you feel like I've been snooping about, but there's a jacket hanging over there, and a pair—"

"James," she said, thickly, staring at the middle of the table, unwilling to meet anyone's eyes for fear of what she might find there. For fear that if she saw an ounce of compassion in anyone's gaze, she might break down. "His name was James. He was my husband."

Jax placed a finger thoughtfully to his lips and nodded slowly. "Well. It means very little from a stranger, but I'm sorry for your loss. Stranger or not, I know what it's like to lose someone you love."

She nodded, rigidly, unable to speak as a hard fist of grief choked her throat.

A rapid pounding on the door reverberated through the whole structure, causing them all to jump.

Lincoln's voice: "Contact! Movement! Let me in!"

Chapter 10

The second Lee heard it, he was moving. "Jones, get the door," he snapped, ignoring the stabbing pain arcing up his left hip as he swung himself rapidly over to where his rifle was leaning against his plate carrier.

By the time Lee had slung into his rifle, Jones was already lifting the crossbeam from the door, hollering through the metal as he did: "Are they on you?"

Lee slid to the side of the door, shouldering his rifle and taking an angle where he could shoot over Abe's shoulder if he had company on his ass.

"No, not yet," came Abe's voice, strained but relatively calm.

Jones heaved the door out of the way. Lee brought his optic up to his eye, the red dot swinging over Abe's urgent face as he slipped through. As soon as he was in, Abe spun and helped Jones seat the door back in place, slamming the crossbeam home.

Lee let his rifle dip and glanced over his shoulder, taking stock of the situation. Marie and Sam were on opposite sides of the box, both with their rifles shouldered. Jones and Abe moved towards their packs, going for their rifles.

"Primals?" Lee demanded at Abe's back.

"No positive ID," Abe returned, slinging into his rifle. "Just saw some movement coming over a ridge a few hundred yards out."

"Bea," Lee grunted, scanning the walls around them for anything that might be considered a weak point. "How secure are these boxes against primals?"

Bea blinked a few times at him, as though she couldn't quite remember what 'primals' meant, but then seemed to recall that's what Lee and his crew called the newer generations of infected—bigger, meaner, faster, and smarter than the plain old crazy people.

"Uh...we've never had them get in?" she said, almost as a question.

"Well, that's good," Lee remarked. "How often do they try?"

"Uh...well..." she was blinking rapidly again.

"Bea," he said again, sharper.

Her eyes hit his. "I've never seen them actually try."

Lee raised his brows. "Wait a minute. You guys have been out here in the middle of nowhere, with no perimeter defenses, and the primals haven't even come in and *tried* to open up these sardine cans?"

Bea seemed to remember the whole *imminent threat* thing, and angled for where she'd leaned her rifle up against the table on the far wall. "It's complicated," she grunted, checking the bolt, then snugging it back into place.

The facts swirled around in Lee's head, not making a whole lot of sense at the moment. But there were bigger problems to deal with. He could peel layers off the Redoubt later.

"Any other entrance to this thing that I don't know about?" Lee asked, finishing his circumspection of the box and returning his attention to the door.

"No," Bea said, taking up a position in the center of the box, her rifle shouldered but the muzzle held low. "One way in, one way out."

Sam pressed his ear to the side of the metal box and listened. Apparently not hearing anything, he pulled his head away and frowned at Bea. "So this has never happened to you before?"

She shook her head. "Not here. Not *inside* the settlement."

Jones was stalking around, searching the walls in vain. "Any windows or gunports or anything? Something to shoot out of?"

"No," Bea answered, an odd brand of worry flittering across her features.

Lee squinted at her. What wasn't she telling them? Simple, stupid secrets? Or shit that could get them killed? She claimed the boxes were secure against the primals, but she had no experience to support that.

Most settlements had learned rather quickly that the only effective barrier to the primals was high-voltage electrical wires. The settlements that didn't have the electrical infrastructure to support this—such as old wind or solar farms that they could splice into—soon wound up as ghost towns, either because everyone living there had come to their senses and moved to a place with high-voltage fencing, or because they got overrun.

The fact that the Redoubt had no perimeter was one of the first things Lee noticed when they drove in. He'd written it off under the assumption that the Conex boxes were secure enough. But now he learned that they'd never even been tested.

Which made absolutely no sense. Primals were hunters, and they hunted everything, but seemed to treat humans as their primary prey, either because they were easier to catch than wild animals, or because they were often found bunched together in large numbers. Herds, essentially. The fact that everyone called them *settlements* didn't change the reality of what it was to a primal: a target rich environment.

So here was a target rich environment, with no barriers to keep them out, and...what? The primals just randomly decided to leave the Redoubt alone?

Lee had never even heard of such a thing.

Both Abe and Marie had their ears to the wall, listening. Abe frowned. Then his eyes widened.

He looked to Lee. "I think I hear them," he whispered.

Marie nodded. "That wasn't a coyote howl."

"Shit, shit, shit," Bea breathed out. "Should we be talking?"

"That howl sounded like it was still a ways away," Abe said.

That went without saying—they howled to organize their pack when they were on the scent of something. When they went quiet, that was when you needed to worry.

Lee looked at Bea again. "Besides, you said these things were secure."

"Yeah, but I don't know that for sure!" she hissed.

Abe pulled his head off the wall and scowled at her. "Yeah, I feel like that begs the question: How have y'all never been overrun by primals? You've got no defenses outside of these boxes, and they just leave you guys alone?"

Bea looked conflicted, which was not a look Lee wanted to see on her face.

"Bea," he said, with a warning tone. "Where we come from, the only way to keep the primals from crawling all over your shit every night is high-voltage fencing. You guys got some trick to keep them away that we don't know about? Because, if you do, I'm all ears."

Bea licked her lips, then moved them with a few unuttered syllables. Then she shook her head. "You guys seem to know a lot about these things."

It was so clearly a diversion, that Lee almost laughed at it. What the hell was she trying to hide from them?

If Sam picked up on that, he didn't show it. Or maybe he was just eager to sound knowledgeable in front of Bea. God, you could literally be in a life-or-death situation, and a young man would still try to impress a pretty woman.

"Back east, the primals learned to form large hordes," Sam said. "We had to do a bit of studying on them just to survive. We haven't seen much of that behavior in the Interior States, or out here. Do you know the numbers of these primals?"

"The numbers?"

"Yes, numbers," Abe interrupted. "Counting? One, two, three? Christ. We talking packs of a dozen? Less? More?"

"More."

"Should I keep guessing? Price Is Right rules? Closest without going over? Or would you like to just give me your best estimate?"

Bea flushed. "It's—it's a hundred or so. I think. Maybe more."

Lee shook his head. "That qualifies as a horde, in my opinion. And that's a lot for out here in the middle of nowhere. Hordes like that usually have a colony, or a nest, and it's usually in an abandoned urban area. You got anything like that around here?"

Bea nodded. "There's a town in the Valley, just a few miles north of here. That's where their nest is."

"That last howl was close," Marie remarked, pulling her ear from the wall. "Probably the last noise they're gonna make before they're right on top of us." She turned and addressed the door. "Hope this thing's as sturdy as it looks."

Lee held up a finger and put it to his lips, lowering his voice. "Now's when we do want to be quiet."

"But they'll still smell us," Bea hissed.

"Yeah, but there's no point in riling them up further."

Everyone went quiet.

And that's when the horn from their truck started blaring.

For a second, Lee couldn't even believe that it was his truck sounding off. He even did a rapid headcount, as though maybe he'd missed one of his team and they were out screwing with the truck.

"That our truck?" Jones yelped.

"Turn it off!" Abe snapped.

"Who's got the keys?" Jones demanded, jutting his hand out to anybody that might have them.

"You do, fuckwit!" Marie spat.

"Oh." Jones dove into the cargo pocket of his pants and yanked them out, stabbing at the buttons on the key fob. The horn continued honking. "It's not working! Which button am I supposed to press? I've pressed all of them!"

"Double-click the lock button!" Sam offered.

Jones repeatedly jammed at the lock button, to no effect.

"It's the metal box we're in," Lee said. "It's blocking the signal."

Jones looked at him, horrified. "I'm not fucking going out there!"

"Goddammit," Lee growled, stalking across to Jones and snatching the keys from his hand. He'd already made a decision, and he was going to roll with it. The primals were close, but if he waited, they'd only get closer, and the last thing he needed was them ripping his truck apart in a rage.

Abe, seeing him angling for the door and clearly not to be dissuaded, threw the crossbeam and pushed the door open by the time Lee reached it. Marie, Sam, and Jones were right on Lee's heels, rifles shouldered.

Lee clutched the fob in his support hand and hefted his rifle as the door opened, scanning the outside. As dim as the lanterns in the box were, they'd toasted his vision enough that all he could see was charcoal sky and the black bulks of the other boxes. He didn't dare flash his weaponlight for fear of drawing more attention to himself. He saw no immediate movement, nor heard any nearby sounds, so he slipped through the doorway, but didn't fully leave it.

He peered around the corner of Bea's Conex box to where his truck sat in the middle of their main drag, the lights flashing and the horn honking, like it was purpose-built to get primals pissed off.

But what shocked Lee the most when he caught sight of his truck, wasn't how loud and bright it was. It was the face staring back at him from the driver's seat, illuminated by the dome light.

"The fuck is Ted doing in my truck?" Lee barked, then stabbed the lock button on the fob. The headlights flashed once and the truck went silent and dark.

A surreal moment, dominated by the lengthy eye contact between Lee and Ted.

Lee thought he heard the huff of a ragged breath from out in the darkness. The sound lit off his adrenaline, sending arcs of electricity along his spine. He did not want to be outside right now. But what the hell was he supposed to do? Just leave the asshole hanging out in his truck? Batten down the hatches and deal with it later?

"Fuck that," Lee grunted. "Hey, asshole! Get the fuck out of my truck!"

In response, Ted jerked, and must have stepped on the brakes. Red light bloomed to the rear of the vehicle, illuminating two shapes loping towards it. It only took that half second for Lee to know what he was looking at. Hideously-wide mouths filled with unnaturally-elongated teeth. Rippling, fatless muscles churning. Ropes of dreadlocked hair flying.

"Contact!" Lee raised his optic to his eye, flicking his select fire all the way over to automatic. The red dot wiggled in the air. Lee eked out his clenched breath, and the dot stilled, centering on the primal closest to Ted, even now reaching the truck bed on the driver's side. He squeezed the trigger.

Four suppressed rifle shots. Four rounds zipped out and smashed into the chest and shoulders of that lead primal. He knew he'd gotten the hits, because he saw the dust and blood come flying off of the creature, but it only staggered, then kept on coming, thrashing into the side of the truck.

Ted recoiled from the driver's door as the primal began smashing its fists into the glass. He backpedaled across the front bench seat, not even realizing that the second primal was coming up on the passenger's side.

Lee just kept on breathing out, lungs nearly empty now, and squeezed the trigger again. This time the five-round burst shattered the first primal's head. It teetered and wallowed about for a second before crumpling bonelessly to the dirt.

"Your left!" he heard Marie shout in his ear. "Got it!"

Even as he swung his muzzle to the other side of the truck, he felt Marie lean her rifle on the back of his shoulder and fire. The suppressor spit heat against the side of his face. Every instinct in his body screamed at him to get back inside, but he just sucked in another breath as the second primal slammed into the passenger's-side door of his truck.

Marie fired again and again. He wanted to twist and look at the threat to his left, but he had to trust Marie to get it done, even as he heard a gurgling, inhuman bark from frighteningly close, and the thud of a body hitting the dirt.

Focus. Breathe.

The jiggling red dot steadied on the primal just as it reared back to smash its fist through the glass—which was something Lee had witnessed them do on several occasions. He didn't have time to go for body shots that might take minutes to kill the thing. He needed it dead *right fucking now*, or it was going to rip Ted out of the truck.

At the last second, he shifted the red dot up and sent a single round through its temple.

"Multiple contacts!" Marie shouted at him, firing as she did, and he could feel her shifting rapidly back and forth, tracking this threat, and then that one. "Too many! We gotta button up!"

"Ted!" Lee bellowed. "Run to me!"

He had no way to know if Ted could hear anything from inside the truck, but if he hadn't heard, he must've come up with the same idea, because he kicked the passenger's door open and came flying out, stumbling over the dead primal at his feet.

The shadows at the other end of the main drag moved. More contacts than Lee could count.

"Run, motherfucker!" Lee urged, though Ted was already running—just not fast enough for Lee.

He raised his rifle and targeted just over Ted's shoulder. Ted noticed the rifle pointed in his direction and faltered, but when Lee pulled the trigger and the shots flew over, he jerked his head to look back and saw the multitude of shapes pouring out of the darkness towards him. Then he managed to find a little extra reserve of speed, and dumped it out all in one mad dash to Lee's side.

The second Ted reached him, Lee's concern for the man's welfare disappeared. He "helped" Ted inside, with a strong elbow to the back of the guy's neck, and if Lee's hips hadn't been shit, he'd've kicked him in the ass too.

"Back inside!" Lee belted out, swinging to his left and seeing what he'd forced himself to ignore: Two bodies, no more than a solid loping stride from Lee. Another that was wounded, limping off to the side and yowling in pain. And behind them, dozens, coming in fast.

"Shitshitshit!" Marie snarled as Lee added his rifle to hers, both of them shoulder to shoulder, raking the moving darkness with automatic fire until they felt Abe's hands seize their shoulders and haul them backwards into the Conex box.

The second they were clear, Sam and Jones yanked the metal doors back into place.

"Hold it!" Jones yelled, reaching for the crossbeam.

Something hit the door on the other side, causing Sam to yip like a spooked dog and stagger back, the door panel opening just a few inches. An arm shot through the opening and snatched ahold of Jones's wrist.

Lee, Abe, and Marie all rushed forward, grabbing whatever handhold they could and pulling on the door, while Jones wrenched at his hand, screaming and cursing his head off. The door crushed into the arm, but it wouldn't release its grip on Jones's wrist. He grappled his free left arm across his body, trying to get ahold of the sidearm on his right hip.

"Pull it again!" Lee shouted, and, as one, he and the others let a tiny bit of slack into the door, then yanked backwards again.

Jones managed to slip his pistol out of its holster, but his grip was wonky and when he tried to correct it, the pistol came tumbling out of his hand.

Then a rifle muzzle came jutting between Lee and Abe. It hit the metal door and discharged in the same instant, a deep, skull-ringing blast, made all the worse by the close quarters. The bullet punched straight through the sheet metal. Something on the other side grunted and gagged, and the arm in the door went limp. Jones ripped out of its grip, backed up a step, and then kicked the arm savagely until he'd ejected it from the opening, and the door snugged shut.

"Jones! Latch it!" Abe barked.

The crossbeam slammed down into place, and Lee pulled back from the door, sucking wind and snatching his rifle up again, just in case the door wasn't as secure as he thought it was. But it didn't budge. Something knocked into it hard on the other side, but it barely shuddered.

Only then did Lee crane his neck to look behind him, and found Bea standing there with her scoped rifle, jacking the spent shell from the chamber with trembling fingers. Her eyes were stretched wide enough to see the whites all around, her lips pale and clammy.

Behind her, Ted had somehow wound up on the floor, gasping for breath.

Jones swore, stamping his feet, and then bent to snatch up his pistol, which he clutched in front of his face as though it had betrayed him. He screamed at it: "Fuuuuuuck! Youuuuuuu!"

"I told you to work on your off-hand draw," Lee growled at him, shoving him in the shoulder. "A waste of time, you said. When am I ever going to need to draw my secondary weapon with my off-hand, you said."

"I've *been* practicing it!" Jones complained. "Just not...you know...with a primal attached to me!"

"Fuckin' Butter Finger Jones over here," Abe griped at him.

"Are we safe?" a plaintive voice cried out. "Will the door hold?"

Lee spun around and stared hate and discontent straight into Ted, which shut him up real quick. Now that Lee's adrenaline had topped out, here came the headache, and the shakes, and the pain in his left hip. He hobbled forward, baring his teeth against it all.

Ted rocketed to his feet, like he thought Lee might try to stomp him to death. Which he might have, had he been possessed of better leg mobility. Ted's eyes jagged to the rifle still in Lee's hands.

"Look..."

"What in the fuck," Lee grated over him. "Were you doing in my truck?"

Chapter 11

"We'll get to the truck thing in a second," Marie barked out, having to speak loudly over the sound of grunting and growling and claws scraping at the door. She jacked a thumb over her shoulder. "Is everyone else in the settlement buttoned up?"

Bea passed the question to Ted like it was too hot to touch. Ted goggled about, seeming to realize that all eyes were now on him. And five of those pairs belonged to five very irritable-looking people with guns.

"Uh…" His lips worked loosely for a breath, and then he nodded. "Yeah, they're all built the same. Everyone knows to lock up at dusk. No one should be out after dark."

Lee figured that answered Marie's question pretty well, and he was still very much pissed about the incursion into his truck. "Oh, no one's supposed to be out after dark? Except for you? Snooping around my shit?"

Ted held up a shaky hand. "No, no! It's not like that."

"How about you tell us what it's like," Abe shot back.

Ted swallowed thickly and gathered himself. "I was just making sure that everyone was locked in for the night, and then I heard the howl, and it sounded so close, I didn't think I'd have time to get back to my house, so I jumped in the truck."

"Bullshit," Lee spat. "That truck was locked." He frowned and looked at Jones. "It was locked, right?"

Jones looked offended. "Of course it was locked. I wouldn't forget something like that."

"Well, you forgot you had the keys in your pocket, so pardon me for having some doubts." Lee spun back to Ted. "How'd you get in? Did you break one of my windows? I swear to God, if you broke one of my windows—"

"I didn't break a window!" Ted practically shouted.

A tense quiet followed, with Lee just staring at him, waiting for him to work up the intestinal fortitude to come clean. Lee wasn't entirely sure how far he was willing to go to get him to admit it. Perhaps some light slapping around. Then again, Lee was in a bit of a tough spot now—he had every intention to stay and help these people. If he roughed Ted up...well, that wouldn't garner him any goodwill with the Redoubters.

Ted took a few steadying breaths through flared nostrils, calming himself and dealing with some internal struggle. He stared into the middle distance as he did it, and Lee let him take his time. It looked like the constipated truth was going to come out eventually.

"I..." Ted tried. False start. He couldn't quite get it out. But then he muscled it up from wherever it was hiding in his chest and spat it out. "I used a wedge and a piece of wire."

"Wait," Bea's face clouded. "You broke into their truck?"

"Well, that much is pretty obvious," Lee simmered. "What I'd like to know is why?"

"Because I didn't believe you, alright?" Ted bit out. "Who the hell just comes along with all the shit you claim to have? It was too much. Too hard to believe. I had to...to see if you were bullshitting."

Lee narrowed his eyes and leaned back, folding his hands on the buttstock of his hanging rifle. "Well. Have your doubts been allayed?"

Ted glanced apologetically at Bea, and gave a small nod. "They have what they claim to have." And then his face twisted up all over again. "And now they've gone and shot a half dozen infected."

Marie tilted her head. "You say that like it's a bad thing."

Ted raked fingers through his hair, pulling the skin of his face taut so his eyes bugged out. "You have no idea what you've done!"

"Hey," Lee stepped into him and jabbed a knife-hand to his chest. "I believe that what we've done is save your ass."

Ted shook his head, looking haunted. "For now, maybe! But you don't know the trouble that you've gotten us into. You can't just go around shooting those things!"

"Hold up," Abe said, waving a hand through the air as though calling a cease fire. "Is this one of those 'they were people once and we should treat them with respect' things? Because I can promise you, treating the primals like humans only gets you ripped apart. At best."

"No, it's not..." Ted made a strangled noise of frustration. "It's not that. You don't understand how the Valley works."

"Well, I sure as shit would like to be educated," Lee grated.

Ted thrust a hand at the door. "Those infected—primals, whatever—they were sent by Colin Horner. But they're not *owned* by him. And now we've only pissed off Colin even worse, and we've pissed off the wizard along with it, and *that's* the real fucking problem!"

Lee blinked rapidly, shaking his head, unable to compute. "That's a bit too much crazy all at once. I'm gonna need you to slow down and take it piece by piece. How the hell did Colin make the primals attack? Last I checked, they don't speak English, and you certainly can't train them like dogs."

Ted looked pleadingly to Bea. The young woman stared back at her settlement leader with lips pursed tight, a silent conversation of secret knowledge passing between them.

Bea caved to Ted's desperation and turned to face her strange new house guests. When she spoke, her voice was quiet, and dead level, an artificial calm that she'd blanketed over herself that spoke of all sorts of bad feelings lying just under the surface.

"It's not Colin that controls them. It's Kat. The girl that was here earlier with Bran."

Lee gave that a moment to percolate in his brain. "Alright," he said, cautiously. "But we still arrive back at the same point: Primals don't listen to people. They can't be controlled like that."

"Kat," Bea said, with care usually reserved for handling toxic waste. "Is not a person. Well, I mean, she is. I guess. But she's…different."

"Different how?"

Bea glanced at Sam. "You said you guys did some studying of the primals, didn't you?"

Sam nodded. "Some. What we could do safely."

"And did you guys ever see any…" she cringed and seemed to be searching for the right way to put something. "Crossbreeding? Between the primals and regular humans?"

Sam's face went slack. "A while back, we had problems with hordes of primals busting into settlements and…taking people alive. They'd break the victim's arms and legs so they couldn't get away. We found evidence of them storing people like this—keeping them as food for later. But then we realized the ones they kept for food were only men."

Lee's stomach churned at the remembered horror of what they'd discovered.

"We found one of their nests in an old warehouse," Sam continued, voice quiet. "And that's where we found the women. They'd had their legs and arms broken, too. But unlike the men, they were kept fed." He glanced at Lee, who had been right there with Sam when they'd made the discovery. "Because they were all pregnant. The primals were…raping them. To make hybrids. Hybrids that had all the physical abilities of the primals, and a good bit of the cognition abilities of regular humans. Some language abilities, too," he added, almost as an afterthought.

Lee looked back to Bea. "Are you saying that Kat's half primal?"

Bea shook her head. "No. Not half. I don't know who her parents were, but I do know that she came from a regular human male, and a hybrid female."

"So she's a quarter primal," Lee said, not sure if he felt fascinated or disgusted.

"That explains why she didn't talk much," Jones observed.

"And the face covering," Lee realized. "If she's a quarter primal, chances are her jaws aren't close to looking like a human's." Another thought occurred to him. He glanced between Ted and Bea. "Was it Colin?"

"That fathered her?" Bea shook her head. "No, it wasn't him."

"Well, how'd he find her then? How'd she wind up working for him?"

Bea let out a soft, disgruntled sound, and lowered her rifle's buttstock to the ground, leaning on the barrel like a staff. She looked to Ted. "We need to tell them about the wizard."

"Oh, yes," Abe snapped his finger. "The wizard. Right. Because there's a wizard." He gave Lee a bewildered look. "The fuck have you gotten us into?"

Despite an immense welling of morbid curiosity, Lee felt exhaustion crawling all over him. God, but he hated adrenaline dumps. Or maybe he was just getting old.

He grumbled wordlessly and shoved between Ted and Bea. He stopped at the table and sank down onto his pack again, stretching his left leg out under the table and kneading at his hip. "Ted. Bea. Grab a seat. Y'all need to explain some shit."

"He's not a wizard," Bea said, with a distinct note of bitterness. "That's just what people started calling him before they really knew who he was, and the name stuck. His real name is Lander Hollis, and he's from one of the settlements in the Valley. Well, one of the settlements that *used* to be here."

"How many settlements were there?" Marie asked.

"There were five. Horner's Peak, obviously, is the ranch that Colin Horner owns. Then there were the Townies that lived down in that little city I was telling you about—used to be called Cedar Grove, but everyone just calls it the Town. Then there was the Commune, which was a bunch of hippies, and Camperland." Bea made a face and shook her head. "We're the only ones left now. Besides Horner's Peak."

"What happened to them?" Marie questioned.

"Colin Horner happened to some of them," Bea said. "But not all of them. And that's where Lander Hollis comes in. He used to live in the Commune, but he got caught...having sex with a younger girl. He was in his forties, I think, and she was only fifteen. The Commune banished him, but the girl's father went after him with a few of his buddies and beat him half to death. I imagine they thought they were leaving him to die."

"I take it he didn't," Lee said. "The shitty ones never do."

Bea shook her head again. "I don't know what happened to him after he was beaten. But a few months later, he shows up to the Commune, alive and well, and demands to be let back in. I don't think he even wanted them to let him back in. I think he wanted them to say no, so he could justify what he did next."

"Which was?"

Bea's brow crinkled like she couldn't quite figure something out. "The Commune got overrun by primals. It was completely destroyed. Everyone in it was killed. And that's when people started calling him the wizard, because they thought he had some sort of power over the primals."

"Now," Ted put in. "A lot of this is patchy information, but what I've come to understand is that Lander was, I guess, taken in by a small pack of hybrid primals—females." He glanced to Lee. "I don't know if you guys have seen the same thing, but it seems like all the primal-human hybrids come out female."

Lee had nothing to say to that, but found it interesting that Ted had used the word *all*. How many hybrids did they have around here?

"Anyway," Ted trudged on. "Apparently, they took him in, and...well...I guess he mated with them. Or they mated with him. He's not at all sane, and I don't think he has a problem with his...current living arrangements."

Lee leaned back and folded his hands on the table. "Gestation for primals is quick. I can't speak to the hybrids, but I know primals conceive and birth within three months." He nodded to Bea. "That makes sense, according to your timeline. He disappeared for a few months. That would have been long enough for them to give birth."

"Yeah, but how mature would they be so soon after birth?" Abe asked. "It takes the juveniles a year to become really dangerous. And how many offspring could he have sired? Not enough to wipe out a whole settlement."

Bea shook her head. "It wasn't his offspring that wiped out the Commune. And he only has one that I know of. It's a female. She's just like Kat. And just like Kat, she might not speak a lot of English, but she knows how to communicate with the primals."

Jones held up his hands. "So he used his hybrid daughter to make the primals attack the Commune." Jones blew out a breath that flapped his lips. "Christ, y'all got some messed up shit going on around here."

"Is Kat his daughter too?" Sam asked.

Ted shook his head. "No. Or, at least, he denies it."

Bea fixed Lee with a hard look and then panned it around to each of the others. "Lander Hollis is bat shit crazy. He now views every primal in the Valley as *his*. His pack. He calls them his *family*."

Ted buried his face in his hands, his voice coming out muffled behind them. "Which is why we're screwed. Because you killed some of his family."

"We were defending ourselves," Lee pointed out.

"It won't matter. Everyone in the Valley knows how it is. Everyone here knows you can't kill primals." Ted smeared his hands down his face and looked at Lee with haunted, bloodshot eyes. "He won't forgive this. He never has. Bea can tell you that."

Bea shot him a look so severe that Lee thought she might come off the table and cold-cock him.

Ted pulled back from her. "Oh, shit. I'm sorry. I didn't think—"

"Just drop it," she snapped. Glanced at the others. "That is not up for discussion."

Lee held up a placating hand, even as he filed that little oddity away for future perusal. "What happened to the Town? And Camperland?"

"Oh yeah," Ted gruffed. "That. Well, sometime after Lander got his shit kicked in, and sometime before he showed up to the Commune, he'd gone to the Town. I guess he thought he could just smarm his way in there, but they weren't having it. Word gets around the settlements, and they'd already found out that he was...well...a perv. They wouldn't take him in. So after he knocked off the Commune, he went right over to the Town and wiped them out too."

"As for Camperland," Bea said tightly. "That was Colin. Or Bran and Kat, anyway, working on his orders."

"Same thing though?" Lee asked. "Kat called in the primals and had them overrun the settlement?"

Bea nodded. "And now Colin's coming for us. And Lander's going to come for us too. We don't have any allies in this place anymore."

"You have five," Lee noted. "And besides." He gestured to the door again, where the sounds of primals without had faded. They weren't mindless creatures—they might not cognate like humans, but they were clever enough, and they wouldn't spend all night trying to get into a steel box they knew they couldn't bust open. "Your defenses held."

Ted groaned. "He sent them at night, I don't know why—he knows we lock ourselves in at night. Maybe he's just sending a message. Or maybe he just didn't think about it. But he won't make that mistake again. And Lander will be on the warpath.

Colin or Lander, it doesn't matter which one. They'll send the primals after us during the day. They'll keep hounding us until they get what they want. Which is us, dead and gone."

Lee rubbed a hand along his chin, fingers playing over the scars that cut through his stubble. "Is there some sort of relationship between Colin Horner and Lander Hollis?"

Again, Ted and Bea looked at each other, but this time Bea shook her head. "I haven't dealt with Colin like you have, Ted. I don't know the man."

Ted's shoulders sagged. "Yeah, there's a relationship there. I don't know exactly what kind, though. I know that Colin got Kat from Lander. I don't know what kind of deal they struck, but that was three years ago, and right afterwards is when Colin built the dam on his river and started charging everyone a water tax to keep the river flowing."

Lee arched an eyebrow at Marie and Abe. "That adds up. Seems like Colin wants control of the Valley. I'd imagine he'd be attracted to having the power to use the primals to threaten and coerce people. Or just kill them, apparently. Once he had Kat, he had the means to enforce something like a water tax, so he built the dam." Lee frowned. "What I'm not seeing is what Lander Hollis gets out of it."

Sam, standing just behind Lee, leaned into the table. "I don't wanna digress, but you said this all went down about three years ago?"

Ted nodded. "Thereabouts."

Sam squinted. "So, how old *is* Kat?"

Ted's eyes flickered with something that Lee couldn't quite place. Maybe it was pity? Maybe it was disgust? "Three years old," he said. Then swallowed, and amended: "Best I can figure."

Jones made a low whistle. "A three year old that looks like a teenager and has the ability to communicate with primals. That's not a recipe for disaster at all."

Sam crossed his arms over his chest, looking thoughtful. "I mean, I know the primals mature very rapidly. But I'd've thought a quarter primal, or even one of the half primals would develop slower."

"Who knows what the hell's getting expressed in those genetics?" Marie observed. "That's a question for scientists. Which we're not."

Lee propped his elbows on the table and rested his forehead on two steepled index fingers. "So. We've got a crazy guy that thinks he's the patriarch for primals, and is busy making hybrids to use to control the horde in the Valley. One of which he's given over to Colin, who is using her to enforce his water tax, which he doesn't really care about, because he just wants everyone off his land."

Ted considered it with pursed lips. "Yeah, that pretty much sums it up."

"Well." Lee smiled with scant humor. "Quite a crap cake we've walked into, huh?"

Chapter 12

Kat stood in the darkness, staring at all those metal boxes. Behind her, the sounds of the pack that she'd called upon faded into the night. There were many packs that made up the colony. This one she didn't care for. The Alpha had taken an intense interest in her, and she'd had to growl and bare her teeth at him.

The Alphas always treated her strangely. Like they couldn't decide whether she was something to eat, or rut, or obey.

The fact that the pack hadn't fed only made it worse. It made them harder to control. Kat had known it would be a bad idea to send them to the Redoubt at night. She knew the people there locked themselves into their metal boxes. Her father should have known it as well. But she wasn't in the habit of correcting his mistakes.

Her father had no affection for her. He did not want to hear her. He did not want to see her. He only wanted her to obey him.

It was strange to her to have a father that showed no affection. Even the pack members showed affection to each other, and their pups. They would groom each other. Nuzzle each other. Curl around each other at night.

Weren't humans supposed to be superior to them?

She knew that she was different from the regular humans in many ways. Her father made sure to remind her of that. She was a mixed breed. Or, as he called it, a mutt. Or sometimes an uh-bomb-nation, whatever that meant. She could tell from context it wasn't meant to be kind.

One of the ways she was different was her eyesight at night. It'd never been explained to her, but she saw how the regular humans bumbled about in the dark, and had to use flashlights and lanterns to get around. Kat didn't need any of those things. The only thing that she lost at night was her perception of color—everything turned to blues and grays. But she could see plenty well enough. And if there was a moon, as there was tonight, it might as well be broad daylight.

She picked her way through the dry grasses, making only the slightest rustle as she did. She could have moved silently—another thing that regular humans couldn't seem to do—but there was no need for silence. She did not need to stay hidden from primals. And all the humans in the vicinity were in their boxes. Not that they could hear that well anyway.

She moved with purpose into the settlement, knowing exactly where she was going, because she'd been here so many times before. In amongst the buildings, the scents of all the people came alive. She could taste their scents, and see them, in a way. They left it wherever they went, in little trails that hung above the ground like low-lying tendrils of fog.

She was passingly familiar with most of the scents in the Redoubt. Now there were five that she was unfamiliar with, but recognized them as belonging to the five strangers she'd seen here earlier in the day. She was unconcerned with them.

But there was one smell, out of all the others, that teased her in a way she couldn't figure out.

She found that scent and followed it straight to the door of one of the boxes. She knew this box. She'd been inside of it before. And she knew who lived there.

She crouched down, inhaling deeply as she did.

His name was Ted. And his scent...well, she didn't know why his scent was so intriguing to her. But it lit off something in her brain, and that something compelled her. It filled her with a mix of feelings that she didn't understand. Like a hunger for something she'd never tasted, and could not be fulfilled by eating.

She wanted him. She just didn't know what she wanted him for.

The one time she'd been alone with Ted, she'd tried to rut him. She remembered him backpedaling, telling her to calm down, trying to push her off of him. But that was another thing about her that was different from regular humans: Other human girls that looked the same size as her were weak, and a man like Ted could have shoved them around easily. Kat was apparently built of sturdier stuff, because no matter how hard he tried, he couldn't quite overpower her.

It was only after she'd clawed him and smelled his blood that she came to herself and thought that rutting him wasn't what she wanted after all.

To this day, she hadn't figured out what exactly it *was* that she wanted from him.

Something. And someday she'd have it. If she could figure out what it was.

She pressed her nose to the door and scented. Her bandana hung around her neck. There was no need for it now, and it only made scenting harder.

She frowned and pulled her head back.

The scent from inside the box was stale. Old. He wasn't in there.

In her low squat, she panned her head around, going to all fours to make it easier to get her nose close to the ground. As she did, the trail of his scent became apparent. She followed it on all fours for a moment, realizing it was getting fresher as she moved.

Fresh enough that it had to have been after dark when he'd made it.

What was Ted doing out here after dark?

Something in her brain wondered if he hadn't been waiting for her. She dismissed it, knowing it for what it was: fantasy. Now *there* was something that was wholly from the human part of her. From what she could tell, the creatures with whom she shared her blood—Bran and her father called them "infected," though she didn't know what that meant—didn't have much in the way of imagination. They simply perceived reality, and acted upon it, their minds never going to what-ifs and maybes.

Humans, on the other hand—and Kat with them—were remarkably vulnerable to daydreaming. Conjuring up images of what the future might bring, what other people were thinking, and what they might do with those thoughts, and how you might respond to them if they did.

Fairly useless stuff.

And dangerous. Because sometimes those fantasies had a way of feeling real. And when they felt so real, people sometimes acted on their imaginations, rather than reality. In fact, people did that a lot. And Kat was not immune to it. She recalled one time in particular that she maybe shouldn't have acted on her imaginings.

She could still feel the sensation of her teeth breaking that woman's flesh. The look in her eyes as she begged for mercy. The gurgle as that begging was cut off when Kat closed her jaws around the woman's throat.

And she remembered wondering in that moment if she'd made a mistake. She'd imagined that moment so many times, while under that woman's spiteful, fearful gaze. She didn't like Kat, and Kat didn't like her, and so Kat imagined how satisfying it would be to rip her apart. And then she did.

Part of her was immensely satisfied afterwards. That was probably the "infected" part of her. Another part had felt...well, she wasn't entirely sure what it was that she'd felt, but it was like being afraid of a punishment that you might or might not get. And she assumed that was the human part of her.

Fantasy: Dangerous stuff.

The trail stopped in a muddled wash of scents. She pulled her hands off the ground and rested them on her knees, surveying the scene. She was in front of the white pickup truck that the strangers had come in. Several bodies lay in the dirt. Not human bodies, but she'd already known that.

A small growl worked its way out of her throat, as the smells of blood and bowels overpowered the trace of Ted's scent.

She rose to her full height to get a better vantage point, and spotted more bodies clustered around another one of the metal boxes. She strode casually over, still sniffing as she did, but there was too much to get a read on any one particular thing.

Around the door of the metal box were two bodies. Five more scattered about, a little further away.

That was nearly half the pack.

Lander Hollis was going to be angry.

Standing so close to the metal box, she heard the murmurs of voices from within, but largely ignored it. All of these boxes were full of murmuring voices—most of them more excited than usual, probably due to the gunfire. But her ears pricked at a single word.

Kat.

Her? Were they talking about her?

She leaned in closer. Not that she had to. Her hearing was keen enough to pick out the words without trying. She immediately recognized Ted's voice. He was talking about Kat, and Lander Hollis, and her father.

The details were a bit lost on her. Oh, she could hear the words clear enough, but people had the habit of talking so rapidly, and using so many words to do it, that sometimes she struggled to keep them all in her head and string them into sentences that made sense.

There were words about her, and her father, and the dam, and deals, and arrangements, and water taxes. Those all jumped out to her, because she was familiar with those phrases and heard them often. But the finer points of what exactly they were saying about those things were inscrutable to her.

Interesting that Ted would be talking about her.

Was he as obsessed with her as she was with him? The feeling made a part of her glow, which made her frown and look down at her chest, because she'd never really felt that before. Except, maybe to a lesser extent, when Bran said nice things to her.

Distracted by that, she lost the tenuous thread of what she'd been able to make sense of, and then lost interest.

It was only as she started to walk back out into the night that it struck her: Ted could have died tonight. And it would have been her that called in the infected that did it. She hadn't even thought about that before, because she knew that the Redoubt buttoned up at night.

But Ted had been outside. Ted had been near the strangers' truck. Ted was now in another person's metal box, as though he'd run there to hide.

And she realized something very strange as she thought about all that.

The idea of Ted dying *scared* her.

Chapter 13

Dawn came, bright and clear, and in the time it took Lee to wake, stretch his disgruntled limbs, and gather his gear, the box had become uncomfortably hot.

"Christ, can we open this thing up?" Abe asked, face already beading with sweat. The air in the box had been stuffy all night, but that was to be expected with seven bodies huffing out hot air.

Bea, who'd been the first up and woke everyone else by not-so-quietly clattering about the kitchen area, gave a dismissive nod to the door. "Go ahead."

Abe let out a thankful breath and tossed the crossbeam to the side, then shoved open the door. The air outside wasn't any cooler, but at least it was dry and moving.

Lee's skin felt like it was covered in a film of oil and dirt. His clothes were beginning to have that stick-to-your-skin feel. God, had it really been four days since he bathed? Well, it'd have to be a little longer, because he had shit to do this morning.

As he moved towards the door, he fell in step with Marie, both with their packs on their shoulders and their armor lugged in one hand, rifles in the other. "Think he'll be bothered by our smell?"

"Probably," Marie answered.

"Think it'll ruin our chances?"

Marie only shrugged.

"Uh, Ted?" Abe called from just outside the door. "You have some folks out here that clearly have questions about last night."

As Lee shouldered around Abe, he found what looked like the entire settlement hanging around Bea's Conex box. Some children were poking at one of the dead primals with a stick, until their mother shouted at them to get away from it. They leaped back like it hadn't been dead for eight hours already.

Lee half expected to get barraged by questions the second he showed his face, but the citizens of the Redoubt just eyeballed him in silence. Lee gave them a smile, then nudged Abe in the direction of the pickup truck.

"Let's let these folks hash things out. We don't need to be in the middle of it."

Marie, Jones, and Sam followed them out, bleary eyed and blinking in the sunlight.

Lee didn't bother looking around when all the voices erupted. Obviously, Ted had showed his face, and the dam of hesitant silence had broken.

"Who killed the infected?"

"What are we gonna do about Lander?"

"Did Colin try to wipe us out last night? Is that what this was about?"

"Are they leaving? I thought they were going to help."

Guess that last one was directed at him. Lee still didn't bother to turn around, but cast a good-humored cringe in Abe's direction.

"Folks," Ted's voice rang out, with an unimpeachable calm that belied pretty much every action he'd taken last night. And then he began to explain to them what had happened, conveniently leaving out anything that reflected poorly on him.

"You sure you wanna roll in with just you and Marie?" Abe asked as they reached the truck.

"Gotta open a dialogue at some point in time," Lee answered, hefting his pack and his armor onto the hood of the truck and giving the vehicle a quick once over for bullet holes. There weren't any. Well...not any new ones anyway. "Rolling in five deep can be interpreted as a little threatening. I wanna try to keep things mellow as much as possible."

Reaching the rear of the vehicle, Lee dropped the tailgate and Abe helped him drag out the crate of what Abe referred to as "minion rifles." Basic M4's with nothing fancy on them except the red-dot optic. There were ten in the crate. They could distribute those to the Redoubt's strongest fighters, then fill in the gaps after they got a supply drop from Colorado.

"Yeah," Abe said as they lugged the crate a few steps to the side of the truck and set it down. "But no overwatch?"

"You heard Ted's brief on the terrain last night," Lee replied, not terribly thrilled with the idea of going to meet this Colin Horner guy without overwatch, but already having decided there was nothing to be done for it.

The terrain around the ranch was unfavorable for snipers to stay hidden. According to Ted, it was mostly rolling, grassy hills. Tall grass wasn't hard to *hide* in, but it was hard to see through, which meant that you could either stay hidden, or you could see your target, but you couldn't do both.

And if the overwatch was spotted…well, Lee guessed it would sour the whole "we come in peace" vibe he was going for.

"I'm taking the ESR," Lee continued, referring to the precision rifle that Abe usually manned. "If I see a decent piece of concealment, I can go overwatch for Marie, and she can try to make contact on her own."

They stepped back to the truck bed and Abe gestured to the other crates and boxes of various equipment. "What about the rest of this shit?"

Lee rubbed his chin thoughtfully. "Well, I wanted to bring a peace offering. I was originally thinking ammo, but, if peace is not in the cards, that seems like a bad idea."

"Not a whole lotta shit that you can give as a gift that couldn't be used against us in the future."

"True. But besides the peace offering aspect of it, I also need something to show this Horner guy that I have access to resources. Otherwise he won't believe I'm worth making a deal with."

Abe considered it for a moment, then shrugged. "Stick some grenades in you and Marie's rigs. People are always impressed with grenades. That way, he can see it, but he doesn't get to have it."

Lee was hoping for something a bit more tantalizing—something that would motivate Horner to make a deal—but Abe was right. If peace didn't work out, Lee didn't want his tantalizing gift being used against them.

Sam and Jones arrived and began helping them offload their gear from the truck, leaving only Lee and Marie's personal packs, and the ESR in its tan Pelican case.

After they were done, the team gathered around the hood of the truck where Lee and Marie's gear still lay.

Abe was not quite done worrying. "Peace talks. The night after he tried to kill us?"

"That's exactly why I want to go right now. The night after he tries to kill us, we show up at Colin's doorstep? I think it'll put him off kilter. Maybe give us a leg up."

"That, or he'll just kill you when you get there."

"Sounds like he's a business guy," Lee said, slinging his rifle over his armor. "I think he'll feel us out for a deal first. And we might be able to oblige. End this whole thing without any bloodshed. Wouldn't that be nice?"

Abe leaned on the truck. "And if things go wrong?"

"That's why I'm taking Marie."

"I thought you were taking Marie because she's better than you at diplomacy."

"Yes. And she's got a gun."

"I have a gun too."

"Yeah, but you're salty and you put people on the defensive."

"Didn't you just say you wanted him on the defensive?"

"Yes, but not like *you'd* put him on the defensive. I want to put him on the defensive without *looking* like I'm putting him on the defensive." Lee patted Abe condescendingly on the shoulder. "See, Marie knows these things. That's why I'm taking her and not you."

Abe grunted and shrugged him off. Then stared balefully out at the gathered people, who were now packed in so tight, Lee could barely see Ted trying his hardest to field the same questions posed in different ways.

"So I have to stay back here with these idiots," Abe sighed.

Lee grabbed his pack from the hood and walked around to the side, tossing it into the bed. "Well, my dear Sweet and Salty Abe, you don't have to do anything you don't want to do. If you're not feeling up to training them, maybe you can just lay in the shade and finger your belly button."

"There is no fucking shade," Abe grumped.

"Well, I guess you'll just have to train them, then."

Abe shot him a dark look. "Oh, I'll train them."

"Be nice," Lee advised, wagging his finger at Abe as he made his way to the driver's door. "Try not to give anyone heat stroke." He opened the door and looked at the two younger members of the team. "Sam and Jones, don't let Abe kill any of the people we're trying to help."

"We've still got three IV bags," Jones noted, smirking at Abe. "So you'll have to limit yourself to three heat stroke victims."

"Speaking of," Sam said, coming around to the driver's door as Lee settled in behind the wheel. "We could use a resupply."

"Yeah, I need to make that call tonight."

Sam gave him a hooded look.

Lee nodded, dismissively. "Relax. I left the satphone in Abe's pack. Come on, Sam. You really think I'd take it into an unknown situation?"

Sam held up a hand, patting the air. "Just wanted to make sure."

With no idea how their attempt at diplomacy might go, it was safest if the satphone didn't go with him. It was the lifeline of the team, and if Lee and Marie happened to go down, at least Sam, Jones, and Abe would still have contact with Colorado.

Lee shut his door. Marie was already in the passenger seat, waiting.

"For fuckssake, get the air cranking," she said, leaning back, a somewhat comical picture, dressed in combat gear with a rifle strapped to her chest, but fanning herself delicately.

Lee started the engine. The air was already cranked to the max from the day before. He rolled his window down and thrust a thumb out to the others. "You boys be good. Have fun. Better not be bodies when I get back."

Sam, who was nearest to Lee's window gave him a cautious look. "You just worry about getting back."

Marie eyed Lee from the passenger seat while he was distracted with backing the truck out of the Redoubt. Knowing she only had a moment, she really studied him, trying to find the thing that had changed.

Of course, he'd changed a lot over the years. Her earliest memories of him were probably the least flattering. The first time she'd met him, he was banged up to all hell from a fight the day before in which he'd entirely had his shit kicked in. He didn't even have clothes that weren't shredded or bloody, so he'd been laying there in a borrowed T-shirt and gym shorts, looking more like a piece of carrion than a skilled operative.

She witnessed what he was capable of rather quickly after that first impression, so it hadn't held much sway in her mind. But even so, when she looked back at the Lee she'd known then, he was markedly different from the one she knew now. Back then, he'd been relatively scarless and clean cut, but clearly experienced enough to handle bad situations.

But the bad situations just kept coming, hard and fast, and what might have been seen as "experienced" became a rough, callused shell around his personality. And then that rough shell had turned into a jagged, stony edifice, as likely to harm anyone who came near, as it was to protect the man inside.

And then all that hard stuff he'd built up over the years got blasted away, enormous piece after enormous piece, until Lee was left stripped of his old defenses, naked and exposed.

When that happens, you have two options. You can curl up and die. Or you can be reborn. Become something else entirely. Learn from the past, and construct a new self, playing to your strengths, and mitigating your weaknesses.

Lee was not the type to curl up and die, and so he had been reborn.

"You know, I still have peripheral vision on my right," Lee said, finishing a three-point turn. He glanced at her with his good right eye. "I can see you staring at me."

Marie looked forward again. "Just tryna figure you out," she said, deciding to be forthcoming right out the gate. They'd end up talking about it eventually. They always did.

"I might could be of some assistance there," he said, accelerating out of the Redoubt.

"Oh, I'm just musing on your ever-changing nature."

"Ever changing?"

She cast him a suspicious sidelong look. "The Lee I knew from North Carolina woulda been the one advocating for rough training. Weed the pussies out, you know?"

He smiled softly and nodded. "That's probably accurate."

"So..." She adjusted her shoulders so she could look at him easier. "Are you just getting old? Or is it something else?"

Lee squinted at the road ahead. "Well, I can't pretend that age doesn't have something to do with it. But when you say 'something else' it has a distinct flavor." He looked at her dryly. "Like you got an idea of what that something else is, but you don't wanna say it."

Marie sighed. "We can't be friends with these people, Lee."

He pulled his head back and frowned. "What makes you think that I'm trying to be friends with them?"

"Let's just go with the obvious and say it's because you're going softer on them than usual."

"Am I?" he mused, eyebrows arching.

"That's not how you did it with Rampart on the Border."

"Do I need to point out how that ended?"

"That's not how you did it with *anyone* before now."

Lee shrugged. "Fair point. What's your concern?"

"What's my concern?" Marie huffed, jamming her elbow onto the center console. "My concern is that you're trying to make friends instead of doing your damn job."

"Why would I do that?"

"Stop answering my questions with questions."

"Alright," Lee said, unperturbed. "I am *not* trying to make friends."

Marie looked skyward, exasperated. "So why do I feel like you're doing things differently here than you've done before?"

"Well, now, that's a different question, isn't it?"

"Lee," she said, in her most *I'm-about-to-punch-you* voice.

"I *am* doing things differently," he finally conceded. "Because the usual way of doing things hasn't been giving us the results we want, has it?"

"No," she admitted, slowly. "Not recently."

"So, what? You want me to just keep ramming my head against the wall? Or see the writing on it and switch tactics?"

"You said it yourself, Lee," Marie came back with renewed conviction. "Just last night. We have a great success rate. I'm afraid you're throwing that out the window because of a few bad hands, when you should just stick it out a little longer."

"I *was* sticking it out a little longer," Lee replied, his voice going a bit flat. "I stuck it out in Rampart. Now I've decided to try something different."

"It worked plenty of times before," Marie grumbled. "What's changed?"

"You mean besides watching a whole settlement get murdered right in front of our eyes?"

Marie's lips tightened. "None of us liked what happened there, Lee. But sometimes that's just the way it goes. You can't save everyone. You can't win every battle."

"No. But you can try." He let out a long breath through his nose, squinting into the sun-bright hills as they drove their way along ridgelines, heading east towards Horner's Peak.

The silence stretched, and Marie let it. She could tell Lee was mulling things over. He'd always been quick, and usually sharp, with his responses. Nowadays, he took more time. Yet another change that she'd seen develop over the years, often leaving her wondering whether it should concern her.

Was he still the man of action that he'd been? Maybe he was wasting away into self-doubt and hesitation. Or maybe he was just trying to shoot from the hip a little less, and direct his aim a little more.

Finally, Lee had out with it. "You know, one of my old instructors used to say that people only learn in one of two ways: repetition, or deep emotional experience. When we set out to learn something, we either hammer it in over thousands of repetitions, or we learn it once, and painfully. Either way, the lesson gets internalized. I've had a lot of both types of learning experiences in my past. Except they taught me all the wrong things."

He looked at her earnestly. "I used to fantasize about killing myself."

Marie shifted in her seat, discomfited. In a world gone mad, suicidal ideation wasn't exactly rare, and they all knew it. Hell, they'd all had fantasies of their own. However, it was also one of those things that they just tended not to talk about. Talking about it only made it more real. Maybe even more tempting.

Lee continued, his words thoughtful. "I'd imagine putting a pistol to my temple, and I'd imagine all the inner workings of it. The break of the trigger. The firing pin hitting the primer. The propellant igniting. Pushing the bullet down the bore, and then—splash. Lights out. Release." The way he said it—almost dreamily, with the ghost of smile on his lips.

Marie swallowed thickly. "At this point, I think anyone that *hasn't* thought about suck-starting their gun is probably a psychopath."

Lee allowed it with a minimal shrug. "When we were down in that tunnel, and that bomb went off over our heads, I was so completely sure that it was lights out for us."

Marie suppressed an involuntary shudder at the memory of it. They'd been hunting then-Acting-President Erwin Briggs, who'd holed up in a bunker beneath the town of Greeley, Colorado. They'd known at the time that a nuclear warhead was inbound. They'd decided to finish their business with Briggs anyway. They'd *all* been sure they were dead.

"A five-kiloton warhead going off over your head," Lee said with an odd chuckle. "Is a helluva deep emotional experience, don't you think?"

"I still have nightmares about being buried in that tunnel," Marie grunted.

Lee nodded at the windshield. "Any time something like that happens to a person, you gotta wonder what they found out about themselves. You asked me what's different? Me. I've changed. My thinking has changed. And maybe it took a while to manifest to the point that you can see it, but that's when my brain got rearranged, Marie. A whole lotta learning, in the span of just a few seconds."

She watched him, not bothering to ask him what he learned, because she could see he was finding the words himself, just taking his time doing so.

"For me, I realized I didn't want release from life," Lee went on. "I wanted a release from the paradigm that had guided my life up to that point. The paradigm that had taken everything from me, and all but killed me, inside and out."

"What paradigm was that?"

"The mission," Lee said, simply. "The idea that the mission comes before everything else. That completing the mission is justification enough for all the shit you did to get there. Death before dishonor. Die in a pile of brass. All that horseshit that makes you treat human beings like chess pieces. Including yourself.

"The mission became my god. My master. And I was just its slave. I sacrificed everything to it. And the worst part about it, Marie? My hands weren't tied. I wasn't *forced* to sacrifice. I was *willing* to sacrifice...everything. I was willing to sacrifice people that I loved." He gave her a glance that didn't quite reach eye contact. "I was willing to sacrifice you. And Abe. And Sam. And Jones. Everyone and everything became expendable."

"We knew the risks," Marie said, quietly.

"I know you did."

"You told us we might not come back from hunting Briggs, and we went anyway."

"I know you did," Lee repeated. "But for what? To put a bullet in the head of a man that'd already lost all his power?"

"I like to think of it as justice."

Lee smiled without much humor. "Justice don't live around here no more."

"So, what?" Marie turned back to him. "Screw the world and let it tear itself to pieces?"

"Does it look like that's what I'm doing?"

"No," she conceded. "But the mission *does* take priority."

"Over what?" Lee asked. "Over my personal comfort? Sure. Over my life and the lives of others? Sometimes. But not always."

"Do you regret not standing by Rampart when the cartel came knocking?"

"I regret that they died," Lee said. "I don't regret that we decided not to die with them."

"It was the right call," Marie agreed.

"I know it was," Lee sighed. "And that's my point. All those people in Rampart? They'd become slaves to the mission as well. They let that old paradigm lead them right into the grave. Except they didn't get graves. They just got beheaded and piled up to rot out in the desert. They believed that dying in a pile of brass was their highest calling. They believed in death before dishonor.

Except...who's around to honor them? Who remembers them as heroes? No one. Not even us. We only remember them as people who couldn't see the writing on the wall."

"I see you've brought us around full circle," Marie commented with a mirthless smirk.

"Quite deftly, I might add."

"So, why are you going soft on the Redoubt?"

"Not soft. Just...more circumspect."

"These people need to be taught how to fight."

"Do they?" Lee asked. "Can they?" Lee swiveled his head to her again, good eye ranging over her face, the scarred remnants of his left eye socket giving him an oddly intense look. "We've been trying to teach these settlements to fight like us. But they can't. They don't have the combat experience we have. And a few weeks—or even a few months of training—won't get them there."

"Well, we can't do everything for them, Lee. At some point in time, they got to learn to stand up for themselves. I thought that was the whole point."

"Mm," Lee said, nodding in a satisfied way that told Marie she'd just walked into a verbal trap. "And how do people learn, Marie?"

She rolled her eyes and looked out her window. "Repetition, or deep emotional experience. Still doesn't explain why you've gone soft."

"You're really trying to shame me, aren't you?"

"Is it working?"

"Not even a little bit," Lee replied, lightly. "Soft is just a bullshit word that's used to get folks with more fight than sense to submit to that old paradigm. Be hard. Be rough. Be callused." He snorted in derision. "Why? I'll tell you why. So those that don't know any better will exalt the mission above life itself, and sacrifice everything that makes this existence meaningful on an altar to their own sense of honor. When we took The Deal, I'd already decided that I'd never submit to that paradigm again. And since I won't submit to it myself, I certainly won't train others to."

"We took The Deal three years ago, Lee, and in all that time, you've just now decided to change your strategy?"

Lee just shrugged again. "I guess you could say old habits die hard. What other way did I know how to train people when we started? Maybe I didn't even realize I was doing it. Not until I saw Rampart decide to sacrifice everything. Everything, Marie. Themselves. Their elderly. Their children. Everything. Gone. For nothing."

"That's not on you," Marie said. "They made their choice."

"You're half right," Lee replied. "They did make their choice. Everyone has to make their own choice, and there ain't shit you can do about that. But you're wrong that it's not on me. You think Rampart would have done that shit if I'd never trained them up?" He shook his head. "I don't believe they would have. And I'm not going to keep training people to put the mission ahead of life itself. I'll be the first to admit that sometimes life takes killing. Sometimes, in order to preserve life for some, you have to take it away from others. I'm...immensely comfortable with that fact." He looked at her, very seriously. "But I'm not gonna train folks to fight to the death. I'm not gonna train them to be rough and callused. I'll train them how to fight—if they want it. But I'll train them to fight *right.* Fight—if you have to—to preserve your life and the lives of those around you. But don't forget that you're fighting for *life.*"

Marie stared at him long and hard as they trundled over the uneven ground. "So, you don't want to teach folks to fight to the death, because that negates the whole purpose of us being here, which is to make sure they survive. Okay. I'll accept that, Lee. But what's that got to do with Abe running their asses off?"

"Personally, I don't give a fuck if Abe runs their asses off. However, professionally...what's the point? To make them physically tough? We don't have the time for hard physical training to actually pay any dividends. To make them mentally tough?" He shook his head. "These people are already tough, Marie. They're out here living in metal boxes, baking in the sun, freezing in the cold, and getting by on rainwater and whatever food they can pry out of the ground. These aren't soft-ass first-worlders anymore. They've proven they're mentally tough by virtue of the fact that they're still alive.

"They don't need hazing, as fun as it is for Abe." He glanced at her with a twinkle in his eyes. "And maybe for me, too. But it doesn't do us much good in the long run, and in the short run, it's probably just going to piss people off that are probably already pretty reticent about us. Last thing I want is to come back to the Redoubt and have to soothe a bunch of hurt butts. So then we're left with, what *do* we train them in? Weapons mechanics. Tactics. Strategy. Will they listen? I hope so. Because we don't have the time for the repetitions to really work their way into full learning. But my hope is that the little scare from last night was just enough of a deep emotional experience to make them realize how much they need to pay attention."

"And if it wasn't enough?" Marie questioned.

Lee rapped his thumb against the steering wheel a few times. "Well, then I hope Colin Horner isn't the asshole they make him out to be."

Chapter 14

Horner's Peak, Lee realized when they came in sight of it, was not actually at the peak of anything, but instead sprawled across a nicely flat valley at the base of a small ridgeline of mountains. One of those ridges jutted up just slightly higher than the others, and Lee intuited that this was the ranch's namesake.

Lee let his gaze fall from the peak to the ranch below it. They'd passed no fencing on the way in, but that wasn't particularly surprising—free range had taken on a new meaning in a world where most of your neighbors were dead and all the land was up for grabs. But the ranch itself was bordered by a long stretch of post-and-barbed-wire fencing, encircling what must have been close to fifty acres.

Inside that ranch were all manner of structures. Some of them were clearly old and had been old when the world went to shit. Some of them looked newer. Many of them looked both old and new—cobbled together recently from whatever scraps could be scavenged.

Lee had allowed the truck to coast to a slower speed, both to avoid spooking any itchy trigger fingers with an overly-aggressive approach, and to give Marie time to take notes on the little pad she'd pulled out and was already scribbling on.

"Alright," Lee murmured, leaning forward in his seat. "Got four obvious barns, more or less at cardinal points. One big ranch house a bit north of center. Looks like he's got solar panels on the roof." He waited for the scratching of Marie's pen to pause before he continued. "Another house near the east side. Not as nice as the big house. Maybe a bunkhouse for the ranch hands? And maybe two dozen smaller structures of unknown purpose. Stables on the west side, near the main gate. Lots of fencing—combination of wood, wood and barbed wire, and cattle panels."

"Vehicles?"

Lee peered around for them. "There's a few pickups between the big house and the bunkhouse. Looks like some tractors, though I doubt they have any fuel." Lee frowned. "Unless…"

Marie glanced up from her notes. "Anything that looks like a diesel reactor?"

Lee searched the grounds, smirking. "You're so smart."

"That's why you keep me around."

"What appears to be a diesel reactor over by the eastern barn, which I now believe to actually be a slaughter house." It was a large, silver, vat-like construction that Lee had initially passed over as one of the several grain silos dotting the ranch. "Can you get enough fat off of cows to make biodiesel?"

Marie frowned but didn't look up from her notes. "How the hell would I know that? But those people with the pigs did it," she said, recalling a settlement they'd helped a year or so back.

"Yeah. Pigs have a lot more fat on them, though."

"Cows are a lot bigger than pigs."

"True. Alright. So they possibly have access to fuel. Good to know."

"Personnel?"

"Ohhh," Lee intoned as he guesstimated at all the small figures moving around the ranch. "A good bit. About a dozen visible right now. And, hey, look. They're coming out to say hello."

Marie glanced up from her notepad and spotted what Lee had just seen.

The road they were on was little more than two pitted tire ruts. It led straight to the front gate of the ranch. The front gate was nothing impressive. It wasn't even fortified. Just your average steel-pole gates that you might find on any ranch, with two, big, wooden timbers holding up an arched sign that bore the ranch's brand: A big H inside a circle.

At that gate, Lee counted two figures with what appeared to be long guns, which they'd shouldered but weren't pointing directly at the incoming truck. Behind them, from inside the gate, a pack of five more figures were rushing to back them up—also with long guns.

"Seven armed combatants," Marie noted, clinically.

Lee clucked his tongue. "Not combatants just yet, Marie. Let's give them the benefit of the doubt, huh?"

She gave him a scouring look.

He flashed her a grin. "But...you know...be ready."

She nodded, flipping the notepad closed as they drew within a few hundred yards of the gate. She stowed her notepad and let her hands sink down into her lap, gripping the rifle between her legs.

"You wanna pull up short?" she asked, situating herself in her seat, angling her body towards the door in case a quick bail-out was called for. She touched the door lock to make sure it was disengaged, and lowered her window, a blast of dry, hot air immediately filling the cab. "Meet them in the middle?"

"Yup," Lee said, slowing to a crawl and lowering his own window. "I'll walk out to meet them."

Marie sighed through her nose. "I'll shoot them when they try to kill you."

"Mighty thoughtful of you."

He stuck his left hand out the window and splayed the damaged fingers as best he could—the universal sign for *we come in peace.* He slowed to a stop about fifty yards shy of the gate. He could hear them hollering things at him, but it was muddled past the sound of his own engine and the blowing A/C. Their weapons were now definitely pointing in his direction. Two scoped, bolt-action rifles, one M1A with iron sights, two AR variants with optics, and one AK variant with so many unnecessary attachments on it that Lee was surprised the man could lift it.

Yet another poor soul that thought more gear would save him, instead of more training.

Then, from the back of the pack came a man lugging what sure looked to Lee like an M60.

He grunted a warning tone. "You clock that guy with The Pig?"

"Yeah, I see him," Marie replied, a bit more tension in her voice than before.

"Wonder where they picked *that* piece up from," Lee pushed the shifter into park, leaving the truck running.

"Or how much ammo they actually have for it," Marie added.

Lee kneed the door open and slid out, the sounds of all the ruckus from the gate getting clearer the instant he put his feet on the dusty ground.

"Hands up!" someone was shouting repeatedly, like they couldn't figure out anything else to say.

Lee raised his hands to about chest height, showing they were empty. He'd left his rifle in the truck, but he made no attempt to hide the pistol still on his hip. He faced the gaggle of guards at the gate and began walking towards them.

For a moment, their commands faltered. Glances were exchanged between the men. He of the overwrought AK seemed to be in charge, which Lee found darkly amusing. The man stepped forward with all the swagger of someone who believes they know the lay of the land and leveled the contraption at Lee. It'd almost be an indignity to be shot by it.

"You!" the man shouted, clearly about to follow up with something else, but Lee cut him off with a big, sunny smile.

"Yes! Me!"

The man was a rather hefty individual for these times, though Lee figured they had plenty of beef to eat around here. He looked well-muscled enough, but all of it was coated with a thick layer of blubber that gave him a puffy, porcine look. Particularly in his moonish face, with two uncomprehending and irritable eyes peering out.

After a moment of mental upset, the man—Lee decided to dub him Porky—recentered himself. "Tell the other one to get out of the vehicle!"

"Tell her yourself," Lee suggested.

Again, Porky seemed taken aback, but then returned with the renewed vigor of righteous anger, directing his gaze back to the truck.

"You!" he shouted. "Get out of the vehicle!"

Marie's voice was a distant snap of irritation: "No."

"Ah, well," Lee said. "So much for that. But you can talk to me."

Porky redirected his gaze to Lee and actually shook his rifle at him. "Stop right there!"

Lee stopped, waiting patiently for Porky to get his shit together.

Porky's eyes roved over Lee and alighted on his holstered sidearm. "With your left hand, reach across and unholster that sidearm and throw it away from you."

"First off," Lee said. "Is this how you treat all your visitors? It's no wonder everyone hates you. Second, I'm not throwing my pistol in the dirt. It's got enough scuffs and dings on it without me tossing it around all willy-nilly. Besides, I'm not going to disarm myself. You might as well not ask anymore. The topic is closed."

Porky goggled at him for a half second before his shock at being denied turned to rage. "I'll put a fucking bullet through your head!"

"Well, that'd be a damn shame," Lee said. "Seeing as how we're here to see if we can help Mr. Horner."

"Mr. Horner dudn't need any help!"

"You sure you don't want to ask him about that first?" Lee inquired. "Also, can I lower my hands?"

"No!"

"Are you going to shoot me if I do?"

"You're damn right I will!"

"So you're determined to piss off your boss today, huh? Sucks for you. I hear he's not the most forgiving sort."

A few of the other guards had gotten too antsy to keep their mouths shut and called for Porky to beat the shit out of Lee, or shoot him, depending on the leanings of the speaker. Porky seemed pretty convinced by his comrades, and started to aggress on Lee, growling as he did: "I'mma beat the wheels off of you, old man."

Lee didn't move. Just let him come, still smiling languidly. When Porky was about three strides off, Lee leaned in and asked, "When?"

Porky faltered. "When, what?"

"When are you going to beat the wheels off of me? Now? Or later?"

"You must think you're fuckin' somethin', you—"

Porky's bad training, presaged by his terrible treatment of an otherwise reliable weapon system, came to its inevitable end point when he thrust the muzzle of the rifle at Lee, intending to spear his face with it. But then, in a blink, everything went very poorly for Porky.

Lee seized the muzzle of the rifle, pushing it away from his face as he moved. In the same instant, he scooped his right hand up and hooked the buttstock. In a single, fluid move, Lee ripped the rifle out of Porky's grip, gave him a crack in the face with the buttstock to stun him, let go of the rifle, and swept up behind the reeling man with his pistol unholstered and trained on the man's temple.

The AK-abomination hit the ground.

Shouts abounded from the other guards at the gate, but despite their bustling and hollering, none of them had a shot on Lee. He'd positioned himself neatly behind Porky's ample bulk, the man's sweaty head cinched tightly in the crook of Lee's elbow, only the right side of Lee's face peering out from around Porky's.

"You're right," Lee hissed in his ear, his voice entirely changed. "I am fucking something. And you? You're just one more sack of meat between me and what I want. I'll give more thought to swatting a fly than I will to hollowing your skull out. But..." And then his voice changed yet again, back to the friendly tone of before. "You don't have to die right now, sweating and stinking and shitting your pants on a dusty road. So, congratulations! Life is still an option for you. Which is more than can be said for a whole lot of other meat sacks that got in my way. Now, tell your gaggle of pissants to shut the fuck up."

Shaking and wriggling, Porky held up his hands at his fellow guards, his voice trembling and cracking as he shouted at them. "Shut up! Fucking shut up! Everyone shut the fuck up!"

Everyone quite rapidly shut up. Except for one guy still hollering for Lee to drop his pistol. Until he was elbowed roughly by the man next to him. And then it was silent.

"Good," Lee said, giving Porky a light pat on his sweaty cheek. "Now. I would like this to be a peaceful meeting, without the need for threats and guns pointing at each other. But clearly there are few cool heads in this lot. So, what I want you to do now is tell one of your guys to go get Bran and have him come out here."

"You...you know Bran?" Porky stammered.

"Oh, yeah. We go way back," Lee said. "To eighteen hours ago. Now stop jaw-jacking and tell them to get Bran."

"I..." Porky seemed to be wrestling with something. Likely his desire for life against his desire not to look like a complete turd in front of Bran.

"As soon as Bran gets out here, I'll let you go."

"Bran'll kill you for this!" Porky seethed.

Lee sighed, exasperated. "Well, how about we let him decide that when he gets out here?" He seized the man's jaw and squeezed it—as damaged as his left hand was, it could still squeeze, even though it hurt all down his wrist. "Now, *speak*."

Porky's mouth shuddered open in Lee's grip, but he never got the chance to yell out. A voice erupted from the gate: "What in the actual fuck is happening out here?!"

"Oh, look at that," Lee said. "He came on his own."

Bran came through the gathering of guards like a storm wind through a wheat field, his face like a thunderhead, that same old shotgun gripped in his right hand. Behind him, and moving lateral to him along the outskirts of the guards, Lee spotted Kat, her feral eyes fixed on him, moving like a cat that's seen a rustle in the grass.

She made Lee more nervous than Bran did. Though, in all honesty, he was starting to get an inkling that maybe this whole situation had gone tits up.

Bran was battered on all sides by a bunch of overeager guys, all trying to be the one to bring him up to speed. He ignored them, not needing an answer to his question, as he could see it with his own eyes.

Bran stalked straight down the drive towards Lee, his shotgun in hand, but pointed at the ground. Lee had already pegged him as smart. Not that you had to be terribly brilliant to know that a shotgun isn't the best tool for a hostage standoff, but at least he had the presence of mind to realize that, and didn't even bother pointing it.

Lee's eyes snapped over to Kat, who continued to move diagonally, carving away more and more of the protection provided by his unwilling pork shield. He searched her hands and beltline for any sort of firearm, but couldn't see one. He wondered if she knew how to use them, or if she just preferred to tear people apart with her bare hands.

Bran stopped when he was about three or four strides away, hiking one hand onto his hip and letting the shotgun hang loose in his other. He stared at Porky. Then squinted at the side of Lee's face. Lee doubted he'd recognize him just by that sliver, but Bran then craned his neck to the side, taking in the white pickup truck, which he likely *did* recognize.

"Sorry, boss," Porky muttered. "I...I..."

"He put his muzzle in my face," Lee explained, calmly. "I was trying to be diplomatic, but I guess I didn't do all that good of a job. Anyway. What's a guy to do when someone shoves a rifle muzzle right in his face? I felt I didn't have many options. Also, he said he was going to beat the wheels off of me. And I'm really not feeling like pissing blood today. Skipping, skipping. Here we are."

Bran sucked on his teeth, peering at Lee from under hooded brows. "Jax, I think it was?"

"Yeah, it's me."

"Alright. What're you doing right now?"

"Well. I was trying to talk to Colin Horner. Peaceably, mind you. Back in the day, we had diplomatic channels so contending parties could come to agreements. I see that those don't exist in the Valley. So, this is me, opening a diplomatic channel."

"By putting a gun to my guy's head?"

"I only put a gun to his head after he put a gun to mine," Lee noted. "I didn't create the situation, Bran. I just responded to it."

Bran squeezed his eyes shut as though a headache had struck him, and thumbed a bead of sweat from one eyebrow, and then the other. He opened his eyes with a disgruntled sigh. "That's real nice, Jax. Real nice. But what I meant when I asked what you're doing, is what are you doing with my guy?"

"I am using him as a meat shield. As, I believe, is self-evident."

"Well. Will you let him go?"

"Will you promise that I won't be shot if I do?"

"Would you even believe me if I made that promise?"

"Generally? No. However, we are at somewhat of an impasse, and someone's going to have to take a leap here. I'll trust your word as a gesture of good faith."

Bran scoffed and mumbled "Good faith" under his breath. He looked back over Lee's shoulder to the pickup. "That the lady in the truck? The one from yesterday?"

"It is."

"She's pointing a rifle at me."

"I'd imagine so."

Bran considered this for another few beats, then took a big fortifying breath through his nose and turned to the guards at the gate. "Everyone hold your fire. No one shoots. If anyone fires a shot..." He trailed off, then waved lackadaisically at them. "Y'all get it." He turned back to Lee. "Alright then. Let him go."

Lee immediately released Porky, giving him a pat on the shoulder as he sullenly shuffled away. He made sure that his pistol remained pointed in a non-threatening direction, and when no cavalcade of gunshots greeted him, he slowly holstered it.

"Well," Lee remarked, feeling a little awkward now. "I can't say that went great, but at least we're talking now and not just shouting and pointing guns. That's progress, don't you think?"

Bran neither replied, nor moved, for a very long moment. Lee got the distinct sense that Bran was weighing what it would mean to go back on his word. And perhaps what it would mean if he kept it.

Lee kept his eyes on the man, but noted that Kat had stopped, maybe fifteen yards to Lee's right. Her figure hovered there in his peripheral, oddly disconcerting.

A slight tilt of his head was all that preceded Bran's simple, direct question: "Why do you want to talk to Mr. Horner?"

"Hoping we could reach a mutually-beneficial agreement," Lee replied. "One that doesn't involve a massacre."

"That ship may have sailed," Bran observed, evenly.

"May have doesn't mean it has."

"All this?" Bran said, flicking a careless finger towards Lee, and then making a circle to encompass the ground they stood on—and presumably the debacle that ground had just witnessed. "He ain't gonna like this."

"Wasn't a fan myself," Lee agreed. "I don't know your boss, Bran. From what little I've heard, though, he strikes me as a businessman and a pragmatist."

"Mm," Bran grunted, noncommittally.

"I am in a unique position to be able to offer him something that might make it worthwhile to at least sit and listen to me. And that's all I'm asking, Bran. An opportunity to talk. If nothing comes of it, then nothing comes of it."

"Yeah?" Bran looked off towards a random horizon point. "And what happens when diplomacy fails, Jax?"

Lee favored him with a small smile, with just a breath of pity in it. "You seem like a smart guy, Bran. You know what happens when diplomacy fails. But let's not focus on that today, because it hasn't failed just yet."

Bran chuckled mirthlessly. "Haven't met a genuine optimist in quite a while."

"And you still haven't," Lee said. "I'm only speaking the truth."

Bran lifted a cautiously-hopeful eyebrow. "Will you disarm?"

"I will not."

"Yeah, that figures." Bran nodded slowly. "Alright then. Here's how this is going to work..."

Lee sat back into the driver's seat of the truck. The blasting A/C chilled his sweat-soaked body. He blew out a long breath as he eyed the column of guards spreading to either side of the road to permit the truck through.

"They're just gonna let us roll in?" Marie asked, dumbfounded.

"Not quite," Lee said, taking the shifter and pulling it into drive, his motions slow and deliberate. "We maintain a walking speed with guards to either side of the vehicle. We follow Bran and Kat. We do anything funky...well. You get the picture. Oh, you'll wanna lower that rifle."

Still staring at him, Marie yanked the rifle from where it rested between the truck and the sideview mirror, then thrust it to the ground between her feet. "The fuck was that, Lee?"

Lee took his foot off the brake and let the truck coast forward. He glanced at her, innocently. "What?"

She chuffed without humor and shook her head. "You go on and on about life and fighting for the right reasons and not fighting to the death and all that shit, and then in the next breath, you snatch some asshole up and create a standoff?"

Lee hissed out a breath, wincing as he did. "Well. You know. Like I said, old habits die hard."

"Oh, you don't even know what happened, because the training took over?" Marie said, scornfully.

"Look. I'll admit: It could have been done better," Lee conceded. "I am *trying* to be a better person, Marie. I didn't say I *was* a better person. And besides, he had it coming. What was I supposed to do?"

"Let the intelligent woman to your right do the talking? Which is the entire reason I'm here?"

Lee wagged a finger at her. "No, no. I'm saving your silver tongue for the big fish. And also..." He gave her a sarcastic glare. "Before you get too high and mighty, can I point out that no one died?"

Chapter 15

With his truck now parked in front of the ranch house, Lee stepped out and eased the driver's door shut behind him. Glancing around at all the guys with guns, he considered the likelihood of his survival if things went south. He concluded it wasn't great.

They'd left a few of the guards at the gate, but six of them had continued to walk alongside the truck as it entered the ranch. The guy with the M60 was one of them. Bran and Kat were two others.

Lee noted that the four guards seemed to be holding their position around the truck, while Bran and Kat mounted the wooden steps of the porch. At the top stood two other men, one extremely sharp and sour looking, like a half-moldered lemon that's shriveled up and gone hard on the outside. The other seemed a bit wide-eyed and gormless. While the shriveled-lemon-man kept his beady eyes locked onto Lee, the gormless one kept glancing at Bran, as though waiting for directions.

Bran didn't provide any. He strode between the two men, with Kat in tow. Gormless took a big sideways step to accommodate a wide berth for Kat. Even Shriveled Lemon backed off, as though neither of them wanted to be within arm's reach of her.

Lee traded a glance with Marie. "I'm assuming we're supposed to follow you, Bran? Or would you prefer we wait out here?"

Bran just waved a hand, a single finger flicking in a beckoning gesture. He opened the front door and he and Kat stepped through. They left the door open behind them.

Lee directed a smile at Shriveled Lemon as he mounted the steps. "Seems like he wants us to follow him."

No response.

Lee and Marie slipped between the two men on the porch, and Lee noted with a slight tingling at the base of his spine that they fell in behind. Another sidelong glance to Marie. A wealth of information passed in a single look. An entire conversation spoken in silence.

Her eyes and the set of her mouth: *Why do I let you put me in these situations?*

A glimmer of bravado from Lee: *It'll be alright.*

A slight roll of the eyes from Marie: *Asshole.*

A small shrug from Lee: *You got me there.*

The interior was dim for the few moments it took for Lee's eyes to adjust from the daylight. The floor beneath his feet was gray flagstones set into a beige grout. The walls were mostly wood-paneled. The ceiling vaulted high over their heads, held up at intervals by massive pine timbers. The whole place gave a feel of some high-dollar mountain getaway.

Ahead of them, Bran and Kat wound their way through a spacious living area with plush couches and chairs of dark leather arranged around a truly magnificent stone fireplace. Huge windows dominated the living area, the daylight diffused by thin, cream-colored curtains.

On the other side of the living area, Bran and Kat stopped at another wooden door and turned to look at their guests.

"Wait here," Bran said, then started to turn back to the door. He paused. Looked back over his shoulder at Lee, as though he wanted to say something else.

Lee held up his hands. "We won't get into trouble. This is your house. We're on our best behavior."

Bran regarded him for a moment longer, then sniffed, turned to the door, and knocked. "Boss, it's me. Need to talk."

There was a pause, and then the sound of a voice from the other side, too low for Lee to make out. Bran shoved his way through the door, Kat sticking by his side. Lee caught a flash of a very tall, very thin man in a white long-sleeve button-down. And then the door was closed again.

The two men who'd accompanied Lee and Marie moved around them and took up positions on either side of the door. Lee didn't ignore Gormless, as quiet, unassuming guys had the tendency to be worse than the ones who put a lot of effort into looking like hardasses. But he found himself focusing more on Shriveled Lemon. There was something about him that Lee didn't like. A brand of cruelty. Perhaps even sadism. The type of person that could hurt another human being just to see what sounds they'd make.

How do you break the tension with someone like that? *So...how many kittens have you dissected lately?*

Shriveled Lemon broke the silence for him.

"You must be the jackass trying to save the Redoubt."

Lee smiled. "Name's Jax. Should be easy for you to remember—Jax, jackass. They sound alike. And you are?"

"You don't need to know my name," the man replied, sourly.

"Well, if you don't tell me your name, I'll just have to keep thinking of you as Shriveled Lemon."

Marie cleared her throat, not-so-subtly.

Shriveled Lemon glowered. Gormless glanced rapidly between his partner and Lee, the ghost of an "oh-shit" smile tugging at the corners of his mouth.

Marie spoke up, and Lee figured that was about the right time to shut his mouth and let her take over. "I'm Marie. And we're not here to do anything but talk. That's all."

"You can run your mouth all you want," Shriveled Lemon said. "But it's already been decided."

Marie gave him a flat smile. "Well, I suppose that's up to Mr. Horner, isn't it?" She let Shriveled Lemon stew on that and turned her attention to the other man, her smile becoming slightly more genuine. "And what's your name, Hon?"

The man glanced at Shriveled Lemon as though unsure whether he should respond. Shriveled Lemon gave no guidance on the matter, and the man just shrugged. "I'm Darryl. Uh...nice to meet you?"

Though Marie wasn't what most men would find attractive, she did occasionally let loose a brilliant smile, which she chose to favor Darryl with. "Nice to meet you, too."

Shriveled Lemon snorted.

"So," Darryl said, fidgeting like a boy in an awkward social situation. "Uh...where y'all from?"

Shriveled Lemon growled: "You don't need to know where they're from."

Marie ignored him. "Oh, all over the place, really. How long have you been working on the ranch, Darryl?"

"Don't answer that," Shriveled Lemon snapped. "They're just fishing for intel. Keep your mouth shut. They're not your friends."

Marie squinted at Shriveled Lemon. "I'm just making conversation, sir. That's what friendly people do. And friendly people have friends because they're friendly."

Shriveled Lemon took a step toward Lee and Marie, hands on his hips. He opened his mouth, but whatever he wanted to say was cut off by a loud voice from behind the closed door.

Darryl and Shriveled Lemon both twitched at the evident anger in that voice, though Lee still couldn't tell what it'd said. Darryl glanced worriedly at the door. Shriveled Lemon, after his initial jerk, remained completely still.

A long silence fell, all four of them straining to hear what else might come from behind that door. But nothing else did.

The rattle of the doorknob.

The door swung open.

Bran stood there, glaring at Lee as though it were all his fault. "Mr. Horner will see you now."

Lee turned to Marie and gestured for her to take the lead. She drew herself up and strode forward, offering Darryl one more polite smile, and Shriveled Lemon a caustic side-eye. Lee chose to smile and nod at both. Mostly because he knew it would piss Shriveled Lemon off.

The second that Lee passed him, the man was forgotten, and all of Lee's attention turned forward.

He took in the room and its occupants. Besides him and Marie, it was only Bran, Kat, and the tall strip of jerky that Lee figured was Colin Horner.

The man seemed made of rawhide. While the rest of them were sweating enough to dampen their clothes, there wasn't even the shimmer of perspiration upon this man's brow. As lean as he was, he exuded an intense strength. This wasn't a man that could lift the most weight, but he was absolutely a man that would never quit. And people that never quit were extremely dangerous.

His eyes hit Lee's like a silent whip-crack, and Lee found himself unable to be anything but impressed. In the time it took to take a single step into the room and make eye contact with Colin Horner, the stakes became immediately and abundantly clear.

And what were those stakes?

All or nothing.

Because Colin Horner was not a man to play for anything less.

Lee felt something inside of him turn. Twist. Like a wet rag. Except what it exuded wasn't moisture, but wrath.

It wasn't a heady or energizing experience. Lee had felt rage and anger before. He'd felt it animate his body as though possessed. This was different. This was cold. Tired. Frustrated. Like climbing a mountain, switchback after switchback, hoping with every turn along the way that the crest would be there—but no. Only another switchback.

They never end do they?

No. They never did. They just kept coming, people like Colin Horner. They seemed a mindless horde to Lee, as bad as the primals. Perhaps worse, because they knew better. And yet they kept doing it anyway.

Reason would fail. Diplomacy would flounder. Eventually, the guns would come out. The blood would be spilled. The final answer would be found—the most final answer human beings could fathom. The only answer that men like this respected.

Jumping to a lot of conclusions there, aren't you, Old Boy? Lee admonished himself as he stopped, and heard Bran close the door behind him.

Perhaps. Always best to be patient. Always best to wait and see.

But he held his opinions because they'd been proven right, time and again.

"Mr. Horner," Bran said, stepping to Lee's left side, but remaining just behind him. "This is the man called Jax. And...?"

"Marie," she introduced herself in an immaculately neutral tone.

Horner didn't take his eyes off of Lee. The longer he stared at Lee, the more tired Lee became. And the surer he was that his first impressions would prove true.

It was obvious that Horner wasn't going to say anything until he got what he wanted from Lee. And what he wanted was for Lee to buckle under the weight of his domineering stare.

Lee gave him what he wanted and looked away.

Horner gave a soft, derisive snort. "So. Bran tells me you're the ones that are going to plead the Redoubt's case."

"Not entirely accurate," Marie said.

"Oh?"

"We're not here to plead a case. That would imply there's some sort of legal basis for any of this, and that's a false premise to start from. There's no law out here."

"There is," Horner corrected. "What you call 'out here' is my land. And on my land, what I say goes."

"That's fair, sir," Marie acquiesced. "It is your land, after all."

Eyes back on Lee. "So what *are* you here for?"

Again, Lee remained silent, and Marie spoke: "We're here to see if we can make a deal."

Horner stared at Lee for another beat before dragging his eyes back to Marie, frowning. "I'm sorry, ma'am. But why are you talking?"

Marie's jaw tensed. "Well, sir—"

Back to Lee again. "Why aren't *you* talking? I gather that you're the leader. Shouldn't *you* be the one talking?"

Lee took a big, rib-stretching breath and pasted on a smile. "We're more like partners, Mr. Horner. Whatever she says, she says for me and the rest of my team."

A sly look of satisfaction. "Ah. But it is...*your* team."

"Calling them mine is more of a term of endearment, rather than a statement of command." Lee turned to Marie and nodded for her to continue.

"As I was saying," Marie said, evenly. "Our hope is that we can reach an arrangement that is mutually beneficial to all parties involved."

Horner gave her the same long, piercing stare he'd given Lee. Unlike Lee, she chose not to look away. When Horner spoke, his words were slow and direct, as though he were speaking to a frustratingly dull-witted child. "I...would like to hear...from your boss."

Marie smiled. "I don't have one, Mr. Horner. So I'll just have to do."

Horner leaned forward, placing his hands on his desk. Despite being three strides away from them, he still seemed to be trying to loom over Marie. As though a bit of looming could have any effect on her. Lee actually felt a little embarrassed for him. If he only knew who he was speaking to.

"Then I would like to hear from *Jax*."

Marie turned her head, eyes just a tad wider than normal, as though to ask Lee, *Is this guy serious?*

"You won't hear anything different from me," Lee said.

"Nevertheless," Horner grated. "I'd like to hear it from you."

Lee smacked his lips. "Actually, scratch that. You *will* hear something different from me. But I don't think you're going to like what I have to say. Perhaps it's best if I stay quiet and Marie does the talking. Which is precisely what we have already decided. Hence, why she is talking, and I am not."

Horner's eyes glittered with spiteful amusement. "But now you *are* talking. And I think you should continue."

Lee just kept that same veneer of a smile on his mouth. "I don't think I should."

"Why not?"

Lee opened his mouth to answer, but Horner cut him off.

"Because she's better at diplomacy than you?"

"Yes," Lee said. "That's accurate."

"Good," Horner announced, as though the matter had been settled. He straightened up again. "All the more reason for her to shut up and for you to talk. I don't have the time or inclination to listen to bullshit, and I won't suffer someone to stand in my office and try to feed it to me. One thing that's better about the world nowadays?" His eyebrows arched in dark mirth. "All the politicians are dead." The mirth left his eyes as quick as it had come, and he was all cold, brimming challenge again. "So cut the shit and get to business, or get the fuck out of my office."

As Lee often did when butting heads with the endless chain of assholes that created the timeline of his life, he checked himself. His emotions were unruffled. His heart was calm. His breathing even.

Lee left the issue up to Marie. She met his gaze and another silent conversation passed.

Lee arched his brows. *Your call.*

Marie flattened her lips. *What a bastard.*

Lee tilted his head. *Agreed.*

Marie tilted her head back. *Go on, then.*

Only after it was clear that Marie had voluntarily abdicated, did Lee turn back to Horner, who looked smugly satisfied. "Alright, Mr. Horner. Have it your way."

Horner smiled as though to say, *Yes, I always do.*

"You want to destroy the Redoubt and its inhabitants, yes?"

"I want them gone from my land. If they refuse to do so voluntarily, then I'm within my rights to dispose of them."

Like trash, Lee thought, bitterly, but held back. "Well, I *don't* want you to do that."

"Well. Tough."

"I anticipated that would be your stance," Lee sighed. "Which is why I'm here, prepared to make a deal with you—as Marie has already said."

"Yes, she already said that. So how about you get to the part where you explain to me what you're going to give me that will suddenly make everything different."

"Well, what do you need?"

Horner laughed. As with everything else about him, it was dry and joyless. "What do I need? That's such…a stupid fucking question."

Lee grinned as though he was in on the joke, and not the butt of it. "Yeah, yeah. Such a stupid question that you can't manage to give me a straight answer."

Horner's smile fell, but didn't depart completely. "Jax, you strike me as a military man."

"You're truly a prodigy of perception."

Horner waved off the barb. "I'm sure you'll appreciate my lack of desire to tell you what I need. Need is weakness. Weakness is vulnerability that you might try to exploit."

"You're right. I am trying to exploit it. I'm trying to exploit it by offering you a solution, so that you get what you need, and I get what I want. Isn't that the essence of making a deal?"

"I suppose it is. But I'm still not going to just up and reveal weaknesses to you."

"What if I reveal a weakness of my own first? Would that help?"

Horner gave no answer, but seemed intrigued. Or maybe he thought he was just giving Lee the rope to hang himself with. That was okay. Horner could think whatever he liked.

"My weakness is patience, Mr. Horner." Lee held up his hands and let them flop to his sides. "I don't think I was born with enough of it. I try to do the right thing, but in doing the right thing, it sure seems like everyone tries real hard to take advantage of me. And when that happens, the tiny little sliver of patience that I've been able to cling to thus far just goes *pfft*." Lee mimed smoke in the air and watched it drift away with a forlorn look. "And then all I really want to do is all the things I know I shouldn't do."

Horner crossed his arms over his chest. "And what are all these terrible things that you know you shouldn't do? Please. Shake my confidence. Frighten me."

"Nah," Lee said with a dismissive wave. "I can see that would be pointless. And I wasn't trying to threaten you anyway. I just want you to know that you're not special, Mr. Horner. You're just one more guy in a long line. I wanted you to have a clear picture of where both of us stand, right at the get go. Always best to negotiate with complete honesty, yeah?"

"No," Horner shook his head. "But by all means, you go right ahead. Tell me all about yourself."

"Sure. My name is Jax, and I have access to an abundance of resources."

"I could just kill you now and take whatever you have in your truck."

Lee gave an earnest laugh. "The truck? That's like robbing a rich man for the spare change in his pocket. No, I have *access* to an abundance of resources—as in, I can get them for you."

"Color me intrigued," Horner said, raising one hand and perching a finger on his chin. "What type of resources?"

"It's kind of a large menu, so it's easier if you just tell me what you need. Which is why I asked you that earlier. And here we are again."

Horner grunted and then slowly sat back into his chair behind the desk. Leather creaked. He steepled his hands in front of his face. "Let's try this instead. You tell me what you think I need. It'll be educational for all of us."

Lee hitched his thumbs into the front of his armor and relaxed his stance, taking the weight off his bum leg. "At first glance, I look around and see a whole lot of guys with guns, and I think, man, he must need some ammunition for all those guns. But then I think, why would a guy like Colin Horner worry about guns and ammo, when he's got hordes of infected to do his bidding? That's a much better weapon, I think. And it seems that you agree."

Horner didn't look overly pleased that Lee knew this, but he didn't bother denying it.

Lee looked up to the ceiling with a frown. "But *then* I think, well, maybe he *does* want weapons and ammunition. Because..." he looked back down to Horner. "How much control does he really have over all those infected? Does he actually have any control at all? I mean, you've got a shaky deal that I can't quite fathom with some weird guy that fucks and breeds with them—which, in my humble opinion, shows a certain brand of insanity that I personally wouldn't want to get into bed with. And I guess you've got Kat over there, who calls the shots for you. But how much control do you *really* have, Mr. Horner? Does it ever make you even the slightest bit concerned that your grasp on this power is...slippery?"

Horner's face was as hard and dead as a flatiron skillet. He retracted his steepled fingers. Placed them very deliberately on his armrests. Pressed himself up to standing. "I see Ted's been running his mouth again."

Lee shrugged. "He is the leader of the settlement I'm trying to save from extinction."

"And did he tell you how he knows all these things?"

"Local rumor mill, as I gather. Would you care to make any corrections?"

Horner moved around his desk and stood at the front corner. "No. I'll only say that...well...you may want to dig a bit deeper into who you ally yourself with in the future." Horner drew himself up, placing his hands on his hips. "Now. As for whether or not I have control of these...animals." He turned his eyes to Kat and pointed at her. "You. Come."

Lee felt himself wince. His good eye shot to the right, just quick enough to see the way Kat's body stiffened. Shoulders rising up defensively. Head lowering aggressively. Hands tensing at her sides. Every molecule of her body screaming rebellion.

But she moved forward.

One step. Two steps. Then she stopped at Horner's side and turned around, her head hanging.

Horner wasn't even looking at Kat anymore. He was staring at Lee again, just the very corners of his mouth twisted upwards. "Take off your bandana."

Kat looked sharply at Horner, her tan skin flushing around her forehead.

Horner swung his gaze to her, eyes intense. The second he made eye contact with her, she flinched away from it, dropping her gaze to the floor. Horner said nothing further. Obedience had been demanded, and the command would not be repeated.

She raised a hand to her face. Her hands weren't the oddly-elongated appendages of a full primal. They were rough, but looked mostly human, save for the fingertips. Those tapered to unnatural points, the nails thick and strong and curved. More like claws. She pinched the lowest corner of the bandana, right near her chin, and dragged it off her face.

Lee had already known what to expect. What he saw did not surprise him at all, and neither he nor Marie gave any reaction to it.

It was not as though the top half of her face was human, and the bottom half primal. But the mix of mutated genetics was nonetheless obvious. Her mandible was wider and longer than normal. Her lips thin and much too wide, the corners stretching all the way back, nearly to her jaw. Her nose was flat, and beneath that, her mouth protruded in an almost ape-like fashion, creating more of a snout. Where she normally wore her bandana had created a drastic tan line. From her cheekbones up, her skin was darkly tanned. From the cheekbones down, it was pale almost to the point of ghostliness.

"There we are," Horner said in a low tone. He looked back to Lee. "Does this make you uncomfortable, Jax?"

"Her face?" Lee asked. "No. What you're doing? Yes."

Horner shook his head. "That's because you think she's human. But she's not."

"Three quarters has to count for something."

"Oh, that's where you're wrong. She's...tainted. Anything human in her is drowned by the animal that's flowing through her veins. Yes, she can speak—not much, but a few words. And yes, she can understand them. But that's really where the similarities end. You should see the things I've seen her do. Just trust me: it's best not to think of her as human. She's more like...a very intelligent dog. And just like a dog, she does what her master commands her."

"I have a dog," Lee ground out. "And I'm pretty sure he's smarter than most people. You've made your point, Mr. Horner."

"Have I?" Horner said, quirking his head to one side.

"Yes. You clearly don't need guns and ammunition. So let's talk—"

"Sit."

For just a flash, Lee thought he was being commanded to sit. But then he realized Horner was looking at Kat again. And pointing to the ground at his feet.

"Can we talk business, Mr. Horner? I'm not really in the mood for tricks."

Horner ignored him. "Kat," he said, his voice a deadly little sing-song. "Did you hear me?"

Kat's lips trembled. Contorted. Forming words.

"Not...a dog."

Horner's eyes widened, sparking like pilot lights in a room full of gas.

Kat's eyes turned to his, all murder and defiance, a low growl rippling its way across her mouth.

"Mr. Horner—" Lee snapped, but it was too late.

Horner's fist flashed out, as quick as a snake, and connected squarely with Kat's face. It was a fast punch, but a hard one that Lee thought would have rocked him, had he been on the receiving end. Kat spun with a grunt and hit the floor on all fours.

"Did you just fucking *growl* at me?!" Horner roared, standing over her, fists clenched at his sides.

"Mr. Horner!" Lee bellowed, rocking the room with a voice he rarely used.

Horner thrust a finger at him. "You stay the fuck out of this!" he seethed. "She needs *correction*!"

The cold wrath that Lee had felt upon first laying eyes on Colin Horner had inundated every corner of his mind and every cell of his body. His limbs thrummed with it. He looked at that man's wild eyes and thought of bending him backward over his own desk until his spine snapped. Thought about wedging his fingers between that asshole's teeth and prying his jaws open until they broke off.

All in a flash.

But he didn't. He was trying not to be that guy anymore.

When Lee spoke, he deliberately chose not to utter any of the things that had run through his brain a microsecond before. He didn't even yell. He just said it.

"Don't do that again."

Horner paused for the span of a few heartbeats. He looked right at Lee, evaluating him. Evaluating how seriously to take him. And then he reared a foot back and slammed his boot into Kat's stomach.

I'm gonna rip his jaw off, Lee decided, as all notions of diplomacy fled him and he surged forward.

A gunshot blasted the room.

Lee spun to the sound of a shotgun racking. Saw the spent shell spinning away, trailing smoke. Saw the gaping hole in the ceiling still raining dust and splinters down on a flinching Marie.

The shotgun racked and Bran swung it towards Marie. Considering what had happened to Porky, Marie must've seemed like a softer target to hold at gunpoint.

His error was immediately corrected.

The muzzle of the shotgun never even came in line with any part of Marie. She dipped under it even as she jolted forward, body-checking Bran as she seized the long gun and ripped it away. The shotgun discharged as she pulled it from his fingers, taking a chunk out of the wood wall just to the left of the door.

Bran staggered back and righted himself, preparing to lunge for Marie, but she was too quick and too practiced. She'd already backed out of his reach, and re-racked the shotgun. Bran skidded to a stop, hands up, eyes wide.

Lee didn't even recall unholstering his sidearm, but there it was in his hands.

A shift of movement behind him.

Lee swung, bringing the pistol in tight to his body.

Horner pulled up short, just out of reach of Lee.

"I told you not to do that again," Lee hissed at him.

Horner's face writhed as though there was something trying to get out of him.

The office door burst open.

Lee caught the briefest glimpse of Shriveled Lemon charging in, all fire and fury with a pistol in his hand. He got about to the frame of the door before a third blast from the shotgun sent an explosion of wooden shards peppering his face. He yelped and leapt back through the doorway, scooting to the left and taking cover on the other side of the door.

Marie racked the shotgun.

"Boss!" Shriveled Lemon growled from behind the doorway. "You okay?"

Marie's voice: "You show so much as a toe and I'm taking it off."

Bran: "Alright! Everybody be easy! Let's figure out a way out of this!"

Lee held Horner's gaze, even as the other man's eyes darted about, assessing the situation, trying to catch up. But he was on the back foot. This was a catastrophe to him. To Lee...well, it wasn't that great, but it wasn't all that unexpected either. Now he just had to keep his opponent on the ropes until he could figure out how to extricate himself without Marie and him getting hung up on butcher's hooks.

The most likely option was to use Horner as a hostage to get them out of the ranch.

"I'm pointing a gun at Mr. Horner," Lee announced. "You outside the door—drop your weapons, or I put a hole in—"

Something hit him in the left side, hard. A savage snarl of breath in his ear. He hit the desk and tried to thrust himself off of it, but then there was a mad scramble of limbs all over him, too fast for him to even cognate. His pistol was wrenched from his grip and went flying across the room. He caught the barest glimpse of a mouth full of inhuman teeth, and then a palm came out of the bottom of his vision and hit his nose with a crack he felt all through his skull. Everything became dark starlight.

He could feel his body moving, but he wasn't moving it. Felt iron hands gripping him, arms like steel cables squeezing his ribs. Something clamped down on his windpipe, but it wasn't trying to choke him. He could feel claw-tipped fingers squeezing in, wrapping *around* his windpipe.

He gulped a ragged breath. His vision cleared enough to see Marie, huddled in a nook between a large cabinet and the wall, the shotgun in her hands pointed right at Lee. No—at the person holding him.

The *hybrid* holding him.

Shit. That's Kat.

Colin Horner's voice screeched through the room: "You drop that shotgun or she's gonna rip his throat out! Drop it! Drop it now!"

Marie knew she couldn't make that shot. Kat was in way too tight to Lee, and, as Lee had noted quite recently, a shotgun is not a great tool for a hostage standoff.

If she didn't drop the shotgun, they were both going to die.

If she did...well, they were probably still going to die. But at least it wasn't a certainty, as it was now.

Marie must have run her mind along the exact same track, because right as Lee came to that inevitable conclusion, she tossed the shotgun to the ground and stood up, hands raised.

Despite the fact that it was an inevitable conclusion, Lee hated to hear that weapon hit the ground. Now he was in no-man's land. Now he was dandelion fluff at the mercy of a hurricane wind. He was out of options, and could do nothing but hope that one might present itself between this instant and whenever they took the life out of him.

Shit and fuck.

"Joaquin! Darryl!" Horner screamed. "Get in here!"

Bran was already scuttling across the room, snatching up the relinquished shotgun and training it on Marie. Darryl and Shriveled Lemon—apparently Joaquin—came piling in, each with a pistol, but looking like they didn't know quite where to point them.

A scramble of boot heels.

Horner's face loomed into Lee's still-woozy vision. He could feel the warm blood flowing down his upper lip, the salty, metallic taste on his tongue. He considered spitting it in Horner's face, but wasn't quite to the point of petulant defiance just yet.

Pay attention, he told himself. *Watch for an opening.*

That was their only chance now.

Horner's face was all twisted up, too incensed to even be gleeful in victory. He seized the hair on top of Lee's head and wrenched him out of Kat's grasp. Given how strong she'd been, Lee doubted Horner could have done it if she hadn't allowed him. Then again, as his face was bounced off the hardwood desk and the stars coalesced again, he learned that Horner was no weakling himself.

"You make a move on me," Horner hissed in his ear. "They're gonna blow your girl apart."

His fingers twisted, ripping Lee's hair out in chunks as Horner rammed his elbow repeatedly into the back of Lee's head until everything was a dull, sightless roar.

Words in the darkness. Hot breath on his face.

"Control, motherfucker. I'll show you control."

He was ripped from the desk and thrown to the ground.

"Beat them both until they can't move."

More footfalls, vibrating the floorboards against Lee's face. He breathed and sputtered and spat blood.

His vision cleared once more, just in time to see two faces looming over him.

"Ah, fuck," Lee murmured, as Joaquin and Porky smirked meanly down at him.

Just dandelion fluff in a hurricane.

Keep watch. Pay atten—

Joaquin's hard-soled boot came down on his face.

Chapter 16

They say what doesn't kill you makes you stronger.

What they don't tell you is that, while the things that don't kill you do in fact make you stronger, that strength is all garnered by the mind. The body, unfortunately, is never quite the same.

So, as Lee groggily perceived his beating tapering off, and all the damage reports started localizing the pain all through his body, his one, big, background thought was, *How much more broken am I going to be?*

Nose smeared all over his face. More missing teeth. Probably some broken ribs.

But in the strange relativity that Lee lived his life, these were minor concerns that he had to focus past. He couldn't distract himself with thoughts of how much worse off his body was going to be, because if he didn't pay attention, he wasn't going to *be* anything but dead.

Curled around his throbbing torso, trying hard not to breathe too deep lest his ribs send mind-numbing electric jolts through his system, Lee heard voices, but the roaring and ringing in his ears caused them all to muddle together.

Hands grabbed at him. Shoved him around. The weight of his armor was torn away from him. More hands, roughly frisking him. Someone rammed the edge of their hand into his crotch, making him grunt and curl up again, but other hands grappled his legs apart again and continued their search. His boots came off. Then his socks. Pockets turned inside out. Belt stripped away.

He tried to open his eye, but no matter how wide he stretched, it was just dim, red darkness.

His one good eye was swollen shut. He was left only with his sense of hearing to know what was going on around him. And after so many years of gunfighting, that sense wasn't the sharpest.

Regret came like an unwanted visitor, knocking at the doors of his mind, ready to explain to him all the ways that he'd messed this up. He refused to open the door. He could have that conversation later. Right now it was only another distraction.

Something collapsed into him. Slack weight, and body heat, and sweat.

Marie's voice was a broken croak: "Jax..."

Before he could respond, there was a sharp slap.

"You shut the fuck up, bitch!"

"I got the rope!" someone declared, like they'd won a scavenger hunt.

Lee's hands were wrenched behind his back. Rough cordage wrapped tight around his wrists, again and again. He felt them feed a loop of cord around the bindings on his wrist. Felt it pulled towards his feet.

The bastards were hogtying him.

"Put 'em in my truck." That was Horner, Lee thought, still sounding snappy and pissed. "Bran, Kat, Joaquin, and Darryl, you're coming with me. The rest of you double up the guards and patrols. Be ready in case their friends try some shit. We'll be back before noon."

The bed of the truck was screaming hot.

Lee forced himself to lie still and take it. If he moved too much, they'd only start beating him again.

They'd tossed him in on his side, which was a mercy, in a way. Nothing sucked more than being hogtied and laid on your stomach.

Lee found himself distantly amused by the fact that he had developed preferences related to being hogtied.

This is what you get! His regret again, now hollering through that locked mental door. *You stay in the game long enough, you get to walk with a limp, and have a missing eye like a fucking pirate, and become a connoisseur of being restrained in shitty positions. What a wonderful life of adventure you've discovered!*

Shallow breaths, but steady. Trying to center himself.

Skidding tires and growling gravel. He slid towards the tailgate with the sudden acceleration, and went Marie with him.

They were facing each other. Their knees were knocking together, and their foreheads were touching. He just couldn't see her. He wondered if she could see him.

"You alright?" he husked, too low to be overheard by the others.

They hit a divot in the road. The truck bed bucked. Lee felt his body leave the hot sheet metal for a brief moment, then slam back down. Marie hissed out a curse, then grunted, "Pretty busted. You gonna make it?"

"For now. Can you see?"

A pause.

"Yeah," she murmured. "Kinda."

"How many in the bed with us?"

Pause.

"Three."

"Tailgate down?"

"No."

"Shit." Probably wouldn't have done them any good anyway. Even if they could gyrate themselves over the tailgate before getting nabbed, they'd still hit the ground going fast, and they'd still be hogtied.

"They get your boot knife?" he whispered.

"Yeah. Yours?"

"Uh-huh."
"You got anything useful?"
"No."
"Me neither."
"Hey. You can see. That's something."
"I'm gonna wait until later to cuss you out."
"That's helpful."
"The fuck were you thinking?"
"I thought you were going to wait."

Marie growled, but said nothing else.

Lee set to gently straining at the ropes that bound him. There was no give in them at all. But it gave him a chance to test his limbs for any obvious breaks. Every muscle hurt, but it didn't seem like he had any clearly-broken bones. The ribs on his right side felt more bruised than anything. The ribs on his left, though…those felt worse.

So. The good news was that he could still move around. It might hurt, but there was no mechanical reason why he couldn't.

The bad news was that he still had no clue how he was going to extricate himself from this.

He felt when the truck left the road. Or at least what counted for a road around here. It hadn't been a comfortable ride up to that point, but once the tires left the trail and started going over rough terrain, he felt like a bug in a jar being shaken by some snot-nosed kid with a cruel streak. Perhaps a young Joaquin.

He was starting to get pissed about it when the brakes went on and the truck skidded through the dirt and came to a rocking halt. He felt a wash of relief that the ride was over, but it didn't last long. They'd gotten to where they were going. And that meant Lee was out of time.

The sound of doors opening and closing. The truck still thrumming at an idle. The tailgate dropped with a metallic *bang* that felt all too final. Someone seized ahold of the rope that bound his wrists to his ankles and yanked him out.

Lee tried his best to tuck his head in, but it still bounced off the tailgate as his body dropped off the end. He hit the dirt, pain exploding through his ribs.

He heard—and felt—Marie hit the ground next to him with a hiss and a yelp of pain.

Dry grass prickled at his face and neck. He pried at his eyelid again, and this time got the tiniest sliver of daylight. Then the daylight was blotted out. Someone was standing over him.

Horner's voice, mean and low and close to his face: "End of the road for you, motherfucker."

Marie was not in a good way. Besides being beat to all hell, she was fucking livid. She'd done a good job of keeping that anger out of her voice when she'd whispered to Lee, mostly because it was not the time to hash things out. But, oh, was she irate.

Scared, too, of course. But even that wound up curdling into anger, because it's way more palatable to be pissed than terrified, and it's a pretty easy transition to make. Instead of focusing on how shitty your situation is, you just focus on the asshole that got you *into* that situation.

Her right eye was swollen up to the point that all she could make out was a blurry, impressionist image of what was immediately around her. Which, at that point, was grass, dirt, a truck, five erect figures, and one figure on the ground beside her.

Her left eye wasn't quite as bad, and if she opened it wide enough, she could see most of the details.

For a moment, she had a hard time differentiating between Colin Horner and Joaquin, as they were both long and lean, and they'd both donned white cowboy hats. Then she recognized Horner's white, long-sleeve shirt.

Horner squatted down over Lee, knuckling the brim of his hat up. "End of the road for you, motherfucker."

"Any chance for one last appeal to reason?" Lee's voice was strained and dry.

Horner chuffed and stood up, putting his hands on his hips. "Yeah, sure. Why not? But make it quick."

Marie twisted her head to get a better look at Lee. His face was barely recognizable, between the swelling, the re-located nose, and the blood smeared all over it. His split and swollen lips were parted, revealing teeth tinted red—and one gaping hole where one of his right bicuspids should have been.

"Mercy has a way of coming back around to you," Lee said. "So does cruelty."

Horner pulled his head back with a snort. "Your one last appeal to reason is…karma?"

Lee managed something like a shrug. "Not karma. More like justice."

Horner shook his head. "See, you're getting it all wrong again, Jax. Around here, justice is whatever I say it is. And right now, justice means you, getting eaten alive."

"Perhaps," Lee admitted. "I realize you don't really know who I am. But for the sake of my own conscience, I want you to understand that, if you leave us here to die, there will be no mercy for you, or any of your men."

"Wow," Horner said. "You are so…full of shit. It's embarrassing, actually. I'm embarrassed for you."

Lee's head relaxed back to the ground. "Well, you go on and make your choice then, Mr. Horner. I've given you fair warning. You know what the consequences will be."

"Is that it?" Horner said, leaning forward slightly. "Are you done?"

"Yeah, I'm done."

Joaquin sidled in close to his boss. "Lemme just pop 'em in the head."

Horner put his hand on Joaquin's shoulder. "But then he wouldn't learn anything." He swiveled a hard pair of eyes on Kat, who stood over Marie, the bandana masking her face again. "And neither will she."

Kat's eyes were downcast, staring into the dirt between Marie and Lee. But there was a hardness there, too. A slight twinge of insolence. And her whole body posture was clenched and hunched, like an animal backed into a corner.

Horner stepped around Lee's feet and ate up the distance between him and his "daughter" in two lengthy strides. He stood so close that the brim of his hat nearly touched her temple.

"Go ahead, Kat," he said, almost challenging her to defy him again. "Call them in."

Kat blinked slowly, but otherwise did not respond, nor did the expression on her face change.

Bran, who was standing near the truck bed, cleared his throat.

Horner was as still as stone. Dry, hot wind rippled his shirt, and that was the only motion around him.

Some tiny modicum of pity bled through Marie's own self-preservation. But it wasn't enough for her to stop silently begging Kat to defy her father.

And then Kat yanked the bandana down from over her mouth, tilted her head back, and let out an eerie, ululating howl. Marie winced as the sound washed over her, somehow both terrifyingly familiar, and utterly alien.

Marie's pulse began to race.

Horner smiled at Kat as she lowered her head again and pinched the bandana back up over her nose. Then he turned, his eyes skipping over Marie and going to Lee.

"You hear that, Jax?" Horner said. "*That* is control."

Strangely, no one moved after that. No one spoke. Marie's eyes darted about from person to person, and found them all kind of staring off in various directions, as though they were all waiting for something.

It came a moment later: a distant response. An answering howl, carried on the hot wind.

"They heard it," Bran announced, unnecessarily. He seemed all too eager to get the hell out of there and was already walking around the truck to the passenger's side. "We should leave."

Joaquin's hand flashed out and caught Bran's elbow, halting him. "S'matter? You scared?"

Bran quirked an eyebrow. "Well, I was born with half a brain, so...yes." He yanked his arm free of Joaquin.

"He's right," Horner said, hitching up his belt line as he stepped over Marie's body. "I got no desire for those things to take an interest in us and follow us back to the ranch. I got a hard enough time keeping those fuckers away from my cattle—I'm not gonna give them a reason to trail us back."

No one needed to be told twice. Feet hustled. Doors were opened. Doors were slammed.

The engine shifted into gear, and the tires spun, spraying Marie and Lee with dust and grit and chunks of a chewed-up grass. She coughed and spat, rolling as best she could to try to get some clean air.

"Lee!" she croaked, as the sound of the engine faded. "We gotta get outta this shit!"

"C'mere," Lee rasped out.

When she rolled to face him, she found him on his side, trying to squirm towards her. His face was all coated in pale dust, streamers of saliva hanging from his lips as he tried to get the rest of the dirt out of his mouth.

"You got an idea?"

"Yeah, I got an idea," he said. "I'mma chew the rope off of you, and then you're gonna untie me."

For the first time since having the shit kicked out of her, a tiny little ray of hope shone down on her.

Lee stopped and jerked his head. "Roll over. Lemme get at the rope on your back."

Marie rolled onto her other side, craning her neck up and searching the horizon line for the shape of primals loping towards them. Where had that answering call come from? Marie hadn't been able to tell. And how close had it been? Sounds can be tricky sometimes. But if it was close enough to be heard, it was too damn close.

"Ah, shit."

Heart in her throat. "What? What's wrong?"

"They're rawhide!"

"What is?"

"The ropes!"

"I don't give a fuck if they're made outta steel, you better start chewing or come up with some other brilliant idea!"

"I'm gonna fucking chew it," Lee shot back. "It just might take a bit longer."

"Quit talking and start chewing!"

Before she'd even managed to finish the sentence, she felt Lee's head press against her back and the rope tying her wrists to her ankles began to jerk.

It was, perhaps, a tad cruel that she waited for his mouth to be full of rawhide before lighting into him. "What were you *thinking*, Lee? What part of 'diplomatic' includes pointing your gun at someone?"

Lee groaned, but didn't take his mouth off the leather rope to speak.

"What'd you think was gonna happen, huh?" She demanded, her eyes still scanning around for the primals that would be there at any moment. "Did you think you could have a standoff with a guy like Colin Horner and then walk away like everything's hunky-dory? No, I know you didn't think that, because I know you're not *stupid*, Lee! Which means you *knew* what would happen, and you chose to do it anyway! For what? Because some asshat was beating a primal in front of you?"

Lee freed his mouth just long enough to growl, "*Quarter* primal." And then he went back to chewing.

"Oh, a *quarter* primal! A *quarter*, he says! As though that makes a fucking difference! I don't give a fuck if it was an adorable little girl with pink fucking ribbons, Lee! You've seen plenty of nasty bastards do nasty shit to innocent people, and you've never screwed yourself over that hard for them! Why choose now, when we're in the middle of nowhere, alone, and surrounded by bad guys, to suddenly decide that you're going to be the heroic protector of the weak? And she wasn't even weak! She kicked your ass! And now she's called the primals on us!"

Lee head-butted her in the spine. It wasn't hard, but it was enough to let her know that he meant it. "I am well aware of all of this, Marie!"

"Why aren't you chewing the rope?" she cried.

"Because it's not doing anything!" he roared back. "This ain't gonna work. Look around for a rock. Something sharp. Anything."

With the dim hope of chewing through their bindings extinguished, Marie's ire was overcome by a blast of panic. She swore under dry breaths as she searched around for anything that might be sharp enough to whittle away at the leather.

"Had to do it, Marie," Lee said as he tried again to pry his eye open with no success.

"Don't distract me," she snapped.

"Oh, no, you're gonna listen, after all that shit you just laid on me," he said. "You're just pissed, and that's understandable. I'm pissed too. But I'm pissed because I was put in a situation where I didn't have a choice, and you know it. I'm not gonna watch this guy beat some girl in front of me—no matter what she is. Fuck him."

"No, fuck *us*," Marie retorted. "Because that's what you did!"

"We ain't dead yet."

And that was when Marie caught sight of a line of shapes moving quickly through the dry grass in their direction.

Chapter 17

When Marie said, "Oh, shit," Lee immediately knew what she'd seen.

He swore and tried his eye again. He could see a little bit more this time, but everything was cloudy and indistinct.

"How many?" he asked, as though that mattered. In their current condition, one would be enough.

"Dozen or so," she replied, much quieter now.

Even if they weren't hogtied, their chances would be practically nil. Two people against a dozen primals were as good as dead.

He still wished his hands were free. This was somehow far worse. To simply be trussed up like a bit of meat, waiting to be torn open—that was a torture in and of itself. To be able to fight, even if he was destined to lose, would at least allow him some small bit of agency in his last moments.

But here he was, as helpless as a newborn.

And Marie, too. God, that was the part that hurt the worst—the fact that he'd doomed her along with himself.

"Marie."

"Yeah."

"Look at me."

It took her a moment. She didn't want to tear her eyes off of their incoming doom. But then she twisted and faced him. He couldn't see her face clearly, but even the blur of it was a comfort he didn't deserve.

"I'm sorry I got you into this," Lee said, the words quiet, but fast, as he felt his time running out, and facing a backlog of things he suddenly felt compelled to say. "I'm just so fucking tired of watching this shit happen, Marie. I'm tired of watching bad people do whatever the fuck they want, just because no one will stop them. But at least we tried."

He couldn't be sure, but he felt like Marie's eyes were searching his face.

In the end, she seemed not to have anything to say back, but instead just nodded at him. And he didn't know how he felt about that. Didn't know if that nod was absolution, or if she couldn't find anything to say because she didn't want to die telling him what an asshole he was.

"Is there a good way to do this?" she asked after a few seconds.

Now Lee was the one who had nothing to say. Was there a good way to get eaten alive? Sure—pray they go for the throat right at the get-go, and don't start eating you when you're still conscious. But he didn't want to say that.

"It's gonna be alright," Marie said in a whisp of a voice. "We'll go into shock. Won't we? We won't actually feel that much. Will we?"

Lee didn't know about all that. But he said, "Yeah. Adrenaline will mask most of the pain, and by the time it starts to get through, your body will be in shock. You probably won't feel much at all." That was a flat-out lie. And maybe they both knew it, because they'd both heard people being torn apart by primals. It was not fast. It was not painless. They screamed. Some of them screamed for a long, long time.

They said nothing else. It was like they both knew that they only had moments, but didn't know how many. To be cut off in the middle of saying something important was worse than not even saying it at all.

The silence rang on interminably.

How far away had the primals been when she'd seen them? Shouldn't they have been on them already?

Lee had let his swollen eye close, but now stretched it painfully open again. Marie was still on her side, facing him, though he couldn't tell if she was looking at him. He could see the tops of the dry grasses, swaying in the wind, creating a quiet whisper all around them.

Lee was about to break the silence, when Marie's head picked up off the dirt, the cords of her neck standing out.

"The fuck...?" she breathed.

"What?" Lee tried to crane his neck around to see what she'd spotted, but couldn't get that much of an angle.

"Two..." Marie started, and then seemed to choke. Her mouth opened and closed as though trying to get a feel for the words. "Shit, I think those are people."

"Help me out here, Marie," Lee hissed, confusion and fear combining to make irritation. "Tell me what you're seeing!"

Marie refocused through her shock and nodded in a direction too far to Lee's left for him to see. "There's two figures approaching. They're walking. Upright, like people."

"Primals can walk when they want to," Lee snapped. "Are you sure they're people? Do you recognize them?"

"I woulda said if I recognized them! They're not primals. They're wearing clothes."

Lee wrestled himself onto his left side. As soon as he did, his muddy vision picked up an impression of what Marie had told him: two figures—what looked like a man and a woman—with only their head and shoulders visible above the grass, about twenty yards away and striding towards them.

How in the hell could two people walk so casually in the midst of a pack of primals without being shredded to bits?

Did they even see Lee and Marie lying there? Should they call out for help? Should they warn them that there were primals close by? Should they just stay silent?

"Is this a good thing or a bad thing?" Marie whispered.

"No clue," Lee murmured.

The question of good or bad remained unknown, but the question of whether the newcomers were aware of them was answered when the man raised his hand and waved.

"Hullooooo!" an oddly cheery voice proclaimed.

Lee did not echo the greeting. As the two figures drew closer, more details began to emerge through his hazy vision. As Marie had observed, they were wearing clothes. If "clothes" encompassed any fabric used to cover the body. The man appeared to be wearing a thin, tan serape that pasted to his body in the wind—thin enough that it was apparent he wasn't wearing anything else. To make things even more disorientingly surreal, the woman was wearing what looked to him like a camouflage sundress, but with dull pink splotches all over it.

"You seeing this?" Marie's voice sounded as bewildered as Lee felt.

"I am seeing, and not believing," Lee muttered.

As the two figures drew within a few paces of them, everything about them was now visible above the knees. Lee's eye went to the woman—some instinct tickling his brain, telling him that something was not right. The way she moved was not masculine, and yet was not feminine either.

Her face...

It was the same as Kat's: Not fully primal, but not entirely human either. The evidence of mutated genetics was pronounced most clearly in her too-large jaw and too-wide mouth.

The two figures stopped when they were about a pace shy of Lee's side. His eye darted to the man now, and was surprised to see what seemed like a pleasant smile on the man's lips. But the eyes. Oh, the eyes were all wrong.

He's insane.

The odd man was scruffy-faced, though it seemed he kept his beard trimmed. He had dark hair with an even sprinkling of grays, and what had appeared to be incredibly *thick* hair, turned out to simply be dirt that colored his scalp dark.

The man took another step forward, his feet coming into view out of the grass. They looked like they hadn't been acquainted with shoes in a very long time. He squatted down in front of Lee—thankfully draping his weathered serape between his legs. Unfortunately, the serape did not block the stink of the man, which hit Lee so hard he barely restrained his broken nose from curling.

Hell, Lee didn't even know his nose could work so well broken. Or maybe the smell was just that bad—even a broken sensory organ could detect it.

The man grinned at Lee, showing surprisingly straight, white teeth. "Well. This is a bit odd, don't you think?"

Lee couldn't agree more, but there was a slightly more pressing matter on his mind. "Where are the primals?" He saw the confusion in the man's creased brow and corrected himself: "Infected. Crazies. Where are they?"

"Oh." The man raised his head. Nodded in one direction. "Well, there's a few right there." He panned his gaze, and nodded again. "And a few more right there." Back to Lee with a slight frown. "You call them infected and crazies. That is very...closed-minded."

"Well..." Lee was momentarily blank. He'd never been called out for being politically incorrect towards primals. "I called them primals first," Lee noted. Everything was so off its rails at that point that Lee couldn't even extrapolate a possible destination. He was just winging it at this point, until he felt something a little more solid under his feet.

"Huh." The man squinted up at the sky. "Primals." He seemed to be prodding at the word. Testing it. Then he beamed out that highly unstable grin again. "I like it. It's strong. And yet, not insulting."

Lee's gaze strayed to the woman again. He realized that what he'd mistaken for a camouflage fabric on the sundress, was in fact just a very filthy floral pattern—which also explained the discordant pink splotches. Rips and holes and frayed edges abounded.

Unlike the man, her attention remained outwards, a mane of frizzy, almost white-blonde hair tossing about in the wind.

"She's keeping them from attacking," Lee realized.

The man let out a sudden guffaw, so loud and sharp that adrenaline snapped through Lee's system. The man stood up again. "No, no. It's *me* who keeps them from attacking. They know my voice. They know my scent."

Dear God, Lee thought. *Everyone knows your scent.*

The man's eyes widened just a bit more, creating the impression of burning fervor. "They know their *father*."

What had started in the back of Lee's mind as an oddball possibility, now elbowed its way front and center. "You must be Lander Hollis," Lee said, glad to pull at least two of the thousand flapping threads back together, but aware that it still didn't tell him whether meeting Lander Hollis was a good thing or a bad thing.

On the one hand...they weren't dead yet. That was definitely good.

On the other hand...Lander Hollis was exactly as advertised—bat shit crazy. And that would seem to be bad.

"Heard about me, have you?" Lander Hollis did not appear overly excited to be recognized. He squinted into the distance. "They never can stop talking about me, can they?" He whipped back to Lee. "You know what I truly despise about it? When you're famous—or infamous, as the case may be—" Lander spread his hands and put on a face that was somehow both irritable and self-pitying. "You never get the chance to make a good first impression."

Lee wanted to get a reading off of Marie, but didn't dare take his eyes off of Lander. The man's sanity felt like a house of cards, and the smallest slight—even looking away—might be like plucking the bottom card out from under the whole thing.

"Is that what you want?" Lee asked. "You want to make a good first impression? With us?"

Lander's hands flopped down to his side. "Well, it's kinda hard now. If you hadn't been poisoned against me already, then you'd think I was amazing for saving your life. You'd be relieved and ecstatic! You'd consider me a benevolent man with some awesome supernatural powers." Lander sighed and looked disgusted. "But now you're interpreting everything in the light of what they've told you. No matter what I do, you're just going to dismiss it as the ravings of a madman, and a rapist, and a..." He searched the sky for the word, his finger ticking in the air. "What do you call someone involved in bestiality? A bestialist?" That finger suddenly jutted at Lee, backed up by a very stern expression. "*NOT* that that's what it is!"

"Yeah, so," Lee allowed his physical discomfort to show on his face. It wasn't difficult. "I'm really less concerned about a bunch of rumors, and I'm really a *lot* more concerned with getting these ropes off of me."

Finally, the female next to Lander lowered her gaze to Lee. She had ice-gray eyes, flat and uniform in color, so that all that was readily apparent were the two lightless dots of her pupils.

Lander tilted his head to one side. "Mm. Well, I'm not immediately opposed to it. However...I have some questions."

"Maybe I can give you some answers."

"Maybe not." Lander squatted again so he was sitting on his right heel with his left knee propped up. "Do you know why you're not dead right now?"

"Be...cause...you're keeping them from killing us?"

Lander waved a hand. "Right, yeah, right *now* I am. But they're faster than I can keep up with. If they'd've wanted to kill you, they'd've done it before I caught up." Lander gave him a sly, searching glance. "You were over at Horner's Peak, weren't you?"

"Yes, we were," Lee said, trying to be as unambiguous as possible, lest ambiguity cause any more delay in getting free.

Lander nodded, knowingly. "It was Kat that made that call, wasn't it?"

"Yes, it was. What's your point again?"

"My point is..." Lander frowned, as though puzzled. "Why on earth would Kat save you?"

"Save us?" Lee grunted, not bothering to hide his grimace as a cramp seized his hamstring. "She called the primals on us."

"Sure, she called them on you," Lander allowed. "But she didn't make the usual call that she makes. I'm sure it doesn't make a difference to you, but I can hear it." He pointed proudly to his ears.

Lee twisted a bit, unsuccessful in relieving the cramp. What did this guy need to hear to cut the restraints? "She made a different call?"

"Yeah, you know, normally it's a call that means 'Hey, dinner is served.' But this one was a call that meant 'Hey, check this out, but keep your distance.'"

A moment of clarity lightened the pain just a bit. Kat had effectively saved their lives by issuing the wrong howl. Because he'd stopped Horner from beating her? Lee finally twisted his head and looked pointedly at Marie.

She scowled back.

"What I don't understand," Lander continued. "Is why on earth she would do that? I mean, you're all hogtied with cattle ropes, man. I don't think Colin Horner likes you!" Lander laughed again, long and loud and relaxed. "I'm pretty sure Colin wanted her to make the *other* call. And chances are, he didn't know the difference. But it's just pretty odd for Kat to go against Colin's wishes, you know what I'm saying? Pretty odd."

Lee grit his teeth. It was all he could do to speak clearly and distinctly. "We stopped Colin from beating the fuck out of her. Please. Untie us."

Something came over Lander's face. It was hard to determine—partially because the pain in Lee's leg was blotting out his more finely tuned perceptions. It was a mix of emotions that Lee couldn't quite pin down, but gave him the sense that he'd said the right thing, and Lander was looking at him in a new light.

Then Lander smiled. And shrugged. "Okay."

Chapter 18

"How far of a drive is Horner's Peak again?" Sam asked.

The kid named Asher looked at him as though the question made no sense.

Sam blinked and took stock of himself. They were instructing the residents of the Redoubt on the basics of an L-shaped ambush—you know, L-shaped, so you don't shoot your friend across the way? He had just physically adjusted Asher from crowding his cover, and then looked off to the east, wondering why Lee and Marie hadn't returned yet.

He removed his hands from Asher's shoulders. "Sorry. Just...gathering my thoughts."

Asher nodded, seeming to realize what had Sam worried. "It's maybe thirty minutes away?" Then, trying to be reassuring: "But, you know, maybe they talked for a long time. Colin Horner can be a difficult person, as I hear."

"Right, yeah." Sam gave the kid a confident smile. "No worries. Just curious."

It struck him at that moment that he'd been thinking of Asher as a "kid." But Asher was sixteen years old. Only two years shy of Sam himself.

In Sam's defense, Asher wasn't the keenest pupil. He seemed incapable of both guile and malice—both of which were qualities you'd like to see in a person executing an ambush—and it gave him the air of being much younger than he was. He had wide, brown eyes that watched everything as though for the first time, and widened even more when Sam or Abe or Jonesy would say things like, "You do that shit, you're gonna get your noggin popped," or, in response to a question about enemies that were down, but not out: "Well, I mean, if they're still moving...you know...make them not move anymore."

Sam glanced out to where Abe stood in the middle of the main drag, all bushly and glowering. "Just, uh...gimme a minute."

Then, without waiting for a response, Sam strode across the dusty main drag to Abe.

Abe gave him a questioning tilt of the head, but said nothing.

Sam scratched at his temple, squinting against the sun. "When should we start worrying?"

"Two hours ago," Abe said.

Sam spotted Jonesy, jogging over to them.

"Team meeting?" Jones ventured as he stopped in front of them.

"We've started to worry," Sam said.

Jones nodded and glanced to the horizon. "Been four hours, hasn't it?"

"Almost five," Sam said. He hiked a thumb towards Asher. "Guy says Horner's Peak is only a thirty-minute drive. Realistically, could they have been negotiating for almost four hours?"

Abe shook his head. "Not if things went well."

"How un-well do you think they've gone?"

"No idea," Abe admitted. "But I feel like it's time to do something."

"Like what?" Jones asked, blank-faced. "We gonna show up and ask politely what happened to our friends? Or, you know, murder-death-kill?"

"Hey! Sam!"

The voice came from behind him, but he didn't immediately recognize who it was. "Yeah, just give us a minute," he called over his shoulder, then turned back to Abe. "We at least need to get some eyes on Horner's Peak."

Abe started to respond but was cut off.

"Sam!" The voice more indignant now. More urgent. "I'm talking to you!"

A flash of irritation, until he realized that it was Bea. Then he twisted, his eyes shooting up to where Bea was stationed in the lookout.

She had her scoped rifle raised to her shoulder and was staring over the buttstock with severe eyes. "Dust cloud!"

Immediate relief. Which, as Sam began jogging for the lookout, soured quickly into dread. Just because there was a dust cloud didn't mean that it was Lee and Marie making it. If Horner's Peak chose now to launch some sort of attack, the Redoubt was fucked. Sure, they'd rehearsed some basics, but they hadn't drilled them enough to even come close to being remembered in the midst of combat.

"Who is it?" Sam called up as he began to ascend the ladder.

"No visual yet," she replied. "Just the dust cloud."

Abe and Jones reached the ladder just as Sam topped it, but they didn't come up. There wasn't room for all of them, so they just stared after him, waiting for information.

As Sam scrambled into the lookout with Bea, he realized he didn't have any magnified optics of his own. He sidled up next to her and touched her arm. "Mind if I get eyes on?"

He thought she would bristle, but she handed the scoped rifle over without protest.

Sam shouldered it and raised the scope to his eye. He immediately felt a rise of hope. A white vehicle was cresting a hill, maybe a thousand yards out. And as more of the vehicle rose above the ridgeline, that hope turned into relief again.

"It's Jax and Marie," Sam said—confirmed, as he spotted the tell-tale missing panel from the front left bumper, where Jonesy had taken it into a ditch during some escape driving.

"Well, shit," Jones sighed out from below.

"The fuck took them four hours to talk about?" Abe already sounded like he was going to make a thing of it.

"Who the hell knows," Sam griped. Now that he wasn't so damn worried, he was starting to share Abe's irritation. Those negotiations better have been worth it.

Sam handed the rifle back to Bea. He momentarily considered finding something to have a pleasant exchange about, but came up blank. And he didn't just want to stand there like a dolt, so he grabbed the ladder and started to descend.

"Hold up," Bea said.

What's this? Did she finally have some reciprocal flirtation for Sam?

But when he looked up, she was peering through the scope again.

"Uhhh," she said, uncertainty plain in that single, drawn-out tone. "They're stopping. Right on top of that hill. And…there's something in the bed."

Sam frowned, more intrigued than anything, and pulled himself off the ladder to stand next to Bea again. With his naked eye, he could only see the pickup and its rapidly-dispersing dust cloud. There did appear to be something in the bed of the truck…

"I think that's Bran and Kat's ATV," Bea uttered, as though she couldn't comprehend it.

"What the hell do they…?" Sam trailed off as he saw the front doors of the truck open, and simultaneously heard a sharp intake of breath from Bea.

"Shit," Bea spat. "That's Bran and Kat that just got out."

Sam could do nothing but ask the dumbest question in the history of questions, so often quoted by the blindsided: "Wait—what?"

"What's happening, Sam?" Abe called up with threadbare patience.

Sam ignored him, because Bea was speaking again: "That wasn't Jax and Marie driving, it was Bran and Kat. I have no visual on Jax or Marie."

"Are they in the back?" Sam asked—a question only mildly more intelligent than the last.

"I said I can't see them!" Bea practically snarled. "They're moving to the bed."

Sam shook himself into movement and looked down through the hole in the floor of the lookout. Abe and Jones still stood there, gazing fervently upwards. "It's Bran and Kat in that truck. No sign of Jax or Marie."

Abe and Jones spewed a few sharp swears.

"They're pulling out a ramp from the bed," Bea continued to narrate. "They're getting in their ATV. I think they're going to drive away." Bea pulled back from the scope and looked at Sam with a strange expression. "Should I...?"

Sam considered it, but shook his head. "No. Hold coverage. We're going out there."

Sam had already hit the ladder as he said the last words, and scrambled down, his fingers and toes tingling with dread-fueled adrenaline. "Abe, we gotta run out there. Bran and Kat are—"

"I heard," Abe snarled, already on the move as Sam hit the ground. Sam and Jones followed, breaking into a sprint to catch up as Abe darted to the side of the box where they'd laid their rifles and armor.

The Redoubters stood about, uncomprehending, but knowing enough to realize it wasn't good. Hands wrung at rifles like they'd suddenly forgotten what they were. Eyes darted like they'd suddenly forgotten what constituted cover. Feet shuffled like they'd suddenly forgotten where they should be when shit hit the fan.

Sam, Abe, and Jones all hit their individual rigs, snatching them up as they changed directions, now running towards the hill a half mile in the distance.

"Jones! Watch right!" Abe ordered as they charged out into the open. "I'll take left! Sam, clear the vehicle!"

Sam managed to get his armor up and over his head. Didn't bother to mess with the belly straps. The plates swung and flapped against his chest with the rhythm of his rapid stride, full magazines rattling. He got his arm looped into his sling and finally got both hands on the rifle.

It only takes a few minutes to sprint a half mile. But in those few minutes, Sam had what felt like days to consider what he would find in that truck.

Mostly, his brain kept coming back to an image of Lee and Marie's sightless eyes staring up into nothing, faces splashed with livid gore.

He forced himself to focus on the possibility of threats.

As the three of them ran, they drifted into positions to cover their respective areas: Abe on the left; Jones on the right; and Sam in the middle. Sam ran with his eyes locked onto the vehicle, searching for any sign of movement. There was none.

Closing within fifty yards, Sam pulled back on his pace, his chest heaving as he shouldered the rifle and addressed it to the vehicle. The muzzle played steadily back and forth across the vehicle, belying how shaky and unsure Sam felt.

Funny, they never tell you that. None of the warfighters that Sam had trained and operated with had ever pointed out that you could train your body to move a certain way, and you could train your mind not to give into panic, but you could never train your adrenal system not to dump harrowing payloads of its specialty concoction into your bloodstream. That, Sam had eventually realized, never went away.

Jones, of all people, had been the only one to ever even remotely touch on the subject: "Amateurs think of that feeling as 'being nervous.' Pros think of that feeling as being 'excited.' How well you handle it all depends on how you imagine it."

Sam liked to hold himself to professional standards, so he tried hard to tell himself that this was exciting, but it was real hard to get excited about the possibility that he might soon find Lee and Marie in pieces.

They approached the last fifteen yards, slowing to a purposeful walk now. Abe began angling for the rear axle, and Jones the front axle. Sam pushed forward to clear the interior, going low to keep his head below the line of the windows until he was close enough to pop up and scan the inside with a quick peek.

The front was clear.

Sam tried to gird himself up for what he would find in the back. His movements were quick and precise as he pivoted away from the front passenger's window and sidestepped to the back.

Where he found nothing.

"Truck's clear," Sam said, almost mystified by it.

"Hold what you got," Abe called out, now hunkering at the rear axle, just the top of his head and the muzzle of his rifle above the line of the truck bed, scanning the other side of the ridgeline as best he could.

Abe skirted around the back of the vehicle and got himself a better vantage point down the slope of the other side. After a few agonizing moments of inspecting every clump of brush big enough to hide a person, Abe called back, "Ridgeline's clear."

He immediately swung around to the truck again. "Don't open the doors."

Sam and Jones held back as Abe dropped down to all fours. He moved slowly, checking the undercarriage all the way around the vehicle. Sam knew what he was looking for—anything that didn't look like it belonged. Such as wires and explosives.

After nearly five minutes, Abe stood up, sweating and red-faced. "Nothing on the undercarriage I can see." He was on the driver's side of the vehicle, speaking over the hood to Sam and Jones on the passenger's side. He jerked his head and sidled over to the door. Sam followed so they were staring at each other through the front windows.

Abe's eyes scoured the interior on Sam's side, and Sam did the same for Abe's side.

"Don't open that fucking door," Sam suddenly said, his heart lurching into his throat. He jabbed a finger at what he was seeing. "There's something stuck between the seat cushion and the door."

Abe nodded. "Same on your side. Can you tell what it is?"

"No—I can just see something's pressing on the seat cushion." It was such a slight rumple in the fabric, that if Sam hadn't been intimately familiar with this particular vehicle, he might not have even noticed it.

Jones had backed up a few paces from the truck. "Didn't Lee and Marie both take grenades?"

"Fuck, fuck, fuckity-fuck," Abe summarized the situation, then fell silent.

Sam shifted to the back windows and saw the exact same thing. Abe followed his lead and confirmed it was the same on Sam's side, too. All four doors of the vehicle were booby-trapped.

"We're gonna have to break a window," Sam decided.

"Break a window?" Jones practically gasped. "You're high."

"We gotta get in there somehow. If we break a window, we can reach in and pull the grenade out without letting the spoon pop off."

"Uh-uh. Screw the truck. I say we leave it here forever."

"It's our only mode of transportation right now," Abe said.

"We got the satphone, don't we?" Jones insisted. "Let's just call Colorado and have them airdrop a new truck."

"For chrissake, Jonesey," Sam snapped over his shoulder. "Breaking the glass ain't gonna blow up the fucking truck."

"So you *think*!"

Abe apparently had made up his mind on the issue, because he stepped to the driver's side and speared the muzzle of his rifle into the upper corner of the window.

"Jesus!" Jones leapt backwards.

The glass took another hit and then erupted in a cascade of pebbles.

For a moment, no one moved.

"You fucking psychopath!" Jones wheezed.

Abe didn't respond, not wanting to jinx himself. He leaned carefully into the broken window and peered down at the gap between the seat and the door. "Yeah, it's a grenade. De-pinned." He let his rifle hang, his hands held up like a freshly-scrubbed surgeon entering the operating room. They made a few hesitant motions, as though Abe were visualizing how he was going to extract the grenade. Then he went in.

Sam decided to take a big step back with Jones. He had absolute faith in Abe. But why tempt fate?

Very carefully, Abe seized the grenade, keeping the spoon clamped tight to the body, and pulled it out. Completely focused on the explosive in his hand, he crossed to the passenger's side of the vehicle, turned, and then wound up like a major league pitcher. He hurled the grenade over the truck and down the hill.

All three of them hunched down and plugged their ears.

The explosion rattled the truck, briefly igniting a fear in Sam's chest that the vibrations had dislodged one of the other grenades. But after a steady five count, and no exploding truck, Sam let himself breathe.

Abe returned to the driver's-side window. The keys had been left in the ignition and he reached in, clicking them into the ON position, then lowered the rest of the windows from the driver's controls. Sam and Jones were all too happy to let Abe play EOD, and stood back as he repeated the process at the other three doors.

Three explosions later, and about ten minutes of Abe sticking his head through the open windows and inspecting the doors from every angle he could crane his neck, and they were able to open the doors.

Jones, who was the most mechanically-minded of the team, gave the engine compartment another solid inspection for any other surprises. Nothing turned up. Which made sense. Because Lee and Marie had both loaded two grenades into their rigs.

Horner had only booby-trapped the truck with what he'd taken from Lee and Marie.

Which meant that Lee and Marie had *definitely* been captured.

"What did they do with them?" Jones said, still posted up over the engine block.

"I don't fucking know," Abe said, his tone implying it was an idiotic question.

None of them knew shit-all at this point.

Except for one thing: The negotiations had not gone according to plan.

Chapter 19

It was nice to be free of the ropes and all, but for Lee, moving around was no great joy either. His joints creaked and ground. Deeply bruised muscles that had stiffened in his hogtied position screamed as he forced them back into motion. Hands and feet that had gone numb under the squeeze of the restraints came roaring back to life with nothing but pain signals to offer.

As Lander shuffled over to Marie and began cutting through her rawhide bindings with a little pearl-handled pocket knife, Lee rose cautiously to his bare feet. He was keenly aware that the hybrid female in the incongruous sundress had not taken her eyes off him since Lander began sawing at his restraints.

He regretted standing. His feet felt like they were swarming with ants. And he was pretty damn sure he'd just slipped a disc. But when you have an entity that is at least one-quarter inclined to eat you, and that entity is staring at you like a cat at a mouse hole, you try your best not to show any weakness.

Should he say something to her? It felt like a moment when he should say something.

"Hey," he said with a curt nod. "How's it goin'?"

It was as good as anything.

The female tilted her head. Eyes never wavering.

Lee held her gaze, but turned his head slightly, speaking over his shoulder. "Does she understand me?"

Her eyes narrowed and her lips curled back, flashing predator's teeth. A voice like a harsh whisper came out of her, the single syllable oddly formed in a mouth too large to be human. "Yes."

He shouldn't have been surprised, and yet he had to restrain himself from recoiling slightly as an uncomfortable sensation skittered down his spine.

Behind him, he heard Lander snicker. Then there was the sound of the last tendril of rawhide snapping, followed by a long, sibilant noise of pain from Marie.

"Do you have a name?" Lee asked, using his limited peripheral vision to get an idea of where the other primals were. He could see shapes in the grasses all around him, and wanted badly to look, but felt very motivated to make some sort of human connection with the hybrid before he unlocked eyes with her.

"Her name's Freya," Lander said with a grunt as he stood up. "I'll help her out on that one. She has a hard time with it. Sounds like Frooh-Hah the way she mumbles it."

Lee watched Freya's eyes jag over his shoulder, presumably at Lander. And was he mistaken or was that just the slightest little shift of resentment that worked across her face?

When she looked back to him, he had the sense that something had been released between them. The intensity in her gaze had pulled back a great deal. She was still paying attention to him, but was no longer fixated.

Lee felt just comfortable enough to disengage from her and pan his gaze around, finally taking in the creatures that had them surrounded.

A memory took hold of him in that moment. A snippet from his childhood. His parents had taken him to the Asheboro Zoo in North Carolina one summer. He didn't remember much from that outing, as he'd only been about eight years old at the time, but he distinctly remembered the lion habitat. There was a window at the habitat's ground level, maybe four-by-four, and if you tapped on the glass, as annoying zoo-goer's are wont to do, the biggest feline you've ever encountered would come stalking down. Lee remembered standing there, inches from the glass, and staring into those yellow eyes in which there was nothing but instinct. Even at eight years old, he'd understood on an instinctive level that if that glass were to disappear by some magical happenstance, he would be ripped apart.

He remembered telling himself, very rationally, that such a thing was impossible, and that he was perfectly safe. And yet he also remembered feeling that the situation was so very precarious.

He felt exactly the same way now.

Lee counted ten of them as he turned in a slow circle, finding that they created a complete circle. Some of them stood, their postures odd and forward-slumped with their arms hanging loosely at their sides. Others crouched so that only their heads peered up above the tops of the grass.

They did not move or mill about. They uttered no sound. Every single one of them was entirely focused on either Lee or Marie, their gazes steady and intense. Just like that lion. Powerful instinct fettered only by a seemingly inconsequential barrier—in this case, Lander and Freya's supposed control over them.

Lee decided he would not be making any sudden movements, and would be as friendly as he could manage with Lander and Freya.

Lander stood and slipped the closed pocket-knife into what looked like a pouch of some sort around his waist. He squinted up at the sky, shading his face from the sun with an outstretched hand. "Just a bit after noon," he said, as though this were some picnic outing and he'd determined that they had plenty of time to kill. "Walk with me."

Lee turned his attention to Marie, who was staring at Lander from underneath arched eyebrows and rubbing her red-chafed wrists.

"Where are we going?" Marie asked.

Lander stopped and looked at her. "Does it really matter to you? You're safe as long as I say you're safe. If I were in your position, I'd swallow my questions and do my best to go along with things."

Lee waited until Marie gave him a questioning glance. He nodded to her and said, a little pointedly, "Sounds fair."

Lander smiled and started walking again, Freya falling into step with him.

The primals around them began moving to keep pace. They kept their distance, but maintained their wide ring around Lee and Marie.

Lee sidled a little closer to Marie. "How's your body? Anything broken?"

She shook her head stiffly. "Feels like mostly soft-tissue damage." She glanced down at her bare right foot as she picked her way around sharp stones and other stabby things. "Think one of those toes might be broken, but there ain't shit to be done about that."

Lee gave her a thorough inspection—especially her head and face. She had a few knots and cuts, and a noticeable goose egg that had stained her scalp red and trickled down her temple. "Your head okay? Any signs of concussion?"

"Oh, I'm definitely concussed," she said. "But it's not the worst I've ever had. You?"

"About the same."

Feeling marginally better about his companion's physical condition, Lee put his focus back on their strange escort. "So, by swallowing my questions and going along to get along," Lee hazarded. "Does that mean no questions at all?"

Lander's shoulders bobbed in a shrug. "I suppose I'll answer what I feel like answering."

"Why are you helping us?"

Lander sighed heavily. "Is it so hard to believe that I'm not a man of violence?"

Lee didn't immediately answer, because it *was* hard to believe.

"I'm not," Lander said, a little defensively. "I don't *want* to kill anyone. I want everyone to live in peace. It's just...challenging at this point in time. But, if I had my druthers, we'd live in a world where humans and primals coexist. You might call that my life's work. After all, *I've* learned to coexist with them, haven't I? I've proven that it's possible. Now I just have to convince everyone else to get along." Lander grimaced then. "But Colin Horner is a bit of an issue there. He just wants to kill everybody because he's obsessed with his land and his cattle."

"I was under the impression that you were closely allied with him," Lee said.

"I try to keep the peace." He gave Lee a shrewd look. "Why were you at Horner's Peak?"

Lee briefly considered lying. But in circumstances where you have no idea what is motivating the other party, lies can be as harmful as the truth. Lee had found that, most of the time, it really was best to let the chips fall where they may.

"We were there on behalf of the Redoubt," Lee said. "To try to broker a peace between them and Horner's Peak."

Lander's pace stalled for just a moment of unguarded surprise, but he never stopped, nor did he turn around. "I wasn't aware they were at war."

"I wouldn't characterize it that way," Lee said. "More like Colin Horner is trying to steamroll people off his land. The Redoubt is just the next in line. Were you aware of what he did to Camperland?"

"Oh, I'm well aware," Lander said, with a bit of a mocking laugh in his voice. "Who do you think did his dirty work for him?"

"You?"

Lander finally turned his head to fix Lee with an irritable look. "No, not me. I don't do the man's dirty work for him. That's why he has Kat." His face took on that airy look of uncaring again. "But it was my...*primals*...that did the work."

Lee chose not to point out that Lander claimed to control the primals and could have stopped it, if he really didn't want to be used as a tool. Instead, he countered with, "So, you must know that Kat called your primals in on the Redoubt last night."

Lander stopped and turned, but he didn't seem angry. More…bemused. "I realize I never asked your name. How rude. You are?"

"Jax," Lee replied, deciding that this particular lie was of no real consequence. He gestured to his side. "And this is Marie."

Lander put on a smile that Lee supposed was intended to be dazzling, but just came off as unhinged in its intensity. "Delighted!" he proclaimed. Then refocused on Lee. "Now, Jax and Marie, you need to understand something about the Valley. I control the primals here. But I do not control Colin. It is not my place to tell him what he can and can't do with Kat. If he chooses to use her for nefarious purposes, well, that's on him. It's not my preference to see him use my family to destroy entire settlements of people, but I'm not going to go to war with him over it, you know?"

Lander continued walking, gesticulating lazily as he spoke. "I could overrun his ranch, you know. I could send all my family in there, and I know we'd win, eventually. But that wouldn't really help human-primal relations, now would it? If I really want us to coexist, then what good would it do me to kill Colin and his men for killing all the rest of the humans in the Valley? Then there'd be no humans left in the Valley. And then the day would never come when the Valley would be a shining example of humans and primals living peaceably together." He smiled beatifically. "We could be an example to the *world*, Jax!"

Lee didn't quite know what to follow up with, but Marie broke in, speaking with extreme care. "May I ask what your intentions are with us?"

A scoff. "You mean am I going to kill you?"

"It would be nice to know if we're speaking to a friend," Marie admitted, leaving out the implied ending: *or an enemy.*

Lander looked briefly put-upon. "I already told you I'm not a man of violence."

"Very forward thinking for our current times," Marie noted, diplomatically.

Lander swung his hands absently at a fluffy seed head, causing it to burst into a cloud. "So, I take it the peace talks didn't go well over at Horner's Peak, huh?"

"Well," Lee said, wincing a bit at the memory. "Marie is much better at talking than I am, but Mr. Horner insisted on talking to me. And I suppose I was a bit more honest than he liked."

"You said he tried to beat Kat."

"He *did* beat her. Until we intervened."

"You realize she could have saved herself if she wanted to."

"I realize she's physically capable," Lee said, remembering how fast she'd moved on him, and how iron-strong her arms had been around his neck. "But I wonder if she's mentally capable of going against Mr. Horner. He seems to have quite a hold on her."

"She didn't call the primals in to kill you," Lander pointed out. "That was going against him."

"She thinks he's her father," Lee said. "Or at least, that's what I've been told."

Lander didn't answer, and Lee swapped another look with Marie.

There wasn't much in the way of landscape features, so Lee had already seen the single big tree standing at the top of a low hill, and realized they were heading for it. Lander didn't speak as they approached it, and Lee felt their precarious position might topple if he kept nudging for answers, so he kept his mouth shut, and tried to parse through what he already knew.

The problem was, he knew jack shit. Oh, sure, he knew who the players were. But he needed to know their motivations. From Ted and Bea over in The Redoubt, to Colin Horner and Bran and Kat, to Lander himself, everyone was either downright inscrutable, or holding back enough that Lee couldn't be sure of anything they said.

He was missing an intrinsic part of the big picture. He could sense the shape of it, but he was missing some important piece of information that would bind it all together into one cohesive, understandable whole.

A heartless rancher, a crazy wild man, and the poor scared villagers caught in the middle.

That made sense. In a children's story.

Real life tended to be more complicated.

What was Lee missing?

Lee didn't quite appreciate how massive the tree was until he was standing beneath its shading branches. There were no cattle in sight, but there were plenty of old cow patties and hoof-prints to reveal they pastured there, and took refuge in the shade of this tree.

"We'll rest here," Lander said, stopping inside the shade and placing his hands on his hips. "Always best to rest during the hottest part of the day."

Despite Lee's bruised and broken body, he found himself blessedly relaxed by the sudden coolness of the shade. He'd just been plugging away, focused on the weirdness of his situation. That was great for taking his mind off his pain, but he hadn't realized how tired the hike in the sun had made him. His thighs felt quivery, his hands shaky, and his skin had that uncomfortable prickle to it that told him that he was getting dehydrated. Taking a rest in the shade sounded downright heavenly.

That lasted for about the span of a single breath, until he saw the primals filing into the shade as well. It wasn't that they necessarily drew any closer, but somehow, within the confines of the shade, Lee felt like he was stuck in a room with them.

Lander seemed to notice his concern. "I assure you, they won't attack. Not unless Freya or I tell them to." A smirk, with twinkling eyes. "Or if you were to try to attack us. Or if you tried to run away—don't try to run. You know how dogs are when something runs from them?"

Lee nodded, still watching the creatures as they watched him back. "Yeah, I'm familiar."

Lander made a gesture as though to indicate enough had been said on the matter. Then he fluffed out his serape, crossed his feet, and lowered himself into something like a meditative pose. Freya stood behind him for a moment and then squatted down, so that her knees were against her chest. She looked like she could hold that position for hours.

Stiff and aching, neither Lee nor Marie were so nimble. Lee navigated himself to the ground and sat, with his legs splayed out in front of him, favoring his broken ribs. Wincing, Marie lowered herself into a similar position.

"Why are you helping the Redoubt?" Lander asked.

Lee looked up and found the other man watching him, his face as blank as a professional card player. What was this guy's deal anyway? Colin Horner might be a bit of a puzzle, but this guy was so far beyond the pale, how could Lee possibly nail down what made him tick?

"It's what we do," Lee answered. "We find folks with problems, and then we try to solve them." He immediately followed with a question of his own. "Does it bother you that we're helping the Redoubt?"

Lander frowned up at the leaves over their head, his fingers absently plucking at the low, scraggly grass that grew beneath the tree. "Does it bother me?" he mused aloud. Then shook his head. "No, it doesn't. It complicates things for me, but that's okay. I have plans." He fixed Lee with a serious stare. "There are...things...that I need from them."

Lee tried not to frown at that, despite the twisting sensation in his gut. "What kinds of things?"

The beard at the corners of Lander's mouth twitched up. "What did our mutual friend Ted tell you about Kat and Colin Horner?"

"He said you'd made some sort of deal with Colin Horner. Colin Horner wanted some control over the primals in the area, and you gave him Kat."

"And do you know how Kat came to be?"

Lee quirked an eyebrow. "As in, birds and the bees?"

Lander chuckled. "Yes."

"My understanding is that you..." Lee wasn't quite sure how to phrase it without sounding derisive. "...have some half-primal and half-human hybrids in your...family?"

Lander's smile broadened at Lee's attempt to be subject-matter sensitive. But he didn't interrupt, so Lee took it as a good sign that he hadn't put his foot in his mouth yet.

So he continued. "I kind of assumed that Kat came from a full-human male and one of those half-human females."

Lander gave a nod to indicate Lee was not mistaken. "And who do you assume sired her? Colin?" He raised his eyebrows. "Me?"

Lee raised his hands, palms up. "I was led to believe that Colin was *not* her biological father."

"Hm," Lander grunted, his expression unchanged. "Well, that's telling, now isn't it?"

"Is it?" Lee questioned. Then leaned forward a bit. "Are you saying Colin *is* Kat's father?"

Lander looked off into the middle distance with a sigh that hinted to Lee that his question was about to be dodged. Sure enough, Lander went squirreling off on an unexpected tangent.

"Did you know that Colin had a girlfriend?"

It struck Lee as oddly juvenile the way that Lander had said it. Like they were gossiping in the school yard about who was making out under the bleachers. "Uh...no. I was not aware."

Lander nodded slowly. "Up until about, oh, I guess it was six months or so ago? Yeah. Pretty lady." He trailed off, still staring at nothing in particular. Then he suddenly looked at Lee, and said, casually, "They found her torn apart." He waved a hand at the primals hunkered in the shade, still watching them intently. "By you-know-who."

"Oh."

Lander leaned in, his face suddenly intense again. "At least, that's what they say."

Lee quirked his head. "You think someone else killed her?"

Marie sniffed. "I could see Colin going psycho enough to tear someone apart."

"No," Lander said dismissively. "It wasn't Colin. I can tell you that much right now. Or, at least, I can tell you that I have faith in my sense of people, and my sense of him is that he did not do it. He was quite irate with me. Understandably so. I don't think he's that good of an actor. And besides, why would he need to cover that up? As he's fond of saying, he's the one that runs the Valley. He could've lopped off her head in front of his whole ranch and they would have shrugged and figured he had a good reason. No, it wasn't him. And I'm also fairly sure it wasn't my primals." Lander smiled knowingly at the plucked grass between his legs. "No, it was someone else. Someone capable of killing her like a primal would."

"You think Kat did it," Lee realized, entirely unsure whether to believe it. He could buy it. But what did that mean for his arithmetic concerning the strange trio of Colin, Bran, and Kat? What was the relationship there? And *was* Colin her father?

Rather than answer, Lander raised a hand and pointed off into the distance, in the general direction of south. "You see that little ridge over there? The one right on the horizon with the two trees on it?"

Lee squinted in that direction, but his eye was still too foggy to make much out at that distance. "Marie, you see what he's talking about?"

She took a moment to answer. "Yeah, I see it."

Lander's hand dropped back into his lap. "The Redoubt is just on the other side. If you can make it to that ridge, you'll see them."

"You're letting us go?" Lee asked.

Lander seemed surprised by the question. "What good would it do me to keep you?" His eyes strayed to Marie and stayed there for an uncomfortably long time, as though he was reconsidering what he'd just said. But then he blinked and looked back at Lee. "You should know that Colin's going to make the call again, and soon. He's going to have Kat call in my primals on the Redoubt. And I'm guessing she'll make the correct call this time."

"He tried that last night," Lee said. "Your, uh, *family* can't get in when they're buttoned up."

Lander only shrugged once more. "I would assume Colin has a plan for that. You should too."

"Why are you telling us this if you're going to allow it to happen anyway?"

Lander's eyes took on that feverish cast again. "I want you to deliver a message to Ted. I want you to tell him, from me, that a debt is still owed." A flash of a smile that was anything but friendly. "He'll understand."

Chapter 20

"You're not sweating much," was the first thing that Marie said after they'd walked about two hundred yards from the tree in silence.

Lee swiped at his brow and was disappointed to feel more crusty salt deposit than moisture. He wasn't quite empty just yet, but he was sure heading that direction. "I still got a bit."

"Enough to make it? 'Cause I am not carrying your ass."

He eyed the distance, but still could not really see the ridge with the two trees that Lander had pointed out. "How far you think that ridge is we're heading for?"

Marie paused to judge the distance. "Maybe six miles?" she finally said, and started walking again.

"Yeah, I got that," Lee decided.

"You got that, like you're speaking in faith, or you're confident?"

"I said I got it, Marie," Lee answered, annoyed. "Airing your doubts ain't gonna help."

"Alright. You got this," Marie conceded.

"Thank you."

They walked on for a while, but Lee could sense the space between them filling up with unsaid words, and knew the dam was going to break eventually. And if it was going to happen anyway, Lee figured he might as well give it a little push and get it over with.

"Go on," he prompted. "Get it off your chest."

She was quiet for a few more strides. Lee didn't bother looking over. He knew she was watching him. Measuring him, as though he were a troublesome concoction in a beaker.

Finally, she had out with it. "I get that the only reason we're alive right now is because you intervened on Kat's behalf."

"But," Lee prompted, sensing the word hiding in amongst the others.

"But we wouldn't have been in that situation to begin with if you'd just kept your cool."

"M-hm."

"M-hm? That's it?"

"No. I said 'm-hm' because you clearly have more to say." He gave a beckoning twiddle of his fingers. "Go ahead. Lay out all your charges against me and I'll defend myself when the prosecution rests."

Marie made a disgruntled noise. "I don't have a case against you, Lee. I'm just…You're worrying me. Is this really the time or place for you to be trying to…" Her hands moved like she was trying to get a grip on something without form. "Change? Be a different person? Be a *better* person? Or whatever you're trying to do, Lee. I don't know. All I know is that Lee from three years ago wouldn't have put his team at risk for some stranger. And not just a stranger, Lee—a *hybrid*! And one that's pretty much a primary enemy of the people we're trying to help."

Lee felt heat that had nothing to do with the sun, flushing the back of his neck and making his jaw muscles clench and unclench. But he knew there was yet more to come, and so he let it come.

"This might sound shitty, but here it is," Marie said. "You wanna try to be a new, compassionate individual or some shit? To try to assuage your conscience from all the shit you've done in the past? Fine. That's your own journey to take. But you do that shit on your own time, and not in the middle of an operation."

Lee gave the ensuing silence a few beats. She seemed to be done. "And when exactly am I not in the middle of an operation?"

Marie considered it. Lee knew what answer she'd come to: There was no such time. Lee's entire life *was* an operation. If he was with a settlement, then everything he did was a part of the operation to help them. If he was traveling to a new settlement, then that was an operation in and of itself: Find someone that needed help, all while traveling through unknown territory filled with unknown threats.

"Alright," Marie said. "Then maybe when we're not dealing with a life-threatening scenario? Such as being in enemy territory for peace talks, surrounded by people that want to hurt you?"

"And what would be the point in that?"

"What would be the point?" she echoed, incredulous. "Your survival? Your *team's* survival?"

"Once again, I'll point out that nobody died."

"So, all's well that ends well, huh? The ends justify the means?"

"You know, that phrase is usually used when people do bad shit to achieve a goal. I've never heard it used to tell someone they should be more of an asshole in order to save their own skin."

"Fine line between being an asshole and being smart. Not everything requires a response *right fucking now*."

"Agreed. Not everything requires an immediate response. But that did. He hit her. I wasn't going to allow it. I told him to stop. He did not. I enacted consequences upon him. Which, in turn, had consequences for me and you. Oh well. Doing the right thing always has consequences, Marie. If doing the right thing automatically laid out a highway paved in gold that led you to Nirvana, then a whole lot of folks who are rotting in the ground right now would have been rewarded instead of being slaughtered. You wanna talk about assuaging your guilty conscience? How about all the times we lie to ourselves that our safety is more important than actually doing the right thing? Now *that's* assuaging your conscience. Because here's the shit no one tells you: If your job is to fight? Your life is gonna suck, no matter how you cut it. The question is, do you at least get to feel like a good human being as you slog through it? Or will you add on all the self-loathing of knowing that you're a shitty creature, on top of the weight you're already carrying? I don't know how much time I got left, but when I go out, Marie, I want to go out doing the right thing. What I *do not* want, is to go out with a self-administered bullet, thinking of all the times I did the wrong thing just to save myself, only to wind up despising myself so completely because of those choices that I'd rather end it than take another step forward. So, if you're looking for an apology, you're looking in the wrong place. And if you can't get on board with doing the right thing, even when it means hanging your ass on a limb, then I don't know what you're doing here, because no one ever promised anything from this life except exactly what we're getting: Hanging our asses out in order to do the right thing."

Marie trudged along in sour silence for a moment.

Then, with a grunt, she sallied back into the fray. "How long you been practicing that one?"

"Pure inspiration."

"Well, that's certainly one way to color events—all honorable and shit," she said. "But when you get right down to it, Lee, maybe it's just your pride."

"My pride?"

"Yeah. How you just can't let a man like Colin Horner give you the middle finger without trying to show him who's boss. Instead of just smiling and going along with it, because you know you can get him in the long run." She looked and saw Lee giving her a dubious face. "Oh, don't act like your inflated sense of self hasn't led us down some shit roads in the past."

That smarted enough that it almost blanketed his physical pain. He just about stopped walking, but it was actually his exhaustion that kept his feet moving—if he stopped it would only be that much harder to break his inertia again.

There was some truth to what Marie said. His hubris *had* led them down some bad roads. People had died on those roads, and those that survived were scarred. It was certainly a thought that he'd entertained in his own private headspace. But entertaining it as a possibility, and having a third party affirm it, were two wildly different sensations. One left him uneasy. The other left him burned.

But truth was kind of like moonshine: You always know how pure it is by how much it burns going down.

"Alright," he said. "I earned that. I've made many decisions with a blind trust in my convictions, and that's led to some bad shit. Bad shit that you and the others have had to deal with."

"But?" Marie prompted.

"No buts. I admit that my pride has led me down some bad roads. You characterized it as an inflated sense of self. And while that's not untrue, it kind of carries the connotation of me being a narcissistic asshole."

"You *are* a narcissistic asshole."

"Now you're just jabbing. I have narcissistic tendencies, but so does everyone else. Everyone tries to protect their minds from admitting nasty truths about themselves, because that shit hurts and it's exhausting to fix. I can be slow to admit my own faults, but I think everyone is, and I admit to them more often than your average bear. So I admit that I have a big ball of pride in my chest, and it often takes me places I don't want to go. But I will not admit that I'm self-obsessed, because I don't think that's true at all."

Marie scoffed. "How would you characterize it, then?"

This time Lee did stop, but only because he felt that hamstring edging towards a cramp again. Inertia be damned, he winced and bent at the waist, straightening his knee to try to relieve the growing tension. "I would characterize it as a conviction, whether true or false, that it sure seems to me like the world hinges on my decisions."

Marie eyed him as he stretched, one hand on her hip, the other shading her face. "The world hinges on your decisions," she echoed. "That sounds like delusions of grandeur."

"Does it?" Lee shook his head. "I decide to leave my bunker to recon my area, and I get declared a nonviable asset. I decide to stand up for people, and I wind up leading a civil war. I try to explore the Gulf Coast region, and I end up as an enemy of the *Nuevas Fronteras* cartel. I try to oust a dictator, and I get declared an enemy of the state and a terrorist. You see the pattern here?"

Marie harrumphed but didn't otherwise respond.

"For better or for worse," Lee continued trying to explain. "I perceive that my decisions and actions seem to have consequences disproportionate to how small a player I consider myself to be. Which then makes me feel that perhaps I'm not as small a player as I think. You call this an inflated sense of self-importance. But I think I'm just reading the signs, Marie."

Lee got most of the cramp out and started walking again.

"So," Marie ventured, still sounding unconvinced. "If you really think that your decisions have consequences disproportionate to your overall importance…then why the fuck did you jump in to try to save Kat?"

Lee frowned at her like she was missing the point. "Because it was the right thing to do. We already covered that. Just like it was the right thing to do to recon my area, and to save those people, and to fight back against a dictatorial regime. Doing the right thing sometimes lands you in hot water. That's no reason to stop doing it."

"So what's the right thing now, Lee?" Marie grumbled, bitterly. "How are you going to land yourself—and us—in hot water next?"

Lee's expression turned cold as he trudged on, staring straight ahead. "There is no right thing now. Doing the right thing went out the window as soon as Horner left us for dead. But I warned him, so my conscience is clear. Now I'm going to burn his shit to the ground. No mercy. Just like I promised him."

Chapter 21

Lander and Freya stood outside the main gate of Horner's Peak, staring down the four guards posted there. Freya looked like she was on the verge of pouncing on them, which would have been very bad for everyone involved, including herself.

She couldn't kill them all before the guy with the machine gun mowed her down. And if she did pounce, the pack of ten primals lurking in the tall grasses behind Lander would immediately join the fray and this whole thing would turn into a bloodbath.

That's not what Lander wanted.

"What do you think, Freya?" Lander asked, trying to distract her. "You like the name 'primals'? I'm quite fond of it myself. Been using it in my head. It fits."

Freya quirked her head in his direction, her aggressive tension fading just a hair. She blinked a few times, then uttered a noncommittal grunt and went back to glowering at the guards.

Lander had acted to the man Jax and his lady-friend, Marie, as though he had complete control of the primals in his vicinity. And he *did*!

Except for that one time.

And that other time.

And the three months after he'd first been rescued by his wives, when they and their retinue of female primals had protected him from almost constant aggression from the males.

But they'd learned! They respected him now. They saw him as their father. This was why Lander was so sure that humans and primals could coexist. They were smart enough to see that he was the *true* Alpha, because they were smart enough to recognize the value of someone more intelligent than them.

Hell, there were humans who couldn't manage that.

People just had to stop being so afraid of them. And with someone like Lander in charge of the primals, and keeping them from giving into their predatory instincts, that had become a real possibility.

Lander imagined the Valley becoming a wonderful example to the rest of the world. The first place on earth where humans and primals lived peaceably together. And he would be in charge of it. He would be the godfather of this new relationship. Just as the people of the Valley had once called him a wizard, soon the whole world would think of him that way. A guru. The only man alive who knew how to tame the primals, and set an example for a beautiful future relationship.

He often narrated key moments of his own biography in his head. He just hadn't decided if it was going to be an autobiography, or if he'd let someone else write it. Probably better to let a professional writer do it—if there were any still alive. There had to be, right? And once Lander became who he was destined to become, they'd be beating down his door to be the one to write about him, so he'd have the pick of the litter.

But he also had concerns. Would another person be able to capture the nuance of his genius?

Maybe it was better if he wrote it himself.

At long last, the man Lander had come to see stalked out of the gate. Colin Horner scowled at him from under the brim of his white cowboy hat. But was that a bit of fear in his eyes? And was

Lander mistaken, or were they darting over Lander's shoulders to try to spot the pack that usually accompanied him?

Lander was no fool. He had all the power in this relationship, and he knew it. From Colin's perspective, at least, and that was what mattered. Colin was scared of pissing Lander off, for fear that he would send his entire family after the ranch. He didn't know that Lander was determined that there be at least *one* settlement of humans in the Valley—otherwise his dreams would never come to fruition.

In reality, the power was very balanced. They needed each other. But Lander always made sure to act a little volatile and unstable—all the better to keep Colin on his toes.

"What are you doing here, Lander?" Colin demanded as he stopped in front of him.

Lander glanced over Colin's shoulder at the preparations happening inside the ranch. Colin's ranch hands were bustling about, fueling up two of their diesel pickup trucks, and generally seeming like they were getting ready to start some shit.

"Seems like you're on the warpath, Colin."

"Shouldn't *you* be on the warpath?" Colin said. "They killed some of your family last night."

Lander grimaced at the reminder. Not because he felt any grief, per se. More like *aggrieved*. When people killed his primals, they insulted Lander directly. They might as well spit in his face. And usually, Lander would render punishments for such insolence. But since there were only two settlements of humans left in the Valley, and it sure looked like one was about to kill the other, he'd chosen to forestall his judgment.

Lander sighed and gave Colin a sly look. "Why would I go on the warpath when you're already doing it for me?"

"So you're not here to convince me to leave the Redoubt alone?"

"Would it make a difference if I tried?"

"No."

Lander had figured as much. He shrugged. "Well, then."

Colin huffed and put his hands on his hips. "So what *are* you doing here?"

"I'm here to bargain for a life."

"Whose life?"

Lander almost laughed, because Colin was obviously being intentionally dense. Instead, he lowered his chin and glared up at Colin from under his brows. "You know who."

Colin's nose twitched. The slightest wrinkle of disgust, quickly hidden. "Why are you so obsessed with her?"

Lander's expression became almost dreamy. Remembering that day, three years ago. The day he'd seen the future. "Because she's got *fire*, my friend. And that's what I need. That's what my *family* needs."

Colin shook his head, as though deciding he didn't want to know. "Alright. Bargain then."

Alright then. Down to business. Lander took a big inhale. "What'll it take for you to deliver her to me? Alive, of course."

Colin pursed his lips. Crossed his arms over his chest. "Gonna be difficult to guarantee her safety."

"You're a smart man," Lander smiled. "I'm sure you can figure it out."

Colin made a face. "Risky. I'm risking my people for it. You'd have to make it worth my while."

"Name it."

"That desperate, huh?"

Lander tilted his head. "Desperate? No. Just..." he smiled. "Forward-thinking."

Colin pretended to consider for a while longer, but Lander knew he was just playing hard-to-get. Trying to eke out more favorable terms for a deal he already knew he was going to make. But Lander had arrived, knowing what Colin would ask for, and knowing what he was willing to part with to get what he wanted. He had all the cards.

Colin finally nodded, as though it had been such a tough decision. "Fine. I'll do it. And in exchange, you're going to keep your infected away from my cattle."

Lander winced at the word *infected*. Did they have to be so rude, right to his face? Time to play a little hard-to-get of his own. "I hate to say it, Colin, but your cattle are an important food source for my family."

"Find another fucking food source. Those are mine. And those are my terms. You want the deal or not?"

Lander sighed and stretched his back. "How many head of cattle do they kill?"

"You don't know?"

Lander frowned. He honestly had no idea. "They're not puppets, Colin. They have autonomy, you know. I don't know what every single one of them is doing all the time. Just ballpark it for me."

Colin sucked his teeth. "One or two a week."

Colin was low-balling the real number, Lander realized. He was anticipating that the number of cattle a week would be what they negotiated on. But Lander's family didn't actually *need* Colin's cattle. They were just easy pickings.

Lander looked unsure. "You know, my family requires a lot of food."

"They're omnivores, ain't they?" Colin grouched. "It don't have to be meat, and it certainly don't have to be my cattle."

That was true enough, and a large part of the reason they didn't need Colin's cattle. Their hunting range was actually much larger than just the Valley, and there was plenty of wildlife, not to mention all the abandoned orchards that still produced a scavenge-worthy crop.

But Lander put on a pained face. "You're asking me to starve my family."

Colin barely restrained a roll of his eyes. "You came to me, asking for something. In order for me to give you what you want,

I have to take serious risks. This is what will make the risk worth it. You know, you coulda gone and grabbed her yourself by now."

Lander waved it away. "They'll only hide in their boxes and wait us out. I can't convince my family to lay siege to some metal boxes for a week. I have control over them, but they are still…well, like I said, they're autonomous. They'll lose focus after a while and go off in search of easier prey. It'd be a pointless endeavor."

"So you need me," Colin concluded. "And my price is that you keep your infected away from my cattle."

Lander gazed skyward for a long, awkward moment. Then he lowered his eyes to Colin's once again. "Stillborn calves, sick ones, and old ones."

Colin frowned. "What?"

"That's the deal I'll make with you," Lander explained. "I'll keep my family away from your cattle, provided you give us your stillborn calves, and any other cattle that gets sick or too old. I mean, what do you do with them anyway? You probably just leave them wherever they die. Give them to us." He flashed a smile. "Waste not, want not, that's what I always say."

Colin knew a good thing when he saw it. It cost him nothing, and it gained him security for his herd. "I'll do that deal."

"Splendid," Lander said, grinning. "We'll be back this evening. If you have what I want, then you'll get what you want."

No one in the Redoubt knew how it was going to happen—only that it *was* going to happen, and sooner rather than later.

Colin Horner's patience had run out, and he was coming for them.

The tension had set like a bad pudding, making the air thick and worrisome. The energy was manic and tight-gutted, thin-lipped and dry-mouthed. People clutched rifles in ways that made it oh-so-obvious that they'd only been taught how to properly use one that very day. And they all knew there was a world of difference between being taught how to do something, and actually knowing how to do it.

"Well," Abe said, smiling through the ominous atmosphere. "At least we got a half day of training in."

No one in the gathering of recently armed and briefed residents found that sentiment particularly encouraging, and let Abe know how they felt with a fusillade of disbelieving and disgusted looks.

Abe doffed his smile and donned his customary frown. "Hey. Five hours of training is better than no hours of training."

Still no takers, it seemed. Abe cast an evaluating look at Sam and Jones, who both discreetly shook their heads at him as though to say, *maybe you should let someone else do the pep talks*.

"You're gonna have us set up for an ambush like we practiced," a voice called out, all tinged and strained with worry. Sam was not surprised to find that it was Asher. "But what if they don't come in that way? What if they don't even attack us like that? What if they send the infected after us like they did to everyone else?"

To that, Abe offered a casual shrug. "We have no idea what they're going to do, or when they're going to do it. That's why we're going to set up to execute an ambush, but we're also going to keep our friend Bea in the lookout, so if they come at us another way, we can respond. Adapt and overcome."

"Adapt and overcome?" Asher echoed, as though the core concepts there were deep mysteries of the universe that he couldn't fathom.

Jones swaggered forward, hips swinging like he had a six-shooter on each. Sam could almost hear the spurs jingling with each step. "Alright, check it out, folks. Y'all got all these big old metal containers. If he sends the primals again, then we'll fall back to our Conex boxes. Until then, we're going to remain outside, because if he sends anyone with guns, then those just become family-sized coffins. And if we're going to remain outside of the boxes, we might as well use them as cover and concealment. And if we're using them as cover and concealment, we might as well set up to spring an ambush. Yeah? See? It all works out."

Jones seemed satisfied, though no one in the Redoubt seemed to share that feeling. He looked over his shoulder and nodded at Sam.

"What?" Sam furrowed his brow. "We all gotta say something?"

Jones gave him a severe look and jagged his eyes towards the crowd.

Sam sighed. *I guess this is what we're doing today.*

He stepped forward reluctantly, raising his voice. "Guys, I know you're all nervous. I know you think you'd feel better if we had a plan for every eventuality. That'd make you feel nice and secure. But that would be the wrong decision in this specific situation. Our best course of action is to remain loose and fluid, ready to change gears at a moment's notice. Just pay attention to what's going on around you, don't get sucked into tunnel vision, and listen for a change in orders." He offered them a smile, but unlike Abe's, his was *actually* encouraging. "Trust us, guys. We know what we're doing. Now, how about everyone get into position. You don't need to be hard in the paint and rifle up and all that. Just find yourself a spot of shade and try to stay relaxed and hydrated and listen for commands. Aight?" Sam clapped his hands together and gave the gathered residents a sweeping, dismissive gesture.

Predictable murmuring followed this, but they began to disperse and move towards their assigned positions.

Sam caught Jones's gaze, and then Abe's, and jerked his head towards their recently-reclaimed pickup truck, now parked adjacent to Bea's Conex box. Silently, all three trudged over and got in.

As soon as the final door closed, Jones said what they were all thinking: "We have no idea what we're doing."

Sam, sitting in the front passenger's seat, turned to look at Abe in the driver's seat. "Shouldn't we be doing something about Lee and Marie?"

"Like what?" Abe asked, clearly frustrated.

"Like finding out what happened to them."

"And just leave the Redoubt to their own devices?"

Sam made a grim face and shook his head.

Jones wasn't quite so opposed to the idea. "I mean, Lee and Marie could be strung up in a slaughterhouse right now, waiting for a rescue. And these people? Man, I hate to say it, but is sticking around here really gonna do them any good?"

"Of course it'll do them some good," Sam retorted. "Three good rifles might make the difference."

Jones made a doubtful noise. "We're supposed to be calling audibles, but do you really think these people are up for that? They're gonna be so amped up the second there's a dust cloud on the horizon—" he mimed explosions next to his ears. "—poof. Auditory exclusion. They ain't gonna hear *shit*. And even if they could, they're gonna be too scared to do what we tell them."

Sam twisted in his seat to glare at his friend in the back. "So just leave them? Abandon them? Like we did to Rampart on the Border?"

Jones winced, but leaned forward, elbows on knees. He looked earnestly into Sam's face. "No, dude. This isn't like Rampart at all. Because in Rampart, we had *weeks* to train them. We've only had basic instruction on *one tactic* over the course of five hours. And the shit is hitting the fan. Prognosis is bad, brother. We made the call to get out of Rampart, and as much as it may chap your ass to hear it, that was the right call. Otherwise we'd be dead with them."

"So you're just scared?" Sam challenged.

Jones only blew a raspberry at that. "Don't even try that shit on me, Rough Ryder. It don't work. I'm being a realist."

"Alright," Sam said. "Fuck you, then." He glanced pointedly between Jones and Abe. "I'm fuckin' stayin'. Y'all wanna poof, go right ahead. But I'm not leaving."

Abe gave a derogatory chuff and mushed Sam back into his seat. "Cool your nuts, Rambo, no one's leaving."

"Dammit," Jones muttered. "Thought we were still hashing out our options."

"Well, that ain't one of 'em," Abe shot over his shoulder. "I'm just as worried about Lee and Marie as you, Jonesy, but Sam's right. No way in hell I'm cranking this truck up right now and just driving out of here. I can live with a lot of cold-hearted shit, but that won't be one."

"You sure?" Jones sighed, staring out the side window. "It'd be super easy to do. I can do it for you, if you'd like."

Sam rounded on Jones again. "Seriously, Jones? What's gotten into you? I've never heard you sound like such a flake."

"Uhhh," Jones frowned at him, raising his fingers to tick them off, one by one. "Lee's gone. Marie's gone. The residents don't know what the fuck they're doing." Three fingers. Then he raised a fourth. "And, going back to Lee and Marie being gone—our enemy is clearly not to be underestimated."

Sam opened his mouth to retort, but Jones cut him off, putting all those fingers into a knife hand that jutted at Sam's nose. "And you're sitting here acting like I'm being a coward, but I'm not advocating we tuck tail and run—I'm advocating that we go find out what happened to Lee and Marie, who, I might remind you, could quite possibly be about to fucking die. You care more about these randos than your own team, Sam?"

Sam didn't know how to answer that question, but Jones didn't give him a chance anyway.

"And here's another thing," Jones said, switching his knife hand to Abe, who regarded it like a pro linebacker might regard the Pop Warner kid that's vowed to run him over. "Strategically speaking, the best time to infiltrate Horner's Peak and try to find Lee and Marie is when Horner's got all his men on the warpath. And don't even try to deny that that's smart."

"First of all," Abe said, still staring at the knife hand. He pushed it back towards its owner. "Put that thing away. Second of all, you're right—that's literally the smartest thing you've said since I've known you. Third of all, it doesn't matter, because we're not leaving the Redoubt."

"Bullshit," Jones said, slumping back into his seat. "If you'd've come up with it, we'd already be doing it."

"No, we wouldn't," Abe said. "And don't be churlish."

Jones's face screwed up. "What does that even mean?"

"You," Abe replied. "How you're being right now. *That's* churlish."

"You mean practical, logical, and good-looking, with a dash of well-founded concern for my missing friends?"

"Even now," Sam marveled at him. "You're *still* making jokes."

"No, I'm *seriously* advocating for going after Lee and Marie, because apparently I'm the only one in this truck that gives a shit about them."

"Goddammit, we're not going!" Abe suddenly roared, with a punctuating hammer-fist to the center console.

In the brief moment of silence following Abe's outburst, they all heard it: Bea, in the lookout, yelling, "Contact! Contact! Contact!"

Immediately, the cab turned into a whirl of motion, the doors springing open, boots and gear and knees and elbows clattering in a mad rush.

"Well, we can't go anywhere now!" Jones shouted angrily at them.

As Sam tumbled out of the truck, snatching his rifle from where it was leaning against the fender, he stole a glance at the Redoubters. Despite his best mental efforts, what Jones had said got his brain all tangled up, and he expected them to be flying off into a panic. But, lo and behold and thank the heavens, they were doing what they were supposed to be doing, on their points of cover, rifles shouldered.

Hell, maybe Abe had been right: Five hours of training was better than none.

Abe sprinted ahead of Sam and hit the supports of the lockout first, slapping it twice with a dull metallic ring. "Watcha got, Bea? Talk to me!"

Sam skidded in beside him, checking his bolt and mag.

"Dust cloud," Bea said from above. "Dead east. Two hills away. Maybe three quarters of a mile."

Abe's thick, black brows scrunched together. "That the road straight into here?"

"No, it's too far to the north of the road."

Sam stared at Abe until the other man looked back at him. "Change of plans?"

Abe bared his teeth, but shook his head. "Not yet."

Sam heard the scudding of footsteps behind him and whipped around in time to see Ted tearing up, his ridiculous revolver in hand, pointed at the sky like an '80's movie cop.

"Are they coming straight in?" Ted said, breathlessly, and half at a whisper.

"What?" Abe shouted back, unnecessarily loud. "Why are you whispering? They can't fucking hear you. Talk like you're not scared. Your people are watching."

Ted swallowed. Straightened a bit. "Are they coming straight in?" he repeated, louder. "Is it the ambush? Are we doing the ambush thing?"

Sam could see the way Abe's face seemed to twitch and roil, and decided to step in before any semblance of goodwill was burned to ashes. "We don't know yet, Ted," Sam spoke quickly. "Get back on your position. If the plan changes, we will let you know, I promise."

Ted nodded rapidly and started backpedaling. "Okay. Alright. Shit." Then he spun and high-tailed it back to where he belonged.

"Hold up," Bea said from above. "I got another dust cloud, this one way to the south now."

Sam stepped out from under the lookout, took a glance up to see where Bea was now pointing her rifle, and then turned to follow her gaze. "Yeah, I see it," he said. A tan smudge on the horizon to the south. A straight shot down the Redoubt's main street.

"Bea, keep checking that horizon," Abe instructed. "I wanna know anything else that pops up." Abe snapped his fingers to get Sam's attention, then hiked a thumb upwards. "Climb up there and put eyes on the east while she's scanning."

"Yup," Sam acknowledged, slinging his rifle and catching the pair of binocs that Jones tossed to him. He swung onto the ladder and clambered up.

Bea stood in the center of the lookout, her feet straddling the hole Sam was coming up through. She turned in a slow circle, squinting through her scope. "Clear so far, except for the south and east."

Sam squirmed past her, then knelt at the east-facing wall and propped the binoculars on the lip of the sheet metal. He controlled his breathing and turned the focus knob. The gently rolling hills to the east snapped into sharp relief.

"Eyes on the east," Sam called down to Abe. "Got visual on one, red, midsize pickup. Looks like multiple armed subjects in the truck bed. Heading straight at us over the second ridge out." He paused. Licked his lips. Tried to get a head count as the truck slalomed down the hill, the occupants jostling violently in the bed. "I see a lot of long guns. Can't give you specifics. Maybe...eight dudes? They're dropping into the valley between the hills."

They dropped out of sight. Sam peeked up over the binocs, feeling his pulse in his throat, in his fingertips. When the red truck came up out of that valley, it would be on the nearest ridge, just to their east, maybe a third of a mile out.

"Looks like they're trying for a pincer move," Sam called down. "Bea, whatcha got to the south?"

"Large black dually," she said. "I see people in the back, but I can't tell how many. It's coming straight on. No...wait..."

Sam tore his eyes off his own binoculars to steal a glance at Bea. She was leaning one elbow against one of the lookout's supports, her face scrunched into a frown.

"I think they're stopping," she said, as though mystified. "Yeah, they definitely just stopped."

"They stopped?" Abe called from below.

"Yeah, they stopped and the guys are getting out."

Sam pressed his eyes back into his binoculars as he heard Jones's voice, "They gonna try to take us on foot? I'm not sure how I feel about that."

"Well, that'd be fucking dumb," Abe pointed out. "They'll be exposed on the sides of the hills coming in. I mean, great for us...but dumb."

Sam felt a sinking feeling that he couldn't quite pin to a source, as he stared through his binoculars, wondering if he'd shifted out of line with his target. Because they hadn't come up over the hill yet. He scanned the line of tall grasses cresting the hill but saw nothing. Not even a dust cloud.

"Hey, that red pickup never came up on the other side of the hill," Sam warned.

"They're not coming in," Bea said, her volume climbing. For a moment, Sam thought she was talking about the red pickup to the east, but then she clarified: "All the guys—they're taking positions on the ridge. They're disappearing into the grass."

"Ah, shit," was all Abe said from below.

"Yo, those are not good angles for us," Jones's voice sang out.

Sam rose to his feet, looking down at the Redoubters, and seeing exactly what Jones was saying. Almost all of the boxes in the settlement were aligned north to south, with their broad sides to the east and west. Positioned as the people were now for an ambush, they were exposed to the east. But if they moved, they'd be exposed to the south.

"Hey, Abe, I think—" Sam whipped his gaze to the east, just in time for his eyes to catch the tiniest little puff of gray from amidst the waving grasses on the eastern ridge. Then there was a *zzzzip* and a loud, wet, *whap*.

And then Bea screamed.

Chapter 22

The sound of the single, distant gunshot rolled across the sky.

Lee and Marie both came to an abrupt stop, their hearts immediately hammering, breath caught in their chests. They'd both been shot at enough to know that if you hear the gunshot with no accompanying *zip-crack*, then the bullet wasn't aimed at you. Still, they both instinctively hunched, not quite squatting, but no longer standing erect.

Lee scanned the horizon ahead of them, where the gunshot had seemed to come from, but saw nothing. Then he glanced to Marie, his eyebrows arching.

She nodded. "The Redoubt."

They were only a few hundred yards from the hill with the two trees that Lander Hollis had pointed out to them, beyond which he said they would see the Redoubt. And it suddenly seemed to Lee like there weren't a whole lot of other explanations for that gunshot, aside from the one he didn't want to accept: Colin Horner was attacking the Redoubt.

Still, Lee held up a staying hand. "It was only one shot. Let's not..."

The air suddenly crackled with the sound of a gunbattle—hectic and arrhythmic.

"Motherfucker!" Marie took off at what was probably intended to be a sprint, but was much more of a rapid hobble. Lee couldn't do much better.

They thrashed up the hill through the waist-high grass, forced to wade through it and high-step around clumps. Lee's ribs screamed from the effort, made worse by his heaving breath. That hamstring started to squeal again, but it'd just have to wait, because Lee had no more time to pander to his broken body.

Marie hit a narrow game trail that seemed to lead up the hill to the two trees, and her pace quickened, Lee finding it just seconds after.

As they neared the top of the hill, the tempo of the gunfight in the distance abruptly changed, becoming slow and sporadic.

Lee knew exactly what this shift in tempo was. Everyone had unloaded during the initial clash, but now everything slowed as fighters dug into cover and began to choose their shots.

Marie hit the top of the ridge just ahead of him, and pulled up short, sinking towards the ground so that just her head and shoulders were above the grass. She held up a fist so Lee wouldn't go barging past her. She was seeing something, and it wasn't good.

Lee came abreast of her, hissing air and froth through his teeth, bent at the waist with his hands on his knees.

The ridge they were on was part of a line of hills that formed a rough circle around the Redoubt. The settlement lay in the center of that circle, perhaps a little over a mile south of them.

Of all the parts of his body that had failed him over the years, Lee counted himself blessed to be pushing forty and still have eyesight as keen as he had in his twenties. Of course, he only had the one eye, but at least it wasn't nearsighted.

He spotted a mash of bodies, trying to hold a bit of cover on the far western side of the settlement. It was obvious that they were under fire, and equally obvious that they weren't doing much shooting back.

"There!" Marie snapped, dipping lower in the grass and pointing a finger to the east of the Redoubt.

Lee sidled up next to her, aiming his good eye down her arm and spotting what she was pointing at. From their vantage point, Lee could just make out the top of a red pickup truck, positioned so that the circular ridgeline was between it and the Redoubt.

And then he saw movement in the grass. Right there on the very top of the ridge, just a handful of yards from the red truck: A man leapt up, sprinted a few yards, then went prone again, disappearing into the grass.

Like spotting one ant, and then realizing there are many more, Lee suddenly saw movement in multiple areas along that ridge. The tell-tale twitch as the grass was buffeted by muzzle blasts that spat out barely-perceptible plumes of smoke.

Immediately, Lee's gaze snapped up and scanned the rest of the ridge, knowing what he would find even before he did. And there it was: Another pickup truck, this one not quite so well concealed, but much farther away, to the south of the Redoubt.

Lee's heart slammed with nothing that had to do with exertion. His dehydrated body managed to summon enough moisture to wet his palms. "Shit. You see that other truck to the south?"

"Yeah, I got it."

"They're pinning them down and picking them off."

Marie's head started shaking. "There's no way we can make it in there without getting pegged on the way in."

Lee had already deduced that. They were stuck. And in a horrific flash, memories of Rampart at the Border began to flood his mind. The feeling of powerlessness as you watched people being slaughtered, one by one. People you should have been able to protect.

Except that it wasn't just the people of the Redoubt down there. His team was down there too.

His family—or at least the closest he would ever get in this life.

He couldn't let Rampart happen all over again. And he sure as shit couldn't leave his boys down there to get picked apart. Not today. Not ever.

But what was he going to do in his current physical state, with not a single weapon on him?

Growling, Lee set his teeth and slapped Marie on the shoulder. "Come with me."

Sam's first instinct as he watched Bea crumple to the floor of the lookout was to unload his rifle in the general direction of east. His second, more measured thought, was that doing so would only draw more attention to their little metal death box.

Instead, he immediately dropped, sending up a silent prayer that he hadn't been noticed, and yelled to Abe and Jones below, "Bea's down!"

A bullet punched a hole in the metal siding, just over Sam's left shoulder, then another poked through the wall right above Bea's squirming body.

Squirming—that was a good thing. Also, the fact that she was still screaming.

Sam wrestled the loop of the binos over his neck and crawled towards Bea, his rifle clattering and scraping along the floor underneath him. "Talk to me, Bea! Where you hit?"

She only seethed out another stretch of screams.

Sam skittered up next to her. She was writhing so violently he had to elbow one of her legs down to keep her from kneeing him in the face. She was half on her back, half on her left side, with her right arm flopping, and her left arm clutching her chest.

"Hey!" Sam shouted at her face, trying to pull her hand away so he could check the wound.

Bea's eyes shot open, wide and pouring tears. "My back!" she snarled at him.

She was stronger than she looked. Sam expected her hand to come away from her chest more easily, but she was fighting him. He swore and put more oomph into it. Her hand pulled away, trembling in his grip, revealing a growing patch of blood spreading over the upper right side of her chest, just in the pocket of her shoulder.

"My fucking back!" she screamed at him, face livid and veins popping out in her forehead.

"Your fucking shoulder!" Sam yelled back, not at all surprised that she wasn't clear on where her injuries were. He yanked her shirt open, popping a button that went pinging off the metal wall beside them. Caught sight of the wound. Saw the swollen flesh, with the uneven hole in the middle, bits of muscle tissue hanging out. That was an exit wound if he'd ever seen one.

Bea wasn't wrong about her back—it was just that her brain was only processing the pain of the entry wound. By pulling her onto her side, Sam saw the dribble of dark blood coming from the much neater-looking hole, just between her spine and her right shoulder blade. It'd entered there, and then blown out the front of her shoulder.

They needed to get out of this death box, pronto. "I'm gonna move you," Sam said, as gunshots reverberated through the walls. He grabbed her by her left arm and pulled her towards the hole, still trying to keep his body low.

He stuck his head through the hole, but couldn't see anyone below. "Abe! Jones!"

"Yo!" Jones's voice came back up, followed by the snap of five suppressed rifle shots.

"I'm gonna lower Bea down to you!"

Jones shouted something that Sam couldn't make out. Didn't matter anyhow. Sam was already pushing Bea into the hole.

"Don't drop me!" Bea managed between clenched teeth, her bucking diaphragm causing her words to shake.

"I'm not gonna drop you," Sam said. "I got you. I'm right here. I'm gonna hold on, and Jones is gonna take your feet." He didn't wait for her to be ready. He pushed on her left shoulder, sliding her lower body further into the hole. "Jones, she's coming down!"

"Hurry the fuck up! My ass is in the wind down here!"

Sam wrapped his arm around Bea's left, gripping her tightly just above the elbow and then pushed her all the way through.

She grunted as gravity took her body. The weight came down on her shoulder. Sam lurched and spread his feet, straining to keep himself from being sucked down with her. She gasped, and then squealed, so high-pitched that Sam found himself rattled.

"It's alright! You're okay!" he shouted, though there was no way she could have heard him over her own screaming.

"Bring her down more!" Jones yelled.

Sam shimmied his body. Both of his arms were now through the hole, the edge of it biting into his armpits. He tried to peek down but only caught a flurry of limbs—Jones's hands trying to harness Bea's thrashing legs.

"Stop fucking kicking me!" Jones roared at her, then managed to hug her legs to his chest. "I got her!"

Sam let go.

Jones had tried to position himself so she'd flop over onto his shoulder, all nice and tidy. She did not, instead pitching sideways and pulling Jones off balance. He stumbled, trying to stay under her, but he was going down and knew it. He twisted as he did, turning his own body into a crash pad for hers. The two of them went down in a wallop of flesh.

Sam scrambled his legs through the hole and dropped the ten feet to the ground. He hit the dirt in a forward roll that was anything but graceful, his rifle swinging around and clocking him in the groin. He groaned, but didn't have the time to take a knee and wait for the branching pain to abate. He immediately scrambled towards Jones and Bea, sliding down to one knee, his rifle shouldered.

"Get her to cover!" Sam shouted, then dumped his mag at the eastern ridgeline. He'd hoped for some muzzle flashes to aim for, but there was nothing. He was just spraying and praying.

"Reloading!" Sam shouted, sparing a glance behind him as he dropped his empty mag and went for another. A flurry of suppressed gunshots ripped over his head. Jones had pulled Bea up onto her feet, holding her with his left arm while he backed up, hip-firing his rifle—not towards the east, but straight down the main drag towards their attackers to the south.

They were exposed on both sides.

Sam seated the new mag and dropped the bolt. "I'm up! Crossing!"

Jones held his fire as Sam surged to his feet and put himself between the enemy to the south and his retreating friends. In the distance, he could still make out the very top of the black pickup truck on the southern ridge, and—there! A little puff of gray and a twitch of the surrounding grass.

He shouldered his rifle as he backpedaled, then paused just long enough to bear down on a breath and squeeze the trigger in steady procession—five rounds right on that spot he'd seen. He had no clue if he'd hit anything, but spun around and cut the corner of the box after Jones and Bea.

They now had cover from their attackers to the south, but were still exposed to the east. Sam turned his back on Jones and Bea, right shoulder to the wall, backing up as he covered the eastern ridge.

"Stop fucking dragging me!" Bea shouted with encouraging gusto.

"Then use your fucking feet and run!" Jones yelled back at her.

Sam heard their shuffling stumble turn into pounding feet and figured they'd ghosted for cover, so he gave the eastern ridgeline one more sweep, then turned and sprinted the last few yards to the end of the box.

Sam turned the corner and saw that they were in a convenient nook...with about ten other people. It was the corner between two boxes—Bea's, which happened to be one of the few oriented east-west, corner-to-corner with one of the others which was oriented north-south. The corners didn't touch, leaving about a foot of gap that everyone shied away from, but it was the best bit of cover, given the angles that their attackers had on them. Unfortunately, it was already overcrowded.

Sam scanned the faces for Abe, but he wasn't there. Where had that asshole run off to? Sam reached for the PTT button on his chest, and realized—far too late to do anything about it—that they'd left their radios charging in the pickup.

No contact with Abe.

Bea and Jones were against what would have been the back wall of Bea's Conex box. She groaned and slid down the wall, leaving a smear of blood behind, while Jones shouldered his rifle again and inched towards the gap in the corner.

"They're shooting at us through that gap!" someone said, clearly trying to dissuade Jones.

"It's okay," Jones said, testily. "I'm a professional."

Sam fervently hoped that Jones hadn't just jinxed himself. Keeping one eye on his friend, Sam squatted in front of Bea and took her face in his hands, forcing her to look at him. Her eyes were cinched with pain, the tears still coming, but she wasn't fading.

"You're doing great," Sam said, slinging his rifle off to his left side and ripping the IFAK from the side of his plate carrier. "Bullet went all the way through. I know that sounds bad, but it's actually a good thing."

To which Bea only responded, "Motherfucker!"

He wasn't sure if that was directed at him, or whoever had shot her. "That's good," he said, his hands working rapidly, pulling a pack of hemostatic gauze and two chest seals from the IFAK. "You stay mad. Stay awake. Keep talking."

Bea's version of talking was to unleash every swear she knew.

But that was a good sign. Clearly she wasn't having trouble breathing, so hopefully the bullet had missed her lung. He grabbed her shirt and ripped it so the rest of the buttons came flying off. Sam pulled the shirt down her back and fully off of her limp right arm. It left Bea in only a bra, but she had bigger problems than exposure.

"Can you move that arm?" he asked, as he set the two chest seals on the ground and ripped open the gauze.

If she tried, he couldn't tell.

"I can't move it. Is that bad?"

"Hon, you've been shot," Sam said. "It's definitely not good. But I'm here, and I'm gonna patch you up. I got you. I'm not gonna let anything bad happen to you."

The second those words left his lips, he instantly regretted them. What kind of bullshit was that? He couldn't make those kinds of promises.

He pulled a length of gauze out and wadded it into a ball around his index finger. He caught Bea looking at the gauze, and then looking at him, clearly terrified. He nodded, sympathetically.

"This is gonna suck. Bite down or scream. I gotta do it to stop the bleeding."

"Waitwaitwait!" Bea's good hand shot out and grabbed his. "Don't you have something for the pain?"

Sam hesitated. Just long enough for Jones to let out a yelp as a flurry of projectiles pinged off the corner where his head had just been and lanced into the dirt, sending up a wash of dust.

"I told you—" someone started to shout.

"I don't wanna hear it!" Jones snapped, rolling onto his knees and coming up breathing hard in Sam's face. "They're not pushing on us," he said, his tone full of dread.

"Isn't that a good thing?" one of the other people huddled close to them asked.

"The adults are talking!" Jones shouted over his shoulder, then whipped back to Sam. "Why are they not pushing on us, Sam?"

"I don't fucking know!" Oh, yeah. Something for Bea's pain. He looked at her seriously. "I got morphine, but it might knock you out."

She was breathing hard and fast and shallow.

"You want me to hold her down?" Jones asked, to which Bea looked horrified.

"Bea, I gotta stop the bleeding, and that means packing the wound. I don't think—" He was about to say that he didn't think she should take the morphine in the middle of a fight, but she cut him off, grabbing a handful of his shirtsleeve.

"Give it to me." Her eyes were pleading.

Shouldn't have even told her I had it, he thought, even as his hand dipped back into the IFAK, his fingers finding the set of four, single-use injectables. He pulled one out. Thumbed off the cap, and, without preamble, stuck it straight into Bea's shoulder, right next to the wound.

She winced. Then she frowned, eyes darting between the injection site and Sam, like she thought it should have hit her immediately. By the time Sam got his ball of gauze ready again and placed a steadying hand on her shoulder, it did. Her eyebrows arched as though surprised, all the tension suddenly leaving her face.

"Oh...shit," she murmured.

"Great," Jones grumbled, rising to his feet. "She's a lightweight. Now we're gonna hafta carry her."

Sam pressed the thumb of his free hand against the hole in her shoulder. She didn't react to it. He could feel her blood seeping around his thumb to the rhythm of her pulse.

"Sam," Bea slurred.

He positioned his index finger with its ball of gauze right at the wound opening, but paused long enough to look her in the eyes. Which were half lidded and fluttering.

"Don't leave me," she husked.

Shit.

"I won't," he promised—again, before he could really think about what that promise meant.

Double shit.

Then he pressed the gauze into the wound channel.

Bea let out a low, mournful moan, as though the concept of the pain was only a dream. And then she passed out.

Chapter 23

Abe was not far away.

As soon as the first volleys had erupted, Abe had left Jones with Sam and sprinted for the people all bunched up along the main drag. Their attackers on the eastern ridge had started firing first, causing everyone to instinctively move to cover, clustering with their backs to the main street.

Completely exposed to the shooters on the south ridge.

Their error had not gone unnoticed, and their attackers had not let them off easy.

Dozens of people clustered along the main drag, and as Abe sprinted towards them, already shouting at them to keep moving, he watched them start to fall. Men and women and children, all screaming in unison, their alarm turning to abject panic as they watched friends and family members keel over.

Abe ran straight at a kid who stood as though his feet were rooted to the ground, staring at a fallen friend and yelling out a long, single note of anguish. For a moment he couldn't remember the kid's name, but decided to shout at him anyway.

"Move, motherfucker! Run!"

The kid never even looked up. The back of his head disappeared in a spray and he pitched forward, his expression of grief and terror never leaving his face. It was only after he slumped over the body of his dead friend that Abe remembered his name.

Oh, yeah—Asher.

Rounds zipped down the main drag, targeting the hapless civilians clustered against the boxes. Abe ran straight for them, realizing they didn't even know where they were being shot at from. They were falling, but they didn't know why. Higher-order thinking and problem solving were out the window.

"Move, goddammit!" Abe roared at them, hitting the wall with a metallic bang. He grabbed whoever he could get a hand on and propelled them out into the main drag. "Go! Run! Get to the west side of the settlement! West side! The fucking *west side*!"

The first man that Abe shoved into a run got two steps in before his guts were opened by a flurry of passing rounds, sending him spinning and shrieking. Abe didn't have time to feel guilty for that. He just kept grabbing them and shoving them and screaming in their faces to move, to run to the west side.

He got about five people in before the rest started to realize where the bullets were coming from. All it took was for a few people to launch themselves off the walls and tear across the main drag for the rest to get the picture. A stampede ensued, a few people collapsing in the middle of the road as bullets found them.

Abe finally found the person he'd been looking for. Ted crouched with his face to the wall and both hands to his head, as though trying to cover his ears. His big revolver trembled next to his temple.

Abe posted over Ted, shouldering his rifle and screaming at anyone that might hear him: "Shoot south! Suppressive fire!" They'd taught them what suppressive fire was, and a few people that were tearing across the street were at least sending haphazard shots in the direction of their attackers, but that was about all Abe was going to get out of them, and he knew it.

He targeted the ridgeline and let loose, stitching a steady pattern of single shots from right to left. Then, keeping his rifle trained in that direction, he reached down with his support hand, grabbed

Ted's collar, and hauled him up. Ted let out a wail, as though he thought he were being attacked. Abe pointed him west and shoved him in the back. "Go that way!"

Ted at least had the wherewithal to run, and Abe followed behind him, emptying the last of his magazine to the south. He didn't even bother to call his reload—no one was listening, and no one would have the presence of mind to cover him while he reloaded anyway. He knocked it out in two fluid movements, and got right back to shooting as he crossed the main drag at a sprint.

Something hit his plate carrier, punching his chest and jerking his whole body. One of his mags disintegrated—spring and follower flying off in a fountain of spinning cartridges. He'd never seen a magazine burst like that. Like a fucking Jack-in-the-box. It was almost funny. Except that it scared the shit out of him.

He passed someone trying to drag along a body that was clearly already dead. Abe kicked the woman's arms from what might've been her husband. "Leave him! He's dead!"

He didn't wait to see if she obeyed.

He reached the boxes on the other side of the main drag and squirted down the narrow alley between them, several running figures ahead of him. Bullets ripped the air around them, coming from the east, nipping at their heels and screaming past their ears.

He thought he saw Ted straight ahead. The man was running like he didn't intend to stop until he got to the Pacific.

What's the plan here, Abe? he asked himself as he hurdled a fallen body.

He needed to regroup. He needed to figure out what the hell Colin Horner was trying to accomplish. The initial volleys had been devastating, but if Horner's plan was to just sit on a ridge and take potshots, then this could take a long time. Which was a good thing. With enough time, Abe could find a way to turn things around.

As he reached the last row of boxes on the west end, Abe cut the corner to his right and posted up. He checked the ridgeline to the south. Their current position had edged out their attacker's angles. It was a shallow reprieve, but Abe would take what he could get.

All along the boxes, those that had survived the first attack were keeping their bodies tight to their cover, knowing that if they stepped away from those walls, even just a few yards, they'd be visible again. As many bodies as Abe had seen drop, there still seemed to be plenty amongst the living.

Abe did a rapid count, skipping the people that were clearly unarmed. Of those that bore at least some sort of firearm, Abe guesstimated he had twenty, maybe twenty-five fighters. There had to be others—they just weren't here. And where the hell had Sam and Jones gone? They hadn't even had a chance to get their comms up and running, so coordinating with them would require face-to-face interaction.

God, he hoped they were still alive.

Someone pawed at his back. "What're we gonna do?!"

Abe spun, irritation turning to disgust as he saw Ted huddled there, eyes wide and watery behind glasses that sat askew on his face, speckles of dirt across the lenses.

Abe jerked his shoulder free of Ted's grasp, then rounded on him and grabbed the man by the front of his shirt. "First, I need you to unfuck yourself."

"Unfuck myself?"

"Stand up!" Abe jerked Ted around by his shirt until he was more or less standing upright. "Take a deep breath and stop mewling like a lost kitten."

A flash of indignation was about all the fight that Ted had in him, but at least it was something. His face flushed and his loose-lipped, slack-jawed mouth closed and tensed.

"Where's the rest of your people?" Abe demanded.

"I don't know!" Ted shot back. "There was shooting and then everybody was running and—"

"Alright, shut up." Abe held a finger up to Ted's nose. "Your people still need you. Keep it together."

Ted's nostrils flared. "Tell me what to do."

"Stay with me, and do what I do," Abe grunted, then turned himself back to the people huddled in cover.

The gunfire had slowed dramatically. Only a single shot every few seconds, and even that was slowing. Horner's men had them pinned down on the west end of the Redoubt, and they were keeping them covered, only shooting now when someone showed a piece of themselves.

For what purpose?

Abe stalked down the side of the box. Each person he came to he touched with a firm hand on the shoulder or a slap on the back. "You good?" he asked, and mostly got vacant nods. He glanced over their bodies, checking them for wounds—sometimes people didn't even realize they'd been hit. A few had minor wounds—grazes and such. But, somewhat surprisingly, everyone else seemed whole.

"Everyone top off your ammo!" Abe shouted down the line. "Make sure you got a full mag! Stay in cover unless I tell you different!"

Abe reached the end of one box. A ten-foot gap to the next one. On the other side, another dozen or so people, watching him intently. He turned to Ted. "Cut across the opening and check on your people. Do what I just did."

A bit late in the game for leadership training, but hey, sometimes you have to learn on the fly.

Ted gawped, but, luckily for his face—which Abe intended to smack if he protested—he kept silent, then steeled himself, and bolted across the opening.

A single shot split the air just behind Ted as he reached the other side. He proceeded down the line of people, doing his best to mimic Abe's example.

Alright. So they had twenty-some-odd fighters, with no clue what Horner's strategy was, outside of a protracted engagement of taking shots at each other from a distance. If Horner kept his guys in position on the ridgeline and didn't try to aggress or flank them, then Abe's only reasonable option at this point was to attempt some sort of counter-attack by flanking *them*.

The thought twisted his guts. There was no way Abe could get these people to do any sort of assault maneuver at this point. A bounding assault might've been basic to his thinking, but it was far too advanced for them.

He turned and checked the lay of the land to the west, hoping there was a hill he could exfil the people behind. Because the Universe apparently hated him, the terrain was pretty much flat going straight west. The ridge that encircled the Redoubt was more of a horseshoe shape, and he was staring at the open end of it.

He twisted and looked a little to the north. That was where the horseshoe started. The first ridge was maybe half a mile out. Could they make it over that ridge on foot? If they kept a single-file line and decent tactical spacing, probably not a *lot* of them would get hit.

Probably.

If he pulled everyone out and got them over that ridge, they'd essentially be handing over the Redoubt. But what other options did he have? They were packed in too tight, and were under too much coverage to make any decent counter-assault from their current position. They needed to fall back to some semblance of safety, and the hills to the northwest seemed like the only option.

Any plan was better than sitting here, waiting to get picked off.

"Abe!" Ted's voice barged into his thoughts.

Abe looked to his left, where Ted stood on the other side of the gap between boxes. A random shot struck the metal corner just a foot or so from Abe's face, causing him to flinch as metal fragments nipped at his face.

Ted made a thumbs up when Abe looked at him again. "Everyone's good!" Which was probably an overstatement. "What now?"

Abe waved his hand. "Come back over here!"

Ted's shoulders slumped, then cinched up tight, and he sprinted wildly across. Another bullet chased him, but the shooter's reaction was too late. The bullet hit the dirt well after Ted had already ducked into cover beside Abe.

"Alright," Abe said, grabbing Ted's heaving shoulders and pointing to the hill northwest of them. "We're gonna gather everyone together, and make for that ridge right there. You need to..."

Abe trailed off as a new sound reached him. It was distant, and he almost hadn't even picked it up. But it was a sound that was connected to a whole lot of bad feelings, and Abe's subconscious didn't let him miss it.

A howl.

And suddenly Colin Horner's plan became clear.

Chapter 24

Bran hated that sound.

Also, he hated this plan. Particularly the part where he was required to drive this goddamned ATV ahead of a horde of infected.

Colin wanted things to be *timed* correctly, so they couldn't just sit around and wait for the infected to show up. Colin wanted them to show up at a specific time—namely, after a few volleys of gunfire had pushed all the residents of the Redoubt out of their metal boxes. And that meant that Bran and Kat had to go fetch these damn things and lead them on a chase, keeping them in something of a holding pattern until it was go time.

They'd been positioned about two miles away while the fight broke out at the Redoubt, running the creatures in a huge circle until Colin had transmitted over the little two-way radio: "Bran, send 'em in."

Now, they were hurtling straight at the Redoubt, with Kat standing up in the passenger seat, hands gripping the rollbars, with her head tilted back, howling at the sky.

Bran glanced back and saw the horde trailing them by maybe a hundred yards. It still felt way too close. Then he looked forward again and checked the ATV's battery life for the umpteenth time. They had about a third of a charge left on it. And that also felt way too close.

"Alright, Kat!" Bran said with just a hint of irritation at the ear-jangling howl. "I think we got 'em. Redoubt's just over the next ridge."

Kat dropped back into her seat. Her bandana was pulled down around her neck, and she didn't seem inclined to put it back on again. She was excited. Riding high on the thrill of what they were doing. Bran didn't think she ever really considered the lives she was snuffing out when she did this shit. Not that his hands were clean, but at least he didn't get *excited* about it.

It was moments like this that made him wonder about her. He tried to treat her like a person, because everyone else treated her like an attack dog. But when she got like this, he had to wonder if she deserved it.

He spared a glance at the ATV's little sideview mirrors, seeing the loping shapes in the tall grasses behind him. Flashes of feral eyes and gaping, too-large mouths. Bran remembered the words etched into sideview mirrors: Objects in mirror are closer than they appear. He decided to accelerate.

"You sure they're not gonna try to go after me?" Bran asked. He'd been worried about that particular part of the plan—the part where he actually drove into the Redoubt *with* the pack of creatures behind them. Because Kat had a special mission, and Bran was essentially her driver.

Kat pointed at him, then at her chest. "You. With me? Safe."

Bran clenched his teeth and worked his hands on the steering wheel. "I swear to God, Kat, if you let one of those things chew on me, I'm never going to speak to you again."

"No chewing," was her response. "Safe."

Abe was a man of action. It was a character trait that had been reinforced by his years in combat situations—the old adage that any action was better than no action.

And yet, for the first time, he couldn't figure out what to do.

Horner's plan had hit him in the brain like a cement truck. He'd sent his goons to fire on them from a distance, in order to keep them from taking cover *inside* their boxes. And now he was sending in the primals. The Redoubters couldn't hide in their homes, or they'd be shot to shit. But if they stayed out in the open, they'd be run down and torn to pieces by the primals.

There was a sliver of Abe that grudgingly admitted that it was a good plan. It'd forced them into an untenable position. They couldn't stay where they were, but they had nowhere to run.

Heading for the cover of the ridgeline to the northwest had abruptly lost its already dull patina of hope. There was no way they could outrun the primals.

"What are we gonna do?" Ted demanded of him.

Abe slashed a hand through the air. "I'm thinking," he snapped.

His thoughts were not helpful. Possibilities came flitting into his brain, and they all sucked. Nothing had a reasonable expectation of success. The odds of their survival had become terminally low, and now he was bartering with himself over *certainly dead* and *probably dead.*

It's awfully hard to be imaginative while under fire. In the end, Abe had to cut himself short, and circled back to a thought he'd already dismissed as a nonstarter, but which now provided their only chance. Abe gave it a no-bullshit assessment and reckoned they'd have about a one-in-a-thousand chance of actually living to see another day.

"Alright, fuck it," Abe roared, getting pissed, because that's really all you could do in the face of certain death. He grabbed Ted by the shoulder with a grip that told him there would be no negotiating. "Run and get everyone you can find, and pull them back here." Then he backed up a single step and shouted to those around them, still huddled against the walls of the boxes. "This is it! This is where we make our stand! It's kill or be killed! Pick a lane and shoot anything that's not one of us!"

Ted boggled at him, and Abe felt a plunging feeling in his guts, knowing that he had no more hope to offer than this. He pushed that feeling away. There was just nothing else he could do, and he sure as shit wasn't going to die with a belly full of regrets and fear.

"We're just gonna duke it out with them?" Ted wheedled, his voice pitched high, almost a falsetto.

If Abe were talking to anyone he actually respected, he'd've invited them to speak up if they had a better plan. But he knew that would only be a waste of time here. He'd already considered the options, and he didn't trust Ted to come up with anything but all the shit he'd already dismissed.

"That's what we're doing," Abe confirmed, spinning on a heel and stalking the length of the box towards the north end of the settlement. "It's either that or lay down and suck your thumb." He decided to give the man at least some semblance of hope, not because it was true, but because he figured Ted needed it to remain functional: "It's our best option at this point."

Well. That wasn't exactly *untrue*. He just wasn't detailing how their "best option" was still a godawful crap shoot.

Ted started to say something else, but Abe shouted over him: "Quit fucking around and go get your people!" Then, letting his sling take his rifle, he cupped his hands over his mouth and bellowed, "Sam! Jones! Get your asses over here!"

He hadn't really been expecting a response—just trying to cover his bases—so he was surprised when he saw Jones's helmeted head jut out from around a corner, two boxes down from Abe.

"Yo!" Jones shouted back.

"Where the fuck have you been?" Abe's relief came out as anger.

"Trying not to get shot! Did you hear the howl?"

A smattering of gunfire pinged across the top of the box to Abe's right, making him flinch. He checked behind him and found that Ted was gone. Hopefully doing what Abe had instructed and not huddled in a corner, weeping.

Abe reached the end of the box. An opening, and then another box, and then Jones's face. This shouted conversation was stupid. He considered running to Jones, but then they'd only have to double back and consolidate here again. He cupped his hands over his mouth again. "Pull everyone you can back here!"

Jones flashed a thumbs up, then disappeared.

Another metallic impact to Abe's right. Something hit him in the shoulder.

He hissed and jumped back, twisting to look at his right deltoid, where a little chunk of copper jacketing was protruding from his sweat-dampened shirt. He swore and plucked the thing out. Eyed the box to his right and saw the hole that had sprouted there. Spall was a bitch. But better a piece of fragmented bullet than the whole bullet itself.

He flicked the bit of bullet jacketing from his finger.

A tumult of bodies cut the corner where Jones had been moments before, everybody running in a half squat. A flash of worry hit Abe as he counted heads and saw that Sam and Jones were not with them. Surely they hadn't gotten laid out in the last few seconds. Abe was about to give in to his fear and run to check, when he spotted them. Jones first, backing up, followed by a grim-looking Sam, facing forward. A body carried between them.

As they pushed through the civilians, Abe caught sight of the lolling head and knew that it was Bea. Half of him got irritated that Sam was overfocused on her. But the other half of him instantly felt bad for Sam—it was pretty obvious he had a thing for the woman. For Sam's sake, he hoped she wasn't dead.

Sam and Jones deposited her on the ground, then jogged over, shouldering their rifles. Jones looked like Jones always looked when the shooting started—not really all that different from how he looked normally. But Sam's face was drawn, and Abe could practically see his attention pulling back towards Bea's inert form.

"You with me?" Abe asked him earnestly as they drew up to the other side of the gap between their respective pieces of cover. A lull had overtaken the gunfire, making it possible for them to speak without shouting, but it tickled the back of Abe's mind. Were the shooters pulling back to avoid unwanted attention from the incoming primals?

Sam gave him a hard look, but nodded. "She's still alive. Gave her morphine. She's out."

Just as well, Abe thought. If your fate was to be eaten, being zonked on morphine while it happened wasn't a bad idea.

"Tell me you got a brilliant plan," Jones pleaded.

"I ain't got shit," Abe growled back, then checked around him to see if anyone was listening. Big surprise—no one was. Back to Jones and Sam. "We've gotta stick it out and fight."

"Fuck me," Jones belted out. "You heard the howl, didn't you?"

"Yeah, I heard. Options are severely limited." He gave Sam and Jones the opportunity he hadn't given to Ted. "Y'all got a better idea, I'm all ears."

They traded a glance. It was mournfully blank.

"That's about where I got to," Abe said with a nod. "You two handle the folks on your end. Our one advantage, if you can call it that—" A random shot struck the dirt between them, the ricochet moaning off into the distance. "Fucker," Abe grunted, then continued. "Is that we only gotta cover two angles. So set up a firing line, because that's the shit we're reduced to right now, and keep those rifles firing."

Sam and Jones both nodded, the looks on their faces saying that they knew the math that lay before them, and it was unforgiving.

Either they'd run out of targets, or they'd run out of ammo.

Joaquin stood in the crook of the open driver's-side door, leaning against the red pickup truck. Once he'd figured out that the little sheeple down in the Redoubt weren't going to shoot back, he'd pulled the truck up to the top of the ridge so he could watch them get their shit pushed in.

It wasn't as exciting as he'd hoped. He couldn't even see anything. By the time he'd made it to the top of the ridge, all those people had gone scurrying off to the far side of the settlement, and that's where they'd stayed. Probably where they'd stay until Bran and Kat and their horde of infected got in there to mop things up.

Disappointing. Joaquin sighed and scratched his cheek with a single index finger. It's not like he was a sadist or anything—he didn't *specifically* enjoy watching people get massacred. He didn't mind it either. But really, what he'd wanted to see was Ted dying. Catching a bullet, or being torn apart, either would do. He just hated that weasel.

Glancing to his right, he could just barely make out the five shooters along the ridge. He'd told those idiots to space themselves out more, but then they'd run and only put maybe a couple yards in between them. And then the shooting had started, and the Redoubt wasn't really shooting back, so Joaquin figured *what the hell* and let them be.

Sighing, he turned his head towards the southern ridge. He could just make out the top of Mr. Horner's black dually. Couldn't really see the shooters over there at all, but he could see the tiny figure of Mr. Horner himself, standing similarly to Joaquin—nestled in the angle between the open driver's-side door and the body of the truck. It looked like he was watching the Redoubt through a pair of binoculars.

Joaquin wished he'd thought to bring binoculars. Hell, maybe Ted *had* bit it, and he'd just missed it. That'd be a shame.

Between Joaquin's position and Mr. Horner's, lay the rough, tire-rut road that connected the Redoubt to Horner's Peak. And just at that moment, the little ATV with Bran and Kat was cresting the hill. Looked like Bran was driving pretty fast, kicking up a good bit of dust. Even got a little air when he came off that ridge. Slammed down with a little swerve, but maintained control.

Joaquin smirked at the thought of Bran and Kat losing control of the ATV and watching it go tumbling down the hill. It'd suck for Mr. Horner's plan, but it'd be great for Joaquin. He didn't like Bran because the guy thought he was better than everybody else, always acting like he was more righteous than them, because he got all squeamish about killing trespassers. As though being regretful about murder absolved you.

And Kat? Hell, Joaquin didn't have any strong feelings about her either way. Joaquin had grown up in a little Mexican neighborhood in southern California, right around the corner from one of those pull-a-part places. They had a junkyard dog there. Would scare the bejeezus out of Joaquin every time he walked by—big, nasty, black and tan mutt, come hauling out of nowhere like he'd been lying in wait and hit the chain link hard enough to splatter slobber on Joaquin, snarling and growling and barking.

But it was just a dog, doing dog shit. Joaquin didn't blame the dumb animal. But he didn't like it scaring him. Which is why he'd tossed rat bait at it like they were treats. Little green cubes that he'd pilfered from his uncle's shed. Dumb mutt ignored them at first, but after a while, got curious and scarfed them all up.

He hadn't felt bad about killing the dog. Nor had he felt vindictive or triumphant. He just didn't like being scared like that every time he walked past. And now he wouldn't be.

That was pretty much the same way he saw Kat. A dangerous animal that he bore no direct ill-feelings towards, because she was just being the animal she was. But he didn't like how she made him all edgy, so he wouldn't mind if she got taken out one day.

Didn't look like today would be that day, though.

The ATV sped down the hill, and shortly thereafter came the rush of bodies over the ridge. A wave of them, loping along on all fours. Creeped him out the way they did that. Fucking mutants.

At this point, the Redoubters *had* to have figured out what was coming at them. Joaquin was curious what they planned to do about it. Fight it out? That'd be a blood bath. He'd seen packs of infected half that size take out plenty of people, whether they were armed or not. And if they tried to make a run for it? Well, then they'd only die tired.

When Joaquin felt something hit him, his first thought was a bolt of sheer panic: One of the infected had broken off from the pack and grabbed him! He squealed as he was ripped backwards. An arm clamped around his head like an iron band.

He tried to buck and spin, but it was no use—the thing had him too tight. He thrust backwards, slamming his attacker into the side of the truck. Joaquin began wildly throwing his elbows behind him, catching his attacker in the ribs, and garnering a very human-sounding groan...

And that's when he saw the second attacker, coming straight at him through the grass.

She moved with fierce intent, closing the distance between them in a few strides. Her face was all mangled from the beating he'd given her earlier, but he still recognized her.

And if *she* was alive, then the arms that were holding him must've been—

He was so locked into her eyes that he didn't realize she'd just snatched his buck knife from his belt until he felt the tug and saw the flash of steel.

His mind went blank as she shoved that sliver of steel into him, right under his sternum. He felt it pierce his heart. Felt his heart convulsing around the blade. The pain was blinding.

But he did have one last thought:

Damn bitch knew right where to put it...

Chapter 25

Lee gritted his teeth against the pain in his ribs and held onto the thrashing man. His convulsions didn't last long. Marie kept ramming the blade in, fast as a sewing machine, her teeth bared and eyes savage.

By the time the man went limp in Lee's arms, Marie was already on the move. Lee dropped the man, gasping for the breath he'd held while keeping his core tight against the man's flailing elbows. Marie snatched a bolt gun from the driver's seat and passed it to him.

They wasted no effort on words.

Lee gave the rifle a rapid once-over. Spotted the detachable magazine. Plucked it out. 30-06, FMJs. Four in the magazine. He seated it back and checked the bolt. One in the chamber.

The truck door slammed, the engine revving.

Lee didn't even look, just dropped in place, right there over the dead body. He rolled it so it was laying on its stomach. Propped the rifle on the man's ass like a sand bag, and nestled in tight behind it.

The pickup's engine roared, the tires spinning, sending a gout of dust spraying across Lee's torn up bare feet. He settled into the scope, leveling his breathing as much as he could.

From behind him, the sound of a man screaming in alarm, just audible over the truck's engine. Then a nasty, crunchy impact, as Marie ran him over.

Lee forced his mind to take in only what he needed in that moment, which was everything he could know about the rifle in his hands. The scope was a 3-9x magnification. Basic duplex reticle. He had no idea what the rifle was sighted for. He adjusted the focus, bringing the black pickup to the south of the Redoubt into sharp relief. And found himself looking right at Colin Horner.

Lee felt his heart thudding against the dirt beneath him. The body he was leaning against gave a little death twitch. Sonofabitch. At this distance, another twitch like that could send his round off by several feet.

"Hold still, fucker," Lee seethed.

Another *thud-thud* from behind him, as Marie rolled someone over with both sets of tires.

Where to hold the reticle? He couldn't remember the last time he'd used a 30-06, and his recollection of its ballistics was hazy at best. Everything was a broad estimation.

A hit on Horner was nigh on impossible.

But with five rounds, Lee was reasonably sure he could walk in a hit or two on the big dually truck the man was hanging out of. It wouldn't disable the vehicle, but it might spook the man into drawing back and giving the Redoubt a momentary reprieve.

So Lee ripped the scope back to its lowest magnification and held his reticle so the truck bisected the bottom arm of the crosshair. Shifted just a pinch to the left to account for the light cross-breeze...

The trigger was feather-light—almost too light—and the gun bucked when Lee barely touched the damn thing. At the same instant, a smattering of gunfire cracked the air behind him, followed immediately by another car-on-body impact.

Lee's mind split in two, half of it wondering if Marie had been shot, while the other half focused on the impact of his bullet. It came a heartbeat later: A gout of dust, about six feet below the grill of the truck.

He jacked the bolt, and only then peeked over his shoulder.

The scene that hit his eye was breathtakingly surreal.

The little red pickup, halfway into a donut, spinning up twin rooster-tails of pale dust, the windshield pebbled and white from being smashed in. The spread-eagle body of a man seemed to hang in midair. A glimpse of Marie's face through the driver's-side window as she brought the truck around in a tight spin. And one more guy, running full-tilt down the hill, trying to escape.

She's got it handled.

Lee jerked back into his scope, already doing the computations in his head to account for the first shot's low impact. He raised the reticle so that the truck stood at the bottom third of the lower crosshair arm. This time, knowing how light the trigger was, he gingerly touched the pad of his finger to it and applied surgeon-like pressure.

BOOM

Lee stayed in his scope as it settled from the recoil. This time he saw the splash of gray dust as the bullet disintegrated across the truck's brush guard. He had the satisfaction of watching Horner's tiny figure jolt and scramble.

A man screamed behind him. Lee ignored it as he worked the bolt. Horner leapt into his vehicle, the driver's door swinging shut. Lee edged his reticle just a smidge higher, as the screaming behind him was drowned out by the sound of a red-lining engine. Then another *whump*. Then tires sliding as they locked up. Lee breathed in. Heard the man screaming again—apparently one hit from a truck had not been enough to put him down. Lee breathed out. Horner's black dually started to back up. More roaring engine behind him. He touched off the trigger.

BOOM went the rifle.

THUD-UMP—THUD-UMP went the sound of tires over flesh.

No more screaming.

The windshield of Horner's truck sprouted a gray circle, right in the center.

Lee reloaded and let fly his last two rounds as fast as he could get them off. He saw the first one splash off the top of the windshield. Couldn't see where the second one went, and then Horner's truck was gone, backed down over the ridge.

Lee didn't even bother with the rifle after that. He surged to his feet, leaving the spent rifle where it lay. Down the hill about fifty yards, Marie was cutting the truck in a hard J-turn maneuver, bringing it back around towards Lee, while he sprinted on his wrecked bare feet to where he saw a patch of blue shirt in amongst the grass, about fifteen yards away.

The man inside that shirt was still alive. It was Darryl. He goggled up as Lee gave the guy a quick look over. Darryl's hands were splayed out to his sides, a rifle laying just a few inches beyond his right fingers. His hips turned in the completely wrong direction—his back was on the ground, and so was his crotch. The only thing that moved were his eyes and his mouth, and the sweat trickling down the sides of his face. Or maybe they were tears.

Lee stooped with a grunt and grabbed the rifle. Your basic AR variant with a big, beta drum mag and a too-large scope. Damn thing weighed a ton.

The red pickup came hauling up to Lee's left and skidded to a stop. It was only after Marie let off the accelerator that Lee actually heard Darryl's whisper.

"Please."

Lee checked the drum mag. It had a clear front and he could see it was still half full—fifty-ish rounds. "Please, what?" Lee said, not even looking at the guy, his voice somewhat annoyed. "You're damn near twisted in half. Ain't shit anyone can do for you, and I wouldn't be the one to do it anyhow."

He thought about sparing Darryl a single round to put him out of his misery, but he was already moving off before any semblance of pity could rise in him. Moving rapidly to the next body, this one wearing a white shirt that wasn't so white anymore. The impact of the truck had burst him open like a balloon.

"Lee!" Marie's voice. "Let's go! Primals are running at the Redoubt!"

He didn't bother to yell back at her. He knew they needed to move quick. He also knew they both needed weapons. As effective as Marie had been with it, the red truck didn't count. The second body's rifle had been tossed a bit, and it took a few frustrating seconds for Lee to spot it. It was an FN-FAL. He snatched it up, then grabbed the two mags still in the dead man's chest rig. Then, with his whole bundle, he raced back towards the pickup truck.

He stopped just long enough to give Darryl a sympathetic shot to the brain.

Sam sent people sprinting across the gap between the boxes, trying to get everyone to consolidate in their desperate gamble to withstand the incoming primals. And then he realized that there was no incoming fire—no *ping* and *thwap* of the rounds hitting steel and dirt.

Had their attackers stopped shooting because the primals were almost on them?

Then he heard something unmistakable in the distance: A man screaming for his life. And right along with that screaming was the sound of an engine revving.

Frowning, Sam looked across the gap and caught Jones's eye.

"The fuck's going on out there?" Jones said.

"I'm gonna look," Sam blurted, then dropped to a knee, facing the corner, his rifle up.

Just before leaning out, he heard someone shout, "Infected! Infected!"

Shit, he'd been right—they'd only stopped shooting so the primals could swarm them. But then what was the screaming and engine revving all about?

Sam leaned out, just his head and rifle clearing the corner. Down through the grid of metal containers, Sam could see straight across the Redoubt to the hill beyond. And what he saw made no sense.

"What is it?" Jones demanded, seeing the confusion flickering across Sam's face. "What's going on? Talk to me, Sam!"

"Uh," Sam shook himself out of his momentary shock. "The red pickup is..."

As he said it, the pickup slammed into a body, sending it pinwheeling through the air. The pickup didn't stop. It cut a sharp turn and started chasing another shooter as he fled down the hill on the other side, dropping out of sight.

Sam pulled himself back into cover, his heart hammering, and for once, not from the likelihood of his own demise. Adrenaline hit him full-force as he made a tenuous connection in his brain, and found that it had opened a tiny window of possibility. A way out of this giant shit storm.

"Jesus, Sam!" Jones caterwauled.

But Sam ignored him, instead rocketing to his feet and finding Abe on the other side of the gap. "Abe!" The black-bearded face swung on him. "Someone's taking out the shooters for us! We can move!"

But Sam hadn't said what he'd actually thought. Perhaps because it was silly, or childish, and yes, somehow concerns like that still leak into your head, even when you're on death's door.

But he knew that what he'd thought was right, because it just *felt* right.

It wasn't just *someone* that was taking out the shooters for them.

It was—it *had* to be—Lee and Marie.

Chapter 26

The black-painted bed of the pickup truck was skillet-hot on Lee's bare feet.

He forced himself not to dance. Forced his feet to stay in the same spot, bracing himself against the cab as Marie piloted it down the hill. He could practically feel his toes blistering and cracking.

Burning was a funny thing—of all the types of pain a person could feel, burning caused the most immediate and instinctive reaction. Even the toughest people had a real hard time keeping their wits when something on them was getting burned. It practically short-circuited the brain.

So for the span of four or five seconds, it was all Lee could do to stand there and repeatedly swear.

That's why it took him a few seconds to get back on track, pound the top of the cab and shout to Marie, "Go for the primals! We might be able to draw some of them off!"

Immediately, the pickup changed course, causing Lee to stumble. Unfortunately, this was a working truck, and the bed was not kept clean. His right foot planted itself directly into a smattering of bent, rusty nails.

Lee was all out of fucks, so this time he didn't say shit. Just picked up his foot with a grimace, plucked the offending piece of metal from the ball of his foot, then steadied himself again. He hefted the rifle he'd stolen, with its heavy drum mag, and yanked the scope's magnification down as low as it could go before raising it to his eye.

Through the scope, the pack of primals was just a mad scramble of bodies in various shades of earth. He didn't bother to aim—all the targets were packed in tight. He let loose, giving them a protracted flurry of projectiles as fast as he could control the recoil.

The terrain leveled out as they reached the bottom of the hill, Lee continuing to fire in rapid bursts. They were cutting an angle right at the incoming horde of primals, perhaps two hundred yards from them, with the Redoubt to their right.

Between the recoil, the moving vehicle, and the magnified optic, Lee had no idea if he was hitting anything. He had to be hitting *something*, or at least getting the primals' attention, but it was like they were locked into the ATV that was leading them. They did not divert like he'd hoped.

Lee swore, coming out of his scope as their distance to the horde rapidly shrank. "Marie! Cut us around the outside of them! Cut a big circle!"

They were practically on top of them when Marie yanked them to the left, and Lee pivoted to the right side of the bed, smartly stepping over the nails this time. He planted his feet wide and started hammering any shape that wound up in his crosshairs. And this time he was close enough to see what his rounds were doing.

As Marie gunned the pickup in a wide, clockwise arc around the back of the horde, Lee watched the rounds slam into flesh, watched dirt and blood come flying off of them, watched them jerk and stumble. But these were not human beings anymore. They were simultaneously something more, and something less. They did not go down easy.

Lee guided his fire down to their pelvises, and that's when he started to see bodies drop. Because it didn't matter how wild or tough you were—when the pelvis shatters, you're not running anymore.

Primals went down in heaps, tumbling head over foot. Wild eyes and bared teeth flashed at Lee through clouds of dust as Marie continued their wide arc, and Lee continued to pound into them until the drum mag went empty. Right when he felt the bolt lock to the rear, his eye caught the tail end of the ATV, heading for the main drag of the Redoubt.

Lee didn't spare the AR a second glance, but simply slung it off into the bed. Then he hammered the top of the cab as he sidestepped towards the driver's side. "Marie! Gimme the other rifle!"

The pickup swerved as Marie reached for the big FN FAL she'd posted in the passenger's seat. Lee braced himself on the cab, snapping a glance to the right to see that they were about halfway up the column of primals—and still not a single one had broken off to chase them. Almost like they were displaying *discipline*.

Lee put his eye back on his target. He could see both Bran and Kat in that ATV.

The thought struck him: Did he really want to take Kat out?

"Here!" Marie screamed at him as she juked around a clump of rocks that would have ripped their undercarriage out. The barrel of the long, black rifle waved about, thumping against the side of the cab.

Lee stretched to reach it, ribs squalling as he took hold of the heavy rifle and brought it around.

Was it right to kill Kat after she'd saved his life?

Hell, maybe I am getting soft, Lee thought as he shouldered the rifle. Three years ago, he would've taken the top of her skull off and rationalized it with something like, "play stupid games, get stupid prizes."

Two divergent strains of thought, branching out from Lee's mind.

I'll split the difference, Lee decided, and sighted for Bran.

Bran twisted in his seat at just the right moment—thank God—and saw the guy in the pickup truck shouldering a long, black rifle.

What made that one little peek over his shoulder so suddenly and monumentally important for the continuation of his life, were two little factoids that his brain linked together.

Factoid one: That motherfucker was looking right at him. And, generally speaking, when a guy with a gun, who's shown a marked desire to kill your associates, looks at you, it's pretty safe to assume he's thinking about killing you too.

Factoid two: That motherfucker only had one eye. And the only motherfucker that popped into Bran's head under the category of *one-eyed people my brain has flagged as dangerous*, was the man named Jax.

Who should've been halfway digested at that moment.

So, the first thing that Bran did was swear and swerve. Something cracked through the air, very close, and was immediately followed by a bellowing rifle report. The steering wheel jostled in his grip as the ATV left the road. Directly ahead, the first line of Conex boxes loomed close—too close for him to correct back onto the main drag. So he kept the ATV's momentum going to the left, and skimmed along the outer line of boxes, the corrugated sides whizzing by just outside Kat's door.

The second thing Bran did was look right at Kat and yell, "What the fuck did you do?"

Bran saw the truth in the sudden surprise that shot Kat's eyes wide. Not the surprise of being shocked at an accusation. The surprise of being caught red-handed. And there it was—plain as day, for just that instant: Guilt. Shame.

Humanity?

And then the moment was gone. Kat snarled and twisted in her seat, her eyes locking onto the man in the truck behind them. Then she issued a series of rasping, whooping barks.

Just as Lee was bringing the sights of his rifle back onto the ATV, he watched Kat spin in her seat, look him dead in the eye, and make some sort of call.

No less than a dozen heads with mangy, dreadlocked hair and slavering jaws swiveled on him. They immediately split off from the main group, charging towards the pickup.

Marie spotted them coming and gunned the engine, sending Lee staggering back in the bed. She steered away from the horde, leaving several of the primals in a squall of dust. But two of the smart ones had been further ahead when they'd peeled off, and Lee could already see they were on a perfect intercept course.

Those two primals went all out, the intensity of their four-legged strides growing faster and longer, jaws wide open to gulp air, tongues lolling.

Lee sighted for the nearest, which was just a few yards off the right side of the truck. He fired reflexively. Four, big, .308-caliber rounds punched the primal down into the dirt.

He'd already known he wasn't going to get the second one, but it's still just a terrible sensation to feel the chassis of your vehicle shake as something you definitely don't want onboard decides to jump in with you.

A big mass of darkly-skinned sinews. He swung the rifle towards it. The primal snatched the muzzle as it came around. Whether the primal was just that strong, or Lee was just that spent, the rifle left his grip with such velocity that it left his hands thrumming like he'd grabbed a live wire.

No weapons. Only hands and feet. Lee didn't have time to bemoan the fact. He saw how the primal was perched right on the sidewall of the truck bed, and thought, *yeah, solid front kick might do it*.

And it might have, except for a nasty pothole. The bed lurched just as Lee brought his right leg up to plant it in the primal's chest. He went down, flat on his back.

It was on him instantly. He brought his arms and knees up to defend himself, but the creature hit him with all of its considerable weight, snatching his arms and pinning them down in one dishearteningly-powerful slam, its jaws stretching wide, going for the throat.

Marie hooked a sudden right and hit the brakes in the same instant. The primal went flying off as though it'd been snatched out of the bed by some cosmic hand.

Lee'd had a pretty shitty day so far. Week. Month. Etcetera. But right at that moment, he felt like the luckiest man in the world. If they tried a hundred times, they couldn't have repeated that performance.

He struggled upright, patting the back glass and shouting, "Good one!" as he oriented himself again, seeing that they were heading back towards the Redoubt, where the tail end of the primal horde had just disappeared, sprinting through the grid of boxes.

Bea was dimly aware of the chaos all around her. She was in a strange semi-dream state that she'd never experienced before. She knew it was the drugs that Sam had given her. She'd thought they were going to knock her out completely. But even as everything lost cohesion and consequence, she was still taking in sensory data.

The infected were coming. Everyone was shouting about it, and there were lots of stamping feet and crying and yelling and swearing. Distantly, she recognized that she was helplessly paralyzed on the ground.

Sam's voice over top of her, yelling: "Help me with her!"

Then another voice responded, and Bea was pretty sure it was his friend, Jones: "I can't believe you're doing this!"

A muted note of panic struck her, like hearing a blood-curdling scream from a mile away—*I don't want to die!*

She felt hands hook under her armpits, and thought they must've been Sam's. And then she felt someone else's hands around her legs, and they must have been Jones's. Her body left the ground, while the muted scream of her own panic became louder and louder and louder. Until she realized it wasn't her inner panic. It was the screams of the Redoubters, and their families, and their children.

That was what brought her mind to the surface of the warm morphine sea she'd been drowning in. Her eyes opened on shifting shadows in a wash of light, lines and edges blurred and streaked, only the very center of her vision providing any focus.

She was staring up into Sam's face. His brown skin slick with sweat and pebbled with dirt. His features strained. His dark eyes looking right back at her.

"You with me?"

She could tell he was shouting, but it sounded watery and diffuse. She nodded. Or at least tried to—her shoulders were all scrunched up from the way she was being carried, squeezing her neck in a sort of brace. Then she tried to tell him not to risk his life for her.

All she got out was a few nonsensical consonants in a slurry of groaning vowels.

Why was he doing this? He didn't even know her. She didn't know him. They owed each other nothing. She wouldn't have risked her life to save him. And any gratitude she might have felt for his care at that moment would forever be tainted by resentment if he wound up getting himself killed for her.

Then again, if he got killed, she was probably going to die right alongside him.

She didn't want that.

She didn't want this.

She didn't want any of it.

None of which she could say. She could only watch, a passive observer in her own body.

Sam's eyes darted up and went wide with fear. "They're coming!"

Bea could barely move her head enough to see Jones take a rapid glance over his shoulder. "Oh shit! Oh shit! Get inside!"

She saw them only as fleshy shapes amid others clothed in blues and reds and blacks. The fleshy shapes danced and lunged, and fell upon the clothed shapes, seeming to make them disappear into the ground. And the fleshy shapes were almost the same color as the ground, so it seemed that all the earth around them had sprung up like a violent, roiling sea and was swallowing them up.

Bea could hear them. The people screaming, but also the infected. The huff and grunt of their multitudinous throats. Their snarls and snaps and growls and yips and barks, so unlike any animal she'd ever heard.

And in amongst all of that, like a boat on a heaving sea, came a strange white box, floating through the midst of it all, seeming to speed directly at her...

Sam saw the white frame of the ATV cut straight through the mess of encroaching primals. He saw the grim face of the man behind the steering wheel—Bran. And beside him, Kat, this time without the bandanna to cover her mutated jaws. They were both staring right at him.

As Sam rounded the corner of the Conex box, where people were piling into the open doors, he was suddenly certain that Bran and Kat wanted something specifically from *him*.

And the only thing he had of note was the semi-conscious woman in his arms.

He needed to get inside that box. That was their only way out of this. That was the only way he could save Bea.

Why was he doing this?

Because he was sweet on her? After one day of knowing her?

Or was it because he'd told her he'd stay with her? Because he'd promised her she'd be okay? Neither of which he had any business promising, but that's not really the point, is it? Sometimes we just make stupid promises. Some people were willing to say the stupidity of the promise negated their obligation.

Sam was not one of those people.

He had no one to curse but himself as he was suddenly caught up in the tide of people trying to all cram into that box at once. Even as he churned for the opening, he knew it wouldn't work. He could see it written in the facts all around him.

Dozens of people trying to make it through the open doors of that box, with the primals right on their asses. They wouldn't have time to close and bolt the doors. No one was thinking about that—they were just trying to get away.

There was no time to figure out another option. The ATV was coming in, braking hard, sending waves of dust ahead of it as it yawed sideways, bringing Kat broadside to Sam.

Jones went for his rifle, dropping Bea's legs. At the same moment, Kat launched herself out of the ATV, powered by the vehicle's sliding momentum. Jones got his rifle in both hands, but then Kat smashed into all three of them like a wrecking ball, sending Jones onto his ass and Sam and Bea rolling in a tangle.

Dirt sprayed into Sam's eyes and mouth as he skidded across the ground. He blinked rapidly, catching sight of a single primal loping towards him, thick ropes of frothy saliva streaming from its jaws. But Kat suddenly appeared in front of it, swirling up from where she'd hit the ground, spreading her body out in front of the primal as though she would tackle it, despite the immense size difference.

The primal came skidding to a stop, and then diverted as though it had suddenly forgot all about Sam and Bea.

Sam tried to gain his feet, only to discover that Bea was collapsed on top of him.

Kat spun, her eyes flashing, her teeth bared.

Sam dove his hands between his body and Bea's, trying to grasp his rifle.

Kat saw it and snarled.

"Sam?" Bea slurred. "You needa get oudda here!"

He would have sorely liked to. Would have liked to say something back, too. Witty. Reassuring. Cavalier. Anything would do.

But nothing came to him, because his brain was incredibly preoccupied by the vision of Kat charging him, and the fact that he couldn't get his gun up.

Kat reared back as she reached him and sent a savage stomp right into Sam's face. A sensation too severe to actually be categorized as pain exploded through his skull, his brain reeling into half-conscious space.

Reality became a disjointed collection of bizarre thoughts and sounds and sensations.

He could feel movement all around his body. Thrashing, violent movement.

Am I being eaten? He'd expected more pain. This actually wasn't so bad.

Screaming.

Well, someone's being eaten, and it's very bad for them.

Bea's voice, clearer and sharper than before, as though the fall had jolted her awake: "Sam? Sam!" and then, "No! *No!*"

Something was squeezing his waist, surprisingly hard.

Is that the feeling of them tearing into my guts?

Whatever was squeezing him around the waist started tugging.

His mind's eye painted a perfectly logical picture: A primal with their face buried in his stomach, jerking its head, ripping him open.

More of Bea's voice yelling, "No! No!" Grunting, straining. "No!"

Sam was pretty sure his eyes had been open the entire time, but when vision became a thing for him again, he was staring at Bea, rather than a primal. Bea, with her arms around Sam's waist, and her ass in the air.

...the fuck?

And then it made sense. Her ass was in the air because Kat had *her* around the waist and was trying to pull her free of Sam. That was the jerking he'd felt. It shocked the hell out of Sam for one simple reason: He knew that Kat must have been fiercely strong.

And yet somehow, Bea, fresh out of a morphine nap, wasn't letting go.

Sam's numb hands started to move towards the last known location of his rifle. And that was when a big, dark face came into Sam's vision, blotting out the sky. And for just a second, Sam thought that it was Abe, and he felt a wash of relief.

But it was Bran, with that shotgun held in both hands. Bran, who said these words, all in a tumble: "Fuck it, we'll take him as a hostage!"

And then he slammed the butt of the shotgun into Sam's already smashed face.

Chapter 27

There was no way in hell Marie was going to run their stolen truck straight up the main drag where they'd be pinched in by the Conex boxes, so she cut a wide right around the Redoubt. Still in the bed of the truck, but now weaponless, Lee figured she intended to cut the ATV off on the other side.

"Marie! I got no weapon!" he shouted at her window, wondering what exactly she intended to do when she saw the ATV pop out in front of her.

"Alright!" was all she yelled back.

Lee braced himself firmly behind the cab as she roared along the eastern side of the Redoubt, the structures streaking by on his left. Was she going to ram them? And would that eject him from the truck bed?

He didn't really want to test it out.

"Marie!" Lee called in a warning tone, feeling the truck decelerate under his feet as Marie approached the northeastern corner of the settlement. "Don't—"

The ATV blasted past them, a streak of white from left to right. Lee caught the barest glimpse of Bran in the driver's seat, and Kat, appearing to straddle something in the back utility bed.

Marie yelled "Braking!" about a half second before she slammed on the brakes, ramming Lee's chest into the cab, his ribs crackling.

He gasped and almost gagged, the way his whole body seized up. Couldn't help but clamp his eyes shut against the pain for an instant before forcing them back open to see a hazy image of the ATV zooming off east.

Two thoughts, rapid fire in Lee's mind: *Were those bodies Kat was straddling?*

And then, *Should we go after them?*

But before he had time to consider either of those questions, a dull roar washed over him. He jerked his head to the left.

"Oh, Jesus—Marie!"

"I see them!" she shouted back, yanking the truck into reverse.

The primals were pouring out of the Redoubt, chasing the ATV—and coming straight at Lee and Marie.

"Hold on!" Marie warned, then slammed on the gas.

Lee was jerked into the cab again. It seemed like a tsunami of primals was surging towards him, and no matter how fast Marie accelerated in reverse, Lee couldn't find the end of it. They were getting closer, and closer, and closer, almost on top of them—

One hit the front-left quarter panel. It went spinning into the dirt, but then shot back to its feet and kept running. Behind it, a few more primals slipped between the boxes and went loping off, the entire horde following the fleeing ATV.

And just like that, the horde of primals left the Redoubt.

"Brake slowly!" Lee practically begged, holding his side with his left arm.

She did. Kind of.

As the pickup rocked to a stop, the absence of gunshots and roaring engines left Lee's ears feeling numb. Until he heard the cries. Not cries of fear anymore.

Cries of pain.

And grief.

Don't get sucked in, Lee told himself, even as he felt his stomach churn. There was a fallout coming, but he still had to be one of the ones keeping a head on their shoulders. The scene needed to be secured. Anguish would have to wait.

Lee twisted in the bed to check the southern ridge where the black dually had been. He couldn't see the truck. No movement in the grass of the hilltop. And no one took a shot at him as he stood there, ripe for the reaping.

Guess they're gone then.

"Marie," he ground out between pain-clenched teeth. "Find our boys."

The entire west side of the Redoubt was a mess. From the southern end of the main drag, all the way around to the north end, bodies dotted the grass as though they'd been sprinkled in a great, sweeping arc. It wasn't just primals though. Once you got in amongst the boxes, there were plenty of humans. And parts of them.

Marie pulled the truck to a stop at the northwestern corner, where a mass of people were accumulating, trickling out of whatever boxes they'd managed to lock themselves into—if they'd been so lucky.

Lee scanned through the growing crowd, looking for the familiar faces of his team. As his eyes passed over the people, he realized many of them were injured, and it didn't look like they were bullet wounds. Arms hung limp. Legs were twisted out of joint. People pressed bloody hands over giant divots that'd been ripped out of their flesh—many in the chest, shoulders, and arms.

He slipped out of the bed, though it was a bit of a painstaking process. With the adrenaline receding, the stress he'd placed on his injuries was coming back to haunt him with a vengeance. But even as his bare feet hit the dirt, he was thinking about what a colossal fucking mess he was in.

Worry ratcheted tighter, click by insistent click.

Find your people, he told himself. *That's the important thing right now.* But he knew what was in store for him. He could see it in the gazes all around him.

Anger. Resentment. Mistrust.

A huge swell of guilt rose up in him. *You told these people to trust you, and now they've got dead family and friends.* But he forced himself to relax and float to the top of that cresting wave of condemnation. Let it all pass beneath him.

He set his teeth together and forced his posture straight, forced his lungs to breathe deep and steady, despite the pain that caused him.

Marie stepped in stride with him as they approached the gathering. It seemed all eyes were on him. He'd been the leader. Now he would bear the consequences. And they didn't take long in coming.

Voices stabbed out of the crowd, but Lee couldn't see who was talking. They all started at once, so he couldn't catch what any of them said. He got the gist though. That part was hard to miss.

"They're hurting and they need someone to blame," Marie said, her voice a warning for Lee, but also riddled with an exhaustion born of seeing this play out many times before.

Lee sniffed, his lips pressed into a grimace as the shouted words poured over him and the guilt flowed beneath him.

"What were you thinking?"

"What happened?"

"You did this!"

"This is your fault!"

Sonofabitch. Cocksucker. Motherfucker.

He stopped when his feet came to a dead body. A man with his throat ripped out, lying in mud made from the dusty earth and his own exsanguination. An M4 lay next to his body. Save for a thin layer of dust, it looked new. No frills except the red dot optic. It was one of their "minion rifles."

Lee stooped as the battering of invectives and accusations lulled, the people suddenly curious—and perhaps a little worried—about what he was doing. He took up the rifle. Checked the mag, which was maybe half full. Checked the chamber, which was loaded.

Only then did he look back up at the people.

Did they see his bare feet? Did they see his swollen, cut-up face? Did they notice him favoring his ribs? Anyone with half a brain could see that both Lee and Marie had been through the wringer for this settlement. But their grief and anger blinded them.

A woman shoved to the front of the crowd, holding a shoulder that looked like it'd been dislocated. Tears made glistening streaks through a face coated in dust. Lee wondered if she had lost someone, or if she was weeping for herself.

"Where *were* you?" she cried into the strange pall of silence that had come over the gathering. As though he'd been neglectful by not being here. As though he should be able to be everywhere he was needed, all at once.

Lee held up a finger because it looked like she was about to light into him. She hesitated, balking at his upraised finger as though it was the final insult to a laundry list of injuries.

"Where's Ted?" Lee grated, his voice dry and hoarse.

"Ted?" the woman asked, like she'd never heard the name before. "What do you need *him* for? So you can try to convince him not to kick you out?"

Lee stared back at her, his expression unchanging. *Because shit needs to get done, and I don't think you're gonna take orders from me right now*. But rather than say that, which wouldn't help at all, he let his gaze drift off of the woman and went back to scanning the crowd.

She started to say something else, but Lee raised his voice over her. "Ted! You're needed up front!"

For a flash, he wondered if he was calling to a dead man—wouldn't *that* make things ten times worse—but then he saw a head of bedraggled, sandy hair moving through the crowd, glimpses of Ted's eyes behind dirty glasses. When he emerged from the crowd, he was still holding his revolver in one hand. His posture was strange. Like he'd been beaten down worse than Lee, though Lee couldn't see a mark on him.

Lee glanced to Marie and repeated his earlier command: "Go find our boys." *God, please let them all be alive and whole.* She didn't seem overly pleased to leave Lee in a pot of simmering anger about to boil over. But she nodded and moved out, her gait stiff and unwieldy around her own injuries.

He looked back to Ted.

The man's eyes were filled with hurt and indignation. He raised his arms, then let them flop to his sides. "What happened, Jax?" He raked a hand unsteadily through his sweaty hair. "What happened to the fuckin'...the fuckin'..." he abruptly shouted the last part: "*Peace talks?!*"

Lee closed the distance between them. He wasn't moving quick or aggressive, just trying to be face to face, rather than ten yards separate. But Ted shrank back anyway—one shuffling step before he caught himself and glanced about to see if anyone had noticed.

Lee stopped when he did this and frowned at him. "What? You think I'm gonna hit you or something?"

That's exactly what Ted had thought. Lee could see it in the shame that fell over Ted's face. But people don't like to be shamed in public. It's much easier to get indignant and try to save face with a show of power, which they always seemed to equate with getting mad, for some reason. Ted was no different.

His eyes got all narrow and hot. He jabbed a finger at Lee. "Oh, fuck you, Jax!" The finger swiped up and down, indicating all of Lee. "Fuck you and your...your stupid macho bullshit!"

Lee glanced pointedly down at himself. "I'm just standing here."

"Yeah, you're just standing there!" Ted slavered. "Just standing there, where you randomly appeared, only moments after Horner tried to have those infected wipe us out! And *now* you show up! *Now* you want us to listen to you again!"

Anger came to Lee. A pretty natural response to being dressed down by some ignorant fuck that didn't know what they were talking about. But not every natural response is helpful. Lee let it pass beneath him, just like the guilt. In its wake there was only stillness. And sadness.

He knew there was no point in trying to manage another's emotions. It never worked. It was always ignored, and most of the time led them to resent you even more for not validating their temporary madness. Sometimes they came to the truth on their own. Most of the time they just wallowed in it forever.

There was no point in addressing Ted's emotional outburst. The only thing that mattered now was the truth, and all that it illuminated.

So he didn't bother telling Ted that he couldn't have been there to help them, because he was busy being stripped of his boots, armor, and weapons, beaten senseless, and left as an aperitif for a pack of primals. He didn't bother telling Ted that he and Marie were the only reasons any of them were still alive at that moment.

"You see all this shit?" Ted practically shrieked, waving his arms—and the revolver—all around. "You see all the bodies? Bodies, Jax!" Tears welled in his eyes, his face flushing red. "Those were my people! *My! People!*"

Lee took a step closer to him, his expression finally betraying the tension within him. "Who'd they have in the back of that ATV? 'Cause I swear I saw Kat with two bodies in the back when they drove off. Who'd they take?"

"They took...?" Ted goggled about, eyes flashing between Lee and his people. "I don't...how the hell am I supposed to know?" Defensive now. "I couldn't tell what was happening! I was busy *fighting*, unlike—"

He'd been waving his hands wildly as he talked, and as the revolver came around to point at Lee's face, Lee snatched it deftly out of his grip. He knew Ted hadn't meant to point it at him, but that wasn't why Lee had taken it from him.

Ted gasped and jumped back. A ripple of shock through the crowd, and Lee made sure to be very still for a moment, lest one of these people decide to defend their beloved leader by putting a few rounds into Lee.

"What the fuck?" Ted screamed at him.

Lee opened the revolver's cylinder and looked at the backs of the six cartridges. Gleaming brass, with the little silver primer in the center. Not a single primer had a dent in it from being struck by the firing pin. Ted hadn't fired a shot.

"Mm," Lee grunted, shoving the revolver back towards Ted, with the cylinder still open. "Some fighting you did," he said, but quietly, so the others wouldn't hear.

Ted stared at Lee. Stared at the revolver. Reached out with a shaking hand and tried to take it back, but Lee held on for a second longer.

He waited until Ted looked him in the eye again before speaking. "For your continued good health, don't close that cylinder." His nostrils flared in disgust. "Not like you're gonna use it anyway."

"Jax!" Marie's voice cut through Ted and Lee's staredown, causing both of them to look.

She was jogging back up with Abe and Jones in tow.

Relief damn near took Lee's knees out.

Except...

The look on Marie's face. And Abe's. And Jones's especially.

A cold hollow formed in Lee's chest.

"Where's Sam?" he managed, thickly.

It was Jones that answered, panting as he trooped to a stop in front of Lee and Ted and all the pissed off onlookers. On his face was written only failure and shame. He shook his head.

"They took him," Jones heaved out. "I'm sorry. They took Sam and Bea."

Chapter 28

Colin Horner didn't say a damn word as he drove back towards the ranch. He stared straight ahead, through the spider-webbed glass around two bullet holes in his windshield. His eyes barely moved. Barely even blinked.

His thoughts came at him in an unrelenting series of disjointed snippets. Fragmented scenes from circumstances both real and imagined.

The guys in the back of the truck—two in the back of the crew cab, and four in the truck bed—weren't quite sure if their boss was satisfied with the operation or not. On the one hand, they hadn't managed to wipe the Redoubt off the map. But they had succeeded in capturing the woman Lander Hollis wanted, and that was good, right?

And yet, Colin Horner seemed mighty pissed.

In reality, Colin wasn't even sure what he was feeling. Rage did continue to bubble up in him, but more than that, there was fear. Uncertainty. Anxiety. And a deep, deep chasm of madness that yawned beneath him, always ready to swallow him whole if he didn't keep his guard up.

That's what had happened, he realized: He hadn't kept his guard up. He'd made the foolish mistake of having *expectations*. Expectations that the people under him would do what he told them to do. And then someone—fucking *someone*—had managed to sneak around behind Joaquin and his men and take them all out, and then put bullet holes in Colin's fucking truck.

And who had those someones been? He felt like he knew. But he couldn't possibly. In flashes of mental clarity, he searched his memory for any empirical evidence that would have substantiated this suspicion, but came up empty. They'd been too far away for him to see, let alone recognize.

And yet…he knew.

No, he seethed at himself, the vinyl steering wheel creaking as he strangled it in both hands. *No, you don't know. What you're feeling is paranoia.*

That chasm of blackness, waiting for him. Waiting like an ant lion waits for its prey to slide down into its little sand trap. And he *was* slipping. He was sinking. He knew this feeling, because he'd been dealing with it his entire goddamn life.

And how often has your paranoia been right?

Maybe he'd meant it as a challenge to his own paranoia, but instead, the rage surged up again.

Fucking all the time! All the time I'm fucking right! Motherfuckers try to gaslight me and tell me I don't know what I know, but I know what I fucking know, and I know this!

Those someones had been the man Jax and his bitch Marie.

Because hadn't Kat hesitated for a long time when he'd told her to call the infected in on them? And when she did finally let out that godawful howl, hadn't it sounded different to him than all the other times?

Oh, you speak the language now? You're a regular fucking Doctor Doolittle. You fucking putz, get your head on straight.

And then: *She fucking did something. That little animal bitch did something. I don't know how she did it, or what she did, but I KNOW IT.*

Slipping.

She betrayed you.

—oh, but you've done such a WONDERFUL job making her like you—

I don't fucking need her to like me. Attack dogs don't need to like their masters. They need to be scared, and they need to be mean, and they need to be kept hungry and pissed off.

—maybe she's less of an animal than you think—

Oh, less of an animal than I think?

And now just images: Patty, laying in the grass. Patty, with her throat ripped out and her stomach torn open. Patty, with her right leg and left arm missing, the stumps all shredded with the round bone of the joint protruding and the severed tendons sticking out, like something had chewed them off.

And Kat standing there, telling him that it'd been a small pack of infected that had caught his girlfriend out beyond the fence. Telling him that she'd charged in when she heard Patty screaming and scared them off, but it'd been too late for Patty.

But hadn't she had blood on her hands?

At the time, he'd figured she'd just touched the already-dead body. But later, after he'd played the scene over and over in his mind, he wasn't so sure. He wished he'd told her to take her bandanna off so he could see if her mouth was bloody too.

Lies. Everyone's fucking lying. They lie, and then they gaslight you when you catch them. They tell you that you're crazy. They tell you that you're being irrational. They tell you that you're being paranoid.

He didn't even realize he'd driven the distance back to his ranch until he saw his house looming up in front of him.

Where had those moments gone? He'd been so lost in his own head...

He pulled up in front of the house, braking hard, and then throwing it into park.

"Uh, boss?" one of the guys said from the back—Kyle, or something like that. Or maybe Skylar. He remembered thinking it sounded like a girl's name, so probably Skylar.

Colin ignored him. Thrust his way out of the vehicle. Slammed the door behind him. Marched up the front steps, with his nostrils flaring and everything around him seeming to get a lot closer to him. To stare at him. To watch him. To judge him.

The entire world was fucking with him. Running a game on him.

—remember that little bottle of pills?—

Of course he remembered.

—and what'd you take those for?—

Fuck the diagnosis. Fuck it, and fuck the doctor that gave it to him. You know, he wasn't that different from his father, and his father hadn't been labeled, and had pills shoved at him by some overeager head shrinker. Back then, you were allowed to be pissed and question the loyalty of your family and friends without everyone telling you that you were crazy.

Still, he missed those little pills. Even right at that moment, when he was somehow so sure that his perceptions were true and not delusions at all, he missed the peace and calm he'd felt while taking them. He missed the clarity.

I have clarity right fucking now, part of him insisted. *Just because everyone lies to your face doesn't mean you're not seeing clearly.*

And, of course, part of him just feared that he was losing it. Feet dipping into that cold, dark chaos of unstoppable thoughts that all bore the weight of extreme conviction.

A constant tug of war in the core of him, stretching who he was, threatening to shear his identity in two. The conviction of his perceptions hijacking his sense of truth. But then his rational brain would tell him that truth only came from logic. And then came all the mental contortions of trying to reconcile the two. Trying to make his perception of truth agree with his logical brain, and always coming up just a hair short, like not having quite enough length on two ends of string to tie them together. Because if he couldn't make them agree, then he *was* going to tear, right down the middle. He'd lose himself in that darkness.

He found himself standing in his office, behind his desk. Vaguely recalled stalking through his house to get there. He stared down at the desk, his hands on his hips, breathing slowly but heavily through his nose.

Do it, do it, do it.

Sometimes it was hard to tell whether his mind was goading him or begging him.

He glanced up at movement. Felt his stomach drop as he realized he'd left his office door open, and there was Skylar, creeping towards him, staring at Colin from under his heavy brows.

Had that motherfucker been sneaking up on him?

—maybe he's just scared of you—

Because he's a fucking pussy.

Skylar halted the second Colin looked up at him, and that made it seem like he'd just been caught.

Colin let out weird noise, something between a gasp and a gag, his hands dropping from his waist. "Were you...?"

Skylar blinked, terror leaking into his eyes.

Little rat's been caught. Every rat thinks they've got the run of things until they get—SNAP—caught in a fucking trap! Rats and squirrels and weasels—all ways to describe someone like Skylar.

"Boss—"

Colin's face wrinkled up, and something in him was either stricken, or enraged. "Were you sneaking up on me?"

Skylar's shoulders drooped. Almost like he'd been hoping this wouldn't happen, but expecting that it would.

Hoping *what* wouldn't happen?

—you, going insane—

Losing your grip

—bonkers—

Bananas

—Jesus Christ, could you do the whole world a fucking favor and blow your brains out already?—

"It's not like that, Boss," Skylar tried.

Tried, and failed.

"Huh!" Colin sounded like an offended old woman in his own ears, and he loathed himself for it. If he could, he would've beat himself until his brains came out his ears.

That's what this fucking world always does! They drive you crazy, and then blame you for going crazy! Gaslighting me! Motherfuckers!

And then he was back to hating the world more than he hated himself.

Maybe Skylar saw what was wriggling through his features. His face went all faux-calm, and he spun with a quiet, "No worries, nevermind." Colin was already coming around the desk, but if Skylar heard his heels clacking on the floorboards, he didn't look around.

Colin had the urge to tackle him from behind, the images of him beating his own brains out shifting and melding into him beating *Skylar's* brains out. But the desk was calling to him.

Do it, do it, do it.

He slammed the door on Skylar's retreating figure, causing the wall to shake and the decorations to rattle. The slam seemed to give him a blast of self-reflection. He was losing it. He couldn't afford to lose it. He was losing it more often lately, and losing it for longer, and the only thing that had helped was

—*the pills*—

what he had in the desk

Do it, do it, do it!

If he let his thoughts run amok, they'd spiral out of control. And he couldn't let that happen. Not right now. Not with everything going on.

—*because eeeeeeeeeeeveryone depends on YOU*—

Because they're rats and ticks and leeches! Pests! Bloodsuckers! Gaslighters!

He stalked back to his desk and practically fell into his seat, his hands sliding up and down his thighs, up and down, up and down. He thought about it for the barest of seconds. He knew addiction was a factor—*Do it! Dooooo iiiiiiiiit!*—but it really did help. And help was what he needed. Because he'd run out of pills a long time ago—seventy-five days after the collapse of Western society, to be exact.

He snatched the center drawer open. The contents shifted violently. Pens and pencils. A little pocket pistol and some loose cartridges. Some spare change. An old flash drive with who-knew-what on it. And a little tin that used to hold mints.

He felt better just looking at it. But he'd feel even better after he snorted what was in it.

He grabbed up the tin and slapped it on the desk, then slammed the drawer closed, because everything felt like it needed to happen violently. He took the little tin in both hands and thumbed the lid open.

Dammit it all to hell. There wasn't much left.

Well...not in *here* anyway.

About a year after his pills had run out he'd miraculously found *this* shit.

No...his *ranch hands* had found this shit. They'd gone on a scavenging trip, and come back all hootin' and hollerin' about it. Told him it was meth, and they planned to have a mighty fine party with it—two kilos of it. Colin guessed they thought that since there were no laws anymore, he'd be okay with having all his ranch hands turn into meth-addled shitbags. He wasn't, and told them so in no uncertain terms, and then relieved them of it.

They sulked but got over it.

Colin had intended to burn the stupid shit, but decided to hold onto it. Call it intuition. Because a week later, he was being swallowed up by that chasm, and the only thing that kept him from breaking with reality completely was a big old snort of meth.

It didn't exactly make all the intrusive thoughts go away. But it made him strong enough to withstand them. It sped his mind up to a level that the thoughts didn't seem like disjointed blurs anymore, because he was thinking as fast as they were. He could keep up with those bastards. He could get his hands on them. He could wrangle them into submission.

His thoughts were like stampeding cattle, and without help, he was just one man standing in their path, destined to be trampled to death. But with this stuff, it was like he could be on horseback and run alongside his thoughts and steer them in the direction he wanted them to go.

Yeah. Something like that.

He'd burned through one of the kilos, even trying to ration it. So when he'd started on the second kilo, he'd made a promise to himself: He'd only use it when he *needed* it. He wouldn't let himself get addicted. He'd treat it like medication.

That was when he'd hid the second kilo, and only refilled the tin once a month.

Of course, that'd been some time ago, and that last kilo had been depleted pretty heavily. And maybe he'd fudged it a few times and refilled his tin after three weeks. Or two weeks. But shit, come on. He had to stay in control. And the world was always fucking with him. Always driving him crazy and then gaslighting him.

He tipped the tin until all the white powder shifted to a corner, then spilled it out in more or less a line. It was a fat one. But if he took his normal-sized dose, then there would only be a tiny bit left in the tin that wouldn't even be enough for a *regular* dose. Might as well take it all.

He snapped the tin closed, staring at the line of powder. His mouth was watering like it expected a sweet treat. Vaguely, he perceived some commotion beyond the door of his office. Vaguely, he recognized that he needed to *do it do it do it* or don't do it at all and hide it.

He did it.

Fire in his nose. Fire in his mind.

He rocked back in his chair, pinching his nose and shuddering and squeezing his eyes closed, waiting for the horrendous burn to abate. How could something hurt so bad and feel so fucking fantastic at the same time?

Like a grassfire, it burned hot and quick, and then smoldered out. Left everything in him feeling lightly toasted. It would take a moment for his brain to accelerate to the speed he needed to combat the torrents of thoughts.

Something slammed into his office door.

"Fuck!" Colin exploded, adrenaline coursing out to his fingertips, watering eyes snapping open to stare at the door. It took him a second to realize it hadn't been something slamming into his door. Someone was just knocking.

"Boss, it's me."

Bran.

Colin slapped the tin back in the drawer and slammed it shut. Palmed the white residue from his desktop. Wiped his nose a few times. Took a few steadying breaths as he rose to his feet—carefully, so as not to make himself faint, which he was prone to after a fat rail like that. Blinked and thumbed the tears out of his eyes.

Apparently he'd taken too long in his preparations.

"Boss?" More worried this time.

"What, goddammit?" Colin snapped, maybe a bit louder than was necessary.

Bran opened the door enough that he could stick his head in. An urge to scream at him came over Colin—*Did I tell you to open the fucking door?!*—but he stifled it by literally biting his tongue.

Bran's heavy brow was all worked up with concern. But after a moment's suspicious inspection of his boss, Bran apparently decided nothing was amiss and strode in.

Kat followed behind.

Colin stiffened, his eyes landing on hers. She immediately looked down. But he just kept watching her as they approached his desk. Rudely leaving the door open, Colin noted, which caused his hands to ball into fists.

Bran stopped in front of the desk. "We got her. And one of Jax's guys."

"Why?" Colin said, working hard to maintain a neutral expression.

Bran seemed taken aback. "Be...cause...you told me to?"

Colin jabbed a finger in the air to the rhythm of his words: "I *told* you to *kid*nap *Bea*!"

Bran's face settled into a familiar formation. It was his longsuffering expression. Like a soldier might stand at attention while having his ass chewed by his unreasonable superior. Colin had the brief fantasy of ripping Bran's face clean off his skull. One-handed. Just grabbing it and shucking it like a corn cob.

"It was a split-second judgment call," Bran said, levelly. "I had the opportunity, and I thought we could use a bit of insurance against retaliation."

Colin drummed his fingers against his thigh. It actually made sense. It just pissed him off at the same time. He didn't like it when people didn't do *exactly* what he told them to do.

Oh, that reminds me...

His gaze shifted to Kat. She was looking at him again.

—Is that fucking insolence I see in those bitchy eyes?—

She snapped her eyes down when he caught her.

A new flood of thoughts and images. Ah, but this time he could keep up with them. His brain was starting to gain speed. And he had confidence now. Confidence that he wasn't going insane. Confidence that he could handle this shit. He could see clearly. So fucking clearly. All those thoughts, instead of whizzing by like detritus in a hurricane wind, were all laid out before him like puzzle pieces.

"Take your mask off," Colin grated in a dry throat.

Momentary hesitation—*fucking insolence!*—but then she reached up and tugged it down, revealing her twisted features. God, she was disgusting to look at.

She glanced sharply at him.

Shit. Had he said that out loud? Ah, well, fuck it. Truth hurts, bitch.

And now I'm gonna get the truth out of you. And I can see you, you fucking whore. I can see the truth all over your face. You can't hide your lies behind that fucking bandana now. No, I'm going to see right through you now, and you can't fucking stop me.

Colin leaned forward onto the desk. "I want you to tell me...right now...what you did."

Bran shifted. "Boss, you know she can't talk all that well—"

"She's *mine*!" Colin suddenly roared at Bran, practically coming over the desk at him. He could feel his face flushing with the pressure of how hard he'd screamed, the corners of his vision darkling.

Bran rocked back on his heels, but didn't retreat.

"She belongs to me! I fucking own her! I don't need you to speak for her! She can fucking talk! I don't give a good goddamn if it takes her all fucking night, she's going to say what she did to me!" Back to Kat, incensed beyond the ability to control himself now. "What'd you do to me, you little cunt? Huh? What've you been doing behind my fucking back? I feed you! I clothe you! I put a fucking roof over your head! I give you a job! I welcome you into my house, into my ranch, into my *fucking life*! And you..." he gasped, because he'd run out of air. The fury seemed to run out at the same instant. His gulp of breath seemed cold. Everything in him, suddenly cold. He felt like crying. "...you betrayed me. Didn't you?"

She was looking at him now. Full on. No glancing away. Was that insolence? Or was she just trying to appear honest by meeting his gaze?

Or did the prolonged eye contact mean she was lying?

Everybody's always fucking lying to you!

Her lips split open. Hideously long teeth flashed.

"Didn't," she growled.

Colin felt like his heart was going to break. He couldn't remember the last time he felt so emotionally affected by something. Why was this always happening to him? Why was the world and everyone in it always fucking with him? What had he done to deserve this constant abuse?

He leaned back off the desk, shoulders slumped. His mouth hung open, drying out with the heaving breaths running through it. He couldn't look at her anymore. Couldn't look at Bran either. Decided to stare at the desktop.

"Who was it that killed Joaquin?" Colin finally said, quietly.

Quiet like a spider in a web. Quiet like a coiled snake. Quiet like a gun that only needs a few ounces of trigger pressure to go off.

Silence.

Ringing fucking silence.

Colin smiled forlornly and lifted his head to stare at the ceiling now. He wagged a finger in the air, inclining his ear. "Do you hear that?" He glanced at Kat—her eyes half terrified, half defiant. He glanced at Bran—his eyes hooded and worried. "Mm?" Colin prompted. "Anyone want to tell me what that sound is?"

Predictably, no one did.

"That's the sound of the truth," Colin practically whispered. Then with more force: "I asked you a fucking question, and what I get is fucking...*silence*. And doesn't that just tell me everything I need to know? Doesn't that tell me the truth, right there?"

Still, no one responded.

Colin slammed his fist down on the desk, making them jump. "*DOESN'T IT?!*"

But again they refused to respond.

Colin straightened, frowning as anxieties creeped into the edges of his mind.

What's happening right now?
—you're losing your shit—
Why aren't they talking?
—because you're crazy—
Why won't anyone just tell me the truth?!
—because everyone's fucking lying to you—
Yes, that's true. Everyone always fucking lies.
—unless it really is because you're crazy—
Am I crazy?
—are you crazy?—
Is any of this real?
—no—

Am I just paranoid and lashing out at the only allies I have left in the world?

—perhaps—

His thoughts twisted and turned on themselves, like a bucket of worms. But at least now he had the strength and resolve not to let them tear him in two. His center would hold. For now.

"Was it Jax and Marie?" Colin asked tonelessly.

Was Colin imagining it, or was that a furtive glance between Bran and Kat?

His heart dipped further. *You, too, Bran? Would you lie to me too?*

But then Bran nodded. "Yeah, I got a good look at them. And I'm pretty damn sure it was them. I just…"

"What?" Colin asked, feeling pretty wise and magnanimous for not screaming at that precise moment. He really was a good leader. Wasn't he?

Bran grimaced. "I just don't know how they survived."

Colin's eyes slid to Kat once again. "What about you, Honeybuns? Do *you* know how they survived?"

She shook her head.

"Say it," Colin hissed. "With your fucking words."

"No."

Colin pictured the little pocket pistol in his desk drawer. What would happen if he just pulled it out and shot her right in the face? How would Bran react? Colin was almost curious enough to do it. But then he thought, *If I kill her, I can't control the infected. If I kill her, Lander might get mad.*

Colin didn't like to admit when someone else was stronger than him, but for now he reconciled himself to it. You don't piss off the guy who controls all the infected in a twenty-mile radius of you. That's bad for business. Especially when your business is free-range cattle.

Then another thought came to him.

What if it was Lander? What if he was the one that saved Jax and Marie?

But why? To what end? Why would Lander betray Colin, when Colin was giving him exactly what he asked for? What he'd been wanting for so long now?

"Where are they?" Colin said, a bit absently.

Bran stirred. "Bea and the other guy?"

Colin nodded.

Bran hiked a thumb over his shoulder. "They're in the empty silo. Tied up. Guards posted."

Colin glanced at his office window. The shadows were already lengthening. How long until dark? A few hours. He had time.

"I want to talk to them," Colin said, and, without waiting for a response, stalked around the desk and out of his office, heading for the old, empty silo.

Chapter 29

The time between when Sam had been captured and when he'd been tied up in the old, empty silo had been some of the strangest moments of his life.

The buttstroke from Bran's shotgun hadn't knocked Sam out, though it'd rung his bell something fierce. He remembered still seeing everything around him—albeit blurred and doubled. He heard the screams and barks and gunfire, and tasted the blood pouring down the back of his throat.

But as far as conscious, rational thought? No, he didn't get that back until he was already in the utility bed of the ATV, roaring towards points unknown. He'd been flat on his back. His right shoulder smushed against the sidewall. His left shoulder smushed against Bea's. And Kat, crouching over both of them, her teeth bared, a hand on each of their throats.

The threat had been implicit by the grip Kat had on his windpipe. If he tried something, Kat could—and would—rip his throat out. It was as good as being held at gunpoint.

So Sam had lain there, and gathered his jangled senses, and marshaled his strength. He waited for an opportunity. For Kat to make a mistake. Or for Bran to drive them over a big bump that set her off balance. Something. Anything.

He was not so lucky. Bran drove like he knew every nook and cranny of the terrain, and never once hit a bump so big that it did anything more than jostle them a bit. And Kat? Kat was intensely focused. Not once did her attention wander. Not once did she adjust her tense body to make allowances for a straining muscle. Not once did her grip on their throats shift.

He found himself wondering how the hell she could keep it up. He knew that primals were possessed of some pretty insane strength and endurance. But the drive was long and unstable, and Kat never showed even a hint of fatigue, mental or physical.

It was the mental thing that got him. Because animals couldn't maintain that level of focus for so long. Shit, neither could most humans for that matter. And what did *that* mean?

Hybrid vigor, he thought, with a wash of surrealism that made him feel like if he weren't already flat on his back, he'd've stumbled under the vertigo of it. *Maybe they're stronger AND smarter than us.*

Maybe they're a better species altogether.

Maybe this was just evolution. Maybe *homo sapiens* was destined to be outbred and outperformed until they were extinct. Just like the Neanderthals.

It was an otherworldly experience to lay there, completely at the mercy of a being who was so obviously superior to him. He began to wonder about the other aspects of humanity—the aspects that the primals seemed to be missing. What about a sense of right and wrong? Kindness? Goodness? Compassion?

No other species seemed to be capable of those things in the way that humans were. And yet Sam wondered if those were just the things that were going to get them all killed.

Evolution could punish a species for their mental characteristics just as much as their physical ones. After all, the dodo went extinct because it had no fear of man, and was subsequently hunted mercilessly. Were all those high-minded ideals of the human condition just latent weaknesses lurking inside of them, waiting for some other, tougher version of their species to take advantage of them?

And if humanity went extinct, and no other species was capable of those ideals, would those ideals go extinct too? Would compassion die out with the only species that had ever grown to have a sense of it?

For some reason, that idea burned hot in Sam's chest. Made him want to fight all the harder. Made him want to preserve that precious spark that lay somewhere in the mind of humanity. It was the first and only of its kind. It could not be allowed to go out.

And that was the strangest thing of all: to suddenly be confronted with the knowledge that all of your previous motivations were thin facades, manufactured by the mind to cover what truly animated your actions.

The question was, *Why are you still fighting*? He'd never pressed himself hard enough for the answer. He'd always assumed he was doing it because *It's better to die fighting* and *It's about the guy next to you* and *Never give up, never surrender* and various other gung-ho rationales he'd heard from others along the way.

And so he'd covered the truth with those facades. And only now did they fall away to reveal the plain, terrifying reality that he'd always known, but never wanted to look at: If humanity died out, then everything good about them would cease to be, and never be again.

Perhaps an idealistic notion for someone whose adulthood had been formed in the savagery of the collapse. That he hadn't allowed it to completely rot out the good in him was kind of a miracle. Somehow, through it all, Sam had managed to find beauty where he could. He'd become a sort of emotional camel, sustaining his soul through all-too-infrequent waterings in a desert of cruelty. His oases had been glimpses of the good that still remained.

People who didn't know if they'd make it through the winter, sharing what they had in honor of a holiday barely remembered. People who helped a stranger, even when they knew it could cost them their life. A light-hearted joke passed between friends on a dark day. A pretty girl's passing smile in a wasteland of hardships.

Despite the hand gripping his throat, Sam cast a sidelong glance at Bea, and almost laughed. In a way, the whole thing between them was silly. To risk your life for someone you barely knew, based on a glance, and a moment of attraction. But life doesn't mean much if you lose your soul. And this was how Sam kept his alive.

By not just noticing those beautiful moments, but actively seeking them. After all, Bea had yet to smile at him. But sometimes you have to make the beautiful things happen, even in the unlikeliest of circumstances. Sometimes you have to dig to find water.

He wanted to say something to Bea in that instant, but felt like Kat's hands were heavily suggesting that silence might be the better option. A few moments after that, the strangely cerebral experience was broken by the sudden deceleration of the ATV. It trundled to a stop. Sam couldn't see anything but Kat's face and the bright blue sky, but he could smell manure and livestock. Without the tires rumbling under him, he could hear the sounds of them too. Some bored lowing in the distance.

He guessed they'd taken him and Bea back to the ranch. There was a whole lot of ways that this could go, but trying to formulate a plan at this juncture was just speculating without data. Based on what Bran had said just before walloping him in the face, Sam didn't think he or Bea were in immediate danger of being killed.

That, of course, is an easy thing to realize academically. But it does nothing for the pit of helpless dread you feel when a bunch of strangers with guns rip you out of a utility bed, slam you on the ground, and start tying your hands behind your back.

Just stay calm, Sam told himself, forcing his mind from a nightmarish parade of images. Meat hooks. Cattle prods. Bullwhips. Branding irons. There were a lot of ways to fuck someone up on a ranch.

He focused instead on the moment. *This moment right now. Stay present. Watch. Listen. Absorb.*

All lessons that Lee had taught him. Lee had some experience with these things, but this was the first time Sam had found himself in unfriendly hands.

First time for everything, Sam thought as he was hauled roughly to his feet by someone who immediately snaked their arm through Sam's and torqued his shoulders, forcing him to hobble along, bent over double and staring at the ground. All he saw of his captor was a pair of battered boots.

Had Kat or Bran been wearing boots? He couldn't remember. It probably wasn't Kat. The legs and feet made him think it was a man.

He snuck a glance behind him, and saw Bea being hauled along in a similar position by a guy Sam didn't recognize. A bit further back, the ATV, and Bran and Kat standing beside it, seeming to be in the middle of a heated conversation. Whatever the hell Bran was so mad about, he wasn't advertising it to the rest of the ranch. His voice was just hissing whispers over the sound of Sam's feet scuffing through the fine gravel.

He thought about saying something to his captor, but the way the man was yanking him along told him he'd probably just get a punch in the face as a response.

After twenty-one steps—Sam was counting—they passed into a heavy shadow. It was dark enough that Sam could barely see. They were inside of something. The sounds of the ranch grew suddenly distant. Their breaths and the scuffing of their feet echoed sharply. The smell of horses and cows and manure were replaced by the dingy smell of old grain.

The man pulled Sam deep into the shadows, and then swiped his legs out from under him, sending him face-first into what felt like a concrete floor. Fine dust puffed into Sam's mouth and nose as he inhaled. He coughed it out, thinking, *What a dick—that wasn't necessary.*

Sam rolled onto his side and craned his neck to look at his captor. He couldn't see much but the light from outside glimmering across the side of the man's sweaty face.

"You move," the man growled. "I'll beat you until you can't."

Sam opened his mouth to say, "No problem, Chief," but then thought that might be a bit glib. Best for his captors to think of him as scared and easy-to-control. So he gave the guy a slack-jawed nod instead.

Sam didn't *enjoy* killing other human beings. However, this was one of those moments where he figured that perforating someone's skull with a handful of five-five-six projectiles would probably feel pretty satisfying.

The man who'd been pulling Bea along gave her a similar warning and then departed. Neither man fully left, though. They stepped through the door of what Sam was beginning to realize was a grain silo, and posted themselves on either side. Close enough to keep an eye on them.

Sam let his head rest back on the concrete. A pall of grain particulate swirled in the sunlight coming through the door, stirred up by their passing feet. Above him, the steel walls of the silo disappeared into darkness.

What do I do now?

It hadn't been hard for him to sell being scared to the guy guarding them. He wasn't pissing his pants and shaking, and he certainly intended to fight back if he could, but he *was* scared. And, unfortunately, there weren't many fighting options available.

The door to the silo was maybe ten yards away, and already Sam had seen both of the guards peek in on them. So he'd have to stay put. If he started moving around too much, the guards would notice, and likely beat the shit out of him. Or worse.

Trying to talk to the guards wasn't exactly a guaranteed failure, but it didn't look hopeful. Sam put a mental category on that one: Last Ditch Effort.

Getting free and charging them? That just wasn't going to happen. They'd tied their hands and feet good and tight. Sam could already tell from wrenching his wrists and ankles that there was zero budge in them. And he had no means of cutting himself free.

Besides all that, even if they *did* manage to escape, what were they going to do? It was broad daylight in a ranch filled with armed men that were roughly as irritable as yellowjackets around a kicked nest. Sneaking out wasn't a realistic option. And fighting his way out was such a long shot, he put it about on par with talking his way out.

So, yet again…

What do I do now?

Bea gagged and coughed—probably on the grain dust.

Sam inclined his head in her direction. Saw the line of her body lying on its side, facing away from him, a few yards away. The sunlight coming through the open door illuminated her bare skin. Sam had ripped her shirt off to handle her wound, but now felt bad for leaving her so compromised. Being stripped to her dirty old bra while being held captive would only compound her sense of vulnerability.

After a moment of looking at her, he realized she was shivering hard. He didn't think she'd lost enough blood to be experiencing shock. And the silo was borderline sweltering. But sometimes the pain and trauma alone can set a body to shaking.

"You okay?" he breathed out in a low whisper.

She didn't respond. Had she not heard him, or was she unwilling to talk?

He couldn't let her retreat into herself. She needed to stay with him, whether she liked it or not.

"How's your shoulder?" he pressed.

"It's got a fucking hole in it," she hissed back, not turning to look at him.

Sam wasn't put out by her response. He actually found it encouraging. If she had the energy to get pissed, then she was doing pretty good, all things considered.

Now, how to keep her engaged?

"So," he whispered. "Finally got you alone."

He saw the way her head jerked. She was still for a moment. Then she contorted herself with a grunt, and managed to roll so she was facing him. Just enough sunlight coming in to see the glare on her face.

"Are you fucking serious?" she said, a bit loud.

"Ssh." Sam glanced at the door, but it didn't seem either of their guards had heard. He looked back to Bea. "And no, I'm not serious. Just…trying to bring the mood up."

"This isn't a fucking party."

Sam managed a shrug. "You got a knife?"

The shadows across her face morphed into a frown. "No."

"Anything on you at all that you can use to quietly and discretely cut yourself free?"

She thought about it for a moment. "No."

"Yeah, me neither," Sam grunted. "So, since we have no solution to our current predicament, we can either sit here and obsess about how fucked we are, or we can try to be pleasant for what might be the last hours of our life."

"So that's it? You're giving up?"

"Definitely not. I'm keeping my eyes open."

"For what?"

"Any possibility to get out of here. And if it comes, then we take it. But it hasn't. So…" Sam shifted to get his shoulder in a position where his arm wasn't going numb. "Now, we sit in silence, or we talk. I prefer to talk."

"Maybe I prefer silence."

"That'll just make you more nervous. Or at least it will me. Talking helps."

A pause. "You've been in this situation before?"

"Not precisely this, no," Sam admitted. "But I've been forced to wait for an unknown fate a handful of times. Like I said, talking helps." Then, rather than continue bandying about with whether they were going to talk or not, he decided to say something that might spur Bea on. "Is there any reason why Colin Horner would want to capture you specifically?"

He'd expected a hard negative response. What he got was an unsettling length of silence.

Sam frowned and turned his head to see her better. "Bea? Do you know why they targeted you?"

"Did they target me?" she said, much softer than before. "I was out of it. Still kinda am, to be honest."

"They ignored everyone else and came straight at us."

"Maybe it was just chance. Maybe they would've taken anybody."

The way she said it smacked of deflection.

"Bea, what are you not telling me? Don't try to convince me that they didn't come directly for you. I was just an afterthought. It was you they wanted. And I can tell that you know why. So cut the bullshit. Now's not the time to lie to me."

Another suspiciously long silence.

Then, finally: "We were working a cornfield," she said, somewhat nonsensically. And then she clarified, and it began to take an unpleasant form in Sam's mind. "Me and James. We knew it was getting late. We knew to get inside by the time the sun hit the horizon. But we only had one more section to plant. And the sun had *just* gone down. We...we thought we had more time. And the infected—we hadn't seen a single one in our area for almost a week."

Sam took a heavy breath, realizing where this was going. But still, the shape of it was indistinct. "James was killed by primals?"

"No," Bea answered. "No, we got away. We saw them coming over the ridge. One was much closer than the others. The pack leader, I guess. And James's rifle was right there." A long pause. "There was no way we could have gotten back to safety without shooting that thing. It was too close. So, I took the rifle, and I killed it. Then we ran. Got the doors barred. And we were safe."

Sam frowned, but didn't say anything. Obviously, that was not where the story ended.

"They told us when we came to the Redoubt—Ted, and everybody else—that things were different in the Valley. If we didn't make waves, the infected wouldn't mess with us. We didn't know how it worked at the time, but they told us never to shoot one of the infected. That would be making waves. It seemed crazy, but everyone insisted that was how things worked in the Valley. Don't make waves, and you'll be safe.

"We found out how it all worked the next morning."

Bea remembered it all with the perfect clarity of a life's most traumatic moment. Every detail of it was cut into her, bone deep, and they refused to even scar over, let alone heal. They were as fresh and bloody and raw as the day they had been given to her.

The first cut was betrayal. How quickly the Redoubt turned on her, even as a chiding voice in the back of her head reminded her, *They told you not to make waves*. How foolish she'd been, standing amongst the other people that she lived alongside, thinking they were on the same team, thinking that there would be some solidarity amongst them, that they'd tell this monster who'd shown up with a horde of his beasts, that they didn't know who had done it.

She even remembered worrying about them. Worrying about what Lander would do if no one fessed up. Would he let it be, or would he resort to more draconian measures to get the truth out of them?

She needn't have worried.

Lander stood there, front and center with his horde of creatures lurking behind him, and that bitch, Freya, at his shoulder. Or more appropriately, at his *heel*. Because that's all she was. An attack dog. She'd only seen the man one other time, and that had been from afar. Up close, she could see the strangeness all over him, like an aura that exuded from his pores.

"Someone killed a member of my family," Lander announced, furious eyes scanning the gathering. "You know the rules of the Valley. You take one of mine, I take one of yours. Who did it?"

He didn't even issue a threat. And yet, he'd barely finished the question before one, then two, then four, then twenty, and then every single fucking person who called the Redoubt home was pointing at her and James. And backing away from them. Distancing themselves. Creating a circular no-man's land all around Bea and James.

Bea opened her mouth to protest, but it caught in her throat.

Lander and Freya moved towards them, the gathering of people that should have been their friends parting before him with absolutely no resistance. Not even hard eyes. They couldn't even look at him.

Couldn't look at Bea or James either.

Lander stopped about two paces from them, frowning back and forth.

Bea's heart didn't feel like it was following any pattern, just thrashing about in her chest. Her breathing kept on speeding up until she was practically panting, though her mouth was shut up tight, and it all went whistling through her nose. In-out, in-out, in-out.

She cast a sideways glance at James and saw his fear was no more controlled than hers. And that terrified her.

"Did you both do it?" Lander asked, quietly. "Or just one?" He was looking right at James.

"It was me," James said, almost instantly. "I did it."

And that was the second cut: Shame. Shame that she'd taken a moment to think about the consequences of confession, while James didn't have to think at all. He didn't want her to be punished, even if she was the one that had done it.

Lander's face grew dead cold. "Kill him," he snapped.

Freya lunged.

"No!" Bea didn't even realize what she was doing until she'd rammed her body into Freya's, halting her clawed hands inches from James's throat. But, God! It was like running into a brick wall! Bea rebounded and staggered backwards, her fists swinging wildly and connecting with nothing.

Freya weaved her head away from the blows like it was a minor nuisance, and then flashed out an arm that was almost too quick to see, backhanding Bea across the face. Her vision went mottled and gray and all sense left her for the span of a second or two, until she realized she'd toppled onto her ass…

Scuffling feet. Growling and grunting.

James screamed.

Freya was on top of him, pinning his arms down as easy as if James were a child.

Something erupted in Bea. Or, more accurately, it *imploded*. Like all of her life energy suddenly condensed down into a pinpoint that burned like a newborn star in her chest. She came off the ground like gravity could not grip her and launched herself at Freya's head, not bothering to take wild swings, but instead going for the throat like she was one of Lander's beasts.

The fury in her blotted out any capacity to remember what had actually happened in those few seconds. All Bea knew was that she'd latched onto Freya's head and shoulders, and clawed and bit until she could feel the skin clotting up beneath her nails and taste the bitch's blood in her mouth…

Then came a slam that took the breath out of her. Felt like every disc in her spine had been rearranged. Like she might have been paralyzed. And then a great strain blasted into her consciousness, coming from her right shoulder. She was yanked onto her belly, with a foot in her back, pressing her down, while her arm was wrenched backwards until—

POP

The pain was so huge and immediate that she didn't even cry out. She *couldn't* cry out. Everything in her body seemed to have short-circuited. She couldn't move. Couldn't breathe. Couldn't speak. All she could do was feel, and fear.

And hear.

Snarling. And screaming. And a wet, rending sound.

She knew what it was, but she couldn't do anything about it. And oh, how she tried. Screaming in her own head to *Move! Get up! Fight! Do something, Beatrice, fucking DO SOMETHING!*

Her body chose to give her only tiny increments of control back. First, her hands, but she could not use her right arm—it was dead at the shoulder. And then her lungs, as she began to gulp air. And then her legs.

Her legs writhed against the ground until they'd managed to turn her over onto her back again. Her head lolled to the side, and she saw it.

James. Freya standing over him. Her claws gripping a bloody mass. James, with sightless eyes, staring up at nothing, not moving. A gaping hole in his throat.

No. Absolutely not. He couldn't have died already. He'd been alive only moments before. How was it even possible? Had she been out of it for so long? Had she missed her one and only chance to say goodbye to him?

Goodbye?

The third cut: Severance. A connection to another human being that could never be had again, because they'd been removed from existence. And this was a wholly different pain, a pain that transcended and blotted out the pain in her body. A reality she could not even fathom, even as she stared at it.

This simply wasn't possible. No one had the power to extinguish him. He was...James. He was her husband. They had a past, and a future. Together. All of it, *together*.

Was this even real?

Ever since the collapse, Bea had had nightmares. Ones where she knew she was in a nightmare, even as the panic drenched her, laying heavy on her chest like a blanket made of lead. Entombing her. Paralyzing her. And this was so much like that.

Because she was lucid enough in those nightmares to know they weren't real, she would cry out. In her dreams, she would be screaming, but in reality, it would only come out a low moan. But it would always be enough to wake James. And then he would put his hands on her shoulders and shake her awake, and rescue her from the fear.

She screamed like that now, hoping to wake James up, so he could wake *her* up.

Except it didn't come out a moan. It ripped her throat out. It ripped her heart out.

And James did not wake up. And no one rescued her from the fear.

But she did feel someone's hands on her, as the breath ran out, and she started to hyperventilate, and her throat began spasming and she couldn't tell if she was going to sob or vomit. Someone's hands, cupping her face.

They turned her head, peeling her unwilling eyes off of James's lifeless form. Forcing her to stare up…

At Lander.

Who smiled down at her as though she were a heavenly vision.

"The *fire*," he husked, his voice trembling with excitement. Gripping her head almost painfully between his filthy hands. "You…are the future."

Then he produced a little, pearl-handled pocket knife.

And then she was given her final cut.

For a long moment, Bea said nothing. But Sam could hear the thickness in her shuddering breaths. Then a wet sniff.

Her voice was strained when she spoke again. "They gave us up to Lander almost immediately. They…they didn't even try to protect us. And James…" she sounded like she was being strangled. "What the fuck did I think was going to happen? I just stood there, Sam. I just stood there, and I didn't say a goddamn word. While James took the blame for it."

Sam realized he'd been holding his breath, waiting for this last part. Then he let it out in what would have been a groan, if he'd dared to use his voice. The only thing he felt appropriate to whisper in that moment was "Shit."

He could imagine it. He could imagine her sense of powerlessness.

And then a lot of things about Bea came into focus. The latent resentment towards the people she lived with. Her evident hatred for Lander. Her distrust. All of the things that Sam had simply written off as "prickly."

"That's when I got this scar," Bea uttered. "I remember barely feeling it. Not caring. Just staring at James. And all I could feel was…" she trailed off. When she spoke again, her voice was distant. "It was Lander that did it. Lander who came over and…just stood there. Staring at me. And all I remember is that I just wanted to touch James. I wanted to…I wanted to touch him before he got cold. I don't know why. It was all I could think about. Like if I touched him while he was still warm, then maybe it wasn't real. Maybe I could take it back."

Sam wanted to tell her that there was nothing she could have done, but he already knew what her response would be to that. Because it's what he would have said too: *I could have told the truth. I could have been brave instead of cowering in fear.*

Sam was intimately familiar with the bitterness and self-loathing that came from watching your family members die while you were too scared to do a damn thing about it. He could tell himself that he'd only been a boy, but that never seemed to matter. Just like it wouldn't matter to Bea to point out that James probably would have taken the fall for his wife, whether she'd spoken up or not.

"When he cut my face with that knife," Bea continued, slowly, almost as though she were puzzled by the memories. "He was…marking me. He wanted me. But he left me there. Said my shoulder had to heal before I was any good to him."

A sudden bolt of alarm pierced the fog of shared grief in Sam's mind. "What'd he mean by that?"

But didn't he already know? Hadn't some part of him already known it, and didn't want it to be real?

"You asked why they targeted me," Bea murmured, haunted and bitter. "And that's why. They did it for Lander. Because he wants me. He wants to...breed me."

Chapter 30

Angela Houston let the young woman behind the counter swipe her ration card through the reader, then took her steaming cup of coffee with a smile, and turned to look at the expanse of Colorado mountains all around her.

These days she found it easier and easier to believe that life beyond the enclave of Aspen was just as it should be. Just as it was a little over six years ago. It was a pleasant fiction that Angela felt no need to disrupt. And, apparently, everyone else in Aspen thought the same.

After all, the only reason they "sold" coffee and old-fashioned donuts in a street kiosk, as opposed to making people go through the mess hall, was to maintain that veneer of a peaceful, functioning society.

Angela was just fine with that. She'd done the hard shit. She'd survived three years of it. As a mother, as a liaison between civilians and military, as a representative of North Carolina, and finally, as a president. Madam President, of the United Eastern States. Which was to say, the handful of secure settlements throughout North and South Carolina, Georgia, and Florida.

She'd hated all of that. Now she was just "Mom" again, and perfectly content to be so, thank you very much. Not that "Mom" was without challenges, particularly as the mother of a teenage daughter who was, at least on good days, trying to learn how to walk again after a bullet had partially severed her spine three years ago in Greeley, Colorado.

But the late afternoon was Angela's *me time*. And sorely needed. Abby had been depressed the last few days and hadn't even bothered with the walker. A situation that somehow made Angela both compassionate and infuriated. Compassionate, because...well, it was her daughter for chrissake. Infuriated, because Abby was going to throw away the progress she'd been making, and Angela knew her daughter was going to regret it when she got out of her funk. But she also knew there was shit-all she could say to convince her daughter to tough it out.

Hell, Abby had toughed out enough. And that's really what it came down to. She had a right to feel overwhelmed and depressed, without people trying to convince her that she was wrong to feel that way. Just like Angela had a right to take a goddamned nap and follow it up with an afternoon coffee. Which she'd probably regret around 10 P.M. when she tried to fall asleep.

She smiled at that thought, as she took a sip of the scalding and not-that-great-tasting-but-who-gives-a-fuck brew. It was a wonderful thing when all you had to worry about was whether an afternoon dose of caffeine might prevent you from a full eight hours.

Wonderful, beautiful normality.

And that was when the little two-way radio on Angela's hip chirped, and Abby's voice came over, sounding a bit confused.

"Uh, Mom? You there?"

Angela frowned, shifted the coffee to her left hand, and plucked the radio up with her right. "Yeah, Honey. Do you need something?"

"The, uh..." Abby lowered her voice almost to a whisper. "The thing in your office? It's ringing."

Angela snapped her wrist around and checked her watch. It was four o'clock. That was an hour ahead of time.

She started walking, fast. "I'll be right there."

"Do you want me to answer it?"

"No. Don't answer it. I'll be there in five."

The "thing" in her office was a satellite phone. And the only person that had the number was someone who, on her documentation, was only referenced as "Archangel." But his identity was no secret to Angela. She'd lived and fought and bled alongside him for three years.

He was, in a way, her only remaining connection to the reality of the madness that still lurked beyond the borders of the Interior States.

She tried to sip her coffee twice, but she was walking too fast and only wound up burning her lips. Then, about a quarter mile from her house, she realized the only reason she was walking at all was to try to save the coffee. At which point she swore, dumped it out, and started running.

When she burst in the front door, Abby was in her wheelchair at the base of the stairs. For a flash, Angela wondered, *Damn, if I'd've told her to answer it, would she have had the gumption to try the stairs again?* The curse of parenthood—to forever feel like you fucked up, no matter what decision you make.

"He's calling an hour early," Abby exclaimed, needlessly. She was just nervous and feeling the need to speak. Which was probably why she also said, "What's going on?"

To which Angela snapped, "How the hell should I know?" as she mounted the stairs, and then felt guilty for it by the time she reached the top.

She could hear the muted bleating of the satphone from down the hall. Slowing to a walk now, trying to get her breath back so she wouldn't be huffing into the phone. He called an hour early, and obviously hadn't stopped calling for the last five minutes.

This was bad. Something had gone wrong.

Every single one of their faces flashed through Angela's mind: Lee, Sam, Marie, Abe, Jones. And then back to Sam. And then Lee again. And then Sam once more.

Sam who'd been like a son to her. And Lee who she'd both loved and hated, depending on the day. Of course she loved Marie, and had been friends with Abe, and even the loud-mouthed Jones. But it was Sam and Lee that she couldn't let go of. It was them she feared the most for.

So when she yanked the satphone out of the desk drawer and hurriedly answered it, the voice that came back made her stomach feel like it'd dropped through her feet and out of her body.

"Marie?" Angela said, her voice tight with panic. "Where's Lee? Why didn't he call? What happened?"

"Slow down," Marie said. God, but her voice had changed. Not that she'd ever been particularly sunny, but now she sounded…hard. Rough.

And it caused Angela to obey, despite her thundering heart and nightmarish imaginings. She closed her eyes, pressing the phone painfully to the side of her face. "I'm sorry. Go ahead."

"Lee is…" A breath of hesitation. "Fine."

Why had she hesitated? What did that mean?

Angela pushed a finger to her lips to keep her own mouth shut.

"But shit's gone sideways," Marie continued. She sounded like she was trying to keep her voice down. "We didn't have time to wait for the regular call window. We need help."

Angela opened her eyes and stared at the bland beige wall in front of her. "I…Shit, you know I can't do anything without going direct with Lee."

"Lee's busy."

"Too busy to make sure you get help?"

Marie swore, sounding distant, like she'd pulled the phone away from her face to vent. Then her voice came back, cold and sharp: "And what if I told you he was dead, Angela? What then? Would you just leave us high and dry?"

Angela considered this for a few breaths. Then she spoke as though by rote: "In the event of Archangel's incapacitation, I can accept orders from…the next in command." Technically, that should've meant Abe. But Angela wasn't trying to be stickler. She was just trying not to piss off her secret benefactor, the Interim Commander of American Operations.

"Fine," Marie said. "Lee's been incapacitated."

Angela swallowed. This was her fucking life here. And if she strayed one damn degree from the instructions ICAO Griffin had laid out for her, there was a strong possibility it would result in Angela and Abby being kicked out on their asses.

But then again…Lee and Sam.

And also, *Shit's gone sideways.*

"Fuck it," she spat, then grabbed a pen and put it to the notepad on her desk. "What do you need and where do you need it?"

Ted's demeanor had changed pretty drastically in the last few moments.

After Lee had dispatched Marie to contact Colorado, and Jones to coordinate the gathering and consolidation of weapons and ammunition, he very quietly and politely asked Ted if he would have a private word with Lee and Abe.

Leading them to his personal Conex box, Ted strutted stiffly along, like a riled-up rooster. Even pointed at some of his people and gave them some brisk commands to get a tally of the dead and wounded.

Lee assumed he was trying to reestablish some sense of control—both for himself, and for his frazzled people. Lee let him hold onto that right up to the moment when he and Abe followed Ted into his box.

At which point, Abe shut the door and lowered the security bar over it.

Ted spun, alarm widening his eyes. "What—?"

Lee rammed his fist into Ted's solar plexus. Ted whoofed all the air out of his lungs, and might've staggered back if Lee hadn't held onto him. He stripped the revolver out of Ted's hand—still with its cylinder open—and tossed it into the far corner of the box.

Then, with Ted wheezing and coughing, Lee kicked his legs out from under him and planted the man square on his back.

Lee crouched on one knee over the man's gasping form, his eyes tight and teeth gritted against the screaming pain in his side. He was pretty sure that move had hurt him more than Ted. But he forced his shaking, tingling hand up to Ted's neck. Pressed the heel of his palm into the man's throat, fingers gripping his jaw.

"You scream for help and I'll kill you."

Ted sucked in a rattling breath and then croaked, "They won't let you leave—" Gasp "—if you kill me!"

"I'm willing to deal with those consequences. Are you?"

Ted was silent for a long moment. Strutting cock to fearful supplicant in five seconds flat. He didn't answer that question, so Lee assumed he was, in fact, *not* willing to deal with those consequences.

Abe's approaching footsteps. Unrushed. There'd been no words exchanged between Lee and Abe, but they'd been working with each other for a very long time. Abe had known what Lee was thinking. Probably read it plain as day in how nicely Lee had asked to speak to Ted alone.

"What do you want?" Ted finally rasped.

Lee glanced to his right and saw the suppressor of Abe's rifle hovering there, pointing at Ted's face. He'd pop Ted's noggin if the guy squealed. So Lee let go of Ted's face. And then began thumping his index finger against Ted's forehead.

"I think you've been fucking lying to me," Lee said. "And normally, I'd just let that play out." *Thump, thump, thump.* "But they just took one of my guys, Ted, and I have the sneaking suspicion that it's because you're not telling me something."

Ted flinched and whimpered every time Lee thumped him in the head. Lee had the urge to ram his fist into Ted's face to stop his whimpering. But he was afraid the guy might lose consciousness with anything heavier than a slap.

"I don't know what you're talking about," Ted mewled.

"Well, let's start with this, Ted," Lee spoke slowly and quietly. "I have a message for you. Can you guess who from?"

Ted only shook his head.

"Why, from Lander Hollis," Lee said, feigning amazement. "You know, the crazy wizard that you told us you've never really dealt with? Except that Lander seems to know you pretty well. Or at least well enough to ask me to tell you that a debt is still owed to him."

Ted hadn't been moving around all that much, but now he got downright inanimate. After freezing for long enough that Lee reconsidered hitting him, Ted thawed enough to move his mouth: "I don't know what he's talking about."

"Imagine that," Lee sighed. "You don't know what *I'm* talking about, you don't know what *Lander's* talking about. You don't know what *anybody* is talking about. Christ! I guess you're just an ignorant motherfucker, huh?"

"Or a fucking liar," Abe growled.

"Or a fucking liar," Lee agreed with a nod. He had to appreciate his partner in that moment. Lee hadn't had time to fill Abe in on all that'd happened, but when he mentioned meeting Lander Hollis, Abe didn't even bat an eye. Just rolled with it.

Ted's eyes darted between Lee and the muzzle of Abe's rifle. "Lander's crazy! You can't trust anything he says!"

Lee gave a dubious grunt. "Mmm—crazy? Yes, he's definitely crazy. But I found him to be almost jarringly honest. So, no. I don't think he was lying. I think *you're* lying, Ted. Yes, I legitimately trust the word of a guy who fucks primals more than I trust you. Because you stink of deceit. I've smelled it on you since the second I met you, and like I said, normally I let that play out. But now the life of a very dear friend of mine is on the line, and I don't really have time to fuck around. I need to know what the fuck's going on in this valley."

Lee rose to his feet. "And if you're not going to say shit, then hell, maybe we open those doors and invite your people in here, and we can see if any of *them* might be able to shed some light on why Bea and Sam got snatched, and why Lander seems to think you owe him a debt."

Well, that certainly got a reaction. Ted jolted upright, at which point Abe gave him a light muzzle-thump to the skull, which convinced him to stay down.

Ah, but isn't that the thing about liars? They lie to cover things up. Things that they can't bear the thought of their friends and family knowing about. And then they lie to cover the lies. And so on and so forth. Point being, there's nothing more terrifying to a liar than to have their lies exposed.

But Lee was already at the door to the box. Already grabbing the security bar and raising it.

"Don't!" Ted practically shrieked.

Lee held the security bar there, considering. "I dunno, Ted. I think your people might know some things. Or at least suspect them. After all, they've been watching you. And maybe they like you enough that they haven't come out and voiced their suspicions. But I'd be awful curious to hear what they think."

"You don't need to do that," Ted begged. "Please. Leave them out of this."

Lee looked over his shoulder, still holding the security bar up. "Are you gonna tell me the truth?"

Ted's eyes were wide as full moons in his sweating face. "Promise you won't kill me."

Lee scoffed. "Ted, you fucking ingrate, I only kill folk that *need* killing. And if you give me a full and truthful brief about what is actually going on around here, then I don't see a need to kill you. I mean, don't get me wrong, I have a *desire* to kill you. But I won't. And you can trust me, because, unlike you, I'm not a fucking liar."

Ted considered this with quivering lips and blinking eyes. Then he nodded. "Okay. Okay, deal." He raised his hand, as though to offer a handshake.

"Put your fucking hand down," Abe said.

Ted put his hand down.

Lee put the security bar back in place. Turned. Walked back to Ted. "Well? Talk."

Ted swallowed. "It's a long story."

"Then talk fast," Abe suggested.

"Time's short," Lee said. "And my friend's life is on the line. It'll help if you skip your bullshit rationalizations and just tell us the facts."

Ted struggled like something was caught in his throat. A few false starts: "I...uh...well..."

Abe kicked him in the side. Not hard. More like spurring a horse. "Talk faster."

"I wanted a hybrid!" Ted spat out, shying away from Abe. "I was afraid! I thought I could keep the Redoubt safe if—"

"Kick him," Lee muttered, and Abe kicked him again, garnering a little yelp from Ted. "I told you to skip the bullshit rationalizations. You wanted a hybrid. Keep going."

"I wanted a hybrid. And...so I went to Lander."

"He's surrounded by primals all the time. How'd you get to him?"

"Not all the time," Ted snapped. "Sometimes he just walks around with...with the other one that's like Kat. The one he calls Freya. I would see him sometimes, at a distance. So I decided to approach him and try to make some kind of deal. In exchange for a hybrid of our own. So we wouldn't have any more...incidents."

"Incidents?" Lee pressed.

Ted glanced away. "It was Bea. Bea and her husband, James. Some infected had come around a field they were planting. Bea and James wound up getting away, but not before one of them shot an infected and killed it. Pissed off Lander something fierce. He came the day after, and..." Ted's eyes squinched up. "What was I supposed to do?"

Lee and Abe exchanged a glance, but said nothing.

Ted searched them as though to see if there was any absolution there. There was not. So, looking miserable, he continued. "That's how James died. Freya killed him. Opened his throat right there in front of everyone."

Lee narrowed his eye at Ted. "Keep going."

"So I met Lander to make a deal. But the only deal he would make with me was…" Ted's face got very still again, and his eyes had a haunted look to them. "He needed…I guess…fresh genetics? Maybe his pack of infected were getting inbred or something—I don't fucking know. But that was a part of the deal: I…*I* had to…provide the genetics."

"You had to fuck a primal," Lee clarified with a growing sense of unease. He'd expected almost anything. But this was…well…some fucked up shit.

Ted winced. "Not *primals*. It was Lander's wives. Hybrids."

"So did you?" Abe asked, his voice flat and emotionless.

Ted couldn't look either of them in the eye. Stared off at the wall instead. "Yes." Another dry-sounding swallow. "All three of them. And I could choose the…offspring."

Lee smeared a hand across his face, pinched the bridge of his nose, and peered over his hand at Abe. Abe wasn't even looking. Seemed transfixed by Ted, his nose wrinkled in disgust.

Oddly enough, as disturbing as the concept was, Lee found himself unsurprised. People were animals. Then they evolved society and convinced themselves they were past all that. The last six years had proven that to be a lie. Strip away society, and what did you find? A bunch of animals, doing animal shit to each other.

"Genetics," Lee said quietly. "You said that was *part* of the deal. What was the other part?"

This one took a bit longer for Ted to get out. Sad little soul that he was, at least he had the humanity to feel ashamed. Regardless, Lee was about to tell Abe to kick him again when Ted spoke a single word: "Bea."

"He wanted Bea?" Lee asked, frowning.

"He was obsessed with her since the moment he saw her. That was the day they killed James. He wanted her. For the genetics. Or maybe for himself. But I think for the genetics."

"And you made that deal with him," Lee muttered, his insides doing all kinds of things. Stomach twisting. Heart leaking fire through his veins. "You made that deal. You agreed to fuck his primals, and turn Bea over to him so she could be bred—let's call a spade a spade here, huh?—so she could be fucking *raped*."

"I didn't go through with it!" Ted suddenly raged.

Abe raised his rifle a hair. "Pipe down, muchacho. Don't want your friends outside overhearing this shit, do you?"

Ted shrank in on himself. Said it again, but much quieter: "I didn't go through with it! I didn't turn her over to him! I'll admit, I...I..."

"Fucked three primals," Abe assisted.

"Hybrids," Ted hissed. "Half human." As though that made it all okay.

"Why didn't Lander just take Bea the first time he saw her?" Lee demanded.

"Because she got injured in a fight with Freya." Ted motioned to his shoulder. "Tore her shoulder out of socket. Lander said he couldn't take her when she was injured. After I made the deal with him, he said to bring her to him when she was healed. But I couldn't do that to Bea. I couldn't, because..."

Lee saw it coming. Went ahead and filled in the blank. "Because you *love* her." Said with the most bitter sarcasm with which the word "love" can be spoken.

Ted whimpered and clenched his eyes shut, giving a tiny nod.

"And why didn't he just come grab her as soon as you reneged on the deal?"

"Because he knew I wouldn't give her up," Ted said, opening his eyes and seeming a bit eager. As though he wanted them to be proud of him for being such a brave guardian. "He knew I'd lock down the Redoubt, and he couldn't wait us out forever—his primals would get hungry and wander off."

Abe scowled deeply at him. "Then why didn't you just do that when he came the first time? Why'd you give up Bea and James?"

Ted's face blanked out for a moment, then began to sputter. "Because...I...I..."

Abe's eyes widened. "Oh. Because you wanted James dead so you could move in on his wife. You heartless twat. That's some real David and Bathsheba shit."

Ted didn't confirm or deny. Only started weeping. Big, blubbery sobs.

Lee decided to kick him this time. He endured the pain in his own ribs like cleansing fire, and sent a solid punt straight into Ted's thigh, crunching his common peroneal nerve and making him squawk and moan.

"Stop crying, you piece of shit. You've got no right to be crying. You did all this shit to yourself. If anyone has a reason to cry, it's Bea, who I'll remind you, was captured along with my boy. So, let's get very real here, Ted. Because if you actually do love her—which is really hard to believe, given everything you've done—then you'll want to help us get her back, won't you?"

"Yes!" Ted eked out between snotty sobs. "But how? Horner's taken her and he's going to give her to Lander! Maybe he already has!"

"Why's Horner doing shit for Lander?" Lee demanded.

"They're..." Ted flapped his hands about. "*In league* together! They're allies!"

"And how'd *that* relationship start?" Lee seethed over top of him. "Why'd Lander give him Kat in the first place?"

"To get back at me!" Ted wailed. Watery eyes blinking up at Lee with fear and desperation. If that look had been on any other human's face, Lee would have been moved to pity. But all he felt now was revulsion. "To punish me for going back on our deal!" And then all the strength seemed to leave Ted, and he wilted, only barely holding himself up on one elbow. "Because she's mine. She's my daughter. Kat is my daughter."

Chapter 31

Lee and Abe stepped out of the Conex box and didn't bother to close the door behind them. There was a small gaggle of faithful Ted followers trying not to look like they were lurking, and failing mightily.

Lee caught one of them staring suspiciously at him. He smiled and nodded at the man. He didn't really give a shit what these people did at this point. Didn't really care what Ted did either. If he tried something stupid out of spite, Lee would have no problem putting the man down. And if it didn't rise to the level of killing him? Well, then he'd just air Ted's dirty laundry.

Even his most faithful followers would balk when they heard the shit he'd been up to.

Likely, Ted knew that, and wouldn't do a damn thing.

The missing pieces had fallen into place, and Lee didn't like the picture they showed. Ted and Lander, both obsessed with Bea. Ted lets James take the fall for the dead primal, even though he had to have known Bea was the one that killed it. If James hadn't taken the blame, would Ted have pinned it on him anyway? Lee didn't put it past the slimy bastard to have had some plan in his back pocket for just that instance.

But Ted never suspected that Lander would also become so obsessed with Bea. Probably didn't realize it until Lander made a deal for her. But then Ted backed out of the deal, after already having fathered Kat. Lander couldn't come take Bea, so he gave Kat to Horner out of spite.

And now he'd just used Horner as a tool to do what he never could: get the Redoubt out of their metal boxes.

All for one woman.

That was sickening enough. But now they'd done something to Lee, too.

They'd taken Sam.

It was moments like these that made it so difficult to become a better person. Because all Lee wanted to do in that moment was burn this whole chunk of California to the ground.

Lee approached their white pickup truck and swore under his breath as he saw the bullet holes riddling the side panels and windows. "Can't fucking have anything nice," he griped as he stopped in front of it, yanked the driver's door open, and began sweeping out the glass pebbles, taking care not to cut himself in the process.

"Actually, I was the one that broke that window," Abe admitted.

Lee stared at him. "What the fuck for?"

"They brought it back booby-trapped. Couldn't open the door."

"Goddammit."

"Well," Abe commented, giving the vehicle a sad look. Like it was a horse that'd broken its leg. "It was about time for a new one anyway."

"I didn't want a fucking new one," Lee muttered, spotting Marie as she approached at a fast clip, satphone in hand. "I liked *this* one."

"What? Did you get attached to it?" Abe scoffed.

"I liked it, okay?" Lee said. "It's a good truck. *Was* a good truck."

"Christ, you gonna write a eulogy for it?"

"I fucking might," Lee snapped over his shoulder, then slammed the door irritably, which only caused more glass pebbles to clatter off the window frame and into the seat.

Marie rounded the front of the truck.

Lee met her at the front quarter panel and nodded to the satphone. "What's the verdict?"

Marie's expression was reserved. "She's working on it."

Lee considered that with pursed lips for a moment, then nodded. "Alright. Where's Jones?"

Marie nodded over Lee's shoulder.

He turned and spotted Jones a few boxes down from them, coordinating a couple of guys that were gathering and reloading rifles and spare magazines. Lee hollered at him, got his attention, and waved him over. He seemed all too eager to depart from his retinue with a warning of "Don't fucking shoot yourselves."

Timeless advice.

Lee could see that both Abe and Marie had questions, but they held them until the fourth member of their party jogged up.

"I know we've dealt with some ignorant fucks," Jones huffed. "But...*wow*. I would not be surprised if half the casualties turn out to be blue on blue."

"Yeah, well, we're done with these assholes," Lee announced. "For now, at least."

Jones looked at him sharply. "We going after Sam?"

Lee nodded. "Got to." He looked to Abe. "Glad Horner brought our truck back for us."

Abe smiled. "Mighty kind of him."

"He didn't fuck with the auxiliary gas tank, did he?"

"Well, he drained the gas. But left the good stuff."

"Keys?"

Abe looked to Jones, who then started patting his pockets.

Lee groaned. "You gave them to *him* again?"

"I've got them," Jones said, defensively. "Here. See?" He pulled them from his right cargo pocket and jangled them in the air. "Got 'em."

"Well, that's a miracle," Marie sighed.

"Guys, I'm trustworthy as fuck," Jones asserted.

Lee pointed to the auxiliary tank in the bed, nestled against the cab. "Do me the honors."

Jones vaulted into the truck bed and knelt at the auxiliary tank, riffling through the set of keys.

Abe gave Lee a quick look up and down. "The hell happened to your armor?" Eyes going to his bare feet. "And your boots for that matter?"

"Oh, I'm sure Marie will be happy to tell you all about it," Lee said.

"He fucked up," Marie said. "That's basically it."

"We're alive, aren't we?" Lee groused. "Any chance they left our personal packs?"

Abe shook his head.

"Hold up," Marie said, turning away from them. "I got an idea." She jogged off—also in bare feet.

Abe raised his eyebrows high. "So we're gonna run a rescue op with both you and Marie all busted up, and with no armor, and no shoes?"

Lee eyed his friend. "Better question is, are we *not* gonna run a rescue op because of a few ouchies and some missing gear?"

Abe shrugged, conceding the point.

Jones had the right key pinched in his fingers, his other hand on the underside of the auxiliary tank, looking for the keyhole. He must have found it, because he smiled and brought the key underneath with his other hand. After a few seconds of finagling, the top of the auxiliary tank popped open an inch.

"There we go," Jones said, pushing the lid all the way open. From Lee's vantage on the ground, he couldn't see inside, but he knew what was in there. Hell, he'd designed the thing and filled it himself, though it had actually been fabricated by a very nice welder they'd met in Oregon. It was an insurance policy against just this situation—having their gear swiped.

Jones reached into the hollow tank and drew out a chubby piece of weaponry. An M32, six-shot revolver-style grenade launcher. He handed it to Lee as he drew out a second one from inside.

Lee hefted the weapon and swiveled the cylinder open to reveal six chambers loaded with 40mm high-explosive rounds. He snapped it closed, satisfied.

Abe nodded. "You and Marie can soften the target with those while me and Jones move in."

Jones straddled the sidewall of the bed, holding the second M32 and looking pleased. He nudged at Abe with the toe of his boot. "Hey. You and me. We're gonna be Battle Buddies."

Abe gave him a skeptical look. "Keys?"

Jones's expression flattened. "Goddammit," he muttered, immediately shuffling over to retrieve them from the keyhole where he'd left them.

"Not inspiring my confidence, Jonesy," Abe sang.

"I got 'em, I got 'em," Jones said, sounding put upon. "God. With the judginess, all the time."

Marie returned, holding a pair of boots in one hand, and a pair of flip-flops in the other.

"Those look a bit big for you," Lee commented, eyeing the boots.

Marie shoved them into his spare hand. "They're for you."

"Where'd you get 'em?"

Marie gave him an awkward glance as she dropped the flip-flops and settled her battered feet into them. "They're Bea's. Or at least the flip-flops are. The boots were her husband's."

Lee winced. Then shrugged, and got to pulling them on, socks be damned. He doubted Bea would be that offended if they were used in the course of her rescue. Assuming she didn't die. And assuming her rescue was not at odds with Sam's.

"Oh, and..." Marie paused putting on the flip-flops to dig in her pocket. When her hand came out, it was holding Deuce. Or at least the figurine that represented him. She pushed it towards Lee. "Figured we'd need all the luck we could get."

Lee accepted it gratefully, slipping it into his pocket.

"Damn," Jones commented, looking at Marie's new footwear. "Ma's rocking the Jesus Cruisers. Bold move, Ma."

"Keys," Lee demanded, stomping his feet into the boots. Bit tight, but a few blisters would be better than going barefoot into combat.

Jones slapped the truck keys into Lee's waiting hand and slid down from the bed. "You gonna tell us about your chat with Ted?"

"I'll fill you in on the way," Lee said, climbing into the driver's seat again. "Jones, grab two IV bags and stick Marie and me." He slammed the door behind him, glaring at the Redoubters. "Let's get the fuck outta here."

Major Ronald "Ron" Paige sat at his desk, staring at the handwritten note, with Angela Houston standing on the other side of that desk and watching him like a hawk.

He was leaned way back in his seat, like the paper was radioactive, one hand curled around his mouth and chin.

Angela just stood there and sweated. Literally. She'd run the mile and half to his office in twelve minutes and thanked her lucky stars that A) she'd been keeping up with her workouts, and B) Paige was in his office.

Paige was Angela's only point of contact within the military structure based in Aspen. To everyone else in Aspen, she was Angie Blackburn, because the name Angela Houston came with about as much baggage as the name Lee Harden. Luckily, she'd been a public figure during a time without broadcast media, so no one knew her face.

Except Ron Paige. He knew exactly who she was. But he was also ICAO Griffin's close friend, and the commander of special forces operations in what was generally termed "the American

Theater." He was the only person outside of Angela and Griffin that knew about The Deal.

Angela was praying that would count for something. And she was also praying that the fact that Paige had hunted Lee Harden three years ago, with the intention to kill him for treason, wouldn't count at all.

Paige was not a petty man. Angela actually liked him quite a lot. But when dealing with a dilemma this dicey, she knew that every little factor was being tallied up in Paige's mind. And that *might* include old grudges.

Paige took a deep breath through his nose. Leaned forward, rather slowly, his battered leather office chair creaking. Detached his hand from his face. Placed one index finger on the note. Then said, "No." And slid it back to her.

First, the blood drained out of Angela's head.

Then anger pushed it all back in again.

"Why the fuck not?" she demanded, though, if she were being honest with herself, she already knew why not.

Paige was unruffled by her outburst, though he didn't look particularly pleased. He folded his hands together on his desk and looked at her earnestly. "Because this is *wayyyyy* beyond the parameters."

"Parameters?" Angela acted indignant, but, again, she knew.

"Yes, Angela," Paige said, his tone betraying some irritation. "The parameters that Griffin very *specifically* told me to adhere to. Which I can only assume he established to fend off just this type of request."

"He also gave you discretion," Angela pointed out hotly.

"Not *that* much discretion."

"I don't see how this is any different than usual."

Paige gave her a laconic eyebrow. "I think you do. God, you're like a dog with a bone."

Okay, so it *was* different than usual. But not in any way that really mattered, Angela thought. And she wasn't about to release the proverbial bone. Because if Paige *really* was going to deny her request, he would've already put his foot down, told her he'd made his decision, and asked her to leave. The fact that they were still talking was a glimmer of daylight, peeking through a tiny crack in his "no."

"Explain to me how it's different," Angela tried.

Paige laughed. "I don't need to explain shit to you, Angela. You asked. I said 'no.' That's all there is to it."

Shit, that was very close to shutting her down.

Angela planted her hands on the table and leaned in, lowering her voice. "Ron, it's Lee."

Paige got a flat look. "I'm aware of who it is."

Angela tilted her head. Time to go on the offensive. "Is that what this is about?" She practically whispered it.

Paige glanced in the direction of his office door. Not good.

"Oh, I see," Angela hissed, straightening. "You got a bone to pick, so you're gonna let him die."

Paige grimaced, and Angela felt like she was playing a game of Battleship—*direct hit!* He stood up out of his chair, apparently not liking her looming over him like that, and no longer able to maintain his blasé act. "What the fuck do you want me to do here, Angela?" His voice was heated, but quiet. "I'm not trying to fuck the guy over—I'm trying to follow my goddamn orders."

"Oh, don't try to sell that 'orders' shit to me!" Angela snapped. "There are no *orders*, Paige, and you know it. There are no orders, because this shit isn't actually happening, is it? Lee doesn't exist, right? I don't exist. And we certainly don't have him running around, convincing all the forgotten people outside the Interior that ICAO Griffin gives a shit about them." Angela straightened, eyes going wide as though she'd just realized something. "Oh, wait—yes, that's exactly what we're doing! That's exactly what *Lee's* doing. Out there preaching the gospel about how America isn't quite dead yet, and that we're working on stabilizing the country, and that we haven't forgot about them. And he's done a great job of that, hasn't he? For three fucking years he's done that job, Paige. And not once—not *once*—has he asked for anything more than what was promised him. Not *once* has he rocked the boat, or bucked Griffin, or gone off rez. And now, when he needs us—when his back is really up against the wall—we're gonna hang him out to dry?"

Angela put on a face of mystified frustration. "The guy we have going around telling everyone not to lose hope, that the Interim Government hasn't forgotten about them—*him* we're going to forget about? The first time he asks for something that requires the *slightest* bit of leeway in your so-called *parameters*, we're just gonna tell him, 'sorry, you're SOL'?" Angela let her voice rise into righteous indignation. She spread her arms out as though to encompass everything from sea to shining sea, her eyes casting about as though looking for an answer. "What the fuck are we even doing here? Is this just a giant circle-jerk? Are we just trying to feel good about ourselves but not actually do shit? Because it's been three fucking years, Paige, and we haven't moved the borders. We haven't done a goddamned thing. But *Lee* has. Lee's been doing exactly what he was told to do. Not because he *had* to, Paige—because remember, Griffin gave him an out—but because it's the *right thing to do*. He's out there doing *the right thing*. And then you're gonna sit there in your comfortable fucking leather goddamn armchair, while Lee's team is busted all to hell and trying to survive in a place we can't even be bothered to go, and you're gonna put your little index finger on his request for help and you're just gonna say 'no'?" She was almost shouting at this point. "What the fuck are you supposed to be? What the fuck am *I* supposed to be? What in the actual fuck are *we* supposed to be doing here?"

She ran out of breath.

Took a deep gulp or air. Considered continuing on, but felt her tirade was spent. She didn't have anything else to say. She'd only be repeating herself.

She searched Paige's face, trying to get a read on how well she'd landed her speech, but he gave nothing away. She had no idea where she stood at this point.

Until Paige raised his hands up. And then brought them together in a clap.

Clap...clap...clap.

"Very nice, Angela," Paige said sourly. "I mean, really great performance. Did you practice it, or was it just off the cuff?"

"Fuck you."

Paige made a show of looking around the room, then checking behind him. "Is there an audience? No? No audience?" Back to her. "Nope. Just lil' ol' me. Lemme ask you a question, Angela—if a politician makes a speech, and no one is around to give a fuck, do they actually make a sound?"

Angela glared at him. "If an asshole hears the truth, but refuses to accept it, is he still full of shit?"

Paige pasted on the most flaccid smile she'd ever seen. "I believe we're done here, Angela."

"Oh, I'm not done, *Ronald*," she growled, using his full name only because she knew he didn't prefer it. She had no clue what she was going to do now. Maybe she could go directly to the flight crews?

You're risking everything for this, she told herself. *You're risking Abby's medical care...*

She reached for the note, still staring tracers at Paige.

He slammed his hand down on the note before she could touch it. It happened so fast, and resulted in such a loud bang that Angela flinched back in spite of her anger. He stared right at her and the look in his eyes was...inscrutable.

"Leave it," he seethed.

"Wha—?"

"Ah!" He snapped up his other hand. "Shutthefuckup." He peeled his gaze away like he couldn't stand looking at her.

What did this mean? Why was he keeping the note?

Angela didn't know what she should feel. Had she won or lost the battle? Was Lee going to live or die? Was Sam? Would she ever even hear from them again? And what would she do then? What would she do to keep Abby safe and get her the medical care she needed?

Paige slowly drew the note back across the desk to his side. Picked it up. Folded it. Put it in the chest pocket of his uniform. "I'm going to keep this." He finally deigned to look at her again. "And you're not going to mention it—ever again. Then you're going to walk through that door." He pointed. "You're going to walk your self-righteous ass back to your cushy, first-world house. And you're going to sit by the fucking phone."

"Uhhh...Ohhh-kayyyy..."

Paige stared at her blankly.

Angela frowned. "Are you—"

"Dismissing you? Yes. Yes, that is what I'm doing. You're dismissed." That horrendously bland smile again. "Goodbye, Angela."

Chapter 32

Colin Horner never did make it to the silo.

About a third of the way across the dusty main yard of his ranch, his feet slowed to a stop. He was alone, because he'd growled at Bran and Kat to stay on the porch when they'd tried to follow him.

The empty silo stood straight ahead, maybe another hundred yards. Between Colin and the silos, and a bit to his right, were the holding pens with about fifty head of young bulls awaiting castration. That's what they were supposed to be doing that day. But then all this shit happened.

Colin stared at them for a time. A few of them stared back, their big, black ears framing their faces. Inscrutable black eyes watching him. Did they know they were about to have their balls chopped off? They wouldn't even get anesthetic for it. Just wrangle them down onto their backs, cut open the ball sack, squeeze out the balls, and lop them off with a tool that looked like a hook-billed bolt cutter. A splash of antiseptic solution—they used the byproducts of their whiskey still to do that. And then they just let them go with a slap on the ass.

It was the strangest thing. Colin had spent his entire life doing this job, and yet, all of the sudden, the idea of all those castrations turned his stomach. Not the act of it, specifically, but the fact that it was done without anesthetic.

"They're too dumb to feel it," his father had told him when he'd been a boy.

But then, why did they scream? And a scream is what it was. Sounded like a moo, but it was always higher and sharper and so forceful that their voices would crack when they did it. Not the most terrible noise he'd ever heard from a farm animal—that belonged to injured horses and stuck pigs. But still. The idea of it.

What the fuck are you actually thinking about right now?

Colin blinked and redirected his attention to the silo. The two ranch hands guarding it were watching him curiously. He shifted his weight. Sweaty palms. Clammy fingers twiddling with each other.

Screaming cows. Screaming people.

Howling infected.

Kat, howling.

She betrayed me.

—you got what you wanted; they're sitting in the barn—

Yeah, sure. But what the fuck was he going to say to them? He'd told Bran he wanted to talk to them, but only right then did he actually consider that desire. Because he didn't actually *want* to talk to them. He'd just had an image in his mind of the ranch boss talking to the people that he'd just kidnapped. Because…that seems like something you should do when you kidnap someone.

But there was nothing he actually wanted to say. Because there was nothing to say to them that wasn't either a lie, or simply rubbing in the unpleasant truth. And he was in no mood for lies. And if he told them the terrible truth, then they might scream.

The idea of it came upon him, and felt very real—unavoidable, actually. And if they screamed, then the cows might scream…

This is all bullshit and you know it.

—you're losing it—

No, I'm fine. I'm in control.

—you're not even in the driver's seat, asshole—

But then, who was?

"Boss!" Bran's voice hit him like a smack to the back of the head. But, as he turned back to the Big House, he thought, *Yeah, I'm the boss. See? I'm in the driver's seat...*

When he found Bran, the man was standing on the porch, pointing towards the gate. "He's here!"

Colin's stomach dropped like a trapdoor had been triggered somewhere in his midsection. He looked at the gate. Traced the road with his eyes. And found the two figures approaching. One tall, with a frizzy halo of blonde hair. One shorter, with a tan serape billowing in the breeze.

Behind them, along the top of the nearest hill, a line of figures hunched low in the grass. Maybe a dozen of them.

Lander's "family."

"Shit," Colin hissed under his breath, and began walking back towards the Big House.

The sound of worried nickers and whinnies came from the stables. The scent of Lander's family must've carried on the wind.

Colin's fingers and toes tingled as he stalked stiffly back to the steps of his house. He hesitated at the bottom, but then mounted them and stood next to Bran, simply because it would feel better to stand slightly higher than Lander.

Colin noted that Kat was standing off a bit, with Bran between her and himself. She didn't seem too worried about Colin, though. Her eyes were locked on the two approaching figures, now reaching the gates.

The guards at the gate knew the drill. They also had no desire to prolong any interaction with Lander, or his bottom bitch, Freya. They swung the gates wide when Lander and Freya were still several yards off, and stood far clear of them both as they strode through.

Off of Colin's right shoulder, Bran took a deep breath in and let it out slowly through his nose. Bran might have a soft spot for Kat, but that did not extend to Lander or Freya.

Why's he got a soft spot for Kat?
—because you treat her like shit—

Does he think he has to protect her from me?
—doesn't he?—
Would he kill me to save her?

Colin found himself eyeing Bran sidelong. The air between them seemed to crackle and hiss like a disrupted electrical field. Bran didn't seem to notice, but Colin sure did. He could feel the distorted relationship between them.

Can I trust him?
—of course not—
You can't trust anyone, because everyone's always lying.

"You think Kat made a different call earlier?" Colin said under his breath.

Bran twitched, then turned his head to Colin, realizing the question was directed at him. He faltered for a moment, then said, "What?"

"The howl she made earlier," Colin specified. "On Jax and Marie. Was it the right howl?"

Bran was very still for a moment. Then he smiled, but it was all wrong. Forced. Disingenuous. "Shit, I dunno, Boss. I don't speak the language."

He's lying.
—even your best friend lies to you—
Best friend?
—you're right, that's wrong. Your ONLY friend—
I don't fucking have friends. I have a ranch.

Colin ground his teeth and looked away from Bran, partly because Lander and Freya were now approaching, and partly because he couldn't bear the feeling of betrayal. Looking at Bran only made it worse.

"How goes it?" Lander greeted cheerfully as he stopped, about a yard shy of the front steps. He squinted up at Colin, a smile on his face. So casual. Like he owned the fucking world.

Stupid cocksucker.
—don't you wish you could feel that way, too?—
How?

—confident and in control—

Colin sneered. "We have what you asked for."

Lander's eyebrows raised, his smile falling. But only for a moment. Then he started laughing. Real, solid belly laughs. Completely in earnest. With not a shred of self-consciousness. Not a shred of worry. Like he knew that he was untouchable.

I want to be untouchable, too.

"Christ, man," Lander said through his tapering chuckles. "We're talking about a *person* here, not a bag of feed!"

Colin squinted at him. "A person that you're going to keep captive. Against her will." Not that he really cared. He was just pointing out that Lander had no moral high ground to stand on.

But Lander only bobbled his head and waved his hand, like it was neither here nor there. "Yeah, well, strange times, amiright?" He shrugged. "But we all have to grow and adapt, don't we? We have to evolve. And who knows? Maybe she'll come around and see the good in it."

"The good in it?" Colin practically coughed the words out.

Lander's face flashed momentary irritation, but then settled again. He tilted his head back, looking steadily at Colin, evaluating him. "Oh, dear. I apologize—has your task chapped your morals a bit? I wasn't aware you had any." The humor came back to his face again. "In the future, I'll make sure to accommodate your delicate ethical sensibilities."

Colin sucked on his teeth and thought about another line of meth, but it was too soon, and the tin was empty anyway, and that made him very sad. "You want her or not?" he grunted. "Or did you just come to chat with people that actually speak English?" He maybe should've stopped there, but the rest came out before he had a chance to rein it in. "I imagine it gets old talking in grunts and growls, but this ain't a fucking Sunday social, and I've got shit to do."

The heat of rash words and their looming consequences scorched Colin's scalp.

But Lander only laughed again. "Oh-ho! Damn!" He glanced over his shoulder at Freya, who, Colin noted, was in a staredown with Kat. "I think that was directed at you, lady friend."

Freya's eyes snapped to Colin's, but he could tell that she hadn't been listening. Too busy gazing at Kat with...what? He could never tell whether the intensity in their staredowns was some sort of savage affection, or a promise of violence barely restrained.

Freya made no comment and went back to looking at Kat.

Lander hiked a thumb at her and spoke out of the side of his mouth, sotto voce. "But you're not wrong." He snickered at his own joke, then clapped his hands together. "Aaaanyway. Where is she?"

Roughly eight hundred yards from where Colin Horner and Lander Hollis were talking, Lee and Abe were watching them. As it turned out, there *was* a place in all these rolling, grassy hills where they could stay hidden and maintain a visual on the ranch.

After some careful searching, they'd located a patch of some low, dense shrub that had overtaken the top of a hill directly south of Horner's Peak. Lying on their bellies amidst those shrubs, Lee and Abe had found a decent hide between two clusters of bushes that provided a complete view of the ranch. It wasn't perfect, and the shrubs were prickly, but it was as good as they were going to get.

"You think he's in the silo?" Abe murmured, staring through his scoped rifle at the ranch below them.

Lee glassed the scene below with a pair of binocs. "That'd be my guess. Two guards posted. And it looked like Horner was heading over there before Lander showed up."

Unfortunately, Lander had also brought a dozen primals with him, which complicated things. If they were forced to start shooting from this position, the primals might make a move on them.

The primals were positioned in the tall grass to either side of the road that led into the ranch. They were due west of the ranch, about a thousand yards from Lee, who was due south.

Lee had left their truck two hills further south than their current location. He wondered if they'd have time to fall back to the truck if the primals came at them. Probably not. But a thousand yards *might* be enough to pick them off as they advanced.

Maybe. Hopefully.

"They're moving," Abe said, his voice a low monotone. "Towards the silo. Horner, Bran, Kat, Lander, and his pet primal."

"Oh, that's Freya," Marie corrected from where she was crouching behind them. A little further back from her, Jones sat with his rifle on his knees, watching their rear.

Jones turned to look at Marie with an arched eyebrow. "Freya, like the Norse goddess?"

Marie eyed him. "You know the weirdest shit. And none of it's useful."

Jones shrugged. "What? Everyone was really into Viking shit when I deployed."

Lee shifted his body, making sure not to jostle the shrubs around them. There were a lot of eyes scanning these hills—both Horner's ranch hands, and the primals on the next ridge over. He got himself positioned so he was in line with the silo, then twisted the focus on his binocs.

"Lander and Colin are going into the silo," Abe narrated.

Lee felt a nudge on his ankle, then Marie's hushed voice: "What are we gonna do if Lander takes Sam too?"

"Well, I really would like to wait until dark," Lee murmured. "But if they take Sam, we gotta roll. Y'all down for that?"

"I don't see another choice," Jones agreed. "Can't let the fucker take Sam back to their…nest or whatever. Then we'd have to take on the whole fucking horde."

"None of us are gonna let him take Sam," Marie said, and Lee figured she spoke for Abe as well. "If we have to do it, we gotta wait for Lander to get away from the ranch."

Lee nodded. "Agreed. No point fighting *both* groups of assholes."

No one needed to point out that it was a long shot either way—taking on Lander and his pack of primals was likely to be just as shitty as taking on the ranch, though they presented different tactical problems.

"Next question," Marie pressed on. "Are we going to try to stop him from taking Bea?"

"Fuck no," Abe said. "Sorry for her, but we got enough on our plate just saving our boy."

"I agree he's priority number one," Marie said. "But..."

"It sucks, alright?" Lee said, still staring at the silo. The deep shadows within revealed nothing to him of what was happening inside. All he could see was Bran and Kat and Freya, standing outside and staring at each other. "I know it sucks. No one's saying it doesn't suck. But you're both right. No, we cannot afford to prioritize Bea. But we *will* keep an eye out, and if there's an opportunity to help her that doesn't fuck Sam's chances, then we'll take it."

"What about what we asked for?" Abe said. "Did we ever get confirmation from Angela?"

Marie shook her head. "Nothing."

"So Colorado's hanging us out to dry," Abe grunted. "Great."

"We don't know that," Lee said, even as he felt that Abe was probably correct. "No contact doesn't mean they denied the request. Until I hear a straight 'no,' I'm going to take it on faith that we'll get our time window."

"Which doesn't start for another few hours anyway," Marie pointed out. "Besides, it wouldn't do us any good in a hostage situation."

"Movement." This statement not coming from Abe this time, but from Jones.

Lee twisted to look. Saw the way Jones was angled towards the primals on the next ridge over, and felt everything in him tighten. He reached for the grenade launcher at his side.

"Hold up," Jones said. "Hang on, guys...It's not the primals."

Only Abe remained focused on the ranch, while Lee and Marie both readied their weapons.

"Talk to me," Abe said.

"I don't fuckin' believe this guy," Jones suddenly hissed. His eyes jagged to Lee. "Glass that ridge, right now. Right on the road."

Lee moved as fast as he was able without giving up their position—which wasn't very fast. By the time he'd moved to his knees and gently pressed his binoculars far enough through the shrub to get a glimpse of the road, the object of curiosity was already cresting the ridge.

"Oh, fuck me," Lee grated. "It's fucking Ted."

"Fucking Ted?" Abe jerked, but stayed in his scope. "The fuck's he doing?"

"Riding a fucking bike," Lee said, his heart pounding. "Right through a pack of primals."

Jesus, this guy was completely oblivious. Standing up on the pedals as he topped the rise, either too distracted or too stupid to scan his environment, Lee didn't know which. But he didn't see the dozen pairs of feral eyes watching him.

Lee expected them to lunge at any second. At least *one* of them was going to make a break for Ted, and one was all it would take.

"Are they attacking him?" Marie asked, bewildered.

Lee stared, incredulous, as Ted topped the rise and started flying down the hill towards the ranch. This was when the primals would run at him. They wouldn't be able to resist, now that they had his back. Every instinct in them would tell them to give chase.

And yet...they stayed.

"They are...*not* attacking him," Lee said in wonderment.

Which actually created a whole new set of problems. Lee found himself wishing they *had* tackled the stupid bastard to the ground. Because now he was racing straight at the ranch. And what was he going to do when he got there? Tell Horner that Lee and his team were about to attack them? Would he sell them out just to try to curry favor with Horner?

"Shoulda fuckin' killed him," Lee said, adjusting his body to follow Ted's progress towards the ranch.

"You want me to take him out?" Abe offered. Then: "Oh, hey, they're coming out of the silo. Got Horner, Lander, Bea...and Sam. They're moving Sam too." A pause. "Lee, gimme a range on Ted, just in case."

"Stay with Sam," Lee said, but estimated the distance to Ted. The road in was perpendicular to their position, so the range wouldn't change much. The speed Ted was moving was a factor though. "Looking at eight hundred yards. Moving west to east at twenty miles per hour."

Those were not good numbers, and Lee knew it. Abe was no slouch, and he'd received sniper training, just like Lee had. But that didn't make them professional snipers. And even a professional sniper would have a helluva time hitting at that distance, with that amount of movement. Not to mention eight hundred yards was the max effective distance for Abe's 5.56mm rifle. Not to mention that their range finder, ballistic calculator, and wind gauge, were all in the Pelican case with the ESR, which had been stolen.

In short, the shot was *possible*, but not *probable.*

"Stay on Sam," Lee reiterated. "We can't give ourselves away yet." He lowered himself to the ground, ignoring the pain his ribs, and got the binocs back onto the ranch.

There. Bea and Sam were being hustled along, their arms restrained behind their backs. Bran and Kat were moving them towards the ranch house, with Horner, Lander, and Freya following.

Options tumbled through Lee's mind, none of them attractive.

Take out Lander? Same problems as taking out Ted, minus the twenty mile per hour movement. And that went for Horner too. And even if they *could* make the shot, it'd still turn everything into a mess.

Start the assault now? No good. The primals would come running in, if not by instinct, then by Lander or Freya's command. And Lee and his team would make really nice targets coming down the side of the hill. And the M32 had a maximum effective range of 440 yards. Which meant that Lee would have to make it almost all the way down the hill to even begin firing on the ranch.

Which left the most gut-wrenching option: Wait and see.

But in the meantime...

"Abe," Lee said, taking the binoculars away from his eyes for a moment and looking eastward. "Come out of your scope. Look east. You see that copse of trees?"

Abe turned his head in that direction. It was a cluster of three or four decent sized trees, about fifty yards down from the top of another rise, maybe a half mile from them. "Yeah."

"How fast do you think you and Jones can get into position there?"

"Fifteen, maybe twenty minutes."

That's what Lee had figured. And he didn't think they had that kind of time. But who knew? And if they had to start the assault, it'd be best if they didn't all come running from the same direction. Even if Abe and Jones weren't able to get into position, at least their assault would have more than one angle.

"Alright, go for it," Lee said.

Abe slithered backward from the hilltop until he was able to get up and move. Jones moved to follow and the two of them set off down the hill, first at a crouch, and then straightening and gaining speed the further they went. Marie moved to take up Jones's watch on their six.

Abe's voice through the acoustic tube in Lee's ear: "Comm check. Comm check."

Lee looked at Marie as he touched the PTT clipped to his chest. She gave him a nod to confirm that she'd heard as well. "We got you."

Then he flattened himself out, tried to get comfortable, and waited, watching everything that happened down below.

Chapter 33

Sam blinked into the westering sun as he was marched across the ranch. He guesstimated the sun's distance to the horizon and figured there was about an hour until sunset. Give or take fifteen minutes. Then another hour after that for it to be full dark.

Which meant it would be at least two hours until Lee, Abe, Marie, and Jones came for him. If they were coming at all. But he wanted to believe that they were. He wanted to hold onto that hope.

However, as hopes go, this was one of the forlorn ones. Because he didn't think he had that much time. Bea certainly did not.

He didn't know what he was supposed to do. He was still watching for some possibility of escape, but his options were nil. He hadn't been able to loosen his bindings one bit. And he wasn't sure if Lander was taking him, or just Bea.

In the end, because he was still staring in the direction of the sun, which was directly over the road into the ranch, he spotted what looked like a figure rapidly approaching...on a bicycle.

Sam wound up saying these poignant words: "Uh...who the fuck is that?"

The whole party jolted to a stop, right there in front of the ranch house.

The guards at the gate chose that moment to announce the presence of a newcomer.

"Hey-yo! Someone's coming!"

Horner stepped forward, one pace ahead of Sam, staring at the figure as it came careening up to the gate. "What the hell is *he* doing here?"

Sam wasn't sure who "he" was until Lander said it.

"Ted. Fucking. Foley." Lander said, as though they were archnemeses.

Horner stalked forward, then glanced over his shoulder, his face severe, and pointed a finger at Bran and Kat. "You two stay put."

As he reached the gate, Ted jumped off his bicycle, letting it crash to the ground. He immediately began screaming, and the guards began screaming back. Ted tried to get around them, but they blocked him. Sam found it odd that they didn't even point their rifles at Ted. They didn't seem inclined to use force on him. And after a few seconds of scuffling, Ted broke free. The guards started after him, but Horner snarled and waved a hand at them.

"Let him go!" he roared at his ranch hands.

The guards backed off, seeming perplexed and disappointed.

Ted charged through the gate, waving his arms and continuing to yell words that Sam couldn't quite make out. Horner came to a stop and let the other man approach.

Sam saw it coming from a mile away. He wasn't sure how Ted missed it, but the guy had never struck Sam as terribly observant. Just in the way that Horner bladed his body towards the incoming Ted, spreading his feet and cocking balled fists, he knew what Horner was going to do. As Ted reached him, still alternately gasping and shouting, Horner hit him with a solid fist to the nose.

Ted rocked back, lost his feet, and hit the dirt. He caught himself on an elbow, the other hand holding his face.

To Ted's credit, he didn't stay down long. Didn't even seem terribly fazed by the punch. He swore loudly, but then righted himself. Got to his feet, refocused, and stumbled past Horner.

Towards Sam and Bea.

"Bea!" Ted burbled, his voice muffled and nasally with his fingers pinching his bleeding nose shut. "Bea, are you alright?"

"What are you doing here?" Bea said, but she didn't say it like Sam had expected her to. He'd thought she would be relieved that Ted had come. But she only sounded like his presence pained her in some way.

Bran moved in front of Ted and shoved him back.

"You can't do this!" Ted bawled. "You can't let him take her!"

Horner stalked back into their midst, frowning at Ted like he was coated in shit. "Deal's already done. I gave my word, which still fucking means something. If you're here to beg for Bea, you're talking to the wrong guy."

Sam watched Bea sidelong, but he could not read what was going on behind her eyes. Her expression was hard and downturned, her gaze hopeless. She had zero faith in Ted's ability to do anything to remedy this situation. And yet, she didn't seem inclined to stop him trying.

Sam hadn't been able to think of a way to stall, but maybe this was it. Maybe Ted could enter into some sort of negotiations for Bea. Maybe they'd last for a few hours.

Wishing for the moon, there, Sam, his realistic side told him.

Think. He needed to think. He didn't know how much time Ted was going to buy them, but Sam was going to use it the best he could.

Ted turned his gaze on Lander, and his face seemed to pale at the bottom, and flush at the top. A very unhealthy look. "Lander..."

"Now, what the fuck do you think you have to say to me?" Lander said, moving to Bea's side and gripping her elbow possessively.

Ted's mouth worked silently a few times. "I can...we can...we can make a *new* deal. You and me."

Lander made a fart noise. "That's what I think of your deal. You can't be relied on." Lander looked at Horner. "Is there any need for him to be alive?"

"No," Horner said, flippantly.

"Freya, rip his throat out."

Oh, shit. Sam had really been trying to focus on an avenue of escape, but this was kind of hard to ignore.

Freya jolted forward.

Ted stumbled back. "Wait! No!"

And then, in a blur, Kat was there between Ted and Freya. She had her bandanna pulled down to show her bared teeth as she snarled at the other hybrid female. Freya made as though to move around her. Kat snapped her teeth, inches from Freya's face.

Then the two of them went stone still, like two cats deciding whether or not to maul each other.

"You fucking little bitch!" Horner raged, his eyes going wide and strange. He took two rapid strides towards Kat, but then Bran suddenly intercepted him, standing in his way. Shock flashed across Horner's face—and then it was immediately burned to cinders with an ignition of fury.

This might be it. In microseconds, Sam was primed to make a move, should this whole gathering suddenly devolve into a scrum of violence.

"Hold on, there, Colin," Lander called out in a loud voice. Sharp, but not angry. Almost amused. "I mean, can you really blame her?" he let out a dramatic sigh. "My sweet Katerina..." he said it with the hint of a rolled R, as though trying to affect some sort of accent. "I know why you want to defend this man. But he's not to be trusted. He, in fact, *can't* be trusted."

Kat, who hadn't taken her eyes off of Freya, didn't respond.

"P-please," Ted stammered, backing up a little further. "Lander. I swear. Anything but this. I'll trade anyone else but her."

"Ted!" Bea snapped, aghast.

Lander jerked Bea's elbow to silence her. "I don't *want* another deal with you, Ted. I don't trust you. You reneged on the last one, and why on earth would I ever believe you wouldn't do it again? I don't care what you offer, I'm never making another deal with you again."

Bea stiffened.

Sam did too.

Her eyes snapped between Lander and Ted. "Ted?" her voice was quieter. Filled with growing dread. "What is he talking about? Did you make a deal with him for something? Did you—" Lander jerked her again, but she jerked back, and hard. "—make a deal with this sonofabitch? For *what*?" Lander and Bea, jostling back and forth. Bea's voice turned into a ragged scream. "*What did you make a deal for*?!"

Ted looked pained. "Bea—I—it's—ah—"

"Complicated?" Lander practically hissed, except he had his face all mashed into Bea's hair, like he was trying to speak directly into her ear. "It wasn't complicated at all, was it, Ted?" Definitely talking to Bea now. "Teddy here wanted a hybrid female all his own, just like my Freya. So I let him come and mate with my three wives."

Wait—wives? Sam could barely keep up, battered between shock and disgust.

Bea had gone very still now. Rigid in Lander's grip.

"Two came out stillborn, but one was a healthy little female. Just like Freya. And do you know what I wanted in return? Do you know what Ted *promised* to give me in exchange for letting him fuck my wives?"

Oh, Jesus.

"You, Sweetie," Lander husked into Bea's ear. "He was gonna give me you. Except...he never did. So I made a new deal. With Horner. And now I have you. And you're going to be..." he snuffled the nape of her neck. "...just wonderful!"

All the hardness was gone from Bea's face. The shock had knocked her senses out, because she didn't seem to register Lander groping and nuzzling at her. She just stared blankly across the space at Ted, mouth slightly ajar.

Sam snapped a look at Ted, and saw the guilt all over his face. It didn't matter whether he denied it. The look on his face told Sam the truth.

And he instantly wanted to kill the man.

A dozen things came rising to Sam's mouth. But then he thought, *None of that helps the situation.* Which got him thinking about his situation again. And what he could say that *would* help the situation. Or stall things.

Or cause chaos.

And that's when he thought of the other giant bomb that Lander had just dropped, though it took Sam a few thudding heartbeats to connect the dots.

Ted had mated with Lander's half-primal "wives." And he'd produced three, quarter-primal hybrids. Two had died, stillborn. But one had been a healthy female. Just like Freya.

"Ted," Sam spat it out the second the idea came to him. "You have a daughter?"

He was looking right at Kat when he said it.

Her snarling face slackened, and her eyes became unfocused. She was still staring down Freya, but she wasn't seeing her. Behind that suddenly-vacant stare, Kat was connecting the dots, just like Sam had.

She didn't know.

And then Kat looked right at Sam.

"No one ever told you," Sam said.

Horner pointed at him. "You stay the fuck out of this!"

Lander shook his head. "Jesus, Colin. You never told her?"

The snarl had completely left Kat's face now. She looked blank and bereft. Like things had been stolen from her. And for all her ferocity, Sam found himself pitying her.

Hell, she was only three years old. She *looked* mostly like an adult, but that was the primal genetics in her—they grew fast and died young. She had killer instincts, but what she lacked became exceedingly evident in that moment.

She lacked experience. She was naïve. No matter what she looked like, and no matter the violence her body was capable of, her mind was that of a child's, and it had never thought to doubt.

Kat turned, Freya forgotten. Her feet shuffled, almost stumbled, as she faced Horner.

Horner stood there with his lips pursed like he'd just sucked on a lemon. He didn't say a damn word to the creature that had believed he was her father. There was not an ounce of pity in his face. Only contempt.

Kat said one of her rare words. Said it in almost a whisper, as though mystified.

"Liar."

What was this feeling? Kat had never experienced it before.

She became painfully aware of everyone's eyes upon her. She felt hot and cold all over. Shrunken. Like she couldn't defend herself. Like all of the sudden she'd been rendered powerless.

She stared at the man that she'd called father, and he seemed a stranger to her. Nothing had changed about him. He was still who he'd always been, and his face still held what it always held for her: Hatred. But for so long she'd just assumed that his hatred for her was because she'd been disobedient. Because she'd failed to act like he wanted her to.

Now she saw it for what it was.

Just regular, plain old hatred. Nothing more complex than that. Nothing she couldn't understand. He hated her, not because of what she did, but because of what she *was*.

Not his. Not a part of him. Something foreign. Something despicable.

She realized that her heart was pounding in her chest, and she thought that was odd, because there was no real threat to her safety. There was no reason for her body to be telling her that she was in danger.

This feeling made no sense. This terrible, creeping fear. This whisper in the back of her mind that spoke to her not in the clumsy words that these people used, but with an understanding of the elemental nature of herself.

This was a human fear. It was the fear that you were not a part of something anymore. That you were cast out. Set aside. Left behind.

Rejected.

No one wanted her.

No one ever had.

She was not a part of the beasts whose blood she shared. And she was not a part of the humans. She didn't belong anywhere, with anyone.

Except...maybe...

She turned her gaze on Ted. His scent filled her nostrils, standing out amongst all the other scents of all the other sweating, stinking people around her. She knew that scent. And she knew now why she had always been drawn to it. She'd mistaken it for desire. And it was, in a way. But not a desire to mate with him, like she'd tried that one time. Just a desire to...be *with* him.

Somehow, she'd known they were connected. And she wanted to be with someone—anyone, really—who would understand her. And who would understand her more than the man who had made her?

A new and strange sensation seized ahold of her throat. Seemed she was experiencing many things for the first time. And this one felt like someone was gripping her windpipe, choking her. It made it even harder for her to speak. But she *wanted* to speak. *Needed* to speak.

She needed to connect to something solid, something that would clean away this terrible feeling of not belonging to anyone or anything.

She pressed the word out, and it came from her lips garbled and cracking.

"Father." She reached a hand for him.

She needed him to take it. She needed him to accept her. She needed *someone* to...

He drew back.

In his eyes there was fear, and for a moment, she felt despair—*Don't be afraid of me!*—but then she saw the way his eyes slipped down to her mouth. Down to what she normally kept covered. Out of shame. Out of a desire to be accepted.

His nose wrinkled, just slightly. His head pulled back like he'd smelled something foul. And he looked away from her.

No, she almost begged.

That familiar shame, washing over her head, rolling down her back, making her whole body hunch over, as though to protect something vital at the center of her. Her hands went to her face, as though to cover the terrible maw that seemed to be the reason why everyone hated her. She wanted to be invisible. Because to be seen was to be hated.

Hatred and disgust. From everyone. From all sides.

She realized everything had become blurry. Heat and wet seemed to have consumed her vision. She could feel it, stinging in her eyes, and dripping down her cheeks. She was scared of it for a brief moment, until she remembered that it was a human thing. She only knew that because some humans cried when they were being killed.

Patty had cried when Kat had killed her.

Human, she marveled at herself. *I am human. But humans hate me.*

I am a beast. But the beasts hate me too.

She was neither. She was nothing.

Her brain felt like it was on fire. Her thoughts became ragged and unclear. She glanced sideways and saw Horner's hatred. Then saw Bran's pity. Then saw Bea's horror.

She realized she was turning in a slow circle, trying to find *someone* that wasn't staring at her, or maybe, just maybe, someone that could look at her, could see her as she wished she could be seen.

The man they'd kidnapped—shock.

Lander himself...only passingly amused.

And then all the way back around to Ted.

Who still couldn't even look at her.

And then all of that burning shame turned into something else.

Kat's eyes widened, still leaking tears, but they were drying up fast as though under an immense heat. She pulled her hands away from her face. "I...didn't...*want this*," she struggled out, and the effort that it took for her to speak only infuriated her more. Why couldn't she just be one of them? Or one of the beasts? Why did she have to be in between? Why couldn't she be a whole...*something*?

Ted managed to glance at her again. And again looked away.

Kat took a step towards him, hands turning into claws that raked at her own face. "I didn't want this!" she suddenly screamed. "You did this! You did it! You made me!"

His scent was all around her, and in her. It was *her* scent too. There was a bond between them. So she didn't want to kill him. She only wanted to hurt him. She wanted him to hurt just as bad as she was hurting.

Before she even knew what she was doing, she lunged at him, one clawed hand smashing across his face. He reeled backward with a yelp. The scent of blood hit Kat's nose. Did something strange to her brain, to her thoughts. Like some delicate balance had shifted all to one side. Away from the human in her. Towards the beast.

Ted came up, staring at her in shock now. Three big cuts left the flesh of his face in tatters. Blood streamed down his skin.

Kat felt regret for what she'd done. She hadn't meant to injure him so bad, it was just that she wanted him to hurt...

He backpedaled away from her.

She snarled at him.

He gasped, and turned as though to run.

KILL IT.

And anything in her that might've been human was lost.

Lee watched from eight hundred yards away as Kat suddenly leapt onto Ted's fleeing form, riding him to the ground. They hit the dirt, Ted's legs kicking up a cloud of dust. But he wasn't going anywhere.

"Shit!" Marie hissed from beside him. "Should we—"

"No," Lee said, firmly, not taking his eyes away from the binoculars. "No, we're gonna let this one play out."

As though it wasn't already a foregone conclusion.

A single, high-pitched scream reached them from across the distance. Just the one. And then nothing.

And all around those two thrashing figures in the dirt, not a single person in Horner's Peak moved to put a stop to it.

Chapter 34

Sam watched Ted die. And it wasn't quick.

His thrashing grew weak. Kat had him pinned in something that looked a lot like side control in a jiu-jitsu match. Except for the fact that Kat had her jaws clamped down on Ted's throat.

Ted tried to claw at her face. But she simply grabbed his wrist and flattened that hand out so it couldn't get to her. And then she worked her jaws wider. Tighter. Reminded Sam of a snake trying to get its mouth around something bigger than its own head.

Ted's eyes were open wide. Streaming tears. Emanating terror. He kept trying to breath, his chest hitching, but there was no air getting past his throat. And every time Kat worked her mouth wider and clamped down harder, Sam heard cartilage cracking and liquid squishing.

And then it was only the sound of Kat's own breathing, heavy but steady, in and out through her flaring nostrils.

Sam became dimly aware that the scene had drawn an audience. The ranch hands stood around, but at a distance, with a variety of weapons held in half-ready positions. They'd been all the way ready when it'd first gone down, but when Horner never gave them the command to take her out, their muzzles had slowly drifted down, and now pointed at the ground.

Sam hadn't just been standing there and staring. In the interminable minutes—yes, entire minutes—that it took Ted to die, Sam had been looking around, trying to find a way out of this situation for him and Bea. And while everyone's eyes were certainly on Kat and Ted, that didn't change the fact that Sam and Bea were still surrounded.

And Bea still had Lander attached to one arm. The strange, hermit-like man just stood there watching it all with an expression somewhere between a smirk and a sneer.

And Bea's face...God, it was terrible. Sam watched it cycle through a series of ghastly emotions. Panic. And then pity. And then dread. And then horror. She seemed to want to put a stop to it, but then there was also something else there that seemed callused to the situation. And Sam could imagine that a part of her was thinking that Ted had only got what he'd deserved.

Ted, who'd promised to turn Bea over to Lander to be raped by his primals. Ted, who'd fathered the being that had just strangled the life out of him with her teeth. Ted, who'd created a web of lies that he'd never been able to extricate himself from.

"Alright!" Horner's voice shattered the spell of horror. "He's dead, Kat! Get the fuck off of him!"

Sam marveled at the man's hubris. Who in the world would say that shit to a quarter primal in the midst of an existential crisis? Was he *trying* to get Kat to attack him too?

But she didn't attack him. She unlatched her jaws from around Ted's throat and extricated herself from the limp body. Then she just crouched there for a long moment, staring down at the lifeless figure. She seemed shocked at what she'd done. A moment of humanity stuck in there amidst animal rage.

"Kat!" Horner snapped again, taking a step towards her with his fists balled.

Kat rose to her feet. Her eyes hit Horner's from beneath hooded brows. Her blood-slaked mouth widened, and for a half a second, Sam thought she was grinning. But no. She was only baring her teeth at Horner.

And Horner bared his teeth back. Like one of those shitty dog owners that thinks the best way to control a dog is to act like one.

"You wanna go at me, too?" Horner growled.

Sam could barely believe it. Did this skinny fuck really think he could take her? Did he really think he could stop her if she wanted him dead?

There must have been a part of Kat that thought about doing it. Because Sam watched her head swivel from side to side, those bright, wild eyes taking in all the men with guns standing around them.

Yes, she could take Horner. But then she'd be shot dead.

There was a part of Sam that felt bad for Kat. Felt for the human in her, squashed between a madman that hated her, and the primal instincts that raged for control of her. But the bigger part of Sam mentally urged Kat to lose control of herself. To make a go at Horner. Because then this really would turn into absolute chaos, and while all the ranch hands were focused on saving their boss, maybe Sam and Bea could make a break—

But Kat made her break first.

She let out a weird snarl that turned into something of a howl, and then she spun and took off. The movement surprised everyone—Sam included—and several of the ranch hands yelped and raised their weapons. But she wasn't going after anyone. She was trying to escape.

She ran on two legs at first. But then, as though watching her devolve right before their eyes, she hunched lower and lower as she went, until her hands started clawing at the ground between loping strides, and then she was just running on all fours, like the primals did.

She cut around the side of the ranch house, and went straight on, hurdling the post-and-barbed-wire fence in one lithe jump, and disappearing into the tall grass beyond.

"Fuck her," Horner spat. "We don't need her anymore."

Bran, however, didn't seem so sure. Or maybe it was his own strange affection for the hybrid girl that made him stand there with an aggrieved look on his face and his mouth open like he was on the verge of shouting after her.

But he never did.

"Clean this shit up!" Horner bawled at his men, and they jumped to.

"Actually," Lander said, airily. "If you'd like to simply dump him out beyond your front gate..." he smiled. "I'm sure my family could make good use of him. Waste not, want not. That's what I always say."

Horner regarded him with an inscrutable expression for a few beats as a handful of his men came forward and took Ted up, one man to each limb. "Whatever," Horner grunted. "Fine. Drop him out past the gate."

Horner stepped around his men as they bore Ted up and began shuffling for the gate. "What about this guy? Did you want him or not?"

It took Sam a moment to realize that Horner was talking about him.

Lander moved closer to Sam, pulling Bea reluctantly along with him. Freya moved up to Sam's other side, so he found himself frozen between the two, the subject of everyone's suddenly-intense scrutiny.

Lander peered discerningly at Sam, eyes squinted, head tilted to one side. "What are you?"

Sam blinked. "What do you mean?"

Lander rolled his eyes. "I mean, what's your blood, kid? What's your genetics? You Hispanic or something?"

"Afghanistan," Sam said, not knowing whether honesty would help his situation or not. And did he want to be taken? Just so he could stay with Bea? "My family's from Afghanistan."

"Hm," Lander mumbled, thoughtfully. "He'd certainly bring some fresh genetics."

Shit, do I actually want this to happen?

"But..." Lander continued, making a pained face. "There's something in his eyes. I don't trust him. I don't think he'll...be cool. You know what I mean?"

"No, not really," Horner said, tiredly.

"I think he's a little soft on Bea here," Lander sighed. "Which means he'll be disruptive, at best. Probably won't cooperate with my wives, either. Ah, well. Can't win them all." Lander finally removed his searching gaze from Sam and started forward, dragging Bea with him. "No, I think we'll just let well enough alone for now. I don't want him. You can..." Lander whiffled some fingers over his shoulder at Sam. "...Do whatever you want with him."

Horner stood in Lander's path, forcing him to stop. "Our deal's done, then."

"Yes, yes," Lander said, dismissively. "It's done."

"You'll keep your beasts away from my cattle."

Lander tilted his head to one side. "Uh...yeah. That was the deal. Who do you think I am? Ted?" Then he laughed.

Horner did not. But he stepped aside, and Lander continued on, handing Bea over to Freya.

As though just realizing that her time had come, Bea suddenly thrashed into motion. But she was no match for Freya's preternatural strength. The hybrid woman barely moved as Bea started pulling against her. Just kept marching Bea along, as inexorable as the sunset.

"Sam!" Bea started screaming, trying to look over her shoulder at him. "Sam, don't let them do this! You've got to stop them! Stop them!"

And what was Sam going to say to that? His mouth opened, and his diaphragm pressed the air out of his lungs, but the words just weren't there. Everything he thought of to say tasted like ashes in his mouth.

It'll be okay?

It wasn't going to be okay.

I'll stop them?

He was utterly powerless to do anything.

So he only stared after her as she continued to fight and scream, until Freya reached the limit of her patience, drew Bea into a headlock, and choked her out until she went limp. All the while still making steady progress towards the gate.

"She's a fiery one!" Sam heard Lander guffaw, distantly.

"Bran," Horner said, standing there in front of Sam. "Take the kid into the house. Put him in the living room. Stay with him. And take some other guys with you. Guys you trust not to fuck things up." Horner turned and scanned the ridges surrounding his ranch, as Bran stepped up to Sam, still looking bewildered, and grabbed him by the upper arm.

"You made the right call grabbing him," Horner said. "Got a feeling we're gonna need a hostage."

When Bea came to, the first thing she noticed was the pounding ache in her stomach.

She blinked and gasped, finding it difficult to breathe. She tried to move to alleviate the pain, but something was holding her tight around the waist. And around her legs. She stared at grass and dirt, flying by beneath her.

Feet flashing. Not her feet. These were ghastly things. Dark with dirt. The toes splayed wide, and tipped with thick nails that seemed more like claws. Above those feet were legs so fatless that she could see the striations in every bit of their substantial muscle mass.

And above those legs was a bare ass.

Oh God...

Reality came back like a piercing scream, and she might've echoed it, if she could get more than the tiniest whiff of air. She was being carried by one of them. Slung over its shoulder—that was the ache in her stomach, pounding to the rhythm of the creature's pace, as it ran on two legs instead of four.

Not Freya, but one of the full-blooded infected. Mutated. Evolved. No longer fully human, but not altogether a different species.

Because what was it she'd learned in biology class, so many years ago? It seemed a strange thing to remember right at that particular moment, but her brain alighted on the fact of its own volition.

Things were considered a different species if they could not produce fertile offspring.

But one of these primals could produce a hybrid, when mated with a human. And that hybrid itself was fertile, capable of producing quarter-blooded hybrids, like Freya and Kat.

They were not a different species. At least according to her ninth-grade biology class.

And then she realized *why* she'd thought of all that.

Because that's what they were going to do with her. They were going to mate her with one of these full-blooded primals, in order to produce a half-blooded hybrid. In order to produce more of what Lander called his "wives." Because they grew fast and died young, and Lander's current wives must've been getting old by now. He needed fresh blood. He needed fresh genes.

The horror of it struck her afresh. She thrashed against the grip of the thing holding her, but it only tightened its arms around her. God, it was strong! She couldn't stop it. Couldn't get away from it. Her will was a puny thing in the face of something so monstrous.

"No!" she cried out, little more than a gasp. She began beating at its back, her fists making dull, fleshy thuds against its heavily-muscled frame. She felt, rather than heard the thing growl—a low rumble that reverberated through its chest and into her belly.

It terrified her, but she didn't stop.

"No!" Just kept hammering at its back, trying to hit it on the spine to make it hurt more, then trying to aim for the kidneys, because she'd heard that was supposed to be painful.

She didn't feel like she was able to generate much power in those strikes, but all of the sudden she was sailing through the air, and then landed flat on her back, knocking the wind out of her and setting her to gasping and coughing.

She forced her eyes to stay open despite the racking coughs and the tears that sprang up in them. She couldn't tell where the hell she was, aside from the fact that she was surrounded by tall grass.

A figure loomed in her vision, blotting out the graying sky. She would have cried out, but couldn't draw the air to do it, so she just recoiled, flattening herself into the dirt like she could sink into it and be buried.

Its skin was browned from the sun and covered in a thin sheen of sweat. The hair of its head and beard was a massive mane, clumped at the ends with years of soil. Its brow was beetled into a fearsome scurry of wrinkles, like an animal snarling—and snarling it was. Its mouth parted the thicket of its beard, seeming to stretch from ear to ear, its teeth unnaturally elongated.

The smell of it hit her. The sour smell of a carnivore's skin, and sweat, and dirt.

It must've smelled her too.

The snarl on its face slackened into something like predatory interest. It dipped back, and for a moment, she thought it was going to leave her. Then she realized it was looking at her midsection. Her stomach collapsed into a leaden ball. Panic singed her nerves like fire. She instinctively put both of her hands down over her crotch and only then realized that she'd pissed herself.

The thing reached one huge hand over, grabbed her roughly by one hip, and turned her over with one effortless motion.

"No!" she managed to shout, and tried to kick it, but it seized her legs and pinned them down. "No!" Flattened onto her stomach, she tried to twist and grab its hair or claw its eyes, but she couldn't reach.

She yelped when it smashed its face into her backside. She jerked her legs in a spasm of panic-energized strength, but for all the blinding effort, she barely moved an inch. She was completely powerless. It had her pinned so securely, she was as good as paralyzed.

Oh God! What's it doing?

She felt the heat of its breath in her crotch. Heard it snuffling. Inhaling.

She screamed again, because it was all she had. There was only the stupid idea that if her voice reached a certain, piercing decibel, perhaps it would scare it off. As though it were a skittish animal. But it gave no reaction to her scream. Just kept nuzzling and snuffling at her crotch.

A bark—short, sharp, and unfriendly.

At first, she thought that it'd been the creature that had her pinned. But then the bark came again, louder and closer, and when she looked up, she saw a haze of blonde hair rocketing out of the grass ahead of her.

The pressure on her legs, and the head pushing between her thighs, immediately relented.

Freya stood over her as Bea curled into an instinctive ball. The hybrid growled menacingly, and the creature that had been snuffling at Bea backed away with a plaintive hoot and a grumble, moving sideways on all fours with its head held low.

Bea realized she was hyperventilating when her vision began to shrink and sparkle at the edges. She tried to breathe deeply, but something in her chest wouldn't let her. The fear had overtaken her. Sunk its claws into her deep. Dragged her down into nightmarish dread. Her future was being illustrated for her in sickening detail, and there was no escaping it.

Her hyperventilation was broken with a single sob that wrenched every bit of breath out of her. Just kept pressing it out of her until she thought she'd never be able to breathe again.

A hand settled on her shoulder. She barely felt it. Only really noticed it when it patted her.

Patted her?

Bea's sob finally strangled out, her abdominal muscles aching with strain by the time she sucked in another breath. She twisted and found Freya squatting over her, still patting her on the shoulder like a bored mother whose child has once again fallen to pieces over a skinned knee.

For an instant, Bea almost screamed at her and jerked her shoulder away. But she was too scared. And too taken aback by this strange show of pity.

Freya's face was much like Kat's, in that everything from the nose up looked normal. And everything below was twisted.

And then Freya did a strange thing. Something Bea didn't think possible. She made a very human expression. One corner of her mouth and one eyebrow quirked up. Was she being...sardonic?

Freya's voice came out thick and unwieldy: "Fight. Harder."

What?

And then a very human chortle. Not from Freya, and certainly not from Bea.

Bea whipped her head around and saw Lander standing there, sweating and breathing hard, but smiling. He must've been running with them. Maybe that's why he was so goddamned skinny—from trying to keep up with these creatures, but without the advantage of their mutated genetics.

"Hey, when she's right, she's right," Lander said, grinning. Then he looked over his shoulder. "That wasn't even one of our big boys, Bea. I call that one Bobo, because he's a runt and a fucking idiot." He turned his gaze back on her, and though he was still smiling, everything in his face had changed. "Wouldn't do me much good if you gave into a runt. No, I need better genetics than that. It needs to be one of the big ones. The strong ones. The smart ones. You need to save yourself for one of them. So, like Freya so aptly put it: fight harder."

And before Bea could even wrap her brain around that level of defilement, Lander started running again. Bea was yanked up to her feet by her elbow, and shoved after him.

"Go," Freya growled. "Run."

Chapter 35

Full dark.

Lee had been watching the sky, like a kid wondering how long until the fireworks start. Except his impatience was much less excitement and a lot more nerves.

Funny how that works. When he was a spry, young corporal, he hadn't even been all that scared before his very first engagement. Still full of piss and vinegar, he'd figured he was a badass, trained and equipped by the greatest military in the world, blah-blah-blah. Sure, he was a little jittery—heart definitely got thumping, that's for sure. But other than that, it felt less like going into combat, and more like walking out to his first football game.

But that was because the consequences weren't real to him. Yet.

Over the years, the consequences had become oh-so-clear. The last six years in particular had taught him that no matter your training, your experience, or your equipment, you couldn't account for every variable. Sometimes bad shit happened, and there wasn't a damn thing you could do about it.

And from his vantage point on that hill overlooking the ranch, Lee knew this was far from an ideal situation. Training and experience they had. Equipment was…lacking. He sure as shit would've liked to have his personal pack, with its NVGs and spare boots.

And while he was wishing, he would've liked to have a support platoon. And some air support. And a medevac.

Hell, he and Marie didn't even have their regular rifles. They'd had to go with *minion* rifles.

But, what he had was this: Himself and Abe and Jones and Marie.

One marksman.

One ground pounder.

Two grenadiers.

And a clear sky with a bright half-moon for illumination.

He had every reason in the world to worry, and worry he did. In a combat environment—more specifically, *this* combat environment—rational thinking was no antidote for anxiety. Because his fears were very rational. That was the problem.

So when he thought of the faces of each member of his team, and wondered if they were going to die tonight, he didn't even have the respite of telling himself his fears were unfounded. Casualties were not only possible, but probable.

So, instead of trying to calm himself, which was a fool's errand, he did what he'd learned to do long ago: Stop thinking. Focus only on the moment right in front of you. Let the innumerable possibilities of the future fall away.

It was only his vast experience that allowed him to do this. Because he knew he could trust himself. He didn't need to anticipate every eventuality. If the eventuality arrived, he knew he could handle it in that moment.

He'd had a few special forces instructors that would've shit a brick to hear him say that. But at this point, Lee'd been stuck in the shit for six years straight, without a single break. The experience of those instructors and how they kept themselves alive—as well as sane—wasn't even comparable anymore. Lee's experience had surpassed previous military wisdom.

Probably 'cause humans aren't meant to do this shit for six years straight.

But whatever. He hadn't lost his marbles yet. Hell, he was probably one of the world's leading experts on how not to go apeshit in constant combat.

So, Lee put them all out of his mind. The images of his friends bleeding out and gurgling. The intimate knowledge of how that would mess with his head—not immediately, but later. In the dark. In the quiet. Whenever sleep was hard to find.

He put it all out of his mind, and thought only this:

Twelve armed combatants.

Four assaulters.

One hostage.

That was all that mattered.

He marked the location of the primary threats through his binos, then stowed them. Six of the twelve combatants were currently visible, patrolling or standing guard inside the fenceline of the ranch. The other six consisted of the four men that Lee had seen go into the main ranch house—presumably to guard Sam—along with Bran and Colin Horner himself.

The worst threat came from the two guys with what Lee assumed were coyote rifles. AR platforms with what looked like thermal scopes on them. The frequency with which they kept scanning the dark hills around them through their scopes led Lee to believe his suspicion was correct.

Abe had also weighed in, as the optic on his rifle was higher-powered than Lee's binoculars, and he could see the weapon systems in more detail. Abe concurred that they were probably thermals, so they'd all been very careful to keep their heat signatures out of sight.

Lee slid backwards down the slope until he was confident his heat signature wouldn't be detected, then rolled onto his side. The moonlight on Marie's face cast her expression as severe.

"You ready?" he whispered as he hefted the M32.

"Yuh." Her voice was tight.

"Focus on the moment," Lee said, offering a confident smile that he didn't feel.

Her eyes narrowed at him. "Yeah. Live, laugh, love, and all that horseshit. Let's just fucking go."

Lee sidled up onto his knees, and then into a squat. Keyed his comms. His voice came out a bit strained as he clenched himself against the pain from his earlier beating. "Abe, you good to go?"

"Yeah, we're set," the reply came back.

"Are *you* good?" Marie asked, looking at Lee pointedly.

"Nah, I think I'll just sit here and lick my wounds."

"Smartass."

"Well, what the fuck do you want me to say, Marie?" Lee grouched under his breath. "Doesn't matter if we're fucked up. Still gotta do it."

Marie looked at him for a long time. Or at least, he thought she was looking at him. The shadows across her face turned her eyes into black pits. Eventually she nodded and rose to one knee. "Alright then."

He could tell there was a lot more she wanted to say. He preferred to imagine they would've been kind, encouraging words, recent history be damned.

He turned back in the direction of the ranch, now blocked by the top of the hill. Keyed his comms once more. "We're a go. It's on you, Abe."

Abe took one big breath in through his nose, and let it out slow through pursed lips. At the end of the breath, he murmured into his mic, "Roger that. Standby to move."

Through his scope, the details of the ranch below stood in monochromatic moonlight blue. He would've liked to have some sort of night optic, but a bright moon would have to do. He *did* have his NVGs, as did Jones, but they were unfortunately not compatible with his rifle scope. The ESR had a night-vision attachment, but that didn't do him much good at this point.

God, he wished he had his ESR.

His crosshairs had drifted just a bit as he'd transmitted back to Lee. He eased them back onto target.

His target stood near the ranch's main gate, facing away from Abe. He wore an old ball cap instead of the cowboy hat that the others seemed to prefer. He held a rifle with the front end resting on a fence post. One of the rifles with a thermal optic.

Usually, if Abe were doing a night op, he'd wait until the wee hours of the morning. Two reasons why that wasn't so great in this situation: One, they didn't know how long Sam had; and two, the residual heat of the day would provide *some* cover for Lee and Marie's heat signatures. Or so they hoped. Thermal imaging spotted heat differences, not just heat. Every hour they waited, the ground cooled, and a 98-degree thermal signature became that much more obvious.

Abe spared a moment to glance over his scope at the second thermal-equipped guard. Abe was about four hundred yards away from the east side of the ranch, and that's where the second guy was, more or less facing in their direction.

Beside Abe, Jones shuffled his body around so he was behind one of the tree trunks, then slowly rose to his knees. The guy had been shockingly quiet this whole time, but despite Abe's constant harassment, he knew that Jones could be professional when the situation called for it.

Only when the situation called for it.

Back in his scope, Abe held the reticle on his target's upper back, right between the shoulder blades. "You got the comms, Jonesey," he whispered.

"Got it," Jones confirmed.

Interminable seconds passed. The thermal-equipped guard at the west gate had proven to be Mr. Regular, scanning the terrain at pretty even intervals—about once every minute. Abe waited, counting the seconds. And right on time, Mr. Regular raised his rifle, brought the thermal scope to his eye, and scanned the hills.

"He's scanning again. Get ready," Abe said.

Jones didn't need to reply.

Mr. Regular gave the terrain two passes, then lowered his rifle again.

"Now," Abe said.

"Move," Jones transmitted.

Abe had the urge to glance at the hilltop to see if Lee and Marie were moving, but stayed in his scope. They knew the plan. Move for thirty seconds, then drop into the grass and hope to all hell that it was thick enough to hide their signatures.

This was gonna take a while. Lee and Marie wouldn't be running. In addition to the grenade launchers, they both had rifles strapped to their backs. If they moved too aggressively, the guards in the ranch would hear them rattling all the way down the hill.

Abe kept on counting the seconds. When he reached thirty-two, Lee's voice whispered in his ear: "Down."

They waited again.

Thank God they'd decided on only moving for thirty seconds, because Mr. Regular decided to get squirrelly and scanned the terrain at forty seconds instead of a minute. Abe relayed it to Jones, who relayed it over the comms. Abe wondered if Mr. Regular had heard something to make him break his usual pattern.

"Move," Abe said, when Mr. Regular lowered his rifle again.

"Move."

Thirty seconds later: "Down."

"Distance?" Abe asked through Jones.

"Seven hundred."

Two cycles had eaten up a hundred yards. They'd need to do this six more times. That was a lot to ask of Lady Luck. And Abe could already feel Murphy sniffing around the back of his neck.

On the fifth cycle, everything went to shit.

The only thing Lee heard was the distinctive sound of a bullet hitting flesh.

He dropped, instinctively, and heard Marie do the same. There'd been no accompanying rifle report, and that only meant one thing: Abe's suppressed rifle had just taken out the guy with the thermal scope nearest to Lee's position.

And the only reason Abe would have taken the shot is if the guy had seen them coming.

Then two things happened at once.

Jones's voice erupted in his ear, full volume: "You're compromised! Move and send it!"

And in Lee's other ear, he heard the sound of a half-dozen men all yelling at once.

Lee rolled to his right side, slinging the M32, and bringing the rifle around from his back. "Marie! I'll cover you with the rifle! Move!"

He popped up to a low crouch, just his head, shoulders, and rifle above the grass, as Marie surged to her feet. He had his red dot dialed nearly all the way down. The ghostly reticle swept across the ranch, and the scurrying shadows within. He could see movement, but not much else.

He held his fire as Marie bolted past him, trying to see if any of those shifting shadows looked like they'd spotted them. They had another fifty yards before they were within firing range. It might just be possible that they wouldn't be noticed—

A shout from the gate.

Lee pivoted his reticle in that direction, spotting the faint glimmer of moonlight off of a man's face that sure as hell seemed like it was looking right at Lee. And raising a big gun.

"Marie! Get down!" Lee yelled, then fired three rapid shots at the same instant that he saw the unmistakable muzzle flash of an M60 machine gun, and heard bees buzzing all around him.

He went down.

"Shit-fuck," Abe spat, the second that initial round left his rifle.

The scope jumped, and when it settled again there was the briefest moment where the bullet was still in flight, and the target was still staring through his thermal scope, all his body language saying that he'd seen something he didn't like.

Then the bullet smacked him square in the spine. He crumpled in place.

"Goddammit," Jones seethed, then transmitted, "You're compromised! Move and send it!"

The instant Abe confirmed the target was down, he shifted his hips violently to the left, bringing the east-facing fenceline into view. It took him a half second to find the second guard with the thermal optic, who was, at that moment, just spinning around to see what all the fuss was over on the other side of the ranch.

With his support hand, Abe grabbed the elevation turret of his scope and twisted, feeling each click as he dialed it to 400 yards from memory.

The guard was starting to walk towards the gate. Now starting to run.

Abe led him by a small degree and squeezed the trigger.

The round splashed just in front of the guy's feet, making him skid to a stop and dance sideways in a panic, spinning as he did as though to locate the unseen threat.

Abe swore and brought the reticle to center mass in a brief moment where the guy was stupidly stationary.

A chatter of automatic gunfire hit Abe's ears.

"Shit!" Jones yelped. "They're hitting Lee and Marie!"

Abe fired and forced himself to stay on the guy as the peel of automatic fire continued to pull at Abe's mind, seeming to grow in urgency with every round fired at a cyclic pace.

He saw his target's body jerk. Stumble. Try to run two steps and then keel over, face-first into the dirt.

Abe ripped his rifle back to the gate.

Lee on the comms: "Abe! Take out that gunner!"

Muzzle flashes sparkled all along the gate—both gate guards, and now both of the roving patrol, taking up positions there and firing wildly out into the night. One muzzle flash more obvious than the others.

Abe didn't have time to adjust his reticle. He'd started doing the math in his head the second he knew he'd have to make a rapid transition from the east fenceline to the gate. He held the reticle high over the shadow of a figure behind that automatic muzzle flash, and gently pressed his trigger to the rear.

The snap of his suppressed rifle.

The continued chattering of the machine gun.

Then a spray of red mist that turned the white muzzle flashes pink.

Then the machine gun went silent.

"Gunner's down!" Jones transmitted.

"You're clear on our side," Abe barked at Jones. "Move!"

"Moving!" Jones squalled as he tore around the base of the tree and thrashed out of the copse at a dead sprint, heading for the ranch.

Chapter 36

Aside from all the obvious downsides of missing an eye, one of the worst was that Lee couldn't shoot with both eyes open, and it vastly fucked his situational awareness.

He rocketed to his feet the second the machine gunner was down. There were plenty of bullets flying, but Lee didn't hear any buzzing—the shooters were simply firing randomly into the darkness.

He settled the reticle on one of the shapes that was at least pointing their weapon in the right direction and fired five times, wishing he had the peripheral vision to know what Marie was doing at that moment.

Somewhere in those five rounds, the guy went down, screaming something fierce. Lee followed him to the ground and put two more into his writhing form through the fence.

He dipped his rifle, bringing his eye clear of his optic.

Two more shooters at the gate.

And where was Marie?

He got his answer in the form of a heavy, chest-thumping *whump* from far to his left. Saw the dribble of sparks from the launcher, like a comet tail in the darkness.

For a scant second, even the shooters at the gate paused.

And then the outbuilding directly north of them exploded.

The flash silhouetted the two men. Lee flinched away from the light as it dazzled his eye, leaving a purplish afterimage that obscured everything in Lee's direct line of sight. He swore, bringing his rifle up, trying to sight the two guards. A cumulus cloud of dust and smoke washed over the whole area of the gate.

He couldn't see shit.

WHUMP

In the instant of that second grenade's flight time, Lee saw movement in his peripheral. His eye darted to the movement, but the afterimage obscured it. He got the barest impression of two men running. One lugging something heavy.

The M60?

Lee swore and clenched his eyes shut against the second explosion. When he opened them again, his feet already moving beneath him, the whole gate had been blown open, leaving tattered remnants of wood and twisted metal.

He transmitted as he ran for the breached gate. "Abe! Two running towards the ranch house! I think one of them has the machine gun!"

Ahead of him, and converging on the gate, he saw Marie's figure at full-tilt sprint, M32 pumping in both hands.

Abe's response came back breathless and shaking with the sound of his own running. "I'm already out of position! No visual!"

Lee blinked rapidly as his feet found the dirt road heading into the gate. The ghost of the first explosion that still hung in his vision had thinned, and he could just make out the figure of the man with the machine gun, nearly to the ranch house.

Don't let him get inside!

Lee brought his sights to his eye, but just as his finger dropped to the trigger, Marie hollered "Crossing!" and slipped in front of him.

"Marie! Down!"

She dropped to a knee instantly, her head ducked low.

But the guy was gone.

Lee swore, but there was nothing to be done for it. Now the ranch house would have a machine gun nest in it. "You're clear!" he shouted at Marie. "Hit that bunkhouse!"

He knew that's what she'd already been targeting. She didn't bother to rise—she had a clear shot straight through the gates and right at the bunkhouse. Simply shouldered her weapon, ranged the target, and let fly with three grenades, as fast as the M32 could cycle.

They didn't even know if there was anyone in the bunkhouse. But they knew that *Sam* wasn't in the bunkhouse, and some pissant with a lever action *might* be.

The big barn-style bunkhouse erupted like it'd been built on the mouth of a volcano. The sides of it blew out, and Lee could swear he saw the whole roof lift up, then come caving in on itself.

No pissants anymore.

Lee caught up to Marie and grabbed her up by the shoulder to let her know she was clear to rise. As soon as she was on her feet, he moved away from her so as not to make an easy target of the two of them.

"Everyone hold!" he transmitted. "Gimme your positions!"

He was already angling for the cover of the stables, just inside the gates and to the right. Marie followed. The ruckus had stirred up the horses inside and they were screaming and kicking at the walls with massive reverberating thumps.

"Jones here. Got Abe coming up on my ass. We're on the east end, near the empty grain silo."

Lee rounded the stables and cut in through the main corridor. Horses to either side, all of them in a panic. He slowed his pace. Couldn't hear a damn thing, so he started trying to shush the animals. He had no experience with horses, but he knew to sound calm and gentle. Shockingly, it seemed to have an effect. They didn't immediately go quiet, but their kicking tapered off and their screams turned to indignant huffs and whinnies.

He checked over his shoulder. Saw Marie slinking along the opposite side of the corridor, walking backwards and covering their rear. She'd swapped the M32 for her rifle.

"Hold what you got," Lee said over the comms. "Try to get eyes on that ranch house but don't give away your position. And watch your backs in case we missed anyone."

Did it really need to be said? No, they were probably already doing it out of habit. But long ago they'd all agreed that stating the obvious wasn't an insult. Reminders never hurt, especially in an environment full of distractions.

"Should have a clear shot at the ranch house through this passage," Marie noted.

The stables were oriented so that the main, central corridor pointed just to the right of the ranch house. As Lee approached the last third of the corridor, he saw the side of the ranch house come into view.

"Got it," he murmured, coming to a stop. The horses were getting quieter and quieter as the stillness stretched. He moved very slowly to shave away some angles, more and more of the ranch house coming into view. The porch. A swing hanging listless from two chains. Then the first window.

Light glowed inside, dull and amber. Lanterns or candles.

Lee's target was the rightmost window at the front of the house, if you were looking directly at it. It was also where they heavily suspected Sam was being held, as it was the only window with the curtains drawn.

Lee's rapid-fire thoughts were interrupted by the sound of glass shattering. The curtains twitched and jumped and were ripped aside. And then a machine gun barrel protruded, resting on the sill. A man hunkered behind it.

Two other figures were visible, standing behind the machine gun.

One was Sam himself. And holding Sam in a hostage position, only identifiable by the crown of iron-gray hair peeking over Sam's shoulder, was Colin Horner. Holding a revolver to Sam's head.

Lee's heart started hammering so hard, he felt like it might rip itself apart. He held his position, unmoving, except for the one hand that it took to touch off his comms. His voice came out quiet and direct: "Horner's got a gun to Sam's head, in the window, right behind the machine gun."

Behind him, Marie swore.

"I got no visual," Abe hissed back. "Working on getting a better position. Hang on."

Though Marie was right next to him, Lee spoke over the comms so he could include Jones. "Marie and Jones, start moving towards the back of the ranch house in case we need to make entry."

"Jaaaaax!" Horner bellowed into the night. "Give it up, motherfucker!"

Slowly, ever so slowly, Lee lowered himself into a prone position on the hay-strewn floor. If they took out Horner, would the ranch hands continue to fight, or would they give up?

That said, Horner wasn't an idiot. He was holding Sam good and secure and making effective use of his body as a shield. The tiny dome of gray hair over Sam's right shoulder was not enough for Lee to make a confident shot. Not at a hundred yards with a red dot on a rifle that could only manage three MOA on a good day. Not when one tiny involuntary muscle spasm could wind up taking the side of Sam's face off.

Lee's eye glanced down at the machine gunner. That was another issue. Horner had Sam pressed so close to the guy manning the gun, if they shot the gunner, there was a decent chance the bullet would pass through and hit Sam too.

Shit, shit, shit.

"Jax!" Horner practically shrieked this time. "Come out and face me like a man!" His voice cracked and Lee was surprised at how unstable he sounded. It made a knot cinch just a bit tighter in his chest. Lee had been counting on Horner being cold and practical, as he'd been when they'd met. But this version of the guy sounded unhinged.

Lee didn't think Sam had much time.

He thought about trying to open a dialogue—shouting back and forth with Horner might buy them some time. But then he thought of how volatile Horner sounded. Like a man that might kill his hostage just because he didn't like something that was said.

Keeping silent might be less dangerous for Sam.

Instead, Lee keyed his comms. "Marie and Jones, I need you to get to the front corner of the house, right there next to the window with the machine gun." He could only imagine how much they liked hearing that, but he trusted that they wouldn't waste time arguing. "Abe, I need you to get a *diagonal* angle on that gunner."

"Sounds like you're working something," Abe said.

"I'm gonna give the word," Lee responded. "And when I do, Abe I need you to drop that gunner, and Marie and Jones, I need you take that window."

"Workin' on it," Abe said. "I'll let you know when I'm in position."

After a moment of silence on the radio there came two clicks. Marie and Jones must've gotten close enough to the ranch house that they needed to maintain radio silence. Two clicks of the PTT counted as an acknowledgement.

Through his optic, Lee watched Horner fidgeting around. His head came up a bit, just one eye peeking furtively out from around Sam's neck, searching the darkness. Lee's red dot sat right on that eye, and for just a moment, Lee's finger came off the magazine well of his rifle, and almost went to the trigger.

No. Not yet. Still a bad shot.

Lee switched his focus to Sam for a brief instant. Hard to tell expressions from this distance, but Lee could read Sam's body language well enough. And he felt a welling of pride, because Sam was doing exactly what Lee had taught him to do: Waiting. Watching for an opportunity.

Sam wasn't defeated. He was just being patient.

That feeling of pride devolved into dread.

Don't screw it up, Lee.

And then Lee had to put that out of his mind along with all his other very rational concerns of failure. Focus on the moment. What needed to be done in this moment?

Just keep Horner from shooting Sam.

Horner snugged in tight behind Sam again and started shouting once more, his voice only slightly more controlled this time. "I know you're out there! Let's talk!"

Let's not.

"Alright," Abe whispered in his ear. "In position. Got a good bead on the gunner. Low chance of a pass-through hit on Sam."

Low, not zero. Because you could never perfectly account for what a bullet might do once it hits something. Could punch straight through. Or it could carom around and come out somewhere completely unexpected.

"I copy. Standby for go."

"Alright, motherfucker!" Horner raged into the darkness. "Let's do this! You come out in the open where I can see you or—"

Lee saw the ultimatum coming and knew he couldn't let Horner get it all the way out.

"Why'd you let Kat kill Ted?" Lee bellowed over the last of Horner's words. No real rhyme or reason why he'd gone with that as his opening sally. It was just the first thing he could think of that didn't have to do with Sam. He wanted Horner to *stop* thinking about Sam.

It worked. Kind of. Horner didn't shoot Sam, and he did pause for a few precious seconds.

"You coulda stopped it," Lee pressed, not wanting to give Horner time to see that he was being distracted. And praying to God that he wasn't about to put a spark to Horner's sudden volatility. "You coulda saved him. He wasn't a threat to you. He wasn't even armed."

A temptation to keep going, but Lee put the reins on. He only needed to keep Horner engaged. If he started monologuing, Horner might realize he was being stalled.

"Ted?" Horner let out a nasty chortle. "You're worried about *Ted*? You should be worried about your boy here!"

Well, shit.

Get him off the topic.

"You think Kat's not gonna come back and get her revenge on you?" Lee called out, thinking, *Come on, Marie! Get in position!*

"Revenge on *me*?" Horner sounded insulted. "For what?!"

"For lying to her. For misleading her. For treating her like a dog."

"What the fuck are we even talking about right now? I've got a gun to your boy's head, and you're talking about everything but that! Almost seems like you're trying to stall!"

"I'm trying to figure out a way forward that doesn't require a mountain of dead bodies. I'm kinda tired of making those. I guess you haven't got your fill yet."

"You come out in the open and start talking to me face to face, or I blow your boy's brains out! How about that?"

And there it was. Nothing to do now but force a stalemate.

"You kill him and the very next second I'm gonna drop six high-explosive forty-millimeter grenades on your head. Do to your nice little home what I already did to your bunkhouse. Kill you and every man you got in there with you." A moment of inspiration. "Actually, if any of you guys working for Colin Horner want to turn around and blow his head off for me, I'll let you live."

There came a moment where Horner was no longer yelling at Lee, but dealing with some internal personnel problems. Several men's voices were raised, but unclear.

A subtle shift in shadows at the corner of the ranch house, barely two strides from the window.

"Marie and Jones, gimme two clicks if you're in position and ready."

The voices from inside the ranch house came to a sudden crescendo and then ceased altogether. Lee braced for the sound of a gunshot, but none came.

What did come was two clicks in his ear.

Then Horner, once more: "Nice try, motherfucker! Looks like we're at an impasse! So how do you wanna finish this night, huh? With your boy alive or dead?"

"Standby for go," Lee murmured into his comms, then settled himself nice and flat on the ground, as relaxed as he could be, and then lowered his reticle so that it was hovering over Sam's chest.

Then Lee shouted, louder than before, each word clearly articulated. "Can you hear me loud and clear? Because I have one word for you."

His finger moved to the trigger.

Hesitation. Then: "Yeah, I can hear you. Say what you're gonna say!"

And here's the one word Lee shouted back: "Artichoke!"

Chapter 37

Staring out into the darkness with a revolver pointed at his head, Sam had a curiously distinct memory.

They were in some dingy basement, Sam recalled, but where that was geographically, he couldn't remember. Could've been any number of dingy, dark places where they'd slept on the road between settlements, or in the settlements themselves. Sam only remembered that it was early on in their "career" together, not long after The Deal.

Exposed floor joists made the ceiling, with ancient insulation falling out and forming fuzzy stalactites. A few pipes and conduits that looked like they'd been put there in the previous century, dusty remnants of cobwebs hanging from them.

"Alright!" Jones announced. "Pop quiz, hotshots!"

To which Abe groaned, and Lee smiled, saying, "Nice *Speed* reference."

Marie booed loudly.

Jones looked aghast. "You can't boo Keanu Reeves! He's a national treasure!"

"*Was* a national treasure," Sam observed.

Jones shook his head. "No. He's still alive. I can feel it."

"Whatcha got for us today?" Sam mused. He was tucked into his bivy sack, laying on his side and propped up on one elbow. Jones was sitting cross-legged on his.

Despite the dissenting grumbles from Abe and Marie, these so-called pop quizzes from Jones were a frequent form of entertainment. Abe and Marie were just being killjoys because they'd been winding down to sleep.

It wasn't *just* entertainment. Every once in a while, one of Jones's pop quizzes actually resulted in some good ideas. Mostly, though, they were just crazy fantasies where Jones put the team in extremely compromising hypothetical situations that would never occur in real life, and then demanded they come up with a solution.

Jones spread his hands wide and straightened his back, gazing at everyone with a knowing leer. In the red up-glow of the rechargeable lantern laying in the center of them, he looked kind of like he was about to have a séance.

"It's the simplest of shitty circumstances. I can't believe we haven't already talked about it. Someone's holding me hostage—you know, using me as a meat shield, and they've got a gun to my head. What do you do?"

"Just let him do it," Abe suggested.

"Maybe we'd get more sleep," Marie agreed.

"No, you have to save me," Jones countered. "That's the point of the exercise. You have to save me, and you have to kill the other guy."

"Negotiation?" Sam offered.

"I just said you have to kill the other guy."

"Yeah, I was gonna negotiate you away, and then shoot him."

Jones blew a raspberry. "Boring. That's not even fun. 'Oh, I negotiated Jones away.' You can't just say that. I'm talking about an actionable plan here, Sam, not some fuzzy-wuzzy heart-to-heart."

"Question," Lee said.

Jones pointed to him.

"Is time travel allowed?"

Jones narrowed his eyes at Lee. "Don't make this weird."

Lee held up a placating hand. "It's not weird. Stick with me. You've been taken hostage. That's the situation in the imaginary present, yes?"

Jones looked exceedingly suspicious. "Go on."

"Okay, so if that's the imaginary present, can we imagine that we pre-planned for this event? Effectively, can we imaginarily travel to the imaginary past, and set our imaginary past selves up for success in this scenario?"

"No," Jones said. "Because if you changed the imaginary past, you would change the imaginary present, and the scenario would be different. It's called the Butterfly Effect, Lee. Read a fucking book once in a while."

"But we're planning it right now," Lee said with a twinkle in his eye. "Maybe this scenario isn't the imaginary present, it's the imaginary future, and we're currently in the imaginary past."

"You're just trying to derail me," Jones sighed.

"And if *that's* the case—"

"It's not. This is an adulteration of the core concept of the game."

Lee continued, undeterred. "Then we should come up with a plan now, which is, of course, the imaginary past of your imaginary present scenario that might occur in the future."

Jones ran his hands over his face. "Fuck. Fine. Alright. You win."

Lee smiled. "Code word."

"Code word?"

"Yeah. That's the plan. Have a code word."

And that's when Sam spoke up: "Artichoke. The code word should be 'artichoke.'"

Jones slumped back against the wall, defeated. "Y'all are just destroying my game. Now it's just ridiculous."

"Come on," Sam argued his point. "Who's gonna ever say the word 'artichoke'?"

"Um, an artichoke farmer?" Jones said, as though it were oh-so-obvious.

"Yeah, but we're not farmers. None of us would ever say 'artichoke.'"

"Unless we happen upon a stash of canned artichoke hearts," Jones shot back. "Then one of us says 'Oh, look, artichoke hearts!' and then all the sudden everyone's shooting? Terrible plan."

"No, I like artichoke," Lee pitched in. "Simple. Easy to say. Easy to remember. Hard to mistake as another word. Unlikely to just randomly be said on accident. Perfect code word."

Now, standing in a ranch house with a gun to his head, Sam realized that their imaginary future had become the very real present. And as Horner and Lee began to shout back and forth, Sam felt like he knew where this was going, and his heart started hammering ever faster.

When Lee said "I have one word for you," Sam knew exactly what he had to do.

Because there was only one thing to do when Lee shouted "Artichoke!"

Sam dropped. Just ripped his own legs out from under him and dropped hard to the floor.

And then everything was screaming and gunfire.

The second Sam's chest dropped away from Lee's reticle, he broke the trigger. The rifle was zeroed for 100 yards, and it was point of aim, point of impact. The bullet struck Horner right in the sternum and sent the man staggering back.

At the same instant, the head of the man behind the machine gun snapped to the right in a puff of pink.

Lee perceived two things: The shape of Marie and Jones whipping around that corner, about to come up on the window; and inside that window, a man in a black hoodie, raising a heavily modified AK.

Porky, Lee recognized him the instant before he pumped three shots into him, hitting him center mass. He pulled his finger off the trigger just as the head of both Jones and Marie rose up and filled the frame of the window.

"Moving to the front door!" Lee shouted, keying his comms as he did and hauling his creaking, aching body off the floor of the stables. He could hear Marie and Jones's rifles pounding the interior of that room, and he hoped that if they didn't hear his shout, they'd at least hear it on the comms.

He registered Abe coming around the far side of the empty grain silo with a full head of steam, angling to meet Lee at the front door.

A clatter of unsuppressed gunfire came from inside the house, and Marie dropped out of the window as chunks of wood came flying off the sill and sparking off the M60 that still hung in the window. For a single, terrible stride, Lee thought she'd been hit.

Jones sidestepped to the right of the window, but kept his rifle firing as he moved.

Marie hit the ground on one knee, already swapping magazines.

Relief. Then refocusing.

Abe reached the front porch first, vaulting the steps in a single bound and not even pausing before he rammed the door with a front kick, sending it crashing open on its stoppers.

Lee also took the steps in one jump, but considerably less gracefully. He needed to get to Abe. He needed to cover his back...

Past Abe, a body went toppling into the foyer, and Abe held up right there at the doorstep just long enough to fire three more rounds into the body as it fell, and for Lee to reach his back. His rifle in a high ready, Lee smacked Abe's shoulder with his support hand and they exploded through the door as one.

Abe hooked right—into the room where Sam was.

Lee hooked left, covering Abe's back, and was immediately confronted with a gawky kid that couldn't have been more than eighteen years old. That was all Lee really registered about him—those big, scared eyes. Boyish, pink lips parted in a gape, pronounced Adam's apple bobbing in a twiggy neck.

And the pump shotgun in his hands. Which he then put to his shoulder as his eyes connected with Lee's.

Lee was already on him. Had been on him well before the kid even realized he was there. He had enough time to consider yelling at him to drop it. But not enough time to actually say it. Just a single microsecond of tired regret. Then two rounds to the chest, and two more to the neck and face as he crumpled.

Lee took two strides into the room, sweeping it from left to right as the kid's body hit the ground and the shotgun clattered across stone floors. He knew the layout of the house from being in it earlier, knew this was a sitting room with two chairs. He moved to check behind the chairs, registering Marie's voice shouting, "Coming in the front!"

No one behind the chairs.

Lee stepped to the kid's body on the way out. The shot to the face had struck the kid's cheek bone, and wherever it had gone after that hadn't been enough to offer an instant death. The kid blinked rapidly at the ceiling and issued a long, breathy groan.

Lee moved his muzzle to the kid's forehead. The eyes didn't track it. They weren't even seeing anything. They stopped blinking. The groan ran out of air. The chest didn't move again.

Lee felt momentarily grateful not to have to put him out of his misery.

He kept moving, back into the foyer, falling in behind Marie and Jones.

Marie went straight into the living room where Abe was standing over Sam, but with his rifle covering the downed bodies. Jones had his rifle oriented down the hall that led from the foyer to the back of the house. "One runner!" he shot over his shoulder at Lee. "I tagged him twice, but he squirted out the back!"

Lee held him up by his drag strap. "Hold that hall. Security!"

Only when Marie and Lee flowed into the living room to begin their security sweep did Abe raise his rifle into a high ready and knelt down over Sam, shaking him by the shoulder. "Sam! You good? You okay?"

There were four dead bodies, if you counted the one that had fallen in the foyer. Lee kicked the rifle out of that one's grip, then nudged it over so it was on its back. He was gone. Lee stepped over him and went straight to the body in the center of the room.

Colin Horner lay there, curled on his left side, his back to Lee. He spotted the revolver Horner had been holding to Sam's head, down by the man's boots.

"Two down," Marie noted as she swept over the other two bodies.

As Lee reached Horner, he saw the shoulders shake and a thin wheezy noise came out of the man. Lee booted the revolver and sent it spinning over towards Sam, who was saying, "I'm good, I'm good," in a surprisingly steady voice as Abe ran his hands briskly over Sam's body, checking him for holes anyway.

"Got a live one," Lee called out as he stopped over Horner's form. It figured he'd still be alive. He could see the hole in Horner's chest. Right through the sternum. And yet, it had apparently missed the man's heart. Perhaps an abnormally small target?

Horner's eyes were open. And he was very much awake. Very much seeing everything.

As Lee leaned over him, those pale blue eyes shot up and instantly filled with a hate so venomous that Lee was surprised the dying bastard had the energy to be that pissed.

"You!" Horner managed to wheeze, a spot of blood tinging his lips, staining his teeth.

"Yeah, it's me," Lee said. He glanced up at Jones, still holding coverage on that hallway. "Marie, get with Jones. Clear the back and exterior." As he said it, his eyes ranged across all of the dead bodies and realized that Bran was not among them.

It was Bran that had run.

Horner tried to say something, but it was garbled by too much blood in his throat. Sounded like a phlegmy old man. He choked and spluttered.

Marie met up with Jones and they proceeded down the hall.

Horner kept spluttering until he hacked up a big wad of blood and spat it onto the stones near his face. Then he turned those cold, hateful eyes on Lee again. "Fuck you, you bastard."

Lee shook his head. "I told you this shit was gonna happen, Horner. I warned you, in no uncertain terms. Remember that? I gave you a chance. And you threw it in my face."

"Lee."

He glanced over. Found Sam in a sitting position, rubbing his wrists where raw indents in his skin showed where the restraints had been. Sam's expression was calm. "Just put him down."

Lee squinted at his friend, so glad to find him alive and whole that he wasn't even irritated with being called out. "Sam. I'm allowed to talk to anyone I put a bullet into. It's my kill to reconcile with."

Sam gave only the slightest shrug. Abe took him under the arm and helped him to his feet.

Lee looked back at Horner. "Just trying to give you an opportunity to admit you were wrong. Confession, Horner. It's good for the soul. And you got a lot to confess, and not much time to do it in. But I'm listening, if you want it."

Horner's skin, which had turned waxy, suddenly went livid. The cords in his neck stood out as he jutted his face up at Lee, his bloody lips trembling, a vein protruding under one eye.

"Fuck...you..."

And then Horner seemed surprised by some internal sensation, gave a little twitch, and went out like a light.

Lee sighed and shrugged at the body. "Well. I offered."

"Contact!" Marie suddenly hissed over the comms. "Multiple contacts at the gate!"

Chapter 38

Abe immediately spun towards the window and dropped to a knee, settling the foregrip of his rifle on the sill. Lee moved to his side and snatched up the M60, casting a hasty glance over it to assess its condition. He'd seen a few rounds strike it, but nothing looked busted, and it still had a bit of ammunition belt left.

"Talk to me," Lee growled as he went down on both knees, his slung rifle and grenade launcher clattering against the floor as he shouldered the M60.

He hadn't transmitted—had been speaking to Abe, who was peering through his scope in the direction of the gate—but it was Marie that answered.

"I count at least a dozen, maybe more. Not primals. Looks like people with guns."

What the hell was this about? Lee checked the machine gun's chamber, then slapped the cover down over it again. Had Horner concealed a backup contingent of fighters from them? And where in the hell had he come up with another dozen guys? Lee hadn't seen that many when he'd first been to the ranch, and he'd seen nothing during the last hours of recon to make him believe there was another force hiding out here...

Just as Lee shifted the machine gun to point at the gate, and settled his cheek against the buttstock to aim, Abe's voice came from beside him, as well as over the comms.

"Hold fire! Hold fire!"

"What've you got, Abe?" Lee strained out, seeing nothing past the iron sights of the machine gun but shadowy movement, barely illuminated by the glow of firelight from the outbuilding Marie had blown to bits near the gate.

Again, Abe transmitted his answer for Marie and Jones's benefit: "Everyone hold what you got and stay hidden. But I think…I'm pretty sure they're from the Redoubt."

Lee jerked his head to Abe, who glanced at him over his scope and offered a facial shrug.

"You recognize any of them?" Lee demanded.

"Hard to be positive, but I think so," Abe said, refocusing on his aim.

Lee pulled back from the M60, thinking fast. What did this mean? Just because they might be from the Redoubt—*might be*—didn't mean they were gonna be friendly. But then he wasn't going to just mow them down without knowing.

Which meant someone was going to have to make contact.

"Shit and fuck," Lee grumbled, lowering the M60 back to the ground. "You got a good bead on 'em?"

"Yeah, I got you covered if it breaks bad."

Lee stood up, M32 heavy on his back, rifle heavy on his front. God, he hated hanging his ass out like this, but that was the problem with trying to operate in these strange times, while maintaining some semblance of humanity. You had to take risks. You had to trust your superior training and abilities, and the abilities of your team, and give people a chance.

Would it be easier to shoot first and ask questions later? It certainly would be. And it'd keep you safe. But what would you lose?

Something that was so hard to get back, Lee had long ago decided he'd never risk losing it again.

At some point in time, when you were in the shit for six years straight, you had to make a decision: Risk your life, or risk your soul.

"Sam," Lee said, pointing himself for the front door. "Get on that M60. Just in case." Then he transmitted as he stalked through the foyer. "If shit breaks bad, we're falling back. Regroup at that copse of trees to the east. Y'all copy?"

He got four acknowledgements as he stepped through the front door.

The figures now slinking cautiously through the destruction around the gate must've seen him. Someone let out a holler and everyone stopped where they were, rifles training on Lee. Ironically, several must've been the rifles that he'd given them.

"Hold fire!" Lee bellowed, raising both of his hands as he stepped to the edge of the porch. "Friendly! Friendly!" Then he discretely touched off his PTT again. "Abe, standard duress."

Not one of Jones's crazy scenario games—no, this one they'd trained for since the beginning, because they used it so often. When making contact with an unknown force, they tried to always have someone on overwatch. The visual signal was for the person making contact to rub the back of their head. Then the shooting would start.

"Who is that?" a voice yelled out, more or less in front of Lee. He was pretty sure it was the man standing front and center while his comrades spread out behind him.

"It's Jackson," Lee called back, taking the steps slowly. "There's no hostiles in the area. Only me and my team. Friendlies."

"Lee," Jones murmured in his ear, as though to correct him. "We've got no idea where Bran went. He might still be in here with us."

Lee sighed inwardly, but there was nothing to do about it. His boots hit the dirt of the ranch yard and he kept going at a steady, slow pace. So did the leader from the Redoubt. They slowed, each basing their pace off the other, until they came to a natural stop, about fifteen yards apart.

Lee recognized him, but couldn't remember his name. Just one of the younger guys from the settlement that Lee remembered had a wife and two kids. Which meant it would really suck if Lee had to rub the back of his head.

The guy still had his rifle up, but he wasn't actively aiming at Lee anymore, just kind of pointing it in his direction. Which Lee still wasn't a huge fan of. He nodded, still keeping his hands up. "I'm not pointing my gun at you, how about you not point yours at me?"

In the moonlight, Lee saw the man's eyes jag over Lee's shoulder. "Oh, I think you got some guns on me," he noted, spotting the two figures in the window of the ranch house—Abe on the rifle, and Sam on the machine gun.

"Well, I wasn't real sure what the mood was going to be," Lee admitted. "Are we going to be cool with each other?"

The man considered Lee for a few beats, then lowered his rifle. "We came for Bea and Ted. Were almost here when we heard the shooting start. Ran here as fast as we could." Something wrenched his face. "What...what happened? Are they okay?"

Rather than answer, Lee cast his gaze around to the other figures now inching closer. They'd lowered their rifles too, and relaxed their postures. The worst of the tension had gone out of the moment. Everyone was still cautious, but no one was actively waiting for a gunfight to start.

Back to the man in front of him. "I apologize," Lee said. "Can you refresh me on your name?"

"Gary," the man said, cautiously.

Lee nodded. "Gary, I've got bad news."

Gary's shoulders drooped. "Shit."

"They killed Ted."

Gary glanced away. In the glimmer of firelight on the side of the man's face, Lee could see his jaw muscles pulsing. "Who killed him?"

"Kat."

Gary made a harsh, scoffing noise. "You mean Horner, then."

Lee shook his head. "No, Kat did it all on her own. It's...complicated. And Horner's dead."

Gary's eyes snapped back to Lee. "You killed him?"

Lee nodded.

"What about Bea?"

"Lander Hollis took her."

Gary's shoulders tensed up again. "She's still alive? Where'd they take her?"

"I don't know where they took her. Wherever Lander Hollis and his primals make their home."

"The Town," Gary said, with confidence. Then repeated. "Is she still alive?"

Lee gave a minimal shrug. "I can't say for certain she is, Gary. But given what I know about what Lander wants her for, I'd assume she is."

"Christ," Gary seethed, looking away again. "He's gonna try to...?"

Lee just nodded again.

"Shit." Gary stood there for a long moment, Lee watching him, and wondering what was going through his head. Then: "What are you gonna do about it?"

A small part of Lee wanted to be incredulous with this question—*What am I going to do about it? When did it become* my *problem?* But that initial instinct proved itself to be false, and Lee knew it. It'd become his problem when he'd offered these people help. He'd linked his fate to theirs.

And what of the question itself? What *was* Lee going to do about this?

Nothing. Cut your losses. This entire valley is a deathtrap. You got Sam. Count your blessings and get gone. Move on to some other area that's maybe just a little less fucked up.

That was the smart thing to do. The tactical thing. Because you don't risk an entire team for one, low-value hostage.

But who gets to decide a person's value? What metric do you employ to figure *that* one out? And here were a dozen people who clearly saw Bea as valuable enough to risk their lives for.

Lee gave a long, grating sigh, then turned and looked behind him. Abe, now watching over his scope. And Sam beside him, with the machine gun tilted back so the barrel pointed at the sky.

"Goddammit," Lee muttered. Glanced back at Gary. "Hold that thought." Then he started walking back towards the ranch house, keying his comms as he went. "Alright, y'all. Bring it in. Team meeting."

The other four met him on the front porch. Marie and Jones gave the gaggle of armed civilians a good looking over, then focused themselves on Lee. Something in the set of their faces told Lee that they already knew what this was about.

But really, Lee didn't need to speak to anyone but Sam. So he looked straight at the young man and lowered his chin. "Sam, these folks are here for Bea. The guy I was talking to, Gary, says Lander and his so-called *family* hole up in the Town. That's probably where Bea's at. Surrounded by a whole helluva lot of primals." Lee paused for a slow breath. "And they wanna know what we're planning to do."

There must've been something in the air that night, because any other time there would have been a big discussion, and everyone would have laid out their opinions, liberally sprinkled with their grievances. Lee'd been through it so many times, he almost didn't even need to talk to them to know what they were going to say.

Abe would have gruffed a negative because he liked to play it cautious, but would have ultimately deferred to Marie, who would be a hair more compassionate than Abe, but would have ultimately agreed with him. And Jones may or may not have an actual opinion, but if he did, it would be lost amongst a tangle of digressions. But probably he would also side with Abe.

But tonight…on this night…everyone kept their traps shut, and simply looked at Sam.

And that was the funny thing about Sam, and Lee, and their relationship. Sam was the furthest thing from who Lee had been for most of his adult life. But he was so much like who Lee had become. They'd formed each other, over the years. Lee, the mentor, and Sam, the mentee, but also kind of like a father and a son, and also kind of like brothers, and also kind of like friends.

Sam stared straight back at Lee. He didn't need to glance around to know that everyone was waiting on him. And no one needed to say the obvious: Whatever Sam's decision was, they would have his back.

Risk their lives? Or risk their souls?

"We gotta go after her," Sam finally said.

A strange moment hit them. Lee could practically feel Marie and Abe's guts tighten with an unuttered groan. But it was *unuttered*. Because there was no point in casting doubt on the decision once it's been made. Might as well get fully behind it.

And despite all of that, Lee thought he could also feel a lifting of tension—not the tension of risking your life, because that was still very much there, and coming on quite fresh now that they all wrapped their collective heads around what was ahead of them.

No, this release of tension came from resolving a moral dilemma.

Making the right decision might not always be fun—or survivable—but you know it when you find it because you realize that, if you do survive, you'll be able sleep soundly alongside your own conscience.

Jones raised his hand. Because...Jones.

When all eyes turned to him, he simply said, "How?"

Lee looked at Marie. "How much time?"

"The two-hour window we requested..." She glanced at her watch. "Started forty-five minutes ago."

Lee nodded back to Jones. "Then, to answer your question, I'd say *quickly*."

Bran groaned and collapsed into the dark brush. His breathing came fast and harsh, and his heart was pumping at an alarming rate. He could feel his pulse in his wounds.

It might be noted that Bran held no loyalty whatsoever to Horner's ranch hands. There had been a few okay guys, but mostly they'd kept to themselves. They did cowboy shit. And Bran wasn't a cowboy.

When Kat had done what she did and then run off, Bran hadn't reacted much. Everything had been internal, and mostly hidden behind a face made blank with obedience to Horner. Because Horner was the one that Bran was loyal to. Horner was the one that had given him a job when no one else would.

But as he watched Kat run off into the night, he realized he'd just lost the closest thing he'd had to a friend since…well, since as far back as he could remember. And then Bran began to think about who he actually was to Colin Horner.

It sure didn't feel like they were friends.

At best, Bran was a trusted employee. At worst, Horner saw him precisely how he saw Kat: Just another tool to do dirty jobs Horner didn't want to do himself.

This circus of thoughts put their stakes down in Bran's mind and played to a packed house of his misgivings, all while Bran obediently stood by, and ranch hands tossed Ted's body out like garbage, and Lander took Bea off to do ungodly things. They had an encore performance while Bran stood guard over the kid named Sam, and then put on quite an unexpected finale during the fireworks show that left two of their buildings in flaming tatters, and wound up with Colin Horner holding the kid hostage at the window.

Who am I to him? Bran had thought, over and over as he stared at the back of Horner's gray head. *And what the fuck am I still doing here?*

This all must be articulated so that you understand why, when Horner's spine exploded in Bran's face, he didn't waste another goddamn second on that place. Horner's body was still falling when Bran spun on his heel and took off for the back of the house.

It wasn't cowardice. It was simply that the only thing keeping him there had just died. He'd never given a shit about this ranch to begin with. But he'd fought for it because he felt he owed a debt to Horner. And that debt had just been terminally canceled.

He didn't get off scot-free though.

Laying in a thicket of grass and sage, with the burning buildings of Horner's Peak twinkling distantly below him, Bran cringed and twisted, taking stock of his wounds.

The most painful one drew his attention first. He wasn't even sure how bad it was, only that his whole right shoulder area was screaming and his right arm had gone to pins and needles. No, fuck pins and needles, this was barbed wire and rusty nails. God, how could something feel numb and simultaneously hurt so damn bad?

Craning his neck to look did him little good, save to perceive the glimmer of moonlight off of his blood-sodden shirt. So, with a shaking hand, Bran gingerly probed the area. It was easy enough to find the holes that way, like a game of hot and cold—warmer...warmer...*agony*.

One, swollen, ragged hole, like a fleshy volcano had erupted, right where his pectoral met his armpit. He was pretty sure that was the exit wound. The entrance wound, a smaller hole, but just as swollen, was in the meat of his lat muscle, right next to his shoulder blade.

The second wound was less painful, but easier to locate. The entrance was near the back of his left side, and the exit was just above his left hip bone. He couldn't tell about the depth of it. It could've just gone through fat and muscle, or it might have wrecked an organ. What organs were over there? He didn't have a clue.

He might live, or he might croak in the next few minutes. His only comfort was that he'd just run what had to be the better part of a mile, and most of it uphill, and he hadn't passed out. That meant something, didn't it?

What do you do now?

He had no place to go. He had no friends. He had no supplies. He had only the shotgun still hanging in the grip of his left hand.

Well, he needed to do something about these wounds. But what?

He felt the sticky wetness that had slaked both of his sides. On the right, all the way down his torso. And on the left, all the way down his pant leg. He knew that if any of those bullets had hit an artery, he'd've been dead before he'd even cleared the fence. But he still needed to stop the bleeding.

Bran was not a man of great imagination, nor did he have much experience dealing with wounds. But he'd once seen a movie where some military guys packed their wounds with dirt, presumably to stop the bleeding. He didn't know if that was just some Hollywood bullshit or not, but what he did know was that he had fuckall in the way of a better idea.

So, he grabbed great fistfuls of dirt, grit his teeth, and packed his wounds.

Then he lay there for a long time, staring down at the ranch, and trying to figure out what the rest of his life would look like, and whether he even had much of it left to worry about. Maybe all he had left was tonight.

Everything was uncertain. And Bran hated uncertainty.

Down in the ranch, figures bustled about. There were a lot more of them than Bran had thought. He tried to count, but kept losing track around fifteen, because they were moving around so much. He only recognized one of the figures from this distance, and only by his pronounced limp: the man named Jax.

Bran tried to summon up some ill-will towards the guy, but the best he could do was a sort of dim irritation, primarily because he now had two bullet holes in him because of that bastard. But even then, he couldn't help thinking that it wasn't Jax's fault. It was

Horner's. Because Horner didn't have to do any of the shit that he'd done. He just...did it because he was an asshole.

Bran didn't feel disloyal for thinking that now.

There'd been no need for Horner to beat Kat during that first meeting. He'd done it to prove a point. A point that was unnecessary to make, and, in Bran's opinion, ill-advised. But his opinion hadn't been asked for, as it so rarely was.

No need for him to leave Jax and the woman to Lander's beasts. He'd done it because his pride demanded sacrifice, like some bad-tempered god of the underworld.

No need to hold Sam hostage.

Hell, there was no need to dam up the river in the first fucking place. The guy had a bajillion acres to range his cattle on, and he made a stink about a handful of settlements that probably didn't equal a percentage point of the land he owned.

Horner was just a crazy, bitter old man. He'd sown the wind, and reaped the whirlwind. And Bran had been damn fool enough to help him do it. So who could Bran really blame for his two bullet holes, but the man he'd served, and his own stupid self for serving him?

Bran even thought about giving himself up to the people down in the ranch, but tossed that idea out. Once shit went down, they hadn't seemed keen on taking prisoners. They might be more inclined now that the shooting had stopped and their blood had cooled, but did Bran really wanna toss those dice?

Simply because the man Jax was the only one that Bran knew and could identify, he found himself following the man with his eyes and ignoring the others. Mostly, Jax seemed to be coordinating everyone else. Several people were gathering up the weapons and ammo from the dead. Others seemed to be searching the buildings for anything useful. Two of them took off into the dark hills and returned a short time later with Jax's white pickup truck.

Everyone down there was moving at quite a hustle, Bran thought. Like they had someplace they needed to be, and they were late. Once the truck pulled into the ranch, they all started hauling what they'd gleaned from their searches. Bran noted with some dim, melancholy amusement, two figures lugging the bags and boxes that Bran himself had looted from that truck not twelve hours ago.

After perhaps twenty minutes of all this bustling, it looked like they were packing up to leave, and Bran found himself surprised and grateful that they hadn't decided to burn the buildings down. Not because he gave a shit about Horner's Peak, but because he hoped to find some first aid supplies down there once they left.

Returning to the ranch hadn't been his first inclination, but as the people below began to pile into the truck—and yes, they crammed all of them in there, with six or seven packed in the cab, and maybe ten or so all jumbled in the bed—Bran realized that it was really the only place he had left to go.

As the pickup cut a wide U-turn in the ranch and then headed out the gate with a distant roar of the engine and people clinging for handholds in the bed, Bran struggled his way to his feet. Practically fainted once he got there. Swayed about, blinking and clenching his breath until the stars in his vision subsided.

And once they did, he noted a flicker of movement, down the hill and a few hundred yards to his left. A shadow moving quickly towards the ranch.

He felt suddenly exposed, and infinitely more vulnerable as the movement of that shadow made him think of infected, and how a whole pack of them could be lurking on this hillside. Waiting to swoop in and feed on the dead?

But as the shadow moved closer to the ranch, Bran saw how it would crawl on all fours for a while, then stand up and walk with its head above the grass. Regular infected didn't do that. They could be bipedal when they wanted to, but mostly they didn't want to, and when they poked their heads up to get their bearings in the tall grass, Bran had only ever seen them stand there and look around like meerkats, before dropping down and moving quadrupedally.

Plus, this figure seemed a bit small for an infected.

And…was it wearing clothes?

"Kat!" Bran yelled before he could even consider the wisdom of that action.

The figure halted and spun, but Bran was already certain it was her, and had started moving back down the hill as fast as he could, stumbling over the uneven terrain, his blood feeling thin and miserly in his veins as his heart worked overtime to pump what there was. He gulped air and dried his tongue to jerky.

Somewhere in all his bumbling and gasping, he lost sight of the figure.

Had it really been Kat? What if his eyes were playing tricks on him? It wasn't hard to believe that his dipping blood pressure might cause some wires to be crossed.

Had he seen an infected moving, and imagined that it was Kat?

The thought stopped him in his tracks.

He'd made it down the hill by then, and stood in a flat sea of grass, rippling with a cool night breeze that made his skin pucker into gooseflesh. Except maybe it wasn't the wind. Because he started shivering, and it sure as shit wasn't cold enough for him to be shivering. Especially after exerting himself.

He stared out over the grass, scanning for some sign of movement. A twitch or sway of the grasses, more pronounced than the wind? A dark figure standing up to note his position?

But there was nothing.

His teeth were starting to chatter.

That was definitely not a good sign.

Was he going into shock? But if so, how was he still standing?

Maybe he should just lie down. Lie down and get some rest, and hope that whatever was out there didn't find him.

Unless it really was Kat…

"Bran!"

The word was practically barked at him, sounding like it came from right at his elbow.

He yelped weakly and spun, swinging the shotgun around one handed. But it was so damn heavy in his grip, he could barely lift the muzzle to the shadow that rose up not two strides from him.

Didn't matter anyway.

The moonlight cast that terrible face into even worse shadows. It made the wide mouth seem a bottomless maw that took up nearly the entire head, as though the entire being had been built around its jaw and teeth. It made the eyes seem pale and soulless and devoid of human thought.

And yet, Bran didn't think he'd ever seen a more beautiful face.

The relief quite literally took his knees out.

"Kat," he slurred as he lost his footing and sat down hard in the dirt, the shotgun clattering at his feet.

She sprang forward as he dropped, grabbing his right arm close to the armpit to try and steady him. He gaped at the pain that lanced through him. Didn't even have the strength to pull away. All that came out of his throat was a long wheeze.

Kat seemed to get the picture, or maybe she felt the blood on her hands. She immediately let the arm go. Bran started to teeter over onto his left side, but she grabbed him by the head and held him upright, her hands on either side of his face. An oddly intimate contact.

When the pain receded enough for him to focus, he found himself staring right into her eyes. And they didn't seem so devoid of humanity anymore.

"Hurt," Kat stated.

"Yeah," Bran struggled out. "I'm hurt."

Kat's eyes darted over his body. "Bad?"

"I dunno, but it don't feel good."

Kat blinked a few times and bared her ghastly teeth. And Bran didn't recoil, or even mind at all. It didn't matter how terrifying she could look. She was Bran's friend. The only one he had in the world. And everything about her, even the terrible parts, were a comfort to him.

"ATV," Kat finally said.

"What for?" Bran grunted, trying to remember if he'd even hooked the stupid thing up to its charger or not. And even if it was fully charged, it wouldn't be enough to get them out of the Valley. And even if they could get to someplace that didn't already hate their guts, who was going to accept Kat?

Well, Kat didn't seem to think much of Bran's gloomy assessment, because she was already maneuvering to his left side and gently pulling him up to his feet.

"Kat, there ain't no place to go," Bran said.

But she got his left arm over her shoulder and he didn't feel bad at all about relaxing almost all of his weight onto her, and she took it like he didn't weigh anything. And then she started them towards the ranch again.

"Help," she said as they went. "Find help."

Chapter 39

Bea felt like she was being dragged into hell, and dragged she was, because she could not keep up with these creatures.

No, not creatures. *Demons.* Because if this was hell, then the infected that lived in it must be demons, and Lander Hollis was the devil himself.

In this case, hell was what Bea knew to be the Town. That it had once been a regular burg filled with normal people living out their normal lives, were inconsequential facts. All Bea could see of it now was darkness and shadows and buildings that loomed, their empty, glassless windows leering.

Exhaustion darkened her vision and shrank her peripherals. She didn't know how long her legs could keep moving like this, and whenever she faltered, Freya would shove her hard in the back, or seize her arm and drag her until she picked up the pace again.

Bea was intentionally trying to conserve her energy, but the further along they went, the more pointless it became. She was spent. When they finally let her stand still, she knew she would collapse, and she'd barely be able to move after that.

How was she supposed to defend herself in that state? Would Lander allow her to rest? Get her strength up before…?

She didn't even want to think about it, but she had to. Had to face it head on and call it what it was.

Would she be able to rest before Lander tried to mate her with his primals? He'd said he wanted her to fight harder, so only the strong ones could get to her. But wasn't that all pointless to begin with? Because even if she was fully rested, the weakest male primal was still stronger than any normal human.

Along the darkened streets she went, her throat a miserable, arid tube. The pain in her legs had surpassed the burn of overworked muscles long ago. Her joints felt like they were bone-on-bone, and her hips and thighs and calves were all one big, agonizing cramp. She was shocked at how painful running could be when you're forced to do it far beyond your limits.

As they moved deeper into the Town, a smell began to pervade the air. It was a scent Bea associated with dogs that were kept outside and never bathed. *Their* smell. And the smell of their leavings.

They didn't seem to be taking many turns, Bea dimly noted. They'd come in on the main drag through the town, and just kept on going straight. At moments when she got enough gumption up to actually swivel her head and try to take in her surroundings, she spotted other figures lurking in dark corners, watching them pass.

Some were crouched in the shadows, others perched atop buildings. They made no sound or acknowledgement, but every time Bea caught sight of one, it was staring right at her.

Fresh fish, Bea began to think to herself, as though she were the new prisoner in a cellblock, and the words were being jeered at her. *Fresh fish! Fresh fish!*

There comes a level of exhaustion that, once reached, it becomes nigh on impossible to feel afraid. Bea thought she must've hit that some time ago, because it all just washed over her, and fear was not what she felt anymore. Just sickness, and misery, and resignation.

She just wanted to stop moving. She just wanted to lay down and sleep and never wake up. She had no fight left in her now. Could think of nothing more than just getting to wherever they were taking her, so that she could *stop running*. What happened after that seemed a far-off, muted horror.

So it was almost a relief when she lifted her gaze from the endless slapping of her beaten feet on the blacktop, and saw a large structure ahead of them, which Lander seemed to be heading for. One, big, dark box, that stood out from the other buildings both in size and construction. Like the whole town had been built in quaint brick and brownstone, and then some asshole had plopped this cinderblock and steel monstrosity in this midst of it all.

There was a wide bank of doors and windows on the front, with not a single pane of glass left standing in their frames. Above those black openings, massive letters had been painted on the steel siding in what looked like bright yellow, though the moonlight made it seem to glow silver.

On one side of those letters, a big arrow had been neatly and artistically painted, pointing upwards. The letters themselves—equally artful—read *ASCEND CHURCH*.

In the back of her fatigue-clouded mind, Bea remembered Ascend Church. One of a chain of mega churches that kept popping up all over California in the decade before the collapse, as unstoppable as Starbucks and mushrooms.

It seemed darkly ironic that this branch of Ascend Church now served as the deepest pit in the central circle of hell.

Lander and a few of his primals disappeared into one of the dark openings. Bea hesitated, but was propelled forward by Freya with a muttered growl. Into the blackness she went, her hands instinctively raised, feeling blindly ahead of her.

"Come," Freya rasped in her ear. Then she seized Bea's arm again and began hauling her onward through the soupy darkness. Bea heard movement all around her. The smell became so strong that she could taste it on her tongue, and wished she had the moisture in her mouth to spit it back out again.

Something like a glimmer of light ahead.

Freya pushed her through some sort of doorway, bashing Bea's wounded shoulder against the frame of it as she went. She was too exhausted to even cry out. They seemed to be in a short, narrow corridor. Ahead of them, the light expanded, sepulchral and toad-belly pale.

She felt the ground slope downwards under her feet, and realized she was being ushered through an auditorium that seemed five times too big for a tiny place like the Town. The pale light was emanating from a massive hole in the ceiling, perhaps twenty or thirty feet over her head. Against the blackness all around, the huge shaft of moonlight seemed unnaturally bright.

And there, front and center, stood a stage. It was directly beneath the great hole in the ceiling, so the moon shown down on it like a spotlight, and Bea wondered if this was intentional. Craning her stiff neck up at the gaping hole, she saw the ragged edges of it, how the steel looked like it had been peeled back from the outside, with wiring hanging like jungle vines, and wispy beards of insulation dangling like moss.

The whole place had the feel, not of the modern structure it was, but of some long-forgotten temple, and the moonlit stage was the altar upon which blood and sanctity were sacrificed. And where Bea was being led by Freya's iron grip.

The stage was not empty. Besides the stage lighting hanging skew, and a great wooden cross that lay mournfully on its side, and the vestiges of a drum set that had been half-crushed and pushed against a wall, there were...others.

Three of them. Females. As Bea was pushed closer, they each rose, first to a crouch, and then to their feet. They wore not a scrap of clothing on their bodies, and Bea realized this only surprised her because they did not look like the regular infected, with their hunched postures and over-long arms. When they stood, they did so with a lithe, feline grace far more savage than a human could ever move, and yet, the form of them could not be mistaken for anything else.

These were Lander's wives, Bea realized. Half human, and half primal.

She'd expected them to be far more mutated, but they were actually...beautiful, in a way. In the same way that Bea remembered telling her mother as a child that lionesses were "sexy." A strange thing to think as she was shoved inexorably towards them, their intense gazes on her all the while. But their bodies were as close to physical perfection as Bea had ever seen, covered in long, lean muscles that bore a sort of athletic edge, so that they seemed primed for violence in a way that was unmistakably predatory.

Fear, and something like awe gripped Bea as she stared at them, shocked to find she could feel much at all at this point. Worse than that, Bea was disturbed to realize there was something animalistically alluring about them. Powerful and sinuous, they were somehow both nightmarish and erotic.

Only their faces marred the strange effect. It was as though nature had taken a human face and pressed it out, and flattened the nose, and widened the mandibles, so that it seemed their lips could barely close around all those teeth. It gave the impression of less of a face, and more of a muzzle, and reminded Bea of a baboon.

Lander's three wives were alone upon the stage, but all around the base of it lounged ranks and ranks of primals. They rose as though to meet Bea, and she noticed that they were all female too. These were the Omegas that Jax had talked about. A wall of them, surrounding the three hybrids on the stage.

To protect them? Or to keep them in?

Bea was given one final shove, accompanied by a growl to "Go." She was so spent at that moment that her heart couldn't have even sped up if it wanted to, and all she felt was a twinge of dread as she faced down what must have been two dozen or more Omegas. The ones nearest to Bea snarled and bared their teeth as she stumbled to a halt in front of them.

Freya barked something behind her, and it took Bea a full second to realize it hadn't been a word. Hadn't been meant for her.

The Omegas' eyes darted to Freya, and their flashing teeth were immediately covered. Their heads ducked in something like submission, and they backed away from Bea, but still watched her intently.

Bea swayed on her aching, throbbing feet. She didn't want to move forward, and didn't want to move back. She simply didn't want to exist anymore.

She turned her head to look behind her, dry mouth hanging open, still gulping the sour air. Freya stood a few paces behind her, pointing towards the stage and growling low in her throat. But Bea found her eyes caught onto other movements. All along the dim edges of the moonlight, she could see hunched, muscular forms stalking back and forth like animals in a cage. It was as though they wanted to come closer, but knew that they couldn't.

Bea looked back to the ranks of female primals. So, they weren't keeping Lander's wives from escaping. They were protecting them from the males.

And suddenly it didn't seem like a bad thing to be on that stage.

Her legs had already seized up and Bea could barely bend them as she stumbled through the path that had been cleared by the females. She hit the stage, which came up to her chest, and with one last gasp of effort, hauled herself onto it, and rolled onto her back. But then she hated how exposed she felt just laying there spread eagle, and curled up on her side, panting hard, with her eyes squeezed shut against the horrific world around her.

Breathing, breathing, breathing. Wishing she could be anywhere else. And not daring to open her eyes to see that her wish had been denied.

She didn't know how long she lay there. Her mind was a mess. It seemed no thought could tie itself to another. Linear logic fled her. She was buffeted by waves of emotion that came on strong and then departed a moment later. She thought she might die, laying there on her side, and that thought was the only comfort she had.

"Tss."

She knew the sound had come from very near her. She could feel the body heat of something hovering close. But she only squeezed her eyes tighter. God, why couldn't they just let her die?

"Tss." More insistent, and this time with an accompanying nudge to her forehead.

She ripped her bleary eyes open and stared up at a twisted version of a woman's face, with wild eyes and a massive tangle of dark hair fringed silver in the moonlight. She wanted to recoil, but didn't have the energy to do it. And where would she flee to? Where would she crawl?

"Tss," the creature repeated, pursing its thin lips to make the sound, and Bea realized it was holding something out to her.

A blue, plastic bowl, filled with water.

She was somehow both ravenous for, and disgusted by the water. But the imperative of thirst was the stronger contender, and, almost as though animated against her will, Bea reached out two trembling hands and took the bowl of water. She sniffed it, and it smelled clean, but even before the smell really registered with her, she was already drinking it down.

"Sshu-sshu-sshu," the creature whispered, and began to gently stroke Bea's hair.

"Time check," Lee said, as he lowered himself into the bed of the pickup, beside Abe.

"Forty-eight minutes left," Marie informed him from beside the tailgate.

Abe popped the bipod on his ESR—an M2010 chambered in .300 Winchester Magnum—and settled into the scope. They'd liberated their stolen gear, of which the ESR was a part, along with Lee and Marie's NVGs, which Jones and Sam were currently prepping. Unfortunately, Lee's stolen watch had not been in their gear. He suspected it was on the wrist of a dead body, now laying somewhere in Horner's Peak.

He had, however, gotten his plate carrier and personal rifle back. And his spare boots, which was a relief. He made sure to stow the boots he'd borrowed from Bea's dead husband under the backseat of the truck. In case she wanted them back.

"Copy forty-eight minutes," Lee murmured as he propped himself on his elbows and peered through the thermal spotting scope. Somebody'd been messing with it, and Lee had to toggle it to his preferred "white-hot" setting.

Three quarters of a mile distant, the Town became a mélange of gray geometry. With a sprinkling of white heat signatures.

"Whoo boy," Lee intoned.

"That bad, uh?" Abe grunted. "What're we workin' with?"

Abe had clipped a PVS-30 night vision monocular to his rifle. It had no thermal imaging ability, but the light amplification let him see certain details that Lee's thermal imaging could not. He'd see the targets easy enough once Lee pointed them out, but getting a big picture of the threats presented was definitely easier with the thermal.

Lee did a quick count. "Eight, but those are just the ones I can see. A few on roofs. Few on the street. Mostly stationary."

"Any indication of the nest?"

Lee took a moment before answering. "Welp. My guess would be that big-ass building that's sticking out of downtown like a sore thumb."

"Yeah, I marked that," Abe said. Then seemed to read, with a hint of irony in his voice. "Ascend Church."

Of course, Lee hadn't seen those letters, as they were the same temperature as the wall they were painted on. He'd been thinking the structure was some sort of warehouse, but now recognized it for what it was. Colonies of primals liked to settle in large, man-made structures with open, spacious rooms to congregate in. A megachurch fit that bill quite nicely.

He let out a soft chuff. "Well, that about fits, doesn't it? Besides the size of it, that seems to be where the heat signatures are centered around."

"Any clear way in that you can see?"

"No, not really. And without a birds-eye view, I can't tell what's around corners and shit. I'd say it's a safe bet there's plenty more than eight lounging around where I can't spot them."

"Might wanna check with the locals before we make a plan," Abe counseled. "Hate to get all the way in and find out we chose the wrong building."

Lee felt pretty confident that Ascend Church was their target, but it didn't hurt to ask for confirmation. He pulled away from the spotting scope and pushed his way up so he was standing on his knees.

The Redoubters stood tensely about the truck, watching Lee and Abe with grimly nervous expressions. There were fourteen of them in all, but only twelve hovered around the truck. The other two had appropriated the rifles with the thermal optics from the two guards at Horner's Peak, and were posted a handful of yards away, keeping a lookout for unwanted visitors.

"Anyone got a good idea of what building the primals are calling home?" Lee questioned the group. "Anyone seen it for themselves? Or maybe just heard about it?"

One of their number—a kid that couldn't have been much older than Sam—seemed to check his comrades to see if anyone else was more confident than him, but no one answered up. He made a face and then shuffled forward and raised his hand.

"I haven't seen it myself," he began, hesitantly. "But I heard they were in a church."

Lee lifted his eyebrows. "Any other details?"

"No." The kid looked sheepish, like he'd given the wrong answer. "Just that it was a church. Heard it from some of the guys that used to go scavenging. Said they'd holed up in 'the big, new church.'"

Lee turned his gaze back to Abe, who caught his look from over the scope. Lee shrugged. Abe shrugged back. It wasn't quite as confirmed as would make Lee feel warm and fuzzy about it, but it would have to do. They could lay around all night and confirm it by watching the movements of the primals, but they didn't have all night. They forty-eight minutes. Probably a bit less now.

"Keep an eye on things," Lee said to Abe, pulling himself to his feet. He swung one leg over the pickup bed and sat down, straddling the wheel well. He wanted to ask if anyone had any bright ideas to get them in without being mauled, but feared an avalanche of idiocy. However, they were up against the clock, and their intel was piss-poor. Maybe someone knew something they didn't.

He took a bracing breath and had out with it. "Alright. Anyone know how we can get in there unnoticed?"

A whole lot of downcast eyes was the only response.

Gary leaned an elbow on the truck bed. "Hell, you're the military guy. We were kinda hopin' *you'd* know how."

Lee nodded. "I got an idea. But it don't hurt to ask. Y'all know this area better than we do."

He'd hoped that would stir someone to have the courage to speak out, but nothing came of it.

Marie looked up at him. "What's your plan, then?"

"You remember OP Lillington?"

She frowned, remembering back across the years. "You mean the Camp Ryder Hub? I remember Lillington, but I never went."

Lee squinted. She was right. That'd been before Marie started running with them. Back when Lee's team was Harper and Tomlin and...Julia. Damn, but it still sent a pang through him. All those people that'd run operations with him back then—they were all dead.

He waved a hand as much to clear the confusion away as his own emotion. "Never mind. It's how we used to clear towns about this size. We'd set up on a street that had good roofs to shoot down off of, rig up some claymores, then lure the infected in and wipe them out in one go."

Sam and Jones, who were kneeling beside Marie, fiddling with the NVGs, both looked up. They had to switch them to the head mounts, as Lee and Marie's helmets were another item that'd gone mysteriously missing in the ranch.

"That was before the primals, though," Sam noted.

"Yeah, it was," Lee acknowledged. Back then, they'd called them *hunters* instead of primals, but it was the same creature—those human beings with just the right mix of genetics that their bodies went into a rapid sequence of mutations to accommodate their new, animalistic lifestyle, rather than simply going mad and hyper-aggressive like the rest.

Jones offered up the next concern: "You think the primals would fall for something like that? And even if they did, hell, they can just climb the walls and come at us."

"Yeah, they can." There was no point in denying it. "But that's the foundation of what I'm thinking—draw as many out of the nest as possible. We can accomplish that any number of ways, but what I was thinking was just running the truck straight in and trying to make contact with Lander."

Marie only barely stifled a groan, and didn't stifle her eye roll at all. "Really, Lee? You're gonna do the diplomacy thing again? Because your track record on that is shit."

"Well, I don't imagine it'll work," Lee admitted. "But I figured I could try. Then when things inevitably go south, and he sics his primals on us, we hightail it and lead them away. All while blowing them to bits with the grenade launchers."

"What about Bea?" Sam said, standing up with an NVG half-affixed to its head harness.

"We'd need an infil team to get into the target building once we draw off the primals."

"If," Marie interjected. "He sends *all* of them after us."

"And how's the team gonna exfil?" Abe asked from his rifle.

Lee spread his hands. "Obvious issues. He might not send the whole horde after us. If that's the case, then the infil team's probably SOL." He avoided looking at the disappointment he knew would be on Sam's face. "As for exfil, they'll have to hump it to a rally point where the truck can pick them up."

Gary cleared his throat. "And what about the folks running the ambush? What happens when the primals start climbing the walls after them? How are *they* gonna get out?"

"Yeah, that's another issue," Lee said. "But we might not need the ambush. We don't need to kill all the primals in this place. We just need to get them out of the way. Primary objective isn't to eliminate them—it's to get Bea and get out." He blew a big breath through pursed lips. "With all of that said, I don't see this going down without significant loss of life."

The ensuing silence held for an uncomfortably long time.

Then someone from the Redoubt said, "We can't just leave her." But they said it all forlorn and hopeless, like they knew they were caught in an impossible dilemma.

Lee couldn't tell who'd spoken, but it didn't matter. These words were for everyone standing around the truck. "I'm not trying to convince you to leave her. But if you've got any notions about all nineteen of us walking out of this alive, you can go ahead and banish that thought." He looked around, meeting gazes that seemed to just now realize what they'd gotten themselves into. "There's no plan in the world that'll see us through this unscathed. So if you're waiting for one to come along and make you feel comfortable, well...it ain't coming."

Seemed like a lot of the folks from the Redoubt were re-evaluating their choice to be here. Lee didn't want to see them walk away from this, but he also didn't want them heading in with delusions about their survivability.

Most people, when they think of risking lives and saving lives, they think it's a numbers game. If you risk twenty lives to save one life, that's alright, as long as none of the rescuers get killed. Or maybe if the one life they're saving is an important figure. But when you come out and say you're going to risk twenty lives for one life, and probably lose most of them, if you succeed at all...well, that doesn't make sense to most people.

Lee could see them wavering. And he couldn't blame them one bit. Because it *didn't* make sense, not logically. Lee's arithmetic was just a bit different. In his mind, there were higher costs than just the loss of life and limb. His younger self would've balked to hear it, but screw that pup. Lee'd learned a helluva lot, and his younger self hadn't yet found out what it meant to be haunted by the things you'd turned your back on.

"Guys," one of the older gentlemen in the group said, shuffling a dirty ball cap around on his head. Lee thought he knew what was coming. "I know we all felt bad for Bea, and we were willing to take on Horner and his men to get her back. That was when the odds were evenly matched between us and them. But I'm not sure—"

If he'd gone on any longer, Lee thought every single one of those people from the Redoubt would've turned their backs and walked away. But he never got the chance to finish, and they never got the chance to walk.

Because right at that moment, with every one of them most of the way off the fence they'd been sitting on, one of their sentries shouted, "Someone's coming!" just as headlights blazed from down the road.

Chapter 40

Kat had made a big gamble. Actually, it was several gambles laid on top of each other. She'd seen the man Jax take off in the white pickup truck. It made more sense to her that they'd simply come for the young man named Sam. It made more sense to her that they'd simply return to the Redoubt.

But she'd gambled that they wouldn't. She'd gambled that they'd go after Bea.

Why? Because of what Jax had done. Because he'd tried to stop Colin Horner from beating her. Because he was not the type of man to turn his back on people that needed him.

Or, at least, that's what she hoped. And if she was wrong, she was pretty sure that Bran was going to die, because he'd already lost consciousness, and he smelled sickly and weak, like his body was on the verge of giving out.

So Kat was both shocked and elated when the headlights of the ATV splashed across the white pickup truck and the figures gathered around it.

And then came the next part of her gamble: Would they even let her approach? Or would they just start shooting? And even if they let her approach, would it do any good? They were not her friends. They were enemies. And it made more sense to her that they would just kill her and Bran. That's what she would've done.

But if she wanted to save Bran's life, throwing herself at their mercy was her only option.

The second she saw the truck, she stomped on the brakes. She saw the people around the truck turn and raise rifles, squinting into her headlights. She saw the two other people with rifles, kicked out to the sides a bit, clearly acting as sentries.

The ATV skidded to a halt in cloud of dust, and Kat leapt out, knowing it might be interpreted as aggression, but gambling yet again—would they give her time to talk before they started shooting?

Her feet hit the ground, and her hands came up, and she dredged a single word from her clumsy palette that she hoped would be enough: "Friend!"

In the sudden absence of roaring tires, Kat realized that several people were shouting at her all at once. But she couldn't tell what they wanted her to do. Someone was yelling to shoot her. Another was yelling for her to get back, another for her to get down, and yet another for her to raise her hands, which was confusing, because they were already raised.

She closed her eyes, not wanting to see the muzzle flashes that would end her life, and screamed the word over and over: "Friend! Friend! Friend!"

As the last yell petered out in her throat, she heard the voice she'd wanted to hear.

"Hold fire! Hold fire!" It was Jax, and she opened her eyes in time to see him sliding down from the bed of the pickup and waving his hands at the others. "Stand down! Everyone stand down!"

She almost couldn't believe it. Sure, she'd gambled on mercy, but it still flummoxed her to receive it. These people made no sense to her. They did not think like she thought. They were not the same type of creature. But she was glad they were the way they were, because she needed them.

Bran needed them.

She was tempted to think of Jax as stupid for his mercy. But he wasn't. The second he'd succeeded in getting everyone else to not shoot her, he stepped front and center and raised his own rifle. It wasn't an idle threat. She could see that his eye was centered on the optic, and she could see that the muzzle was clearly pointing right at her face.

"Kat," Jax called out in a clear voice. "Listen to my commands and do exactly what I tell you or I will put you down. Do you understand?"

"Yes," Kat managed. Then, "Help. Please."

"Don't move. Keep your hands up. Keep your feet where they are." Jax approached a handful of steps and stopped, about fifteen yards from her. His aim never wavered. "What are you doing here?"

Kat was very careful not to move her hands or feet. But she did twist her body just a bit, so she could nod at Bran's slumped form in the passenger seat of the ATV. "Bran is hurt," she struggled out. "Shot. Help. Please."

"Marie! Jones! Sam!" Jax called. "With me."

They'd only been a few steps behind, and now came abreast of Jax, rifles up. The other one with the big, black beard was in the bed, with a rifle set on the roof of the cab, pointing at her. "Got Kat covered!" the bearded man said.

Jax swiveled slightly, so his rifle was now pointing at the ATV. "Bran! Lemme see your hands!"

"He's..." Kat tried to form the word *unconscious*, but it just wouldn't take shape in her mouth. "Not awake."

Jax looked back at her. "Kat, take two big steps to your left, away from the ATV."

Kat did so, sparing a glance at Bran's inert form. Was he already dead? She couldn't smell him as clearly from here. Couldn't tell if his chest was still rising and falling.

"Interlace your fingers behind your head," Jax continued. "Now get down on your knees. Cross your ankles over each other.

Now sit back on your heels. Do not move from that position. Lincoln, if she moves, take her out."

"Got it."

Then Jax and his teammates approached.

Jones and Sam moved to the driver's side of the ATV, holding additional coverage on Kat in case she tried anything squirrelly. They trusted Abe's aim, but it never hurt to have a few extra guns on something as dangerous as Kat.

Lee and Marie moved to the passenger side of the ATV. Lee splashed the slouched figure in the passenger seat with his weaponlight. It was definitely Bran. And he was definitely unconscious. There was a whole lot of blood, and Bran's skin looked washed out.

"Got him covered," Lee said, and Marie slung her rifle and ripped open the little side door.

She shoved two fingers into his carotid artery and looked sidelong at Lee. "What are we doing here, Lee?" she whispered.

"I don't know yet. But I got an idea."

"Be still my beating heart," Marie grunted as she retracted her fingers. "He's alive. Pulse is weak and fast. He's lost a lot of blood." She fixed Lee with a serious gaze. "You really wanna save this asshole after what he did to Sam?"

"*Can* you save him?"

Marie gave his wounds a cursory once-over. "Maybe. I don't think he's lost anything vital except for blood. He's in shock. I can try." Back to Lee. "You sure you want me to?"

"Not yet," Lee said, then turned. "Sam, go to Marie." Then he stalked around the front of the ATV. Kat knelt there, a few yards off from Jones. Lee stepped past him, took a glance to make sure he wasn't blocking Abe's shot, then lowered himself—somewhat painfully—into a squat.

Kat's eyes were affixed on Bran, but when Lee lowered himself to her level, she swiveled them on him. There was something achingly human in them: Worry—not for herself, but for her friend. It struck him that she had to have known she might get shot rolling up on them like that. But she'd done it anyway. Because she had no place else to go. And she wanted to save her friend.

For a flash, she did not seem so much like a dangerous animal to Lee. In that moment, she was just another person, trying to save someone they loved. And that was something Lee could understand. That was something he could connect with.

But...Lee still had things that needed to be done.

"You want me to save Bran?" he asked her.

"Yes," she answered, immediately. Then she added, "Please," and it was so plaintive and desperate, that Lee couldn't help feeling a little dirty about what he was about to do.

He nodded. "We've got medical supplies. We can try to save him."

"Please," Kat repeated.

Lee cringed inwardly and spat it out: "But you're going to have to do something for me."

She stared at him for a moment. Then looked back at Bran. Only mulled it over for a second before looking at Lee again and nodding. "Anything."

Lee stood up, no more time left to waste. "Sam, get him out of the ATV. Marie, do what you can for him." As Sam wrestled Bran's body out onto the ground, and Marie ran for her medical pack, Lee stood over Kat, wondering if this was a boon or a curse. "Kat, we're gonna help Bran as much as we can. I can't promise you that he'll live, but we'll try everything we can. But now I need your help. I need your help to save someone else." Lee looked unflinchingly into her face and extended his hand. "Can we trust each other?"

Kat stared at that hand for a long time, and it occurred to Lee that she wasn't so much hesitating, as she was surprised to see this gesture rendered towards her. Who had ever asked to shake her hand? Who had ever even offered it?

Her eyes flitted back to his. "Move my hand?"

Lee had to smile. "Yeah, you can move your hand."

She didn't return the smile—it would have been terrifying if she tried—but she took her right hand from her head and clasped Lee's with it. And damn, but she had a grip.

"You help Bran," she said carefully. "I help you."

And they shook on it.

Then Lee rounded on the others. "Change of plans, folks. Huddle up on me."

Chapter 41

Sam had seen Lee shake hands with Kat, and he guessed that meant they were going to trust each other. But he was still immensely discomfited standing shoulder to shoulder with her in the bed of the ATV as it rumbled quietly along on its electric drive, straight into the dark streets of the Town.

He was trying to stay focused, but that's really hard to do when the girl—*Primal? Hybrid?*—that had almost torn his throat out hours earlier was right next to him. He kept taking sidelong glances at her to make sure she wasn't eyeing him like a pork chop.

He had to do it sidelong, because the NVGs were over his eyes. Through them, the small cityscape through which they traveled was a blur of pale greens and whites, the dot of his rifle's IR laser creating squiggly patterns along the walls of buildings as they passed.

Lee was putting a whole lot of faith in a person that'd been their enemy not too long ago. And there was no guarantee that this would work. Just as Lee couldn't guarantee Bran's survival, Kat couldn't guarantee they wouldn't be pulled apart by the first pack of primals they encountered.

But, as Sam had found in so many other situations...whaddaya gonna do? There were no better options. And even if there were, they couldn't wind back time. They were committed to *this one*.

No turning back. So you might as well nut up and shut up, cross your fingers and toes, and keep your head on a swivel.

Which, Sam thought, was something like faith.

Another glance at Kat. She stared straight ahead, both hands braced against the roof of the ATV. Sam was just about to look away when he saw something in her demeanor change. A tightening. A hardening. An intense focus of the eyes.

He whipped forward and immediately saw it. Called out, "Contact!" at the same instant that Jones called it from the front passenger seat.

"I see it," Lee strained out from the driver's seat.

"Slow," Kat growled. "Go slow."

About a hundred yards ahead of them was an intersection, dark traffic lights hanging low over the roadway. And on that roadway, three shapes were creeping out into the intersection, two on hands and feet, one standing erect.

"Uh, don't we wanna go fast?" Jones said, his voice pitched a little higher than normal.

Sam, for his part, didn't dare speak, because he knew it'd come out in a squeak. His heart was lodged in his throat, and his options were either to yell past it, or stay silent, so he chose to stay silent. Here's where they'd find out if Lee was insane or genius.

"Slow," Kat insisted. "Or they chase."

The ATV decelerated.

Sam flicked the safety off on his rifle. His and Jones's laser designators played over the three figures, Jones's going to the erect one on the far right, Sam's going to the far left. Every instinct screamed for him to start shooting. But he kept his finger off the trigger.

God, how slow were they going to go? This felt too slow. They were sitting ducks in this ATV. It'd take a grand total of two seconds for those three primals to pounce and rip them apart.

Sam's target skittered to the other side of the road, so the ATV would have to pass between them.

"I don't like it," Jones warned.

"It's gonna be fine," Lee said, and Sam knew that if it wasn't, they'd never have a chance to call him a liar.

Sam kept tracking the primal on the left. His heart was hitting so hard it was causing his laser designator to visibly jump to the beat of his pulse. His rifle was cross-body to Kat now, the muzzle right in front of her face, the target only a few yards off. Sam adjusted his aim to account for height-over-bore, and settled it as best he could on the primal's hairline.

Its face snarled. Mouth full of teeth glimmering green in Sam's NVGs. And everything about its posture told Sam it was about to jump, and his finger moved into the trigger guard...

Kat barked without warning, and Sam almost squeezed off the shot.

Everything changed in an instant. The snarling face suddenly hid its teeth. The tension of an imminent pounce went out of the creature and it relaxed back on its haunches, its eyes locked onto Kat, seeming perplexed.

Sam still couldn't take a breath. Still didn't dare to take his aim off the creature, but he had to, for the one second it took to bring his muzzle up and over Kat's head, then continued tracking the primal as it passed behind them.

Kat seemed to give no notice to Sam's maneuverings, and simply turned to the right, issuing the exact same throaty bark to the primals on the right. Sam wanted to turn and look, mainly because having his back to them was making his skin crawl, but he figured the bark had had the same effect, because no one yelled out, and nothing tackled Sam, and the ATV just went right on through the intersection.

"Hoooooooooly shit," Jones breathed out.

Lee's next words were transmitted, and Sam heard them in his earpiece: "First contact, no problems. We're in. How're things looking, Marie?"

Marie paused in her work just long enough to frown at nothing in particular, then key her radio with gloved hands slick with blood. "Well, he's not dead yet, if that's what you mean."

Gary knelt beside her on the other side of Bran's body, and glanced at her with momentary confusion until he realized she was speaking over the radio. He'd pretty much been chosen to assist her because he seemed nominally intelligent and did what he was told without too many annoying questions.

"I think it's getting pretty hot," Gary said, eyeing the bags in his hands.

Marie nodded as she set back to her work. "Alright, go ahead and pull it."

Bran was most definitely in shock. Loss of blood led to low blood pressure, which could be bumped up with IV fluids. Unfortunately, loss of blood also led to hypothermia. Hypothermia could be exacerbated by cold IV fluids. Luckily, Marie had a trick for this. They kept a few MREs in their gear, and each MRE came with a chemical heating pouch to warm up the food without a fire. But they could also be used to heat up an IV bag.

Gary gingerly pulled the IV bag from the steaming pouch. "Where do you want it?"

"Hold onto it for a second," Marie said, squirting more saline solution into the exit wound on Bran's left hip. The idiot had packed his wounds with dirt. She wasn't sure what he'd hoped to accomplish with that, outside of making her job harder. She wasn't going to be able to get all of it out either—not without restarting his bleeding.

She cleared as much as she could until she started to see red rivulets welling up from the wound channel again, then packed it with gauze. She'd already probed the wound channel a bit to see if it had pierced his abdominal cavity, but it didn't seem like it had, so she packed it with gauze until she could pack no longer, then blotted the area dry and slapped an occlusive dressing over it.

"Alright, gimme the bag," she said, shuffling her knees over to reveal the IV port she'd already started in Bran's arm. All she had to do was plug and go. She set the drip high, while Gary stood up and held the bag a few feet over Bran. Then, with one hand, she started pumping the blood pressure cuff still on Bran's arm, while getting her stethoscope back in her ears with her other hand.

"It's called permissive hypotension," Marie said, because, hell, Gary might as well learn something while he was standing there. Maybe it'd come in handy some time. "Hypotension being the fancy word for low blood pressure."

Gary frowned. "Don't you want his blood pressure to come up?"

"I do, but not back to nominal levels yet. I want to keep him about seventy systolic, which is still low, but if we pump it any higher, it can dislodge the clots his body is naturally making to stop the bleeding."

His blood pressure was still bad, but Bran suddenly twitched, flailed one arm, then let out a long, low groan, his eyelids fluttering open.

Marie inwardly swore. That he was conscious again was a good sign, but her job would be a helluva lot easier if he'd stayed out. She abandoned the blood pressure cuff to put a firm hand on his chest, as much to give him a sense of grounding as to keep him from sitting up. She leaned over him, putting a bit of weight on him as his eyes flashed around, clearly not seeing much at first.

"Bran," she said in a stern, clinical voice. "Bran, you with me?"

Gradually, his wild eyes came to center and rested on Marie. His expression was childish in its lack of comprehension. But that didn't last long. They sparked with recognition. Then flared with alarm.

"Easy," Marie said, rubbing and patting his chest. "Be easy, we're trying to help you."

"The fuck?" Bran slurred, his eyes moving to Gary, whom he didn't seem to recognize, then back to Marie with no less alarm than before. "The fuck is...?"

"It's alright," Marie soothed, albeit with a notable lack of compassion in her voice. "Kat brought you to us. You lost consciousness. We're working on your wounds. I've got the bleeding under control, now I'm trying to bring your blood pressure back up." He didn't need to know all that, but sometimes the drone of medicalese lulled people into compliance.

Bran blinked a few times, his pale lips quivering. "Shit," he summarized, and then his eyes went wonky again and his head dropped back and he was out once more.

"Should we move him to the truck?" Gary asked, craning his neck around, as though to point out how horrendously exposed they were.

"Not until I get him stabilized," Marie started to explain as she pumped the blood pressure cuff again.

But right as the last word left her lips, someone shouted, "Oh shit! Movement! Right there!"

And that's when everything went where it always did: Straight to hell.

Abe had just been about to ask his impromptu spotter—a lady named Gwen—for an update on the thermal signatures around Lee's destination, when she jolted, ripped the thermal spotting scope hard to the left, and then after only a half second of pause, shouted, "Oh shit! Movement! Right there!"

Abe's first thought was that he couldn't leave Lee hanging just as he was approaching the megachurch. But how close was *right there*? "Distance?" he barked, hoping to God that Gwen's version of *right there* didn't mean they were about to crawl in the truck bed with them.

Gwen started slapping his shoulder, clearly believing he needed to reorient his rifle. "On the ridge to your left! A hundred yards!"

The sound of hustling feet from all around the truck.

Marie's voice in his earpiece: "Talk to me, Abe!"

Abe was already readjusting. A hundred yards was too close for comfort. As he shifted his hips and shoulders to the right, squashing up against Gwen, he touched off his comms. "Lee, I gotta divert—we got company."

Abe's reticle traced the top of the ridge just to their left until he saw it—a half dozen shapes, moving along the top of the hill and coming straight down at them.

Lee's response was just a background jabber as Abe cranked his elevation turret. "Copy that, keep me updated."

Abe rapidly counted the clockwise clicks to his hundred-yard zero, bringing his reticle onto the leading primal, then expelling his breath and squeezing the trigger. The suppressed rifle let out a muffled crack. The bullet hit the lead primal dead center in the chest. It lurched, did something like a midair mule kick, and changed direction, retreating over the top of the rise with an unsteady gait that told Abe it wasn't going to get far.

"Six primals," Abe squeezed out a transmission to Marie as he worked the bolt and simultaneously found the next primal—which was already following the leader over the far side of the hill. "Hundred yards out and closing fast!"

Unsuppressed rifle fire slammed through the night as the two guys with the thermal optics zeroed in on the primals. Abe saw flurries of dust from a dozen impacts, but no obvious hits. Just before the primal in his sights made it over the hill, Abe loosed a shot that took the back of its head off.

He lurched to his feet, taking his rifle with him. "Marie! Get Bran loaded up!" then, shouting to everyone over the thundering rifle fire, "Everyone get in the truck!" He hefted the rifle to his shoulder and scanned the ridge, confirming that the small pack had disappeared over the hill. But they weren't fleeing. They were just taking cover. They were going to ride the ridgeline all the way down and then pop out right in front of them.

"What do I do?" Gwen shrilled as the first few people vaulted into the truck bed.

"Grab your rifle and get ready to shoot!" Abe snapped back, sweeping his reticle back and forth across the bottom of the ridge, which was far closer than a hundred yards. Probably only about thirty.

I should transition.

No time like the present.

Abe snugged the ESR up against the wall of the pickup bed, then snatched up his regular rifle, shouldered it, and then worked his support arm into the sling. He was going off the moonlight now—his rifle had the IR designator, but he hadn't bothered to put on his NVGs, which would render the laser useless. All he had was the dim point of his red dot, and the moonlight, and the shifting sea of grass around them.

"Someone get in the driver's seat!" Marie's voice shouted as she rounded the back of the truck, holding Bran's feet, while Gary struggled along with his upper half.

"Guys with thermals!" Abe called out. "Holler when you see—"

He didn't need thermal imaging or night vision. They were easy enough to see by moonlight. Four shapes rocketed over the lowest point of the hill, all at once, eating up the thirty yards at a frightening, quadrupedal sprint.

Some idiot tried to jump onto the tailgate, blocking Abe's shot just as his finger dropped to the trigger. He held back, swearing, then grabbed the guy by the back of the neck and drove his head downwards. "Getthefuckdown!" Support hand coming back up while his knees hit the guy's shoulders, making sure he stayed there. The second his red dot touched a fleshy shape, he fired on automatic. One, long string that chipped away at the primal, sending gobbets of it flying, as every rifle that had a clear shot opened up.

Abe's target went whirling to the ground and tumbled, head over heels. Abe swept to the left, saw another target already being hammered, and added a burp of three or four rounds for good measure.

Both eyes open, seeing how the targets were arraying themselves. Two down, and a third getting pummeled as it tried to cut wide to the left, but the fourth was a tricky bastard and somehow squirted between and under firing lines and came up in one fantastic leap that sent it sailing through the air towards the tailgate.

Someone screamed—hell, *everyone* was screaming.

Abe let out a noise like he was straining against a great weight, and put one leg over the guy at his feet. The primal slammed down on the tailgate in an impossible perch, its hands coming down on the guy's legs as it did. The gnarled claw-like digits sank viciously into the flesh. The guy grabbed a hold of Abe's leg and let out a wail that sounded more sad than pained.

Abe squeezed the trigger, and didn't let up, groaning the whole time as his rounds stitched the primal from crotch to clavicle. It jolted back, but held on by the grip it had on the man's leg. It tried to right itself, then lunged gaping jaws at Abe. His next five rounds whittled the skull down to the neck and sent it pitching backwards off the tailgate.

Abe whirled around to see if anyone had taken the damn driver's seat. He realized he was smashed in with quite the scrum of bodies now. The primals were down, and yet rifles were still firing, muzzle blasts still punching in everyone's sinuses, and hot brass smacking them in the face.

Abe got pissed at the lack of discipline and raised his hand, palm out, to wave it in front of his face and bellow for a cease-fire. And that's when he heard Gwen screeching again.

"More coming! There's more coming! Someone get us out of here!"

It took him one sweep of the eyes to see what she'd seen: More than a dozen shapes now, plowing through the grass and tearing down the hill on their left.

He brought his rifle around, but felt the truck rumble to life beneath his feet, and he knew what was next—aggressive acceleration, with a load of people standing in the back. For one horrific moment, Abe imagined the people tumbling out the backend as the pickup charged forward. So he did the first thing he could think of, and sat his ass straight down on top of the guy who was still clinging to his leg. He let the rifle drop from his hands—which rebounded off the guy's head—then lunged forward and grabbed whatever piece he could of the two people closest to the tailgate.

Got someone's shirt, and Gwen's rifle strap.

The pickup's engine roared. Clouds of dust erupted from the spinning tires.

Abe braced his legs as the force of the acceleration threatened to rip the two people from his hands. Gwen would have gone flying, but was arrested by the rifle strap, her feet dangling out over air as two primals swept through the dust cloud and surged towards the back of the truck.

In his left hand, he felt the shirt begin to tear, but the guy it was attached to thought blessedly quick and simply dropped his legs out from under him to keep his momentum from pulling him backwards.

Something hit the sidewall of the truck bed, and someone shouted, and then fired what seemed like an excessive amount of rounds over the side, and Abe caught sight of flailing arms and legs as something went tumbling off the side of the truck.

Gwen hauled herself back into the bed, gasping, her eyes bulging.

Abe let go of her and the other guy and snatched up his rifle again, squirming to get his ass off of the guy he'd sat on, as that individual started thrashing and screaming that he couldn't breathe, which was obviously bullshit, since he was screaming.

In all this mess of confusion, Abe did one sweep with his rifle to confirm there were no more hostiles attached to the vehicle, then pressed his PTT. "Lee, we had to light out! Repeat, we are out of position. You're on your own!"

Chapter 42

If that wasn't the last thing Lee wanted to hear, it was at least in the bottom three.

Abe sounded like he had his hands full—roaring engines and lots of shouting and gunfire in the background—so Lee declined to respond. It kind of felt like he needed to be quiet anyway, as they were rolling very slowly up to the front of the megachurch, where no less than eight primals were milling about.

Through his NVGs—just one tube, for his one eye—Lee could see Jones and Sam's laser designators scanning the crowd like they couldn't decide which of the eight targets to settle on.

"Stop," Kat said firmly from behind him.

Gritting his teeth and clenching his breath, Lee eased the ATV to a gentle stop. The eight primals moved towards them, and there was that kind of tension in the air that suggested things could go very bad if someone so much as cut a loud fart.

When Kat let out that raspy bark, every nerve ending in his fingers and toes lit off. His right hand settled on the shifter, while his left dropped to the rifle slung between his knees.

There was something different about the bark this time. It sounded the same to Lee's ears, but the other two times they'd encountered what Lee could only think of as *primal checkpoints*, she'd simply barked, and then they'd passed through. This time, apparently her bark was less convincing.

One of the primals slunk forward, bipedally, its long, sinewy arms hanging at its sides as it raised its head and snuffled at the air. It issued a sound like a hacking cough, and there seemed to be something unmistakably derisive in its tone.

A low growl from over Lee's shoulder. Kat taking exception to the challenger.

The other primals were still moving as though to encircle them. That did not make Lee feel good. The fingers of his left hand closed around the foregrip of his rifle. He could shove the shifter into reverse, then slam on the accelerator and start firing through the plastic windshield.

The lead primal—an Alpha, perhaps—issued a series of huffs and snorts that didn't sound friendly at all, and were far short of the deference Lee'd seen them give Kat the other two times.

"Kat, what's going on?" Sam murmured. "Do we need to leave?"

Kat snarled and slammed her hands on the roof of the ATV. Lee restrained a jump of surprise, knowing that it might be interpreted as a prey response and cause the whole pack of primals to descend on them in a frenzy.

"No!" Kat seethed, and Lee guessed it was a response to Sam, so he gripped the shifter hard, but didn't punch it into reverse just yet. But damn were his palms getting sweaty.

The ATV shook and Lee snapped his head to the left, wondering if a primal had just launched itself at them. But it was Kat. She'd leapt out of the bed and now stood an arm's length away, her posture low and mean.

That seemed to convince the primals that were trying to encircle them, and they halted, then backed up a step or two. But the Alpha was made of more stubborn stuff. Lee looked at it and saw Sam's laser tracing jittery circles around its nose. It did a strange thing then: It puffed its chest up, and dipped into a low squat, and swayed back and forth on its haunches, its powerful arms sweeping back and forth so the claws scraped across the pavement.

Lee had no idea what he was witnessing, and could do nothing but take it on faith that Kat could handle it. Whatever it was that the Alpha was doing, it must've pissed Kat right off, because she went shooting forward, inhumanly fast, and before Lee could even twitch, she was nose to nose with the Alpha.

For about a half a second.

It was as though Kat had an invisible forcefield around her which no primal wished to desecrate. An undeniable look of shock came over the Alpha as she tore up to it, and as she thrust her face at it, gnashing her teeth, it stumbled back, tucking its ass and scrambling on all fours until it had regained a bit of distance.

It didn't challenge her again.

Whatever had occurred between the Alpha and Kat, she'd won.

The other seven primals backed off even more. Kat eyed them fiercely, her posture relaxing by tiny increments as they retreated. She waited a few beats, then turned and looked at Lee. "Come."

Lee very carefully pushed the shifter into park, and cut the power.

"We really doing this?" Jones whispered.

"Looks that way," Lee husked back, pushing the little door panel open and stepping out. Every movement was slow and measured. He didn't want to do anything that might break the fragile stillness. Even tried to mask his limp, so as not to whet a predator's appetite for wounded prey.

With his left hand, he kept his rifle held tightly to his chest, while his right hand kept his other weapon from clattering as he stood up. He had one of the M32 grenade launchers slung to his other side. Call it a bit of an insurance policy, in case things fell through with Kat.

Not that a handful of forty-mike-mikes will kill them all.

But maybe it could buy them time.

Jones and Sam met him at the front of the ATV. Kat faced the door, gave a final growl that sounded like one last warning not to fuck with her, then strode forward, the three humans trailing behind her. They held their rifles shouldered, but were careful not to point them at any of the primals now.

Into the greenwash of light-amplified gloom. Kat didn't seem to have any trouble seeing at all. She moved confidently through an atrium littered with trash and debris. Lee, Jones, and Sam all panned their heads around, taking the environment in through their NVGs.

They were not alone. Not by a long shot.

Scores of primals inhabited this space, and the smell of them was nearly overpowering. Lee could remember the way the first generation of infected had smelled, pissing and shitting in their clothes, and not having a shred of rationality left, they would stay in those soiled clothes, where their skin would begin to rot.

This smell was not nearly as bad as that. The primals groomed themselves, and each other, and for the most part, it didn't seem like they shit or pissed where they slept. But they had a stink all their own, somewhere between a wet dog and a man that hasn't bathed in months.

The primals all around them perked up as they entered, but none moved to intercept them, or to challenge Kat. A few slunk closer, but never so close as to be threatening, and mostly just to sniff at the air as they passed. Lee was acutely aware of their position here. If the primals charged them, they'd be swallowed up in a tide of claws and teeth. Sure, they'd take out a few before their heads were wrenched off their shoulders. But not enough to save themselves.

Kat continued to move through the atrium like she owned the place. Was her confidence as much of an act as Lee's affected calm? Had she done this before, just waltzing into the colony? Or was she just as desperate as they were? As desperate to save Bran as they were to save Bea?

Kat made for a hallway through which Lee could see an obvious light source brightening his night vision and illuminating a large room beyond. As he moved into the hall behind her, followed by

Jones, with Sam taking up the rear, it became obvious that they were entering the sanctuary.

Sanctuary was a bit humble for this place. It was practically a concert hall. The floor sloped down amid rows and rows of chairs that Lee figured had once been arranged in neat lines, but were now scattered and jumbled and tossed into piles. Clear alleys and pathways weaved through the wreckage, all of them seeming to converge at the front.

"What the ffff—?"

"Ssh," Lee cut Jones off, as quietly as he could manage to silence the other man.

The front of the auditorium was a stage. The illumination that Lee had seen was coming from a massive hole in the ceiling with no apparent natural cause. The moonlight shone down, revealing an unsettling tableau.

All about the stage, now rising from various states of repose, were somewhere in the neighborhood of twenty primals. Lee couldn't count them accurately on account of how closely entangled they were with each other. But he did note that they were all females. A protective wall of Omegas, as though to guard the stage itself.

And upon the stage were four more figures—all of them female, too. But three were clearly not all the way human. And the fourth was Bea.

She lay curled up on her side, with her back to them, but Lee recognized her by the clothes she wore—only pants and a bra—and the bandage covering her shoulder blade.

Lee shifted his attention back to the other three. *Hybrids*, he realized. *Lander's wives*.

Lee had assaulted a primal colony before—albeit a much smaller one—and knew how the hierarchy worked. How the half-human, half-primal females were exalted by the others. Set apart, and protected. Like queen bees in a hive.

What disturbed him most in that moment was how the three hybrid females were crouched around Bea's form, and appeared to be...caring for her. One of them was sitting cross-legged at Bea's head, grooming her hair almost tenderly. The other two were not actively doing anything, but their postures were not menacing towards Bea in any way.

Bea's own posture was stiff. She was not enjoying the attention, only tolerating it, because what else was she supposed to do? The creatures around her might be half-human, but they were still volatile and dangerous. Who knew what wrong move would induce them to turn grooming into a feeding frenzy?

Lee and his column approached the stage down one of the paths that cut a straight-ish line through the detritus and chairs. Kat remained in the lead, but Lee noticed that her pace had slowed. Her eyes were upon the ranks of Omegas around the stage, and Lee sensed that she was not as confident in handling them as she was the males.

The primal hierarchy was matriarchal, so it made sense that females, whether hybrids or full-blooded primals, were given deference by the males. But would Kat's status hold up to the Omegas, guarding their queen bees?

Sam issued the lightest hiss of a whisper: "Bea!"

Lee's stomach tensed as a ripple of reaction went through the primals all around them. And not just the Omegas around the stage, Lee now realized. Shadows were shifting and figures were emerging from what he'd first taken to simply be piles of trash upon a framework of overturned chairs.

The sanctuary was *packed* with primals.

Shit and fuck, Lee thought as he panned slowly from side to side, suppressing his instinct to shoulder his rifle and find a target. He needed to stay calm and unperturbed. If he started giving off aggressive energy, he'd receive it right back.

He needed to act like he belonged there, knowing that one misstep would bring the whole multitude crashing down on them. It felt like being in a tunnel that might collapse at any moment. Or perhaps being in a tunnel and waiting for a nuclear warhead to go off over your head.

At first, Bea seemed not to have heard Sam's whisper. But she must've heard the reaction from her captors, and the stirring of the Omegas around the stage. She rolled, very slowly, very deliberately.

Her eyes peered through the gloom, and Lee realized she might not be able to see them. The shaft of moonlight was coming down right on her, and it must've turned the sanctuary beyond into an ink-blot test of shadows.

Lee's suspicion was confirmed when Bea came up on one elbow and let out a harsh whisper: "Is there someone there?"

Before any of them could answer, a new sound hit Lee's ears. It took him less than a second to recognize it as the sound of something charging on all fours. He twisted for the noise, bringing up his rifle, because he figured the jig was up and this was about to turn into a bloodbath. His thumb flicked the select-fire switch on his rifle, but that was as far as he got.

A shape came hurtling out of a darkened doorway to the right side of the stage. Lee saw a flash of white-blonde hair in the moonlight, and then it leapt with a guttural snarl. He tracked it, but held his finger off the trigger as the figure landed with Jones and Kat blocking his shot.

"Oh shit!" Jones yelped, backpedaling and bringing his rifle up.

But still, no one dared to fire a shot.

Freya came up from a half squat, and Kat hunched down, the two of them facing off. They circled slowly, like a pair of wrestlers waiting to see who would make the first move. If Freya was concerned with Jones and Lee and Sam, she didn't show it. Just as Lee had witnessed at the ranch, Freya and Kat seemed to lock onto each other and forget about everything else around them.

What was the deal with these two? Sibling rivalry?

Speech was clearly not preferred by either of them. They simply stared, baring their teeth and issuing low yowls between them that sounded a helluva lot like two cats about to fight. Not house cats, though. More like pumas.

Lee, Jones, and Sam held their position, about ten yards from the stage. They cinched in tight with each other, pivoting to cover three-hundred and sixty degrees, in an outward-facing circle.

Lee didn't want to be a part of whatever Kat and Freya had going on, but he didn't want to get too far from the bubble of safety that Kat provided them. If she got distracted—or worse, killed—then Lee had no illusions how that would turn out for them.

"The fuck do we do now?" Sam hissed, his head swiveling between the circling hybrids, and Bea on the stage.

Bea was on all fours now, crawling carefully away from Lander's wives, who had stood up and were now making worried hooting noises at Kat and Freya.

"Kat," Lee said, raising his voice just enough that he knew she would hear, even in her distracted state. "Stay on task!"

She gave no indication that she'd heard.

Jones's feet started dancing.

Lee knew what that meant.

"Jones," Lee said in a warning tone.

"Guys, I got this," Jones proclaimed, already moving.

Lee made a move to grab him, but he'd already slipped out of reach. He crossed the distance to Kat and Freya in two bounding strides and did possibly the dumbest thing Lee had ever seen the guy do: Insert his body right between two creatures about to tear each other's throats out.

"Whoa, whoa, whoa!" Jones called out as he planted his feet, rifle in one hand, muzzle pointing at the ceiling, while his other hand pumped the air between Kat and Freya. "Ladies! Cool your jets for a minute, okay?"

Oh, dear God...

"Jones!" Sam seethed through clenched teeth.

"Don't distract me!" Jones snapped over his shoulder. Back to Kat and Freya, who hadn't relaxed their combative postures, but did seem entirely perplexed at this new addition to the situation. "Kat. Freya. Listen to me. Actually, better yet, listen to your mothers. Yeah? Those are your mothers, right? On the stage right there? Or, at least, one of them is? Or two of them? Do you have the same mother?"

Lee did a quick scan, but the rest of the primals were still keeping their distance. He spared a glance at Kat and Freya, whose eyes were darting from Jones, to each other, and then to Lander's wives. Neither of them responded to Jones's query.

"Never mind, it doesn't matter," Jones said, speaking all in a tumble, obviously ad libbing. "Y'all's mothers are right there, watching you two. And I don't understand what they're saying, but it sure sounds to me like they don't want y'all to tear each other apart. I mean, what's the deal with you two anyway? Is there any reason for y'all to hate each other? Or is it just Lander, pitting you guys against each other?"

"Lander..." Freya's voice was harsh and croaking. "Is father."

Kat snarled. "Not. My. Father."

Freya bristled. "*All* father!"

"It's beside the point," Jones hastily interjected, then honed in on Freya. "Freya, listen to me. I had a father too. And he was just like your father."

Lee couldn't help that his ears perked at this. Perhaps the strangest time to take an interest in another's personal history, but as much of a loudmouth as Jones was, he'd declined to open up about his childhood. Maybe he was just making shit up—Lee wouldn't put that past him. But something in the way that Jones spoke said that he was either a way better actor than Lee had ever given him credit for...or he was being earnest.

Jones was now getting the lion's share of Freya's attention. And Lee wasn't entirely sure if that was a good thing or not, but he decided to let this play out—it *probably* wouldn't make the situation worse, and there was a chance Jones might actually diffuse things.

"You and me, Freya," Jones said, his volume coming down a bit. "Our fathers were just alike. Manipulators. Guys that like to play king. My father liked it when everyone around him was working hard to make him happy, and so he'd pit us against each other. He'd pit us against our mother, and our mother against us. Because he liked the feeling of control that it gave him."

Jones fumbled with his NVGs for a moment, then lifted them away from his eyes, so he could look Freya straight in the face.

"It took me a long time to figure out that my sister and my brother and my mother weren't my enemies. It was him, all along. *He* was the enemy. *He* was the one that caused all the fighting, and all the heartache. And maybe you haven't figured that out yet, because, well...you're probably not as old as you look, are you? It doesn't matter, you don't have to answer. The point is, Kat's not your enemy. *We're* not your enemy either, Freya. We're not here to hurt anyone. We're just here for our friend, Bea. That's all we want. And then we'll leave. And no one has to get hurt."

Freya held Jones's gaze for a long moment, then cast a glance at Bea. "Father. Wants her."

"Yeah, I know he does," Jones nodded. "He wants to make more daughters, just like you and Kat. And then he'll pit them against each other, and pit them against you, because he loves the sense of control that he gets from it. It makes him feel important. Special. Because that's what he loves more than anything else—not you, not your mothers, and not any of the others that he calls his *family*. The only thing he loves is himself, and having power over others. You don't mean anything to him, just like Kat didn't mean anything to Colin Horner. You're just...animals to him. You're just useful. And as soon as you're not useful to him anymore? As soon as you're not making him feel special and important? He'll abandon you. Because his whole world is about *him*. It sucks that you love him, Freya. I loved my father, too. But I stopped letting him *control* me. Don't let Lander control you."

Lee was shocked to realize that Freya's posture had become very different. No longer was she hunched into a fighting posture. She was standing up straight now, albeit a bit stooped at the shoulders, as though a heavy burden had been placed there. The snarl had left her face, and she seemed to be deeply convicted by what Jones had said.

Perhaps a normal human would have scoffed and ignored Jones's words. But Lee reminded himself that Kat and Freya, though they might look like women, had the minds of children. For all the violence they were capable of, they were, in a way...innocent.

Freya's mouth worked open and closed a few times, as though she were struggling with some unwieldy words. But the words that finally rang out into the darkness were not hers.

"Freya!" A single, sharp bark.

Lee spun towards the noise, and spotted what he'd missed in the narrow field of view through his NVGs: Lander had emerged from the same dark doorway that Freya had come from moments before. He now stood, a few strides out into the open, not even the affectation of the serape to cover him. The moonlight glowed on his naked skin. His arms were held stiffly at his sides, his hands balled into fists. His lank hair hung in front of his face, through which two wrathful eyes shown, his bearded chin protruding, and his thin lips pulled back to show the white nubs of his bottom teeth.

Freya jerked at the sound of her name. Lee had only a second to glance back at her before returning his attention to Lander, but in that tiny moment, he saw the fear of retribution all over Freya's face, and Lee's stomach bottomed out.

Lander extended an index finger, his hand trembling with fury as he pointed to the ground at his feet. When he spoke again, every syllable was sharp and threatening. "Freya. To. Me."

Freya twitched, like there were strings attached to her limbs, controlled like a puppet, and Lander the puppet-master.

"You don't have to obey him," Jones whispered to her. "He doesn't have any power over you, except what you give him. *You're* in control, Freya. You're the one that actually has the power. Not him."

By slow increments, Lee raised his rifle. The laser designator played around Lander's feet, invisible to the other man's naked eyes. It slowly drifted up his legs. To his knees. To his thighs.

What would happen if Lee put a round through Lander's head? Would everything devolve into chaos? Would the primals attack him for killing their father? Or would he be chopping the head off the snake?

"Sam," Lee breathed, as the laser designator drifted up to Lander's midsection. "We need an out."

"Emergency exit," Sam said immediately. "Left side of the stage."

Lee had clocked it when they'd first entered the sanctuary, but had been hoping that they'd just be able to waltz out the way they came in. Naturally, nothing in Lee's life could ever be *that* easy. He took a look at the left of the stage and saw the darkened emergency exit sign, still hanging over the door. The door itself was closed. Was it locked? And what was on the other side? It wouldn't necessarily just open up to the outside, and given the dimensions of the building, Lee didn't think that it did.

"You're on Bea," Lee quietly instructed. "Me and Jones will cover."

"Freya," Lander's voice had a sing-songy lilt, but there was nothing friendly about it. It was a warning to Freya. But what punishment could he mete out to her? Was it like Horner and Kat? Did Freya just submit to the abuses because she knew no other way? It was like watching a man convince a tigress that he was the one to be feared. "I said...*to me*!"

"Start moving," Lee murmured to Sam, then caught a worried glance from Jones and jerked his head as he and Sam started very slowly easing their feet in the direction of the emergency exit.

Eye back on Freya now. Lee eased his way around Kat's back, who was still completely focused on Freya and Lander. Lander, for his part, only had eyes for Freya. And they were cold, cruel eyes, just as mad and pitiless as Colin Horner's had been. For all their dislike of each other, they were the same type of person. Apparently something they had in common with Jones's father. The type of person to whom others were simply bags of flesh whose worth was determined by their utility.

Lander took a sharp inhale, but before he could start screaming, Freya spun, silencing him.

His eyebrows crept up his face, expectantly. Trembling finger still pointing at the ground beside him. Calling her, quite literally, to heel.

Freya's head dipped, and her shoulders scrunched up even further, giving her a surprisingly child-like look. And then she padded to Lander's side.

"Kat," Lee whispered, sensing their time running out like the last few grains of sand in an hour glass. "We need you with us."

Kat did not turn away from Lander and Freya, but her feet moved, backing up to stay with Lee and Sam and Jones, all four of them moving with tiny, shuffling steps, hoping against hope to just go unnoticed for a bit longer...

They were noticed.

Lander cast his gaze on them, and the smug pleasure that had been written all over his face as Freya submitted to his command turned into a vicious grin. "It seems we have some trespassers in our home, Freya," he said, his voice haughty now that he felt in control again.

Then the smile faded into a toothy grimace.

"Kill them."

Lee's laser designator, right on Lander's face now.

But would taking the shot help or hurt their chances?

Whatever reaction Lander had been expecting, he didn't get it. Freya just stood there with her head bowed, watching Kat slowly retreating with the others. Lander glanced at her. Then turned fully to face her.

"Freya!" he growled, and one hand shot up to seize the hair at the back of her neck. Freya mewled, body twisting as Lander pulled her head towards him. "Make the fucking call!"

"Go for Bea," Lee snapped at Sam. "Now."

Still twenty-some-odd number of not-too-happy-looking Omegas between Sam and Bea.

Every second, Lee kept expecting the howl to come bursting out of Freya's throat, but she only stood there in Lander's grip, head twisted to the side as he now began screaming, and Lee's feet began moving faster and faster.

"Do it! Do it now, you *bitch*!"

Bea was now perched at the edge of the stage, watching Sam get as close as he dared, the look in her eyes saying she knew this was her one and only chance, and she was watching it slip away.

"Bea!" Sam waved at her. "Come to us!"

"I can't!" Bea said, clearly indicating the wall of primals between them like a moat filled with crocodiles.

"Kat, help her!" Lee said, dropping his finger to the trigger and steadying his aim so the dot now swirled over Lander's temple.

Kat moved. The Omegas yowled and refused to stand aside.

"Howl!" Lander was screaming in Freya's face, jerking her head back and forth by her hair. "*Howl*! *HOWL*!"

And then Freya howled.

Chapter 43

Everything, all at once.

That's how it is when shit hits the fan. People say that time slows down, but of course, time doesn't do shit. Your perceptions speed up. In that burst of adrenaline, your mind opens up and drinks from a firehose of data.

And so all the information flooded Lee's brain, all at once.

Freya, with her head jerked to the side, the veins bulging out of her throat as she howled. Lander, getting what he wanted, and now swinging his triumphant gaze right to Lee. And seeing how the muzzle of Lee's rifle was staring right back at him.

An instant of surprise. And then he dragged Freya's head in front of his, using his own daughter as a body shield.

At the same instant that Lee's finger dropped to the trigger, Kat moved with a speed and intent so savage that even the Omegas were taken off guard.

And during all of this, a small hope in the back of Lee's brain: *Maybe Freya didn't make the right howl, just like Kat did—*

An eruption of movement from all around Lee told him his hope was in vain.

Jones and Sam, both pivoting in that instant, hearing the movement, and bringing their rifles up to the horde of threats now coming down on them like an avalanche.

Lee's finger on the trigger, already applying pressure. The laser designator on Lander's nose, but then his face was eclipsed by Freya's.

Don't take that shot.

It wasn't actually a consciously-articulated thought, but more of a feeling in Lee's chest. A big, fat NOPE. And Lee had learned to trust his instincts. He dropped the muzzle. The laser dipped, down off of Freya's face, down her chest, and onto Lander's pelvis.

The shot broke.

Lee saw Lander's body jerk, but nothing else—Lee was already spinning away.

Kat exploded, with only one thing on her mind: *Save Bea, save Bran.*

The howl went up, and it sang through Kat's blood, and if she'd been less human and more beast, she would have been unable to resist that instinctive call to action. But she *was* more human than she was beast. And she had a friend. And she loved him, and wanted to save his life. And the only way to do that was to save Bea's life. And there wasn't a bitch in the bunch that was going to stop her from doing that.

The first Omega lunged, going for Kat's jugular. But Kat already knew it was going to happen—they always went for the jugular first. So she dropped, ramming her shoulder into the Omega's hips and sending her cartwheeling overhead.

She came up, slamming both hands into the neck of another Omega, her fingers bursting through the flesh, closing around the windpipe and the carotid arteries, and ripping them out as she spun away.

Close to the stage now.

Save Bea, save Bran.

A front kick to stop one advancing on her. But this Omega outsized Kat by a good amount, and all the kinetic energy recoiled right back into Kat, sending her staggering back. Right into another Omega. A pair of wiry arms closed around her chest, pinning her arms to her sides.

Teeth sank into the trapezius muscle at the base of Kat's neck. The pain was blinding, but also enraging. Kat flailed and screamed, grabbing anything she could get her hands on. Felt heat and moisture and hair and clamped down with all the grip she could muster, realizing she'd latched onto the Omega's crotch—the only sensitive thing she could reach.

The grip around her chest loosened as a screech vibrated through the teeth in her shoulder. She ripped away, heedless of her own tearing muscles. Broke the grip and spun, swinging her arm with all the force of her body. Her clawed hand smashed the Omega in her face, ripping its jaw clean off.

The stage. Right there.

Bea, right there upon it.

Save Bea, save Bran.

A crush of bodies closing in on her.

Kat grabbed one by the ear and hair. Slammed the head into the edge of the stage. Saw the life go out of its eyes in an instant. Used the falling body as a scaffold and vaulted onto the stage. She landed right at Bea's side.

The woman didn't know what was going on, didn't know who was friend, and who was enemy, and she recoiled, trying to get away from Kat. But she wasn't fast enough. Kat caught her by the arm, then pulled her in. She didn't really know what she was planning to do with Bea until she was already doing it. She moved so fast that Bea didn't even have a chance to resist.

Kat reached down, planted her right forearm between Bea's legs, while her left hand clamped around the back of Bea's neck. Every muscle in Kat's body strained as she heaved the other woman from the ground and then flung her like a bale of hay.

Bea let out one terrified yelp as she flew clear over the heads of the Omegas.

Sam fired on automatic. Marksmanship was unnecessary. The targets were all around them, and closing fast. Through the green world of his NVGs, his laser designator was lost amidst a galaxy of eyes that shined like spotlighted cats.

They were everywhere, appearing out of every shadow, leaping from under every pile of wreckage. Too many to count. Too many to shoot. They'd run out of ammo before they killed even a third of them.

Too many!

Even as he thought it, he felt the terrible sensation of his bolt locking to the rear. The word came out of his throat at the level of a scream, an almost Pavlovian response to the sensation of running dry: "Reloading!"

A scream. A woman's scream. A *human* woman's scream.

As Sam's hand swiped the emergency reload mag from his belt, he saw the shape come flying, seemingly out of nowhere, then crash into the ground at his feet. He got two snippets of visual information that tied it all together: Bea's shirtless form; and Kat, on the stage, in a pose that looked like she'd just hurled something heavy off the stage.

Sam shoved the magazine into his rifle and dropped the bolt, firing one-handed from the hip as he bent and seized Bea's upper arm. The encroaching wave of primals jerked and spasmed as his rounds lanced through them. A few of them fell, but many more took the hits and kept coming. Sam hauled backwards, shouting, "Help! Help! Help!"

"Crossing!" Lee's frame filled Sam's vision. He let go of the trigger and diverted his muzzle to the side. Lee positioned himself in front of Sam and Bea, still moving backward, away from the mob of primals.

Jones swept in, shoulder to shoulder with Lee, their rifles chattering back and forth in bursts of automatic fire, scything down the closest primals, but the gap was rapidly closing.

"Bea!" Sam screamed as he swooped down and hooked his arm under hers. "Get up!"

She stumbled upright with a dazed look in her eyes, blood sheeting down the side of her face. Sam slung her behind him, hoping that he hadn't done it so hard she'd lose her feet again. He hazarded a glance behind him, saw that she was still standing, bobbling on unsteady legs.

"Emergency exit!" Sam shouted at her back, then ripped around to discover that there was barely two yards between Lee and Jones's smoking muzzles and the incoming tide of primals.

Jones went empty.

"Reloading!" Jones sidestepped, opening a gap, and Sam immediately filled it, laying into the seething mass of bodies. They were so close that Sam started deliberately aiming for their heads, knowing he couldn't miss.

"Up!" Jones roared, firing again on Sam's right. At the same instant, Lee peeled away from Sam's left, hollering, "Door!"

Sam didn't know if that was for them or Bea, and it didn't much matter anyway, because if Sam stopped shooting for a single second, they'd be overwhelmed.

And he was about to run dry again...

One good thing about being about to die is that broken ribs and fucked up hips don't really register in the white-hot realization of your imminent mortality.

Lee peeled and then flew for the door like every busted part of his body had just been touched by the hand of God. The emergency exit was five yards away, and between him and it was Bea, who looked like she'd had the sense knocked out of her and was stumbling drunkenly towards it.

Emergency exit doors always open outwards, so as to accommodate a panicked rush of bodies. Lee caught up to Bea in two lengthy strides, dropping his mostly-empty magazine and not bothering to retain it. He reloaded, sending the bolt home just in time to use his rifle like a baton into Bea's back, ramming her into the door.

The door exploded outwards. A short corridor beyond, maybe ten yards long, with another exit door on the far end. Lee planted his foot just inside the doorframe, letting Bea's body continue on its course. Her feet caught each other and she went sprawling, but Lee didn't wait to see what the damage was. He turned on his heel and posted on the doorframe, bellowing so hard it felt like it was ripping his vocal cords: "Peel! Peel! Peel!"

Sam and Jones reacted instantly. They both twisted in mid-backpedal and sprinted for the door. They registered Lee's position and cleared his lane of fire. The second that they stopped shooting, the primals burst forward, snapping at their backs, claws narrowly missing them.

Lee pulled the trigger and held it down, scouring the front row of primals, aiming for their pelvises, hoping to create a log-jam of falling bodies.

Jones in front. Sam right on his heels. And a primal just behind him, loading up for a leap, which would take Sam out, guaranteed.

Lee twitched his shoulders to the side, snapping his string of fire across the thing's chest like a whip. It tried to leap anyway, but fell far short and was immediately trampled by its brethren.

Jones and Sam were both reloading as they moved. Their bolts slammed home with twin *clunks* right as they burst through the doorway, sending the emergency door rebounding off its hinges. Lee jumped out of the way just in time for it to slam closed, and for a bare moment, he searched the area around him for something to brace the door with, then abandoned the idea and hauled ass.

The sound of the door on the far end crashing open—Bea must've got her head back in the game, because she'd recovered her feet and plowed through the emergency exit, revealing a flash of moonlit cityscape beyond.

Sam and Jones squirted through the outer door as it was still on its backswing. Jones pinned the door and posted to the left, Sam to the right, yelling something at Lee that he didn't quite catch but was pretty sure concerned him moving his ass faster. Lee knew he couldn't get any more speed out of his legs, so instead, he slung his rifle to his left side and snatched up the heavy M32.

The door slammed open behind him, amid a roar of voices that sounded like nothing so much as a freight train bearing down on him.

Lee spun, shouldering the launcher and thumbing the safety off. He wasn't entirely sure this was the smartest maneuver in this enclosed space, but if it worked, it would replenish the rapidly-shrinking lead on their pursuers. Lee's chosen gamble immediately became tenfold riskier as he realized he was still wearing his NVG tube, and couldn't aim through the launcher's optic.

If the grenade didn't go straight through the open door, the blast would knock Lee down at best, and kill him at worst.

It was a risk Lee was willing to take, in order to give Sam and Jones the lead they needed to get out of this alive.

By dead reckoning, Lee aimed the launcher for the center of the open doorframe as the horde of primals began to pour through, and fired.

Lander Hollis was just struggling to his feet, hands clutching the bloody hole in his guts, when the air seemed to burst, piercing his eardrums. A pressure wave flattened him out again. He coughed, tried to inhale, but couldn't seem to do it. What little air he did get in past his spasming diaphragm tasted of dust and smelled of acrid smoke. He hacked, tears blotting out his vision, the strain to his stomach causing his wound to bind itself in agonizing knots.

He blinked the tears out of his eyes and tried to resist the urge to cough, though his throat and lungs felt like he'd breathed red pepper. In the dim light from the hole in the ceiling, Lander recognized the familiar landscape of debris and chairs. No movement in the shadows though. And there was so much silence. What had happened to his family? Where had they all gone?

He realized it wasn't actually silent. There was a dull ringing in his ears. And there were sounds underneath that ringing, but they were so muted it was like his head was under water.

Slowly, his locked-up lungs began to loosen, and he drew a full, aching breath. His thoughts cleared with that rush of oxygen. Even his hearing seemed to get a little better, and he registered a mighty tumult behind him.

He rolled onto his side, craning his neck painfully in the direction that the man Jax and his group of thieves had run. All he saw was the tail end of a throng of his children, draining through the exit doors. He could see nothing beyond them. But they were still chasing something, which meant that there was still something to be chased.

Bastards!

With shaky arms, Lander pushed himself weakly off the ground. Got his knees under him. Then slowly, painfully, rose to his feet.

The first thing he noticed once he'd pulled himself from the ground was all the bodies. He couldn't count them all. Many were still moving, still alive. He felt no relief at that. They would be useless, if they even managed to survive.

Closer to the exit door, there was a charred disruption to the surface of the concrete floors that seemed oddly swept clean of bodies. Then he realized it was a blast mark, and the blast had pushed the bodies away in an almost perfect circle. No, actually. Not *pushed*. Those bodies nearest the blast had been ripped apart.

"Bastards!" he yelled. Or at least tried to yell. It came out a hoarse croak and he set to coughing again. Rage filled his belly and leaked into his chest. In it, there was not a shred of grief. He had many children. Even the loss of so many didn't really affect him.

But the *gall*! The absolute *impudence* of these people! To disrespect him in his own house? To come and take what was rightfully his, and what he'd waited so long to have?

Movement, closer at hand.

Lander jerked his head, realizing Freya was no longer beside him. She had retreated to the stage, and now stood leaning against it with a strange, loose posture. Behind her, on the stage, Lander's three wives huddled over Freya. But their eyes were on him.

Lander heaved a breath to scream at her, but the effort of it set his wound on fire and he gasped instead of screaming, both hands clamping down over the wound. His vision darkled at the edges and he felt woozy. He staggered to the side, the rage immediately replaced by fear. How bad was the injury?

He looked down at it, peeling his blood-slicked hands away to reveal a wound that seemed too small to account for this much pain. It was right there, just to the left of his navel.

"Ohh," he groaned. "He...*gutshot* me!" His gaze came up, chills sprouting up all over his naked skin. His expression twisted with pain and anxiety. "Freya!" he gasped weakly, reaching a hand towards her. "Help me! I've been gutshot!"

Freya did not move.

"Diana!" Lander whimpered, looking to one of his wives who'd always been the most affectionate towards him. "Please! Help!"

Diana did not move either.

Rage again. "You fucking cunts! I'm *gutshot*! Do you not understand that? Do you not understand what that *MEANS*?" He screamed the last part so hard that the pain swallowed him whole before he could even see it coming. Hot and cold sensations raced over his skin and swirled over his scalp and his vision went black. Then he didn't feel anything for a moment, until his bare ass hit the cold concrete.

A few panicked breaths brought his vision back. He'd collapsed, and now sat with his legs splayed out, hands still pressing against his wound, blood pulsing through his fingers and leaking through the creases of his palms.

And Freya was there, standing over him.

Blessed relief. His voice became pitiful and pleading again. "I'm hurt. I'm hurt so bad. Help your father, girl. You have to help me."

But Freya just stood there, staring down at him, her frizzy hair turned into a silver halo by the moonlight overhead. In her face there was nothing that he recognized. None of the respect and deific adoration he'd come to expect.

"Freya?" What did he need to say to get her to move her ass and help him? Had she gone deaf from that blast?

She bent at the waist, lowering her face over his. "You. Used. Me."

Movement out of the corner of his eye. He glanced, and saw Tonya—Freya's true mother—sliding down off the stage. They did not usually venture off the stage without their entourage of females around them. But they'd all left. They'd all chased after the thieves who'd taken Bea. The sanctuary was empty, save for Lander, Freya, and his wives.

Diana followed after Tonya, and Sable after her. Slinking towards him on silent feet.

He looked sternly at Freya. "I didn't use you! What could you possibly be jabbering about when I'm laying here *wounded*—agh!" God, but he needed to stop shouting, it hurt more every time.

It was with an obvious effort that Freya spoke, perhaps the longest string of words she'd ever dared to undertake. But her gaze remained locked on his, intense and focused, as she brought each word up and deposited it painstakingly in his ears.

"You. Used. Me. As a shield. You. Hid behind. Me. You. Put me. In front. Of the bullet."

Lander's mouth worked, brain whirring along, trying to spin something useful up. He felt an unfamiliar mix of emotions. There was the anger, of course—the bitch was making spurious accusations! But there was also fear. Because for the first time in her life, Freya looked mad—*at him*. And when he flicked his gaze to the side, he saw something else for the first time. The three half-human creatures that had taken him in when he'd been exiled from humanity, who had cared for him, and mated with him, and set him up as their king...

They looked mad too.

Confusion and self-pity added themselves to the slurry of feelings. He knew they weren't fully human, but even so, how could they be so dense? They might not be able to speak as much as Freya and Kat, but they were perfectly capable of understanding. He was the leader of this family! He was the one with all the power, all the importance! Couldn't they see that his life was more important than any of theirs? More important than Freya's? Because there was only one of him, but he could always make another Freya. All these bitches wanted to do was fuck and make babies. So what was the big deal if he'd tried to save his life by using Freya as a shield?

He was the *human* for fuckssake! And they were barely more than animals! Couldn't they see the hierarchy?

But saying so would have required a bit more honesty than someone as narcissistic as Lander was capable of. So he chose instead to deflect and deny.

"I wasn't using you as a shield!" he whined in his most put-upon voice. "I'm the one that got shot, after all!" He pointed emphatically at his wound. "I was shot! *I* was shot! *I* took the bullet for *you*, Freya! And this is how you repay me? This is how you show your appreciation for me *saving your fucking life*?"

It happened so fast, he couldn't even tell which of his wives had done it. One moment, he was really feeling the heat of his words, and thinking that he could see Freya caving, and the next moment there was a flash of movement and a blinding, tearing pain in his right shoulder.

He cried out, more from the surprise of it than the pain itself. He looked at his shoulder and saw the wide, half-moon chunk of flesh that had just been torn out, the muscles beneath twitching and writhing as blood welled up to cover them.

He gaped at his trio of wives, disbelieving.

All three of them were baring their long teeth at him. But Tonya's teeth were stained red, and her tongue flicked, and out of her mouth fell his missing piece of flesh.

"Y-you!" Lander stammered. "You *bit* me!"

Freya leaned away from him, standing to her full height. He looked into her eyes, expecting to see that his words had had some effect, and how she might rush to him, protect him from her own wily mother. But her expression was blank. Unpitying. Immovable.

She stepped back, and Tonya, Diana, and Sable filled the gap, a chorus of low, threatening growls issuing from their throats. All three of them were crouched low on their muscular haunches, so Lander could still see Freya's head over theirs. She was still looking at him. Still emotionless. Still slowly backing away.

Leaving him. Abandoning him.

And after all that he'd done for her!

He tried to remember what all those things were that he'd done for her, so he could point them out in that moment, but for some reason he couldn't think of a single one.

A clack of gnashing teeth snapped his attention back to his wives.

Fear supplanted self-pity as the dominant emotion now—but only just. He searched their faces for any semblance of affection and found nothing. He singled out Diana. She'd been the first one to find him, the first one to take pity on him, and the first one to mate with him. The others tended to follow her lead. If he could get her to come around...

He raised a hand to her face. "Diana. My dear, sweet, gentle—"

She snapped. Something crunched—*popped*. He jerked his hand back with a gasp. Stared in abject horror at his missing index finger, blood trickling from the stump in a steady stream.

He clutched his hand in front of his boggled face and screamed. "My finger! You bit my fucking finger off!"

His three wives were spreading out now, circling him on all fours. Their nostrils were pulsing with the scent of blood. Their eyes were those of strangers. The humanity that he'd seen in them was gone, and they looked no different than the others. Savage. Base. Primal.

Beyond their circling forms, Freya continued to back away, still watching.

"What are you *doing*?" he screamed, head snapping from left to right and back again as they circled him. He wanted to sound furious and in charge. Wanted to try to cow them into fearing him again. But the façade had been broken. And he realized with mounting terror that his place amongst these creatures had always been fragile—how could he have not seen it?

Something hit him in the back. Pain and rending flesh.

He twisted with a short screech, and saw Sable behind him with a flap of his skin hanging from her teeth. She spat it out, as though the taste of it was repugnant to her.

"Stop!" he cried out. "Stop it right now!"

Wham!—something hit him in the side of his face.

His hand—the one with the missing finger—shot up and felt a stinging, wet crater in the side of his face. He couldn't even tell which one had done it, they were all circling so fast now, jumping in at him, then feinting back. As soon as he looked at one, another would hit him from the other side, and another piece of his flesh was gone.

A piece of his arm.

A piece of his side.

All the chunks spat out and littering the ground around him.

His heart thundered in his ears. He tried to scream, but it either wasn't working or he couldn't hear himself. His lungs ached for air. He felt like he was breathing as fast as he could, and yet couldn't get enough.

The only emotion he felt now was panic.

"No!" he warbled, rolling to his hands and feet. He could see the dark doorway that he'd come through before—the passage to his own private room in the back, what used to be the pastor's office. It had a lock on the door. If he could make it there, he could keep them out—

Teeth sank into his left buttock, but they'd gone deeper than just his skin now. His wail was punctuated rhythmically as the jaws clamped onto his buttock thrashed back and forth, ripping a great chunk of muscle from him.

The pain was so intense that he couldn't move his leg anymore. He collapsed onto his belly. His bloody hands and arms clawed at the concrete floor, moving him by tiny increments, his vision closing in, and all he could see before him was the black opening of the door, so very far away.

They came more rapidly then. A piece of his hamstring. A piece of his calf. A piece of his lower back. But none of them went for the neck. Maybe this was only a punishment. Maybe they did not intend to actually kill him.

But the more he curled in on himself, the faster their attacks became. He could not even keep track of his missing pieces any more. They were hitting him two at a time now. Then all three at once. Growling and snarling and snatching bits of him.

The ground around him became slick with his own blood so that even when he tried to paw himself into motion, his hands went slipping and sliding. Eventually, he just curled up into a ball with his hands over his head, and with each piece gone, began to realize what he could not admit before.

He was being killed.

His wives were *killing him*!

The agony stretched time. It seemed it would never end.

Piece by piece, until, for the first and last time in his life, Lander Hollis wished for it all to be over.

Piece by piece, they took him apart.

Piece by piece.

Chapter 44

The night wind whipped at Abe's face as he held the thermal spotting scope up to his eye, tripod and all. It was a bit hard to get a solid picture as the truck hurtled over uneven terrain, but after a few seconds of shaky scanning, Abe hadn't seen any heat signatures.

He immediately leaned back, stretching over a huddled mass of humanity, bristling with rifles, to slam his hand on the roof of the cab. "Hey! Stop the truck!"

He should've known not to say it with such urgency.

Whoever was driving slammed on the brakes, sending Abe toppling into the jumble of weaponry and limbs. The truck skidded through loose dirt and then rocked to a halt, somewhere in the vast, hilly terrain of the Valley.

Swearing up a storm worthy of a Category Five rating, Abe extricated himself to the nearest side of the bed and hurled himself out onto blessedly-steady ground. Questions chased him from nearly every mouth in the bed of the truck, but he ignored them, taking another scan for good measure, now that he wasn't bobbling around on a moving platform.

He confirmed his earlier assessment: They'd ghosted the pack of primals that'd been chasing them.

Problem was, he had no clue where they were in relation to the Town. They'd been driving for several minutes, but Abe hadn't exactly been keeping track. And he didn't know how fast they'd been going. Fast enough to escape the primals, who could run about thirty miles an hour, so...

Abe gave up on trying to do the math, and instead keyed his comms with a more important question: "Abe to Lee, can we get a sitrep?"

He waited while Marie snapped at the people in the bed to shut up and they gradually fell silent.

Seconds ticked by, each one compounding the dense brick of dread in the pit of Abe's stomach. He turned in a slow circle, looking for the slight glow in the sky that would denote a settlement, but then remembered the Town had no lights.

He keyed the comms again. "Abe to Lee, how copy?"

He counted the seconds this time, and when he got to ten, he cast a worried glance at Marie, who was now standing up in the bed, watching him with a pinched expression.

Had they driven out of radio range?

Shit and fuck. "Abe to anyone on the infiltration team. Sam, Jones, Lee. Come back."

One. Two. Three...

Abe was about to transmit again when his ear practically exploded with sound. Shouts and howls and screams and gunshots and heavy, raspy breathing. Then Lee's voice, straining with effort, bouncing to the rhythm of clattering gear and pounding footsteps.

"Bit busy! Standby!"

Abe immediately swung back to the truck. "Shit's going down. They're gonna need an exfil. Everyone out!"

"Out?" someone goggled at him.

Abe began jamming his thumb over his shoulder. "Out! Out! Out!"

"Abe!" Marie shouted over him. Got his attention. She shook her head. "We can't just leave them out here with a pack of primals running around, chasing their scent!"

"Too many bodies in the bed!" Abe countered hotly. "There's not even room for everyone that's in there, and there won't be room for five more bodies when we extract them!"

"We're gonna hafta make it work!" Marie countered with equal fire. "Figure it the fuck out, Abe! I'm not leaving these people in the dark to get torn up!"

"They have guns!"

"ABE!"

Then someone said, "Who's Abe?"

For some reason, that gave Abe just enough pause that he ran out of steam before he could continue to protest.

"Don't worry about it," Marie quipped at whoever had asked.

"Fuck! Fine!" Abe started crossing around the front of the truck. "Clown car it is! We'll cram as many as we can in the cab! Lay on top of each other if you have to." He reached the driver's door and ripped it open. The dome lights came on, revealing none other than the kid that couldn't have been much more than sixteen, with his hands still clutching the steering wheel. Abe almost laughed, but was too pissed. "Joyride's over, kid. Get out or scoot over."

Lee had bought them time. One 40mm round right into the sanctuary had gained him enough of a gap to get out of the building. It had also sent a chunk of something exploding into the back of his head with such force that it had almost knocked him out. He never did find out what it was, but was pretty sure it had been wet and meaty.

Head ringing from the blow, Lee burst into the outside world, then laid three more rounds into that short hallway, one after the other.

Time. Time to turn around and get his bearings. Time to see Sam and Jones, ten yards up the dark street, covering him. Bea behind them, watching, but looking like she wanted to turn and keep running.

"Go!" Lee yelled. "Get to the ATV!"

Time, and not enough of it.

The roar of the horde came spilling out of the smoking ruins of the hallway. He'd lengthened the gap to fifty yards, but against a creature that could run twice as fast as a man, that fifty yards wouldn't last long.

He had two rounds left in the launcher.

Sam and Jones laid down a few quick bursts of covering fire for Lee, then spun and sprinted for the front of the megachurch, shoving Bea along with them.

Lee pumped out a few more strides as hard and fast as he could go, then spun, shouldering the launcher again. His heart felt like it hit the back of his tongue as he realized his lead had already shrunk to thirty yards.

Whump! Whump!

The last two rounds went out low, Lee intentionally skipping them off the pavement right at the feet of the nearest primals. The first one blew a softball-sized hole in the chest of a primal, then detonated a fraction of a second later, scattering body parts in a burst of blood and fire. Lee didn't wait to see what the second round did. He heard the detonation, and felt the pressure wave smack him in the back, nearly making him stumble.

Up ahead, Sam, Jones, and Bea started to break left around the front of the megachurch. Then they came to a skidding halt, and Lee instantly knew they were fucked. Bea immediately switched directions, fleeing across the street, while Sam and Jones emptied what was left in their mags, backing up as they did. Then they broke, spun, and took off after Bea, reloading as they did.

Lee took the hint. The primals hadn't just mindlessly followed their quarry through the emergency exit. They were cunning creatures, and knew how to outflank their prey. They'd come out the front to cut them off.

Lee would not be getting to the ATV.

He charged across the street at a diagonal, slinging the empty launcher and bringing up his rifle. Adrenaline blotted out the pain of his injuries, but there's only so hard that the mechanism of your muscles can be pushed, and already Lee could feel his stride shortening, eating up less distance.

Distantly, he registered the sound of Abe's voice in his earpiece. Now that it hit his brain, Lee thought that Abe had been transmitting for the last few moments, but Lee'd been too distracted to answer. He wasn't too distracted now, but he needed to save his wind for running.

"Bit busy!" he transmitted in a gasp. "Standby!"

Where could they go? What could they do?

The hopelessness of the situation hit him as fully as the grenade blast. They couldn't outrun the primals. They didn't have enough ammo to hold them off. And their extract wasn't even in the city with them.

Lee hit the opposite side of the street just as the second horde of primals surged around the front of the megachurch.

Sam and Jones, about fifteen yards ahead of him, running with no clear objective.

He spared a glance over his shoulder. Caught the fullness of the threats arrayed against him. The horde that had chased them through the emergency exit was fifteen yards behind him. The horde that had come around the front of the church was maybe twenty yards, but lateral to him.

Hopeless, some part of him screamed.

But the steadier part—the part that had been to hell and back so many times already—said, *Well, you're not dead yet!*

As long as there was breath in his lungs and enough blood for his heart to pump, he was still in the fight. Hopelessness was not a reality—it was a mindset. And if you could have a mindset, then you were still alive. And if you were still alive, then it wasn't hopeless.

Sam and Jones disappeared around the corner of a building just ahead. Lee broke the corner just behind them. Darkened streets. Trash and wreckage. Abandoned vehicles...

He saw it.

To say that it gave him a sense of relief would be stretching the truth. What it gave him was a sense of graduating from *snowball's chance in hell* to *maybe by the hairs of my chinny-chin-chin*.

Ten yards ahead of Sam and Jones, and twenty yards ahead of Lee, stood the hulk of a defunct cement truck that'd crashed into the side of a building, burying the front half in rubble. But the back half was exposed. The back half, with its big, steel drum. The big steel drum, with the very narrow opening. An opening through which only one body could fit at a time.

Well, he had been hoping for a bottleneck of some sort. Beggars can't be choosers, and those with their necks in the hangman's noose can't complain about a stay of execution, even if it's a short one.

"Sam! Jones!" Lee bawled with breath he couldn't afford to lose. "Cement truck!"

They were running straight at the damn thing, but the command was so insane that Jones craned his neck and shouted back, "*What?!*"

"Get-in-the-fucking-cement-truck!" Lee expelled, then dropped his rifle, grabbed up the launcher again, and shucked one, last, specialized 40mm grenade from his chest rig.

"Bea!" Sam screamed at her back, just as she was about to run past the cement truck. "Get in the cement truck!"

Maybe Bea was just not as tactically-minded as to balk at the concept of crawling into something with no exit. Or maybe she was just too exhausted or terrified to question it. But she immediately stopped, grabbed the back of the cement truck, and clambered up, diving headfirst into the small hole at the back of the drum, her feet disappearing after her.

Lee broke the M32's cylinder open, his breath coming in so hard and ragged he was heaving it with every single stride and still feeling like he was about to die. Which he probably was. Just not from hypoxia.

Ten yards to the back of the truck.

He bobbled the 40mm round and almost dropped it.

Jones went up first, Sam posting at the bottom and emptying his magazine, the rounds whining past Lee's ears.

Lee slipped the round into a chamber, spun it into firing position, then snapped it shut.

Jones went into the drum feet-first and held onto the edge with his rifle sticking out, spitting death and buying Lee precious seconds. Then Sam mounted the back of the cement truck, and Jones slipped all the way in to clear the way.

Lee hit the truck, swung onto the back, then raised the muzzle of the launcher to the sky as the horde closed in around him. He fired the round in a high arc, then dropped the launcher and climbed with both hands for the narrow opening above.

The grenade never exploded.

Twenty-thousand feet above where Lee, Sam, Jones, and Bea were clinging to the last seconds of their lives, Major Ronald "Ron" Paige stood before the monitors of the AC-130 gunship's targeting systems, frowning at a whole lot of nothing.

They'd been flying in this fucking holding pattern for two goddamn hours, with nary a peep from the ground below, and Paige. Was. Pissed. After all of Angela's whining and moaning and bitching at him about duty and not leaving guys behind and all that other horseshit, he'd finally caved and decided to oversee this train-wreck of an operation personally.

He'd had the entire crew sign NDAs for this shit. Not to mention the fact that he'd given up dinner with the very attractive British intelligence officer that had recently been assigned to Aspen. And she'd told him that they were going to have a *very* good time—and all that that implied.

Hand to God, he was never doing another favor for Angela. He'd stuck his neck out for this, missed out on a hot night that probably wasn't going to come around again, and—*AND*—he'd still have to get an ass-reaming from Griffin about this whole thing. And he didn't even have a noble rescue to show for it.

"Fuck this shit," Paige grumbled to himself, checking his watch. He'd promised coverage for a two-hour window, and they were already over by two minutes. He spoke over the bulky flight comms on his head, direct to the pilots. "What's the fuel situation looking like?"

"Another ten minutes, and then we gotta head back."

Paige wrestled with himself over that last ten minutes. But, as has already been mentioned, Paige was pissed, and feeling pretty damn put out by this whole fuckfest. He could barely wait to get home. He didn't care how late it was, he was going straight to Angela's house to give her an earful.

"Turn her around," Paige griped into the comms as he turned his back on the monitors. "We're done here."

"Roger that, sir," the pilot replied, sounding pretty bored by the whole thing.

A moment later and the huge plane began to bank out of their holding pattern.

Paige held onto a canvas strap to steady himself and stewed, getting angrier the more he thought about it. Served him right for being a goddamned bleeding heart and not following protocols.

"Uh...sir?"

Paige turned back to where the Combat Systems Officers were perched over their respective displays. The officer at the IR sensors was hunched forward in his seat, with his hand raised, his fingers twiddling the air.

"What?" Paige said, not the least bit curious—only irritated.

"Just got an IR flash from...shit, there it is again." He turned in his seat to look at Paige. "It's an IR signal for sure, sir. Coming from that ghost town we just flew over. I'm getting some visual interference from the angle of the buildings, but..." he turned back to his monitors and jabbed a finger at the screen. "See, there it is again."

For all his mighty piss-offedness of only seconds before, Paige's heart immediately went into his throat. "Turn us back around!" he snapped to the pilots. "New heading!" He pointed at the CSOs. "Target that IR signature and prepare to lay hate."

Chapter 45

As Lee swung himself feet-first into the narrow opening of the cement truck's drum, the M992 Infra-red Illumination Cartridge he'd just launched hit the zenith of its arc and ignited. In the peripheral of his one good eye, the night remained as dark as ever, but through his single NVG tube, the infrared flare caused the display to white out for a moment before it adjusted to the sudden burst of illumination.

Feet in the hole. Sliding down. All the hounds of hell surging towards him.

Hips clattering through, catching on the holster of his sidearm. He grunted and cursed and wiggled until he was free. Chest rig through, trailing the two weapons still strapped to him. Head clipping the edge of the opening and ripping his NVGs right off his head.

He was almost all the way through when something seized his right arm.

"Fuck!" Lee yelped, dragging his head around as the entire weight of the primal came down on his arm. All he could see of it was the thrashing of its long, knotted hair, and its too-wide jaws opening, lunging for his arm.

And all Lee could think in that moment was *Not my good arm!*

He only had one of those left.

With a roar, Lee ripped his left arm out of the hole and jammed his hand into the primal's face, stiff-arming it and halting its lunge for his right arm. His thumb was hooked through the thing's cheek, his fingers clawing at the face.

It yowled at him, pressing against his hand, gaping jaws nearly around his arm.

Lee's left arm had been mauled by a primal several years ago, which had messed up the tendons in his wrist and made his fingers awkward and clumsy. But he didn't need dexterity in that moment, or even grip strength.

All he needed was one, ramrod-straight index finger, which he jammed into the primal's eye with such ferocity, he might've been trying to touch the back of its skull. The creature jerked its head back, but Lee wanted it to be permanently blinded for its transgression, and he just rammed it in all the harder. He felt his fingertip squish through the clenched eyelids. Felt the pop of a fluid-filled sphere.

The primal let out a shiver-inducing scream and let go of him.

Without the weight of it hanging on his arm, gravity took Lee's body and he slid through the hole. It was a short trip that terminated in a sudden, painful stop. The remnants of the concrete in the drum had hardened into a jagged surface that ripped straight through his pants and shredded his left knee.

The interior of the drum was black, save for two tiny flushes of green that illuminated Sam and Jones's eyes from their own NVGs.

"Heads up!" one of them yelled—he couldn't tell which was which.

Lee made himself small, rolling onto his back with his feet towards the opening. There was the slightest glimmer of moonlight through the hole, silhouetting a midnight shadow that was trying to get in there with them. Lee could hear it snarling and snapping.

Pop-pop-pop! Even with the suppressors on their rifles, the sound was painfully loud inside the steel drum.

"Conserve your ammo!" Lee shouted, wrestling his own rifle out from underneath his body.

The dead primal was immediately ripped out of the hole as another came on.

Pop! Pop! More measured this time.

"Last mag!" Sam shouted from Lee's side.

Lee shouldered his rifle and held the red dot at the top of the opening. "Only one of us shooting at a time!"

"I'm up!" Jones said, firing in the same instant. Two more rounds, knocking another primal back. "Shit! Empty!"

"Got it covered!" Lee said, finger on the trigger.

God, but they just kept coming. Primal after primal, trying to get through the hole at them, Lee sometimes getting away with a single shot to the head, but more often having to fire two or three to stop them.

"Why are they still coming?!" Jones screamed.

"I don't know!" Lee shouted back as he fired three more rounds and then went empty. His hand slapped his chest rig for another mag and found all of his pouches empty. Shit—had he already burned through them all? "I'm empty!"

"I got it!" Sam said, and immediately fired.

Why weren't the primals retreating at this point? This was insane behavior for them to just keep coming and coming. They were smart enough to fall back, regroup, and try something else.

But they weren't doing it this time. And there were more of them than they had bullets for.

It's Bea, Lee realized. *They won't stop until they get her back.*

The Machiavellian part of Lee—and yes, it was there—briefly considered giving the woman over to them. But he didn't dwell on that momentary thought. There was no way in hell he could just shove some innocent person at a horde of primals, just to save his own ass.

Pop! Pop! Sam's rifle spat, filling the drum with more acrid gunsmoke. *Pop! Pop!* Another primal slumped, and another came to take its place.

"Did you get the signal off?" Jones demanded.

"Yeah!"

"Then why aren't they blowing this fucking street up?!"

"Give them a minute!"

"We don't have a fucking minute!"

"Transition!" Sam cried out, and the suppressed bark of his rifle was replaced with the ear-splitting *BANG-BANG-BANG* of his pistol.

They were down to sidearms.

Lee swore, already pulling his Glock 17 from its holster.

"What can I do?" Bea's voice quaked from beside Lee. "Tell me how to help!"

BANG!

BANG-BANG-BANG!

Lee covered the hole with his pistol, waiting for Sam to run dry. "Pray, and get ready to fight!"

"With what?" she cried.

"Teeth and nails if you have to!"

BANG-BANG!

Holding the pistol one-handed, Lee keyed his comms, issuing a silent prayer that the steel drum wouldn't block his radio signal. "Lee to Abe, can you copy?"

Abe came back almost immediately, but his transmission was fuzzy. "I got you, Lee! What do you need and where are you at?"

"Extract would be nice! We're two blocks south of the megachurch, and we don't have much time! What's your ETA?"

"I don't even know where the fuck we are! I'm trying to get a visual on the Town, but I got nothing!"

"Use your NVGs!" Lee said. "You should be able to see my IR flare!"

"Lee!" Sam called. "Last few—" *BANG-BANG-BANG!* "Fuck! I'm empty!"

Lee abandoned his radio to put both hands on his pistol.

"Standby, Lee!" Abe said in his ear. "Everything got fucked up—I gotta find my NVGs..."

The circle of moonlit sky above Lee was blotted out.
He pulled the trigger.
And everything exploded.

Abe was cursing so much he realized he was unimaginatively repeating himself. He slammed on the brakes, yelling out the open window to Marie, who was still in the truck bed with everyone else that couldn't stack themselves in the cab like cordwood.

"NVGs! Marie! I need my NVGs!"

"I don't know where your fucking NVGs are!"

"Did you leave them behind?!"

"Did *I* leave them behind? I'm not responsible for your gear! I'm not your fucking mother!"

"Goddammit, woman! Get me some goddamned night vision or—"

It was actually good that Abe was interrupted, as threatening Marie would have had bad consequences for him, and he couldn't come up with a reasonable threat anyway.

His ill-chosen words were halted by the visual of the sky opening up and raining fire. Strings of orange tracer fire and comet-like shells lanced out of the blackness, dead ahead of them. They were followed only seconds later by explosive flares of light from the ground, and a few seconds after that, a rumble of concussive blasts.

"Never mind," Abe shot out the window and slammed on the gas, heading for whatever their aerial artillery support was currently pounding into rubble.

"What the *fuck*!" Bea screamed as the ground shook and the entire steel drum they were encased in bucked and swayed, the sides of it pinging with a hailstorm of shrapnel.

The world through that little hole above Lee's head became daylight-bright with the strobing flashes of explosive shells tearing up the street outside.

"Yes!" Jones screeched wildly. "Get 'em! Kill 'em! Blow 'em the fuck up!"

While Lee prayed, *Please, dear God, don't let them blow us the fuck up!*

Bea kept on screaming for answers, but really, there was no way to give her a reasonable answer in all that apocalyptic ruckus. Sam was trying the old "It's okay, calm down," routine, because he'd never been with a woman long enough to learn that you never tell them to calm down.

Lee did his best to hold his aim on that hole, but the truck was pitching and rocking like a ship in a storm. The flashes of explosions became muddy as clouds of smoke and dust strangled the light, and began to seep in through the hole, adding their lung-clotting stench to the hotbox of gunsmoke they sat in.

Jones was now screaming without words. It was the sound of pure, manic joy. A war cry belted right in death's face, telling it to come again another time, because today was not the day.

Lee was not quite so brazen with fate and chance. Jones could rejoice all he wanted, but Lee was in full pucker-mode, knowing perfectly well that the gunship support had been instructed to target the IR signal and saturate the area with 40mm shells and gatling gun fire, neither of which would have any problem eviscerating the steel drum.

This was pretty much the definition of a *danger close* fire mission. It might feel like salvation, but any one of those rounds could wipe them out at any moment.

So Bea screamed, and Sam tried to soothe, and Jones whooped, and Lee just lay there, covering the hole and puckering.

"Lee," Abe's voice was barely audible over the rain of destruction outside. "I got a visual, and I'm coming in hot as soon as they cease fire!"

Lee didn't bother responding. Twice, a primal appeared in the hole above, perhaps seeking safety more than prey, and twice Lee pulled the slack out of the trigger, but didn't break the shot. Both times the primal thought better of it and leapt away the instant after it had appeared.

Steel hammers beat a constant drumroll from the gunship's 25mm gatling gun, punctuated by the steady *BOOM-BOOM-BOOM* of its Bofors cannon. The gunship's 105mm cannon had not announced itself, and Lee thanked his lucky stars for that. Their chances of being collateral damage would have been immensely increased if *that* thing had started pounding the pavement outside.

The barrage continued into mind-numbing realms, where all the noise became just a dull roar in their battered ears. Jones lost his zeal somewhere in there, and Bea had no more questions, and Sam had no more comforts. Lee's rattled mind couldn't even worry about friendly fire anymore—he just waited for it to end, *Holy hell, how long can they keep this up?*

Every time it seemed the firing would cease, it started back up afresh, until Lee's guts were in high-tensile knots, desperate for the deluge of sensory input to stop.

Gradually, the impacts of the Bofors cannon became more sporadic, and then stopped altogether. The drumbeat of the gatling gun took longer pauses between raking the street with its massive projectiles, until, finally, during one of those pauses, it didn't start up again.

The harried foursome lay in the dark for a long time after that. Or at least it felt like a long time. They'd been tricked so many times by the cannons restarting that they didn't trust it to actually be over.

It was anything but silent, though Lee knew that most of the noise was coming from his own jangled head. His ears felt like they needed to be popped, but he'd had his eardrums perforated enough times to know that wouldn't do shit. The screeching tinnitus would go away only when it chose to.

Beyond that, there was the dull roar of fires burning, shot through with distant shrieks and even more distant howls.

Jones let out a racking cough. "We needa get the fuck outta here."

"Hold that thought," Lee said, his own voice thick and phlegmy. He extracted one shaking hand from his pistol, still holding it on the opening with his other hand, and keyed his comms. "Abe. We're still here. Where you at?"

"We're comin' up on your poz right now," Abe said, his voice tense. "It's gonna be a hot extract."

Lee frowned. "Dare I ask why?"

"You remember that pack that chased us off a little while ago?"

Lee didn't transmit his bitter swear, already seeing where this was going.

"They swung back for home. They've been shadowing us through the streets. They're gonna hit your position right around when we get there, so get ready to move your asses. We're thirty seconds out."

Lee, Sam, and Jones all groaned in chorus.

"Will it never end?" Jones pleaded to the darkness.

"Alright," Lee heaved out, pulling himself to his cut-up knees, and gaining his feet. "I'm out first. I'll hold coverage." Then, as a bitter aside, "With my sixteen fucking rounds of nine-mil."

As Lee clambered up the sloped wall of the drum towards the outside world, Sam took the initiative on the comms: "We're in a cement truck, two blocks south of the megachurch."

"Roger 'at. Twenty seconds."

Lee thrust his hands through the opening and pulled himself up. Heat washed over his face from a hundred small fires, and one very large one, directly across the street. The entire side of the building facing Lee had been struck down, and was now ablaze. The street had been smashed into a cratered moonscape. Smoke hung as heavy as fog, making the twinkling fires bleary and unfocused. Lee couldn't even see more than twenty or thirty yards in any direction.

He pulled himself through the opening by a piece of metal framework, then leveraging his legs out and dropping to the ground. He realized that was a poor choice as his knees buckled on impact. He landed on his ass with a grunt, then quickly hauled himself to his feet again, scanning everywhere for movement.

It was difficult to make sense of the cataclysm that had been wrought. The blacktop was pummeled to chunks. For a moment, it seemed like the jagged remnants of the street was empty of bodies, but as his eyes adjusted to the scene and began picking out details he'd missed on his first pass, he realized that there were great swaths painted in steaming wetness. In amongst the broken hunks of concrete, he could see pieces of bodies. Only knew them for bodies because they were a different shape and texture than the rubble. He couldn't see a single piece bigger than an arm. And it seemed there were as many pieces as there were chunks of concrete.

He could hear the others tumbling out of the cement truck behind him, cursing and slipping and clanking their way to the ground.

The sound of an engine drew Lee's attention back in the direction of the megachurch. Headlights speared the brown gloom of smoke and dust.

"We're passing the church," Abe said. "Ten seconds—oh shit!"

There was the sound of tires chirping. The headlights dipped momentarily, and then rocked up as the truck came to a halt, still two blocks away from them.

"What's the problem?" Lee said, starting to jog in that direction.

"This road is fucked!" Abe said, urgency in his tone. "I can't drive over that shit or I'll rip the undercarriage out! You gotta come to us!"

"Let's move." Lee picked up the pace, his slung rifle and grenade launcher banging dumbly into his thighs as he ran. His shoulders ached. His ribs ached. His knees ached. Aw, hell, everything ached. Two tears in a bucket.

He kept his pistol up, scanning from side to side, but there wasn't much to see outside of smoke and destruction. Just the headlights ahead, a beacon promising safety.

"Can you see us?" Abe transmitted, flashing his high-beams.

"Yeah, we got—"

"Contact," Sam uttered, his voice oddly quiet. Almost defeated. "Two o'clock."

Lee slowed, but didn't stop moving. He panned his pistol in the direction of two o'clock, and saw what he'd taken for shifting smoke, now coalescing into a multitude of shadowy figures. And then he did stop.

He glanced at the headlights again. Distance was hard to judge when all you had was light shining in your eyes, but he figured it was about a hundred yards to their extract vehicle. Almost directly between them and their salvation, a pack of twenty or so primals were emerging from a side street.

They weren't running, but moving hectically about, like a dog trying to find the scent of something. Confused by the smoke and the fires and the disruption to the landscape. They hooted quietly back and forth to each other.

Lee very slowly eased the grenade launcher off his shoulder and set it gently on the ground, careful not to make noise. He kept the rifle, but the damn launcher was heavy, and something told him he was going to want to be light on his feet.

Lee started to move again, but this time slowly, picking his foot placement, and angling for the opposite side of the street from the primals. Maybe they wouldn't notice them through the haze of smoke. Maybe their scents would be covered by it too. "Abe," he transmitted, his voice an urgent whisper. "Kill those headlights—we got company."

Abe didn't respond, but the headlights winked out.

Lee kept his pistol directed at the shadows moving through the smoke, but glanced over his shoulder to confirm the others were staying with him. "Move quietly," he breathed. "They might not notice us."

Agonizing seconds brought them painstakingly to the pummeled sidewalk on their left, hugging the line of ruined buildings. They were approaching the intersection where the primals had emerged. The creatures were still mostly on the far side of the street, but a few had begun to circle wider and wider out into the intersection. They moved on all fours, heads low to the ground as though searching for something. They stopped frequently and seemed to smell things on the ground.

The pieces of their packmates?

Lee was shocked to realize that their worried hoots back and forth had taken on an anguished tone. Did they feel the loss of their family? And why was that so hard to believe? Perhaps because Lee had been fighting these creatures for so long, he'd forgotten that they used to be human. They were still social animals. They cared for each other and, at times, even displayed what Lee had to admit was something like affection.

Strange to see the destruction you've caused sour from a sense of victory into a low sense of guilt. Not that Lee wouldn't do the same damn thing in a heartbeat, especially if it meant saving the lives of actual humans. But wholesale eradication of another species is just a slightly harder pill to swallow when you can hear them mourning for their dead.

He was also well aware that their mourning could turn instantly to rage if Lee and his people were spotted.

"How we looking, Lee?" Abe's voice came, hushed.

The nearest primal was only fifteen yards away. Lee didn't dare speak, so he responded with two clicks of his PTT.

Maybe if Lee hadn't been injured, or perhaps if his legs had been a little fresher, he would have picked that left boot up the inch higher it needed to clear the bit of rebar sticking out of a chunk of rubble. But he *was* injured, and he *was* exhausted, and his left leg *was* his bum leg.

His boot caught on the rebar and he stumbled.

The chunk of concrete shifted.

The primal came upright, its head swiveling to Lee. Through the dense haze, Lee could only just make out the thing's eyes. But they must've seen him too, because they were locked on. The primal snarled and lunged.

Lee had no choice but to fire his pistol. One shot that snapped the primal's head back and sent it tumbling in mid-lunge. But that one shot was like a starter pistol, and the second it went off, every other primal seemed to burst from their strange, mourning ululations with renewed vigor.

"Go!" Lee barked, knowing there was only one thing to do about this. "I'll hold them off!"

There was no time to argue. If there had been, Sam and Jones would have. But with no ammunition, and no time, and with twenty-something primals bearing down on them, they just bolted in the direction of the pickup truck.

Sam was already transmitting: "We're coming in hot! Get ready to peel out!"

Lee fired again and again, choosing his targets, yes, but also trying to gain their attention. *Yes, look at my bright muzzle flashes! Focus on me!* His rounds were steady and evenly paced, two into that shadow, three into that one, always targeting the nearest ones while he moved laterally after the retreating figures of Sam, Jones, and Bea.

He wasn't going to make it—back to *snowball's chance in hell*—but he wasn't just going to stand there in his last moments. If they wanted him, they'd find him a high-priced commodity.

Something came from behind him. It hit him in the shoulder right as he was pulling the trigger, sending his shot into the ground just as a primal was charging straight at him, a dozen of its packmates just behind it. Lee barely had time to register the whirl of white-blonde hair before Freya's arm came down on his gun hand like she was chopping wood. He tried to tuck the weapon into retention, but she moved too fast for him, and the pistol went flying out of his grip.

"Motherf—" Lee stabilized himself after the shoulder-check, targeted the back of Freya's head, and started to launch himself at her—

Wait.

The *back* of Freya's head.

She'd moved past him already, and now stood between him and the charging primals, arms stretched out wide, snarling and barking like Kat had done to the challenging Alpha. The rushing primals skidded to a stop in front of her, their howls of rage turning instantly to plaintive, curious cries.

Another figure launched itself into the midst of this, taking a position shoulder to shoulder with Freya, and facing down the rapidly decelerating pack.

Kat. Standing side by side with her sister.

The primals coalesced into a jumble, forming a small crowd in front of Kat and Freya. They milled about but came no closer to the two hybrids. They craned their necks around and over each other, their feral eyes catching on Lee, and whenever they looked at him, their lips would peel back, revealing all their teeth.

But none of them came at him.

Freya and Kat would not allow it.

Lee's chest worked hard with pent up breath. He glanced to his left, in the direction of the truck, and saw nothing but smoke. Sam and Jones and Bea had disappeared. Had they made it to the truck? Had the truck already left and Lee hadn't heard it because he'd been shooting?

His answer came a split second later.

"Lee!" It was Abe. "You with us? Talk to me, brother!"

Lee very slowly raised his hand to his PTT, but again, didn't dare to speak for fear that his voice would rupture the fragile truce before him. He clicked twice again.

"We got fifteen rifles that can come after you right now!" Abe said. "Gimme two clicks and we'll come in guns blazing!"

Lee's finger trembled on the PTT button, but he didn't press it.

The grunts and growls from the pack of primals had settled now into mutters. Kat and Freya were no longer barking, but simply staring the creatures down, immovable. There was a distinct sense that if Kat and Freya let them, they'd rush Lee and tear him to pieces. They still wanted him. But in the strange hierarchy of the primals, what a hybrid said was law.

After a few more moments, Kat took a step back, then slowly turned her head to face Lee.

Lee met her gaze. Licked a dry tongue onto dry lips. "Uh...Thanks," he croaked with a nod.

Kat blinked a few times, appearing to consider him. Lee didn't care for that look. It bore a flavor of deciding his worth. Deciding whether or not to let him live. Finally, she spoke.

"Bran. Alive?"

Lee held eye contact and pressed his PTT. "Marie. Is Bran still alive?"

Please be alive. Lee suspected Kat's decision hinged largely on that. It was the deal they'd made, after all.

"Standby," Marie replied, sounding choked with relief just to hear his voice.

Lee waited, locked in with Kat, feeling the time drawing taut.

She shifted her feet. Her fingers curling and uncurling.

"He's alive," Marie finally said. "He's alive and awake."

Lee let out a slow breath through pursed lips, then nodded at Kat. "He's alive. And he's awake."

Kat's eyes blinked rapidly, pinched in the corners with an obvious flood of emotion. Her shoulders drooped with relief. "You and me," she said. "We go. See him."

"Okay." Lee was entirely agreeable. Anything to get him off this God-forsaken street and out of this hell hole.

Kat turned to Freya and the two regarded each other for a long time. Then they spoke to each other in words, instead of hoots and barks.

"You come?" Kat asked, hesitant and awkward. "With us?"

Freya seemed to consider this. But then shook her head. "I stay." She turned and looked at the pack of primals before them. "Family. Mothers. Stay for them."

And that was it. There were no other words spoken. No signs of affection between the sisters. Kat simply looked at Freya for another moment, then bobbed her head and turned back to Lee.

He glanced at his pistol on the ground, then questioningly at Kat.

She shook her head. Best to leave the weapon where it had fallen.

Lose a pistol in exchange for his life?

Lee figured that was fair enough.

Chapter 46

This was the weirdest fucking ride Bran had ever been on.

And he'd been shackled in a van that was transporting him to prison, getting stared down by a massive prison guard with a shotgun, who chewed bubblegum like he was imagining it was Bran's liver.

This was way more awkward.

"How are you feeling?" the woman named Marie asked, squatting in front of him in the back of the truck bed.

Bran could do nothing but stare at her for a moment. What an insane question that was. How was he feeling? Well, let's see. He'd just been shot twice by the very people that now surrounded him. And then, apparently they'd patched him up. *Marie* had patched him up. A few hours after he'd been shooting at her. And maybe ten hours since he'd left her for dead.

So, how was he feeling?

"Like a bit of a heel, honestly," he answered. The words were a little sluggish. He was definitely still out of it. And the pain from his wounds had become...extremely distracting. But he wasn't so out of it or addled by his pain that he couldn't feel the shame burning his cheeks and scalp.

Or maybe he was about to faint again?

Marie clearly hadn't forgot about him leaving her for dead, or trying to kill her, or trying to kill the people she was trying to help. Her expression remained implacable. "I meant physically. You feel like you can sit up a bit more? Maybe even stand?" She cast a glance over her shoulder. "For Kat's sake. So she doesn't get pissed at us when she sees you."

"Do I look that bad?"

"You look pretty bad."

Bran chewed on that for a moment, fearing the answer to his next question, but fearing not knowing even more. "Am I gonna live?"

Felt like a fucking hypocrite to ask that question.

Marie shrugged. "I couldn't begin to guess."

"Come on," he said, a little intensely. "Don't leave me in the dark. Gimme something."

Marie sighed through her nose. "Bran, I've seen people die from the dumbest wounds, and other people live after what should have killed them." She got a thoughtful look on her face. "You know, Jax was shot through the lung one time. He actually died. Was dead for a few minutes. But they reinflated his collapsed lung and gave him CPR. Shouldn't have worked. But it did." She looked at him, and her expression was open and frank. "As far as I can tell, the biggest deciding factor is how much the person wants to live."

"I see 'em!" one of Marie's teammates called out. They were all in the truck bed with her, along with a few people Bran recognized from the Redoubt. The one that had spoken was the kid named Sam.

Very strange to be wounded amongst these people. At best, some of them didn't care if he died. At worst, many of them probably wished he *would*.

Marie stood up and offered her hand. "Come on. Kat's walking up. Try to stand."

Bran stared at that hand for a moment, thinking about how standing up sounded like scaling Everest right about then. But Marie was right. Kat was likely to be a tad volatile. If he looked like he was on death's door, she might have a poor reaction. And, frankly, Bran had had enough violence for one night. He'd really like some peace and calm.

He grasped Marie and she pulled him up. Straining, at first, until Bran convinced his legs to wake up, and then he was on his feet. Pins and needles. Waves of hot and cold over his skin. Vision all swirly. He clung to Marie for balance until his head cleared. And she let him.

Bit of a heel, he'd said. But that was an understatement.

Nothing humbled you quite as much as being shown compassion by an enemy.

As the faintness passed, he saw them striding up to the passenger's side of the truck. Kat in the lead, followed by Jax. Kat looked about like she always did, except for the fact that her hands and face and chest were all covered in bright splashes of gore that stood out like neon signs as she walked through the beams of the headlights.

Jax looked like he'd spent the night in a tumble dryer.

The second Kat spotted Bran, her eyes did a strange thing. They filled with...relief. A relief so strong, it could only come from the fear of losing a loved one. And that hit Bran hard. The last time anyone had looked at him like he was anything worth loving was...

Well, shit. He couldn't remember.

Kat vaulted into the truck bed, earning a stir of worry from the Redoubters, though she didn't even spare them a glance. She went straight to Bran, and then just halted, frozen with her arms at her sides, like she didn't know what to do. A few times her hands jerked up, like she was thinking about touching him, or wrapping her arms around him. But she'd never once shown that type of affection.

She'd never once received it.

She swallowed audibly, her mouth working. A lot of words to say, but a limited capacity to express them. Her eyes darted to his wounds. "Better?"

Bran considered that question for a moment, as he felt unfamiliar feelings rising up in him. He'd never felt so high and so low all at once. Nor was he the type of man to really be able to pin down his emotions. He just felt them, and accepted that they were beyond his ability to explain.

Was he better? Fuck no, he wasn't better. But Kat had so much hope in her eyes when she asked it, that Bran didn't have the heart to say the truth, and the love he felt coming off of her was so strong, he didn't have the heart to lie to her either.

Instead he raised his good arm and put it on her shoulder.

When she didn't draw away, he pulled her into him. She smelled of blood and sweat and night wind. She smelled like Kat.

His ears were ringing and his throat was clogged up with mysterious emotions and his eyes were burning and starting to leak. But he still registered Jax's voice.

"They're back there," he said, obviously addressing someone's concern about the pack of infected. "Freya's holding them back, but I don't really wanna hang out."

Bran blinked the tears out of his eyes, separating from Kat before it got weird. She hadn't hugged him back. She'd just stood there. Stiff at first. But then she'd slowly relaxed. Accepted the first modicum of human affection she'd ever received.

There was no room in the cab, so Jax pulled himself into the truck bed, groaning and cursing like an old man as he did. When he'd gotten himself in the bed, he raised a hand, and Bran knew he was about to slap the top of the cab and get them going.

"Where will you take me?" Bran blurted.

Jax paused. Looked at him. "Back to the Redoubt."

Kat shifted so she could look between Jax and Bran, her eyes worried and curious.

Bran swallowed thickly, that odd wave of emotion sinking into something much more familiar: Dread. "Am I being taken prisoner?"

Lee considered Bran's question for probably longer than he should have. The second Bran asked it, Lee could see all eyes turn on him. His team? Well, they just looked mildly curious. But the Redoubters? Their eyes had a bit of bloodlust in them.

This man who they'd just kept from bleeding out, who stood swaying on his feet and looking like he might pass out at any second—he'd tried to kill them. He'd tried to kill every person in this truck. Lee's team could take it in stride, as they were doing at that very moment. But the Redoubters wanted justice.

How much ill will would Lee create if he let Bran and Kat go? But...

"A deal's a deal," Lee said, loud enough for everyone in the cab and the truck bed to hear him. "Kat helped us. I gave her my word I'd help you."

One of the guys from the Redoubt huffed and shuffled his feet. "You said you'd keep him alive," the man growled, glancing at Kat, clearly concerned that his unfriendly opinion might result in her trying to tear his face off. "And you did that. He's still alive. But he needs to pay for what he did."

Lee completely understood where the man was coming from. He'd been there a time or two himself. He'd extracted his revenge—or justice, if you prefer—and despite the admonishments of wise minds the world over, it hadn't left him feeling empty. On the contrary, it'd felt pretty damn good.

But Lee was a man of his word. And that still meant something to him. And one of the things that he considered important was that you didn't weasel your way out of your promises on technicalities. When he'd made that deal with Kat, she hadn't walked away thinking they were going to be prisoners after the deal was concluded. And the thought hadn't really crossed Lee's mind either. When he'd made the deal, he'd made it for *everything*. If Kat helped them save Bea, then the slate was wiped clean.

And she had. And so it was.

Lee ignored the man that had spoken up, and instead looked right at Bran. "No, Bran. You're not a prisoner. Neither are you,

Kat. But you got some pretty nice wounds, and you're gonna need more than just a few bandages to sort all that out. You need medical attention that only we can give you."

Bran was already shaking his head before Lee finished. His face went tight. Pained. But not from his physical wounds. His voice was hushed and shaky when he spoke. "I can't go back there."

Kat looked at him sharply. "Wounds. Need healing." She jabbed a finger at Marie, and then Lee. "Medicine."

Bran looked at her with red-rimmed eyes. "Jesus, Kat. I just spent six years fucking with these people. I don't wanna get to know them." A shame-filled glance at the two Redoubters in the bed with them. "And they don't wanna get to know us."

"Jax," Abe said, waving a hand out the driver's window. "Don't we wanna get the fuck out of here?"

Lee blinked. "Yeah. Yes. Let's go." He raised a hand to Bran's panicked look. "We got miles before we get there. We can talk on the way. But this is not the place to do it."

The truck shifted into reverse, and Abe wasted no time, though he accelerated gently, on account of everyone still standing. Bran bobbled unsteadily as the truck sped up, and Kat grabbed him and eased him into a seated position on the side of the bed.

Abe got enough room to turn around and spun the wheel, guiding their backend straight towards the darkened entryway of Ascend Church, the white-and-black ATV still sitting there where they'd left it.

Abe shifted into drive, preparing to finally get them out of the Town.

"Wait-wait-wait!" Bran snapped with uncommon verve for a wounded man. His head was twisted around, looking out past the tailgate at the ATV. "Is that ours?"

"Yes," Kat answered, a question in her voice.

Bran waved a hand as Abe pressed the accelerator. "Stop!"

Lee slapped the cab. "Hold up, Abe."

The pickup lurched to a halt. "What now?" Abe called, antsy to be free of this place.

Bran struggled to a standing position again. Put his hands on Kat's shoulders, leaning heavily on her. "Kat, we can't go with these people. They've got dead to bury that *we killed*. Do you understand that? Do you understand how much they're going to hate us?"

Maybe Kat *hadn't* really understood that. Because her head drew back, as though the concept were a surprise, and she twisted to look at the baleful glares of the Redoubters. And then the concept became very real to her.

She'd spent enough time with people that hated her. She knew what it looked like.

Bran turned to Lee. "How much battery is left on that thing?"

Lee frowned, remembering that he'd checked as he'd driven into the Town—wondering how long it would last if they had to make a quick getaway. "Around fifty percent, I think."

Kat shook her head. "Not enough."

Bran grimaced. "It might be."

Kat glared. "*You* said. Not enough."

"I know what I fucking said," Bran retorted. "But...I don't know! Maybe we can reach some place. Some place that's not *here*. Some place where the people don't know us and fucking hate us. Some place where we can start fresh and just...be us. Be Bran and Kat. Wouldn't that be better?"

Kat struggled with it for a moment.

Somewhere in those smoke-clotted streets, a primal wailed, long and haunting.

Lee felt an unvoluntary shudder go up his back. "Y'all gonna need to make a decision."

"Your wounds," Kat said to Bran, pleadingly. "Medicine."

"Hey," he said, trying on a haggard smile. "I'll make it, okay? I *want* to survive. I *want* to live." That shame-faced glance that didn't really meet anyone's eyes. "Just not here."

Something like determination came over Kat's face. She gave a nod. "Okay. We go." Then she raised her hand, looking at it with some confusion, as though it were operating of its own volition, and laid it on Bran's unwounded shoulder. "New place. No Dark Mode."

Bran wheezed out a chuckle. "No Dark Mode."

As Lee watched them dismount the truck bed—Kat practically having to carry Bran off like a child—he realized he was relieved to watch them go. Relieved on many different levels, not the least of which was because he wouldn't have to keep the Redoubters from slitting Bran's throat in his sleep. And maybe just a bit relieved that something—some*one*—like Kat could get a second chance.

And, strangely enough, he also felt some worry for them. Bran could die of an infection within the next few days—gunshot wounds almost always got infected if left untreated. Even if they found a settlement, and even if that settlement was willing to take in two strangers, one of which was a hybrid, would they have the medicine he needed?

"Hey!"

Lee snapped his head around and found Marie standing up from her medical pack, a white bottle in hand. She tossed it in a high arc. Kat snatched it deftly out of the air, the pills rattling inside.

"Amoxycillin," Marie called out to them. "Take two a day, morning and evening, for ten days." Then, as though she were in a hurry to avoid any thanks, she twisted and hollered at Abe, "We're done. Let's go."

Abe gratefully accelerated them out of there.

Marie caught Lee's faint smirk as she settled down into the bed, zipping her medical pack back up with jerky movements. "What? You said to do what I could." She waved an irritable hand in the direction of the retreating ATV, the wounded man, and the hybrid that was his friend. "I could."

Lee's smirk turned into a knowing grin. Marie scowled and flipped him off.

Yes, for some odd reason, Lee was worried about those two. And apparently it was infectious, even for someone as stubborn as Marie. But if anyone had a chance out there in this world gone mad, it was Bran and Kat.

Chapter 47

"Doesn't it feel like the Universe has it out for us?"

Jones was in a particularly pensive mood this afternoon, Lee noted as he mashed the detcord into the brick of plastic explosive.

Lee quirked an eyebrow at the younger man. "How so?"

Jones sat straddling the concrete floodgate with its steel door, a pile of C4 next to him. He had a brick of it in one hand, and his knife in the other. He frowned at his work as he cut the brick sidelong, prepping it for the detcord. "I mean, it feels like we're caught in this never-ending cycle of struggle, and just when we think we're going to taste some sweet relief, we're somehow miraculously reborn and forced to do it all again."

Lee chuckled, pushing his detcord-primed package into the hole they'd dug in the soft earth. "I think that's called life." Lee rose from his squat and gestured for the split brick in Jones's hands. "And besides, the Universe isn't forcing you to do anything. You don't have to stay in the struggle."

"Yeah." Jones slapped the brick into Lee's waiting hand. "I could just off myself."

"Well, then you'd just be reborn right back into it." Lee wagged a finger at him. "Your theory, not mine."

Jones mused on that for a moment. "So, there's no way out."

"Of course there's a way out. You simply choose not to struggle."

"Choose not to struggle?" Jones looked aghast. "So...just lie down and take it up the ass? Is that what you're saying? If I stop resisting it'll hurt less? Like prison sex?"

Lee paused in his preparations, a knot of detcord in one hand, C4 in the other. "I'm saying you don't *have* to do anything. Everything's a choice. You *choose* the struggle. Probably because you know that giving up on it will only result in worse struggles in the future."

"But see, that's my point. The future doesn't get any better. It's just...more of this. Another round in the endless cycle."

"I get where you're coming from," Lee allowed. "Sometimes we expect rewards for our labors, but the reality is that pain and struggle are just a part of our human existence. But that doesn't mean you have to be miserable about it."

"Oh, you're not miserable?" Jones looked dubious.

Lee smiled at that and shook his head. "No, I'm really not." He set to mushing the detcord into the split Jones had made. "What is misery anyway? It's subjective. Take two people—one person lived in a shitty little shanty in some war torn, drought-ridden country. The other person is from some nice suburban house in America who's never had to go hungry a day in their life, always had access to healthcare, clean water, and central air conditioning." Lee placed the primed brick in another hole, grunting as he stood up straight again. "Now, take both of those people and force them through the end of the world, and set them both up in one of these shitty little settlements of survivors. Who's more miserable?"

"Well, obviously the suburban American. But they're both still miserable."

Lee shook his head. "No. See, the guy from the war-torn shanty, he sets up in the settlement, and yeah, life is still hard, but he says, 'at least there's rain so I can grow food.' See, he compares it to his worst days in the slum of that drought-ridden country and sees that it's not so bad. Suburban guy, though, his worst day was when he got fired from his cushy job, or lost a bit of his retirement fund in a bad investment, or his wife fucked the pool boy. So, when he compares his current circumstances to that, he says, 'life sucks, and it only seems to get worse.' But it's just a matter of perspective."

Jones pointed at Lee emphatically. "But, see, that's exactly what I'm saying. We're the suburban guy. We had all that nice shit. And now life *does* suck and it seems to only get worse."

Lee shrugged and propped his hands on his hips. "Sure, we have the same background as the suburban guy. But we don't have to share his perspective. We don't have to just compare our life now to our life before. We can also compare our life now to how bad it *could* be."

Jones gave him a deadpan look. "So…it could always be worse. That's your big point?"

"Think about the multiverse."

Jones blinked. "Really? You're going with the multiverse?"

Lee sighed. "It's as valid a theory as any other, Jones."

"Alright," Jones said, cautiously. "How's the multiverse factor in?"

"Because, what if we live in the universe with the best possible outcome? Have you ever thought of that?" Lee smirked at the distrustful look on Jones's face. "Maybe all the universes in the multiverse are complete dumpster fires, *except* for this one. Maybe we live in the best universe. In this moment, in another universe, maybe things are way worse than they are now, and if you were living in that universe, you'd wish you could have the life you're living now. Or maybe, in that other universe, the whole of humanity got wiped out, and there's not even any people left to have existential conversations like this one." Lee looked up at the blue sky, as though appreciating it with a fresh perspective. "And when I look at it like that, I think, well, this moment ain't so bad, all things considered."

Jones squinted disbelievingly at the sky. "So, if your reality sucks balls, just imagine a completely different reality that sucks even worse and then convince yourself to be grateful?"

"Why not?"

Jones chuffed. "Seems like you're deluding yourself because you don't want to face the facts."

Lee blew a raspberry. "The facts don't change. I see all the same facts you do. I'm not putting blinders on. But I choose to see those same facts in a way that doesn't make me miserable. Why is that not valid? Why do we assume that if it makes us miserable, it must be valid?"

Lee gave the other man a discerning look. "Let me ask you a question: Am I deluding myself because I want to be at peace? Or are you deluding yourself because you want to be miserable? Like I said, no matter how you interpret it, the facts remain the same. But one interpretation gives you a sense of peace, and the other makes you miserable. You choose how you want to interpret the facts, so, in effect, you choose whether or not to be miserable, regardless of your circumstances. I personally think it's silly to make myself miserable for no good reason. I've lived that paradigm before and it didn't change a damn thing for the better. It didn't make me a better fighter. It didn't make me quicker to see a threat." Lee smiled and gestured to the scars on his face. "It didn't make me impervious to bullets. All it did was make me miserable and shortsighted. Because when you're miserable you become just an animal that can only think one step ahead because your mind is clouded by past bitterness and future anxiety. If I could go back to my younger self and say one thing, I'd tell myself to stop being so pissy and grow a sense of humor."

Jones grunted, narrowing his eyes at Lee. "What advice would you give me?"

Lee grinned. "Stop being pissy and grow a sense of humor. It's not all that bad, and focusing on the negative aspects of life doesn't make you hard. It just makes you brittle." Lee nodded at the pile of C4. "Now split me another brick."

An hour later, dirt-smeared and sweat-soaked, Lee and Jones spooled out an enormous length of detcord—courtesy of a recent supply drop—and then hunkered down on the other side of a ridge, two hundred yards from where Colin Horner had dammed up the river.

While Jones wired up the detonator, Lee poked his head up and surveyed the dam from afar. Horner—or more likely, his ranch hands—had actually done a pretty good job. The majority of the dam was earthwork, but right in the center of it was the floodgate that could be used to control the flow of the stopped-up river. Lee had no idea where Horner had gotten the concrete for that section, but there was a good bit of it. It leaked a bit more than would probably be accepted if the dam had been made by an engineer, but it had clearly done what Horner had wanted it to do.

Stopped the river, and deprived all the little settlements in the Valley of the water they needed to survive and irrigate their crops.

Lee and his team had had a private sit-down to discuss whether they would leave the dam in place and simply open the floodgate. But the consensus was this: People were shitty, and the second Lee and his team moved on, some other asshole might decide *they* wanted to hold the power of the dam for themselves.

They'd decided it was best to destroy the whole damn thing—pun intended.

Lee settled himself down to the ground, laid on his back, and put his newly-replaced helmet on his head—just in case. A few hundred yards further down, Marie, Sam, and Abe stood at the pickup, weapons in hand. There were still primals in the Valley, after all. And they couldn't rely on Freya to always be there to stop them from chomping on people. Fact was, they hadn't seen or heard from her since they'd narrowly escaped the Town, a week ago.

"Put your lid on," Lee admonished Jones as the other man settled into place beside Lee with the detonator in his lap.

"Oh, right. Good call." Jones put his helmet on, the chin strap dangling. "You ready?"

"Yup," Lee said. "You?"

Jones settled his hand on the detonator's push bar. "On you, Boss."

Lee cupped his hands over his mouth and bellowed the call in three directions: "Fire in the hole! Fire in the hole! Fire in the hole!" Then he plugged his ears, opened his mouth, and closed his eyes, as the earth bucked beneath them.

They got back to the Redoubt just in time to see the first trickles of muddy water wet the dry riverbed that ran alongside the settlement's desiccated crops.

There were about fifty people arrayed along that riverbed. They were all that was left of the Redoubt. They had buried sons and daughters and wives and husbands and parents. They had been disillusioned by the secrets of their leader, but were still somehow heartbroken at Ted's loss.

Lee figured Ted had gotten what was coming to him, but he didn't begrudge the people their need to grieve for what had been, even if it had been a lie.

And yet, through all of that hardship and sadness, the sight of that searching finger of brown water meandering over the arid silt of the riverbed brought a spontaneous cheer from the people. New water meant new life. New life to replace what had been lost and buried. And they rejoiced in the simplicity of that, as only those whose survival depends on the land can rejoice at the sight of water where there had been none before.

Children darted into the riverbed to splash in the water, shrieking and laughing. Adults who hadn't dared to hope for better broke down in tears, or fits of uncontrollable laughter, as the heavy weight they'd been carrying suddenly dissipated.

Smiling at this unchecked display of humanity, Lee searched the crowd for Gary, who had taken over as the leader of the settlement. Lee had thought that Bea would have filled that spot, as he'd kind of seen her as Ted's second in command. But Bea had flatly refused to be put into a leadership position, despite the cajoling of her peers. She'd actually been the one to suggest Gary, and everyone seemed to be mollified by that selection—he was well-liked.

When he found Gary, he kept sight of him until he gained some eye contact, then gave the other man a pointed look and jerked his head in the direction of their settlement. Gary took his meaning and nodded back, then raised his voice over the excited babble.

"Folks! This area here is likely to flood in a bit. Best we get back to our houses and wait for the waters to level out."

No one was put out by the idea. On the contrary, the concept of even *more* water—so much that it would overrun the banks and soak their dead fields—seemed to excite them all the more.

That evening, as the setting sun turned the western sky bright orange, Marie cooked up a truly massive quantity of chicken mac and cheese. That had also been courtesy of yesterday's supply drop, along with the giant seafood pot and the chemical burners she used to cook it in. Sitting on the tailgate of his truck, Lee smiled at the brightness in Marie's eyes as she ladled generous portions on people's plates. She was never so happy as when feeding others.

They'd raided Horner's Peak, cleaning out their stash of homebrewed whiskey, which wasn't all that much, but amongst folks that hadn't had hard liquor in six years, it was plenty to get everyone quite drunk. The atmosphere was festive. Abe was in his cups, and trying to get Marie to go round for round with him, with rather obvious intentions. Jones had garnered a following of young adults, who, Lee noted, were predominantly female. He had a grand time hyperbolizing every dangerous experience he'd ever encountered, and they seemed to hang on every word. With a captive audience, Jones was in his element.

Sam and Bea had both decided to stay sober, and taken to the lookout, ostensibly to keep an eye on their surroundings. Lee kept expecting for them to sneak off for some canoodling, but every time he glanced at the lookout, they were still there. Doing a bit more conversing than watching, but still keeping their heads up.

Ah well, the night was young.

Lee hoped Sam would experience something beautiful that night. If you were going to live the life that they lived, you needed to find those experiences wherever you could. Because even camels had to find water eventually, no matter how far they had to go between oases.

"Goddamn," a gruff voice proclaimed from Lee's side.

He turned to find Gary leaning against the tailgate, staring at the mason jar in his hands, a shallow puddle of amber liquid at the bottom. Gary's eyes looked a little watery and dazed.

"Maybe you should let me handle that last bit for you," Lee said, and when Gary didn't protest, Lee took the mason jar and downed the rest of the contents. It was harsh as hell, but Lee still relished it.

"What'd they put in that shit?" Gary murmured, blinking slowly.

"Alcohol," Lee said, smacking his lips and setting the empty mason jar down. That'd be enough for him. With Jones, Marie, and Abe all drinking, Lee figured he should keep Sam and Bea company in their temperance.

Gary leaned his elbows on the tailgate and hung his head for a long moment. Then, with a great snort, he raised it again and seemed fiercely intent on willing himself back to sobriety. "So. You're leaving."

"In the morning," Lee nodded.

"Sure you don't want to stay a bit longer?"

"Nah," Lee said with a smile. "On to the next sad batch of bastards."

"So, this is really what you do?" Gary frowned. "Just roam about the country, saving people's asses when they get themselves into trouble?"

Lee shrugged. "It's a good life."

Gary looked at him, surprised. Then cracked a smile. "Seriously?"

"Why not?"

"Pfff. 'Cause you have to work with a buncha fuckasses like us."

"Oh, y'all weren't...*that* bad."

Gary tittered, then grew serious and looked away. "Seems tough, though. Never settling down. Always on the move. Always risking your life for others. Never getting any credit for it. Never getting a reward for all your efforts."

"Freedom of the open road," Lee countered. "No one to micromanage how we do things. Always something new. Helping decent folk survive. Sleeping soundly at night because you know you did the right thing." He smiled and winked at Gary. "It's all in how you interpret it. I choose to see it as a good life. So it is."

Gary stared at him for a long time, like he couldn't decide whether Lee was fucking with him or not. Finally he laughed, and shook his head. "You're a weird dude, Jax."

"Oh, I've gotten weirder over the years, that's for sure," Lee agreed, eye twinkling with amusement. "And thank God for that. If it wasn't for getting weird, I'd've lost my shit ages ago."

"We could use y'all's help, you know," Bea said, leaning on the side of the lookout's wall. The sheet metal was so bullet-riddled it looked more like a giant cheese grater.

Standing at the wall opposite her, Sam watched the side of her face in the glow of the setting sun. She'd have a new scar to go with the one that Lander had given her—a two-inch long gash on the right side of her forehead from when Kat had tossed her off the church stage. Marie had stitched it up, the slim black threads still holding the puckered flesh together.

He didn't see the scars though. He was searching her face for any hidden meaning in what she'd said. Was she trying to get *them* to stick around? Or *him* to stick around?

He was hopeful for the latter, but her face gave nothing away. Stony as ever.

Well, it didn't really matter anyway. They were leaving in the morning regardless of what Bea might or might not want.

"Oh, I think y'all will be just fine without us," Sam said.

"The squad could use a helluva lot more training," Bea rejoined, speaking of the ten men and women that had received a bit more focused instruction on fighting over the last week. Bea was their team leader, a concession that she'd made possibly because she felt guilty for turning down Gary's position.

"Training's a bottomless rabbit hole," Sam said. "You can always use more, but there's only so much we can teach at a time. We've given y'all the foundation you need. It's up to you to build on it."

Bea finally deigned to turn her gaze on him. "And what about the ranch?"

Sam scoffed. "What about it? We ain't cowboys. None of us knows the first thing about herding or ranching. Nope." He shook his head. "Y'all gonna have to figure that one out on your own."

"I don't even know how to ride a horse."

Sam shrugged. "Hunger is a great motivator. I suspect some folks will learn cowboying pretty damn quick once they start really thinking about all the beef that's wandering around out there."

"And what about the primals?" Bea asked, pointedly. "What are we gonna do when they start eating the cows again, now that no one's keeping them in check?"

"Honestly?" Sam arched his eyebrows. "I'd let them. That horde's been decimated. I'm pretty sure the twenty that showed up right at the end were all that's left. Shove a cow at them every month to keep them happy and off your backs. I'm sure you can make a deal with Freya. She seems...rational enough."

Bea gave a visible shudder. "Bitch still creeps me out."

Sam bobbed his head. "That's understandable." He sighed and frowned out at the darkening landscape. "It's become a very strange world, hasn't it? Just seems to get stranger and stranger. Is there going to be some point in time when we have to establish diplomatic relationships with this...new species? Is it even possible to coexist with them? Or do we just keep trying to drive each other into extinction?"

Bea didn't answer directly. She eyed him for a moment, then asked a different question. "You ever get tired of it? The constant fighting?"

Sam didn't have to consider that for very long. He nodded. "Of course. I just...don't know what else I would do if I wasn't doing this." He rubbed his face and then settled his hand on the buttstock of his slung rifle. "I don't even know if I *can* do anything else."

"You could settle down if you wanted to," Bea said.

And again, Sam searched her face for what she meant by that. Settle down? Or settle down *here*? The thought was somehow both exciting and terrifying. But, again, Bea's face gave nothing away.

"I could," Sam admitted. "I suppose I could settle down anywhere. But then what?" He slowly shook his head from side to side. "One thing I've learned, Bea, is who I am. And this is it. I'm me. This is what I do. And I think if I ever stopped and tried to settle down, I'd just go stir crazy." He sighed and bowed his head. "I'm *good* at this. But I don't know if I'm good at anything else."

Bea sniffed and looked away. "You won't know until you try."

Sam didn't respond to that. He supposed it was true enough. He wouldn't know how he took to a life of peace until he actually tried it. But he suspected that he'd come to the same conclusion Lee himself had come to, years ago: Some people were simply not built for a life of peace. Those people just had too much fight in them, and that instinct to fight always sought to express itself. In the absence of an enemy, the fighter turns to fighting themselves.

Or worse, the people that they love.

"So," Bea continued, after a long silence. "What's next for Sam Ryder, then?" She cast him a rueful glance over her shoulder. "On to the next settlement? Try to charm the pants off the next girl?"

Sam quirked his head at her. "So, you think I'm charming."

She rolled her eyes and sighed. "You have...some endearing qualities."

"Ah, not enough of them, though." He snapped his fingers with an *aw-shucks* face.

She gave him a questioning glance.

Sam gestured at her lower half. "Your pants are still on."

Her eyes narrowed at him, and he thought, *Well, it was a good effort.*

But then—what was this?—the slightest hint of mirth tightened the corners of her eyes and mouth. She looked like she was actually restraining...a laugh?

"Oh my God," Sam breathed and leaned forward as though witnessing a wondrous spectacle. "Is that...an actual smile trying to come out?"

She shook her head and turned away from him, but not before the grin split the carefully-preserved shell of her face. Long-abandoned smile lines appeared around her mouth and eyes, melding with her scars so that they seemed to go together, turning pain into merriment. Her eyes twinkled, and her nostrils flared with a burgeoning laugh, made irrepressible by the fact that she was trying to stifle it.

Sam's heart did a little stutter step as Bea finally gave up, and laughed. She was actually smiling, and actually laughing, because of him. *For* him. It transformed her face, as he knew it would, and he stood there grinning at her, and marveling at her.

There it is, he thought, as the warmth of the moment washed over him, refreshed him like water to a man in the desert. He savored it, soaked it up, and etched the moment into his memories:

The woman named Bea, with the scars on her face, who hadn't ever cracked a single smile, now laughing in the umber light of the setting sun.

Just that one little moment brought his tired soul back from its long dormancy.

One moment. One experience.

Something beautiful.

That's all we ever really need.

ABOUT THE AUTHOR

D.J. Molles became a New York Times and USA today bestselling author while working full time as a police officer. He's since traded his badge for a keyboard to produce over 20 titles. When he's not writing, he's taking steps to make his North Carolina property self-sustainable, and training to be at least half as hard to kill as Lee Harden (his most popular protagonist). Molles also enjoys playing his guitar and drums, drawing, cooking, and "shredding that green pow" on his Onewheel.

Most nights you can find him sitting on the couch surrounded by his dogs and family, trying to stream an hour of Netflix with his really sketchy satellite internet connection.

Want to be in the know for all things D.J. Molles?
Sign up for the monthly-ish newsletter.
There's a giveaway every month!

djmolles.com/newsletter

ALSO BY D.J. MOLLES

A Harvest of Ash & Blood (Summer 2023)
The Santas
Wolves
Johnny
The Remaining Series
The Remaining
Aftermath
Refugees
Fractured
Allegiance
Extinction
Lee Harden Series
Harden
Southlands
Primal
Defiant
Unbowed
Terminus
Godbreaker Series
Breaking Gods
The Nine
Confluence
and more at djmolles.com!

Printed in Great Britain
by Amazon